THE CONTESTANT

Blake Rudman

A HellBound Books Publishing LLC Book

A HellBound Books LLC
Publication

Copyright © 2025 by HellBound Books Publishing LLC
All Rights Reserved

Cover and art design by Tee N Art
For HellBound Books Publishing LLC

No part of this book may be reproduced, stored in a retrieval system, or transmitted by any means, electronic, mechanical, photocopying, recording or otherwise without written permission from the author This book is a work of fiction. Names, characters, places and incidents are entirely fictitious or are used fictitiously and any resemblance to actual persons, living or dead, events or locales is purely coincidental.

www.hellboundbooks.com

Dedication

My Dear Selah, in pursuit of peace, life will present a labyrinth of shocking and confounding decisions that will only appear to be unscalable. Continue to press on even through the darkness and then suddenly, light will begin to resonate and confound the darkness leading on to new chapters of understanding, increased knowledge and peace.

"There is a tide in the affairs of men, Which taken at the flood, leads on to fortune" William Shakespeare

Love Dad

Prologue

There was only one way out.

Not the motel room's only door, a warped, weather-worn thing made from thin, cheap wood and adorned with peeling green paint; he reckoned the rotting thing was hollow in the middle. The cops would be able to shoulder it open with very little effort, he thought. That was, of course, unless the greasy-haired dyke at the motel reception's front counter had been so kind as to give them the key.

The window, too, was a definite no-no. Stupidly, he'd taken a room on the Sunset Lane Motel's third floor; it had seemed like a smart move the night before, as it was the only vacant room overlooking the main entrance and parking lot. Better for him to keep a watchful eye out for the cops and Christ only knew who else he was aware were hot on his tail.

He'd often wondered who the hell stayed in places like this; he had grown more accustomed to five-star hotels—usually penthouse suites with an endless minibar, twenty-four-hour room service, and steaming rooftop hot tub—than grubby, off-the-beaten-track crapholes. But that had been before.

The solitary window opened wide enough for him to squeeze through—David John Shownes being a mere five-feet-seven inches and weighing in at a lean one-fifty-two pounds; he'd tried it out pretty much the moment he'd checked in for just in case. But, three floors down was a long way, although, sadly, not enough of a drop to guarantee a clean death.

Nope, he'd likely be left flopping around with broken legs on the cracked, weed-festooned blacktop below while the cops cuffed him and manhandled him into one of their blacked-out vans. Then, he'd face the rest of his life on death row for crimes he'd not even committed—right up until they stuck those three needles in his arm and put him down like some sick old dog while friends and relatives of his supposed victims gawked teary-eyed through an unbreakable plexiglass window.

They still did that in Texas.

Or was he still in Louisiana?

Honestly, Shownes couldn't be sure any more; he'd been on the run for what felt like a lifetime, even though it had been less than a week since things had gone all wrong.

From then, it had been one nasty bolt hole to the next as he tried his best to stay one step ahead of law enforcement. There'd been so many across the country, he'd lost track of where he was or where he was supposed to be. The fact that all of those places looked pretty much the same, right down to the overflowing roach traps beneath the bed and curly hairs around the toilet bowl, didn't help with his disorientation.

Still, if Shownes recalled correctly, they also had the death penalty in Louisiana, so it was down to petty semantics at the end of the day.

Of course they did; why else would they have brought him here?

So, yeah, he could fathom there really was only one the way out of the unholy mess he'd managed to sign himself up for.

Heart heavy with defeat, stomach roiling with nausea, Shownes stared at the ancient credenza that dominated the cramped motel room. Fashioned from solid, dark wood—now a long time faded—it appeared startlingly out of place in such a run-down motel room. As a piece of furniture, it clearly had a story to tell, if only Shownes had the time to sit and ponder what that might be. Given any other circumstances, it might have been an amusing way to pass the time.

His eyes crawled over the credenza, from the deep gouge marks its small, square feet had made in the sticky linoleum floor to the thick layer of dust that covered its top. And there, nestled comfortably next to the flat screen, 4K TV, which sat on thin plastic feet and glowed with a muted news feed featuring Shownes's very own, inappropriately smiling face, sat his only means of escape. Funny how the strangest details stuck in the mind at such times: the TV *smelled* new.

Shownes's mouth dried, his tongue glued uncomfortably to its roof, as he studied with growing distaste the small, brown pill bottle, length of rough hemp rope—he reckoned six, maybe seven feet—and shiny, silver snub-nosed Taurus 38-Special, complete with black extra-grip handle.

The pills were Phenazepam; it was written on the otherwise plain, white label on the bottle's side. Whomever had put them there had wanted Shownes to know precisely what he'd be taking, should he decide to bow out that way. From what he could remember from his time in pharma, so many, many years ago, Shownes knew the benzodiazepine-based drug had a similar effect to Valium and remained in the system for several days.

It was also ridiculously easy to obtain off the Internet without prescription and had become a drug of choice for suicides—mostly female, interestingly enough—because an overdose just simply sent you off into a deep sleep from which you would never awake. It really was one of the nicer ways to end your life.

Only, Shownes knew he didn't have the luxury of *nice* or time—the cops would be at the motel and crashing through that flimsy door any minute; they'd drag his sorry ass to the nearest ER to pump his stomach and have him in County Jail before he'd even had time to nod off peacefully.

Of course, the rope was a definite non-starter. There was nowhere at all to tie it to in the small, musty room—unless he tried to end his life David Carradine-style in the tiny built-in closet alongside the mold-ridden ironing board, that was—and he was less than confident about the ability of the tarnished metal clothes rail in there to hold his weight.

Sure, he could try hooking one end of the rope around the credenza's leg and jumping out the window, but the rope seemed far too short for that. Try that, and Shownes figured he'd end up dangling by his neck, legs dancing against the motel's crumbling sidings, slowly choking out, until they cut him down and hauled him off to await the inevitable.

Which left the Taurus.

Small, deadly efficient, it would definitely do the job. Whoever left it in the motel room along with the pills and rope had quite thoughtfully provided a half dozen shiny brass bullets, all neatly stood on their ends like tiny soldiers standing to attention. It was safe to assume, even if not obvious, Shownes mused, they'd be protection hollowed protection rounds rather than range rounds—much more effective, you see, and likely to take out the whole back of a man's head when used point-blank.

"It's pretty much my only choice, then, you psycho," Shownes growled, heart pounding hard in his chest as that realization sank in. "I'll bet you planned it to end like this, too, you manipulating—"

A noise outside startled him.

Stealing a glance through the grubby, once-white net curtains, Shownes espied a quartet of black, unmarked panel vans peel into the Sunset Lane's cracked parking lot.

"Oh no," he groaned.

As Shownes watched, the side doors opened and, before the vehicles had even fully ground to a halt, a small army of black-clad, armed shapes clambered out and fanned out across the lot. They all had FBI printed in bright yellow on the back of their Kevlar vests and carried semi-automatics. The unavoidable Shownes had been dreading for what seemed an eternity was happening: the big guns had *finally* caught up with him.

Behind the FBI vans came a small fleet of a dozen or so police cars, followed, somewhat ominously, by a couple ambulances—lights flashing—and a coroner's vehicle.

Whether it was a last-ditch attempt at escaping the fate he'd had coming since he signed the contract he'd wished he'd never set eyes on—a desperate attempt to cling onto life just a few moments longer—or a simple, primeval, reaction to the overwhelming amounts of adrenaline pumping through his body, David Shownes decided to run.

Grabbing the revolver from beside the TV, Shownes loaded the ammunition into the barrel, his trembling hands fumbling the bullets as two hit the floor and roll beneath the ever-present credenza. He didn't fret too much about them, though, as he knew in his gut four rounds were actually three more than he'd need when the time came; it wasn't as if he had any chance of shooting his way through a veritable army of highly-trained FBI agents and their rifles, especially with only six rounds of ammunition to his name.

No.

Zero chance of that ever happening, Dave, old buddy.

Shownes raced for the door, unhooked the woefully inadequate security chain, and dashed out into the dim hallway; it was already uncomfortably hot and humid out there, even though the time on the TV had informed him it was still some time to go before eight in the morning.

Gun clutched tight in his left hand, Shownes hurried toward the elevator around the corner at the end of the hallway; he hoped and prayed to whatever gods may have been listening that the elevator was still working. By the way it had rattled and protested the evening before as it transported him up the three floors to his room, it would have come as little surprise had it died quietly in the night.

He had to try, at least.

Turning the sharp corner, Shownes all but ran headlong into a smartly dressed woman walking the other way. Mid to late thirties, petite, slim, with a spiked, bottle-black, pixie-cut hair style, she had a face Shownes's mother would have described as *handsome*.

The spark of odd familiarity triggered panic deep in Shownes's gut: his mother had been found brutally murdered and mutilated a couple of weeks ago, and the cops were after him as prime suspect. It was just one of the increasingly bizarre string of events that had led David Shownes to that particular dingy corridor at the Sunset Lane Motel.

The woman's skirt suit hugged her body to tailored perfection, the skirt's hem resting mid-thigh to showcase taut, shapely legs adorned by black spiked heels. Had circumstances been different, with Shownes not running for his life, he may well have taken a chance on picking her up; he still had his looks and a mountain of money, after all.

"Pardon me, ma'am," Shownes grunted as he dodged around the woman in his single-minded hurry to get to that rickety old elevator. He held the gun behind his back in the hope she'd not spot it and scream—broadcasting his whereabouts to the approaching law enforcement was the last thing he needed.

Shownes thought he heard her say something along the lines of *it's okay* or maybe even *good morning*, but all he could think was she looked so strangely out of place in a craphole like the Sunset Lane Motel.

In a heartbeat, the woman turned the corner and was gone.

With a furtive glance along the long hallway to see if the woman had *actually* gone, and with the sound of heavy, booted, footsteps on the motel's concrete stairs growing ever closer, Shownes stabbed at the elevator's tarnished silver call button with his thumb. Since he was a little kid, he'd always firmly believed the more you jabbed an elevator's button, and the faster, the quicker the car would come.

After what seemed an unbearable age, the elevator doors finally wobbled open.

Shownes got in.

From what he could recall, the elevator would take its own sweet time making its way down the three floors to the motel's lobby; it was as if the thing was operating in some sky-scraping Vegas hotel and not a crappy backwater place out in the middle of nowhere.

Even so, Shownes didn't have much time, he figuring the FBI would station a bunch of armed agents outside the elevator's doors on each floor just in case their quarry was actually stupid enough to use it as a means of escape.

A deep breath.

Shownes held the Taurus tight to his temple, its cold steel muzzle digging into the thin flesh there like an accusing finger.

No, wait.

Shownes lowered the gun.

He'd read somewhere, a lifetime ago, that a bullet to the temple was not guaranteed to kill; it was more likely to cause irreparable brain damage and he'd end up a vegetable. To his mind, that thought was far more terrifying than dying – to live out the rest of his days in some hideous living death was beyond comprehension.

Also, he wasn't well-versed enough in the nuances of ammunition to discern for certain if the bullets left by the revolver *were* for defense or range – that made a difference, too, apparently.

The article, written by one of the poor schmucks who got paid to clean up such messes, had said that to be sure—*very* sure—it was best to aim the shot from inside the mouth and up toward the rear of the skull. That way, the brain stem would be taken out, resulting in a quick and hopefully painless death.

Just like flicking off a light switch.

Another deep breath.

The elevator shuddered to a grinding halt.

This was it: the ground floor.

David John Shownes had very little time to reflect upon the bizarre set of circumstances that had led him to that moment, of the days filled with madness that had brought him so close to the edge there was no other option but to make that final, fatal leap.

The gun's muzzle tasted sour, metallic in his mouth, like maybe it had been fired recently. What did he know? He's only ever read about sucking on a gun's barrel in books and seen it in movies. What he did know was that it felt *awful* in his mouth, pressing against his tongue, his teeth, the chill, round *O* of its end prodding insistently at the ridged palate there.

A subdued *ding* and the elevator doors began to open; he espied the first hint of black-clad figures just a few strides away through the crack that formed.

This was it.

Time to end the misery of the last days of his life, last chance to go out on his own terms and not strapped to a prison gurney with a deadly trio of cannulas snaking from the veins in his arm.

And so, with no further thought, David John Shownes pulled the trigger.

Chapter 1

"I'll be down in just a minute, hun!" Chase Lennon huffed with impatience; once Jilly had a notion in that immaculately coiffured head of hers to go somewhere or do something, she had a habit of nagging him half to death until he fell into line.

Whether he'd agreed to it or not. She already had the kids all packed and ready for their impromptu early spring vacation to Atlantic Beach and had, naturally, fully expected her husband to drop everything to do the same.

"You said that a half hour ago!" Jilly's shrill voice drifted up the stairs and into Lennon's mahogany-paneled home office, her impatience matching his.

"A guy's still gotta work," Lennon grumbled to himself as he jabbed angrily away at his iMac's keyboard as if him being annoyed at his persistent wife was somehow the computer's fault. But no, it was his own fault for having bought the stupid beach front house in the first place; ever since he'd announced to Jilly they were now the proud owners of an exclusive beachside property, she'd wanted to spend every possible minute there.

"Just how *do* you think we pay for all this, *hun*?" It was not something Lennon would ever dare to say to his wife out loud and to her face, and most definitely not in such a disrespectful tone, but there in the sanctuary of his office, *his* space, Lennon allowed the words to slip out.

Truthfully, it had not been entirely his own fault; the Bayside Drive property had only ever been meant as an investment; there were definite benefits to being a top player in the realty game, and getting first dibs on exclusive properties was certainly one of them.

The previous owners of the house—all eight thousand square feet of prime real estate and less than an hour's drive away from his built-in-1910, $40m TriBeCa home—had fallen on hard times post-COVID, and the place had been a steal at just $10.2m.

It really had been an offer Lennon couldn't refuse.

He'd fully intended to flip the place and pocket himself a cool, ridiculously easy five mil or so, but the moment Jilly saw the property, she'd gone and done the unexpected.

She'd fallen in love with the dang place.

It was something that had never happened before with any of the properties Lennon had scooped up over his many incredibly lucrative years in high-end real estate. It just *had* to be 1060 Bayside Drive that turned the woman's head.

Lennon eased back in his high-backed, red leather office chair and ran a hand over the smooth-shaved dome of his head; just a couple more things to get squared away and he'd be ready to take some much-needed time out with his wife and kids.

Of course, he'd still be required to keep an eye on his business and take important calls, but he'd learned in the past couple years to allow himself to disconnect from work a little and take time to enjoy his money and family. The kids were growing up way too fast for his liking—Casey had her first period already, just three days after she became a teenager, and Chad was growing like a weed.

As Jilly was all too fond of reminding her workaholic husband, the pair of them would be out of the house and off to college before either of them knew what was happening.

Best make the most of Casey and Chad while he could, especially while they still enjoyed hanging out with Mom and Dad. Having said that, Casey was already showing signs of preferring to spend time with her friends, on her cell, or in her room—pretty much anything but enjoying the precious family time Jilly craved so much.

One last job to do: Lennon hit send on the email to Leibowitz, his accountant of fifteen years and counting—pun fully intended. The email gave the old boy permission to go ahead and pay the property taxes on the Lennons's 1910-built Reade Street home—well over a million for the year.

Lennon instructed Leibowitz to stick it on the American Express Centurian—the ultra-exclusive Black Amex card with no limit—and it would autopay at the end of the following month. Not that Lennon didn't have the cash in hand to pay for the privilege of living in the Tribeca home he owned, he just preferred to leave paying such things to the last possible minute and having that extra month to *actually* cough up the dough.

It was a hark back to the early days, when he was still building his business empire and money was hand-to-mouth tight; old habits like that just refused to die.

"Okay, just one last thing…" Lennon allowed himself a wry smile as he pictured Jilly's face as she waited downstairs with the kids and Bingo, the family's five-year-old labradoodle; that had been the last time they'd allowed Casey and Chad to name anything.

"Let's make sure you did what I'm paying you to do, knuckleheads." Lennon's habit of talking to himself stemmed from so many lonely years of working alone from home as his business grew; there was literally no one else to talk to back, then. Then came the New York office, the success, all the money, and here he was again: working from his home office and talking to himself.

Lennon clicked on his company website to make sure the web guys had made the updates he'd requested a few days ago; they were pretty efficient at following orders, but Lennon was not one to trust that things would get done simply because he'd asked. That was a lesson he'd learned the hard way a long time ago. No matter how big his company got, founder and CEO, Chase Lennon, would always be checking his instructions were adhered to, and in a timely manner.

The website lit up the computer's screen and there was Lennon in all his handsome glory: six-feet even, a trim 200lbs he didn't have to work too hard at, the tanned dome of his head freshy shaved, baby blue eyes fixed in a determined stare, and a winning smile his overpriced orthodontist was immensely proud of.

Lennon was dressed in his very best, three-thousand-dollar Armani suit—dark blue to complement his eyes, of course—and was surrounded by a dozen or so of his New York office team; of course, the photographer had hand-picked all the best-looking ones to make the picture 'pop.'

In the background, in huge letters, sat the company name he was so damn proud of: Imagine Real Estate.

Sure, he'd heard all the John Lennon jokes, and had even referred to himself as the Fifth Beatle on occasion— surprising just how many people actually believed that claim. He didn't even mind too much that some folks at the office still called him John or Johnny—even Jilly did on the occasions when she'd had a few too many of her favorite mojitos—although many of them were far too young to get the reference and were genuinely surprised to learn Paul McCartney was actually in a band before Wings.

It had taken a lot of long, hard years to build up Imagine Real Estate. Lennon had literally worked every hour the good Lord had sent to create the company that provided so well for his family now. Thankfully, Jilly had stood by his side, even in the years during which she hardly saw him; she'd played the part of office widow with unwavering loyalty and never once complained.

She'd even turned a blind eye to his penchant for a little bet or two—the one vice Lennon had allowed himself to indulge in, even when money had been at its tightest. It was never enough to cause concern in his opinion. Lennon was confident he had his 'habit' nicely under control; just the occasional ball game, the horses, and the black jack tables in the upstate casinos.

He reconciled the money he lost and won with the notion that he was, by nature, a risk-taker. After all, was it not the very trait that made him such a darn good entrepreneur and astute businessman?

He'd built up his realty business single-handedly once the realization hit him there was far more money to be had recruiting realtors and having them work under him than wearing out shoe leather and giving up weekends selling properties himself. Add to that his focus on only the high-end properties, and Chase Lennon had created the perfect storm.

So, yeah, he liked a bet every now and then; it was definitely a small price to pay for such success, especially nowadays with money being no object. He also enjoyed the company of other, younger women, which was nothing uncommon in his line of business.

Lennon figured Jilly had known way back then what great things were coming their way and had chosen to bite her tongue at her husband's occasional infidelities. There were times, though, Lennon couldn't help but wonder if she'd ever found out about, or even suspected, his brief fling back in 2015 with Suzannah Trimaldi, one of the up-and-comers at his newly formed San Francisco office.

Despite all the clues being there like weeks away from home, almost paranoid secrecy over his cell phone, mysterious hotel and restaurant receipts, and lipstick on his underwear, Jilly had not once mentioned any grain of suspicion. The woman was no fool, Lennon knew that, so she'd obviously chosen to willfully ignore that particular weakness, too.

"Looking good, there, Suze." Lennon studied the stunning face smiling from the back of the team picture; her jet-black hair was pulled back into a severe ponytail that made her gorgeous face seem overly severe and, sadly, her figure was hidden by the Imagine employees standing in front of her.

It had been taken back when Ms. Trimaldi had been in New York for training and whatever else Lennon and she happened to come up with together in her hotel suite after hours. He allowed himself the luxury of recalling pulling on her long mane of shiny black hair when they made love; it stretched almost all the way to her perfectly pear-shaped behind, her smooth, olive-hued skin, impossibly toned, tall, slim body, and the way she *smelled.*

Suzannah never did reveal what perfume she wore, but it was always guaranteed to break through Lennon's resolution to make each one of their many trysts the last.

Lennon absently flicked through the company website with sweet memories of Suzannah swirling through his mind; maybe one day he'd forgive her for ditching Imagine

Real Estate—and him—for a rival company in L.A. and look her up.

Maybe.

"We're still waiting for you, Daddy!" Casey sounded even more impatient than Jilly, if that was actually possible; she totally *hated* it when her mother told her what to do, especially when it came to chastising her father. Lennon knew his wife had resorted to getting the girl to nag him; Jilly's patience was about to run out entirely.

"I'm on my way!" Lennon did his best to sound amiable through clenched teeth. He had no desire to start the family weekend at the beach house off in a fight with Jilly, but she was making it difficult. She *always* won, anyway, no matter who was in the right; Lennon had learned over their years together just to suck it up and keep the peace at all costs.

"I'm powering down now!" Lennon hovered the Mac's cursor over the shutdown icon and made ready to disconnect from the digital world to fully embrace the real one with his wife and kids.

A popup caught his attention.

Sent via his LinkedIn account, it actually used his full name, Chase Henry Lennon, which immediately set it apart from the countless other spam, ads, and solicitations that plagued his computer on an infuriatingly regular basis.

It also ran with the hook line, *"Who Wants to be a Billionaire?"*

Humming the 'I do' line from the Sinatra song, Lennon clicked his VPN back on and logged into LinkedIn. There, he located the ad in his messages and maneuvered the cursor over the 'click here' button.

Then, he deleted the message.

"Scammers," Lennon huffed.

The ad appeared again.

Same as before, only, somehow more *insistent.*

Now, Lennon knew that was just his mind playing tricks on him: the ad hadn't changed one iota.

Hitting delete a third and fourth time had the same effect: the ad popped up again, and each time it fueled Lennon's curiosity just a touch more.

Fifth time, he double-checked the VPN was activated and clicked on the ad's 'more information' button.

"Well, hello there, darlin'," Lennon affected his best southern drawl, which never failed to amuse him, even though he knew it was nothing like the real thing. The website that appeared was Spartan, to say the least.

No fancy graphics, no images of scantily-clad, nubile young women to catch and hold the attention—sex sells, right?—just a plain white screen with a couple simple paragraphs explaining what he, Chase Henry Lennon, had to do to become a *billionaire*.

It was $1.2bn, to be precise. An oddly specific number. Perhaps that, along with the far-from-glossy webpage, was to show the originators were not scammers based in Nigeria or some similar place he imagined had entire multi-story buildings crammed with workers dedicated to finagling money from the dumb and the gullible overseas?

Or… could it be scammers doing a good job at not appearing to be scammers?

Undeterred, Lennon skimmed the explanatory paragraphs:

Chase Henry Lennon, here is your once-in-a-lifetime chance to join the billionaire's club. As an already-successful individual accustomed to hard work and very little play, we are more than confident this golden opportunity to join our game and achieve wealth beyond even your wildest dreams will pique your interest at the very least…

"Okay, you've *piqued* me." Chase smiled to himself as the familiar surge of adrenaline teased his body. Naturally, he'd forgotten his wife and kids were *still* waiting for him downstairs.

He read on.

The purchase of just one $10,000 lottery ticket gives you the opportunity to participate in our gameshow with the potential to win over one billion dollars in tax-free prize money!

Had to be a scam.

Didn't it?

Lennon poked around the sparse webpage for a menu or some other buttons to click on for more information.

Nothing.

Going against his better judgement, Lennon reread the couple paragraphs and maneuvered his cursor across the screen in the hopes of hitting something; he'd seen websites use the same ploy before—get the viewer psychologically invested by making them look for the link button instead of spoon-feeding them. Hell, he'd even used the technique on some of his company websites in the past.

The cursor switched to the little hand. It had accidentally located the hidden link in the top left corner of the page.

Before he knew what he was doing, Lennon clicked on the mouse button and the website uploaded a new page.

This one was more minimalist than the landing page… if that was even possible. It had a no-nonsense, navy-blue pay button and the title 'Buy Your Exclusive Lottery Ticket Here' just above that. To Lennon's now intrigued mind, it seemed like more of a *challenge* than a request.

The remainder of the page was plain white and entirely uninteresting.

"What are you doing, Chase, old buddy?" Lennon muttered beneath his breath, his lips barely moving. "You don't need the money *this* badly."

Lennon was right.

He didn't.

He had more money in the bank than he could ever possibly spend in one lifetime, the kids' college funds bulging, and pretty much everything he wanted in life. Becoming a billionaire really wouldn't make any change to his way of life, other than offering what his old man used to call 'bragging rights.'

Idly, he wondered if maybe they gave out certificates or special pins to the 3,381 billionaires across the world? There *had* to be a secret handshake at the very least! Lennon thought back to an old rerun episode of *The Simpsons* he'd watched with Chad and Casey a few years ago.

Jilly had been out clothes shopping with her girlfriends and Lennon had sworn the kids to secrecy: his wife didn't approve of the TV show at the time because she thought it was too subversive for little kids.

It was a *cartoon*, for Christ's sakes!

That particular episode had resonated with Lennon as it involved Mr. Burns losing his iconic billionaire status and being forced to leave the exclusive Billionaire's Club—Branson, Buffet, Gates, and their ilk—and slum it with the lowly millionaires in their down-market club, which just happened to be over an adjoining wall.

The absolute shame Burns felt at such a climb down was palpable.

And that had stuck with Lennon ever since; he would often try to imagine joining the billionaires as they smoked fat Cuban cigars and drank the finest, aged single malt money could buy and made fun of the poor millionaires next door. It sounded good.

It wasn't the money.

Chase Lennon knew that.

It was the thrill of the bet he craved, that electric tingle that spread out from the knot in the gut when he bet on a rank outsider horse at 80:1 or the turn of a casino's Blackjack card on 19. It had been a long, long time since he'd felt anything akin to that. The real estate business just didn't excite him like it used to, no matter how many zeros there were on the commission cheques.

Whoever had designed the scant website announcing the mysterious lottery may well have designed it especially for Lennon: the thrill of the bet, of the *chance* of winning big had him hooked long before he clicked on the link.

It was as if the organizers of the mysterious game behind the website knew he'd lost his edge, that Lennon's wealthy life with a beautiful family had made him soft, taken away the keen appetite for clinching the deal that had driven his success in the first place.

"Besides," Lennon told himself, "it's *only* ten grand."

Chump change indeed.

There had been a time in Lennon's life not so long ago, when such an amount of money was considered 'car-buying money.' Now, though, now it would barely cover the insurance on the Bugatti Veyron and Aston Martin Vanquish he only drove once a year.

"Oh, what the hell…" Lennon's personal mantra had prefaced pretty much every major risk he'd taken in his life, from going it alone in the real estate business to getting down on one knee to Jilly just three weeks after they met, and really hadn't let him down too much over the years.

Just look at where it had gotten him so far!

With a deep breath, Lennon clicked on that *buy now* button and made ready to autofill the Centurian card's information, along with his personal details, in the payment portal.

No need.

As it turned out, they already had all the information on Chase Henry Lennon they needed for him to purchase the mysterious lottery ticket.

Chapter 2

Good god, Jilly *still* looked good enough to eat in a string bikini.

Lennon eased his solid frame back on the sun lounger and eyed his wife over the top of his Aviators. Jilly, oblivious to her husband's scrutiny, pottered around the periphery of the azure-blue swimming pool that took center stage in the beach house's spacious backyard.

In it, the kids swam and splashed around without a care in the world, while Bingo ran up and down one side of the pool, tongue lolling, tail wagging, looking longingly at the cool water.

Lennon knew exactly what the mutt was thinking and inwardly *dared* him to act upon it.

The red, polka-dot bikini Jilly had chosen to wear left very little to the imagination, indeed. It was not really much more than three miniscule triangles of flimsy cloth that covered just enough of the essentials for Jilly to feel comfortable around Casey and Chad.

The spaghetti strings holding the triangles together were thin and tight, and from the back, one could imagine Jilly was almost naked. There had been times when Lennon and Jilly had visited the beach house *sans* children, and she'd spent most of the time proudly naked and showing off her expensive breasts and Brazilian wax.

Seeing their mom in such a state of undress around the pool and at the beach had never fazed the kids; they'd gotten used to it over the years and barely even noticed.

Their father noticed, though.

It was good to have a hot wife who took such great care of herself and was more than happy to show off what the best cosmetologists and plastic surgeons in New York could create. Still, all credit to Jilly, she did put in a lot of effort in the home gymnasium he'd had installed to maintain her husband's investment, and that made the world of difference.

Lennon glanced away from Jilly's beautifully flat, toned, tanned abs to his own belly, which bulged ever so slightly against the waistband of his American flag swim shorts. There was a little more padding there than there should be—*insulation for the six-pack*, he preferred to call it—which he figured he ought to burn off in the gym when he got the time.

Jilly waved over, her breasts, unsupported by the hopelessly inadequate bikini top, jiggled alluringly as she did so; did she know the effect she was having on her husband right now?

Most likely.

And most likely she'd be looking forward to an early night and some much-needed stress relief, courtesy of her husband and a little blue pill.

It *was* Wednesday, after all.

Lennon reveled in playing the voyeur as Jilly paused to pour herself a tall glass of lemonade from the ice-frosted pitcher on the iron table beneath the expansive parasol across the pool. He wondered if she ever looked at him with the same stirrings of lust he still felt from time to time; it had certainly been a long while since he'd seen that raw, wanton look in his wife's eyes.

They still enjoyed sex, sure, but it was always on a schedule Jilly set a couple weeks in advance on their joint calendar. Lennon had heard often enough about how spontaneity goes out of a marriage after the so-called honeymoon period of five to seven years or so, and certainly so once kids come along.

But he'd never expected sex to become an agenda item and feel more like a business arrangement instead of the actions of a horny couple who just couldn't keep their hands of one another. Just like it had been back in the early days of their relationship. The couple of guy friends Lennon had talked to about it had assured him it was all perfectly natural and reiterated Jilly's point that if they didn't plan ahead, they'd never get around to making love the few times a week they actually did.

It seemed good ol' spontaneity just couldn't be relied on once you reached a certain stage of the marriage.

Perhaps that was why so many middle-aged guys bought bright red sports cars and ran off with gals half their age?

"Chase, baby, will you keep an eye on Bingo?" Jilly's soft voice floated across the pool, just loud enough to rise above the kids' shouts, splashing, and the occasional yapping of the dog, who was becoming ever more animated as Casey and Chad played ball, and looked increasingly likely to take a dip to join in all the fun.

"Sure thing! Fix me one of those, while you're at it!" Lennon called after his wife and ogled her firm, sexy behind as she sashayed through the French doors and into the kitchen; it was evidently margarita time already—it had to be five o'clock somewhere, right?

Jilly waved a hand over her head in acknowledgement and disappeared into the cool of the kitchen. Lennon turned his attention to the pool, the kids, and, as instructed, the dog.

"Bingo!" Lennon cringed every time he said the pooch's ridiculous name; six thousand bucks for a designer dog and they named it after a stupid elementary school rhyme. "Quit encouraging him to jump in, Chad!"

"Okay, Dad!" Chad replied, but continued throwing the ball way wide of his sister and ever closer to the dog's side of the pool.

Lennon sighed and forced himself to relax. After all, wasn't that the whole point of the impromptu family trip to the gorgeous beach house he worked so freakin' hard to buy and pay for? It wasn't that he was particularly anal about the dog going in the pool. It was just that the last time Bingo had jumped into the ever-so inviting water was back when he was only six, maybe seven months old, and he'd somehow managed to scare himself enough to take a dump in the water.

That was the time Lennon learned the hard way it wasn't okay to simply fish the crap out with the pool net and carry on as normal: Casey had gotten a nasty dose of pink eye from that harsh lesson and both the doctor *and* the pool guy had chastised Chase like he was some delinquent schoolkid.

Thankfully, the stupid dog had also scared himself from jumping in the water again, despite his apparent desire to do so.

The phone rang.

Startled from his reverie, Lennon jumped a little. He'd given the office strict instructions to only call in the event of an emergency. And by emergency, he made it painfully clear he meant the building had to be falling down or a zombie apocalypse was well under way.

He doubted either scenario would be going down on that balmy Wednesday afternoon, so he was more than a little irritated as he reached for his cell.

Lennon plucked it from the tiny poolside table next to the recliner and glanced at the number on the screen. It was not one he recognized, nor had his phone identified it as the near-ubiquitous *Scam Likely*.

Ignoring his first instinct to just let the call go to voicemail, Lennon jabbed at the green button to pick up the call.

"Mr. Chase Henry Lennon?" The voice, male, baritone, sounded crisp and clear, as if its owner was standing right over his shoulder.

"Who is this?" Lennon remained guarded and waited for the inevitable prerecorded message or Indian call center staffer to cut in.

"I'm calling to offer my congratulations, Mr. Lennon," the voice explained, most matter-of-fact. "You are this month's winner of the lottery."

Lennon snorted out a stifled laugh. He couldn't help but admire the audacity. Scammers were getting bolder by the minute, more cunning every day in their ruses, finding increasingly inventive ways to extract cash from the desperate and the gullible.

This, though, this one was just plain lazy.

"I don't play the lottery," Lennon growled into his phone. "You got the wrong guy, my friend. So why don't you go—"

"You bought a ticket online yesterday for ten thousand dollars using the American Express Centurian card ending in six two. Again, many congratulations, Mr. Lennon."

The penny dropped.

"Oh." Embarrassed, Lennon couldn't think of anything else to say.

"As stated on our website, you have won the opportunity to participate in our gameshow and potentially win $1.2bn."

The guy on the phone sounded dour, straightforward, as if he'd made this same call a thousand times before, yet Lennon's head buzzed with excitement. He heaved himself up off the lounger with the intention of taking the call to the pool house. The last thing he needed was admonishment from Jilly for taking a business call on a day off or, even worse, a barrage of questions and accusations he really didn't want to answer.

"Hey, kids!" Lennon dampened the call with a bare shoulder over the phone's microphone and pointed at Bingo; the dog was going hyper by the side of the pool and had that same happy/stupid expression on his face as the last time he'd made the jump. "Watch him for me!"

"You need to meet with us in Philadelphia at eight o'clock tomorrow morning," the voice said. "We will send you instructions and location by text in the next few minutes."

"Okay." Lennon had questions, but struggled to figure out which one to ask first. "What exactly do I have to—?"

"You will have plenty of opportunity to ask your questions tomorrow, Mr. Lennon." The voice was pleasant enough, but quite firm. "Please, don't be late."

"But—"

"Goodbye, Mr. Lennon."

"Can I just ask…?" He was speaking to dead air. The guy had already hung up on him.

"Chad! Casey!" Lennon shouted across the pool as he lowered his phone. "Keep the dang dog out of the—"

There came a loud splash, accompanied by his children's delighted shrieks, and Lennon resigned himself to retrieving the net from the pool house. He also had to figure out a way to break the news to Jilly he'd be flying out later that evening; so much for a steamy, albeit prescheduled, night relieving the tension that miniscule bikini had built up in him all day.

And he couldn't help but wonder just what the good city of Philadelphia had in store for him.

Chapter 3

It had come as a relief to Lennon, with just a tinge of concern, that Jilly hadn't seemed to mind too much when he'd casually announced he'd be cutting short their family break at Bayside Drive.

She'd crinkled up that cute, six-thousand-dollar, button nose of hers and made some smart-ass comment about having to sort herself out in bed that night.

As if there had ever been a chance of any form of lovemaking at the vacation house. Jilly always maintained the walls were too thin, the kids' rooms too close to the master bedrooms, and he knew how Chad and Casey never slept much on vacation.

It was all just an excuse, and Lennon tried hard to remember just when the sexual spark flickered out in his marriage.

Sometimes he wondered why he just didn't hook up with one of the many eager young women who were attracted to him—and his money, of course—on an almost daily basis. It really would be so easy to take full advantage of any one of them. Or two, or more, if the mood took him.

Maybe one day he would.

"It's for work, sweetheart. I'm sorry." He'd chosen just the right moment to placate his wife: shortly after she'd made a start on her third margarita and was nicely settled down on the sun lounger next to his. "A quick there and back. I'll be home in a coupla days, hun – three at the most. You'll hardly know I was gone."

"Sounds about right." Jilly had smiled when she said that, but there was something in her tone that belied any good humor. Of late, her husband's long working hours and distraction from her and the kids had grown to become a thorny bone of contention. After all, his smart business decision to recruit a small army of realtors to work under him was supposed to have led to less work and more family time. Jilly had made no secret of the fact she considered his near-constant working was nothing more than a deliberate attempt to avoid her, Casey, and Chad.

"You don't mind *too* much?" Lennon pressed, a little put out at his wife's lack of protest; he'd expected some kick back, even if it was her trademarked passive-aggressive cold shoulder. And she *did* look hot in that bikini!

Jilly shrugged. "Why would I mind, Chase?" It was a loaded, rhetorical question, of course. "It's what you do, isn't it? Work?"

Had Lennon not been fabricating the whole work trip thing to fly all the way over to Philadelphia to chase up some sketchy gameshow he'd won a place on, he'd have retorted with his well-worn *I work this freakin' hard so you and the kids can enjoy summer breaks in a $15m beach house* argument.

As it was, he'd been feeling more than a little guilty at abandoning the family since he'd gotten the phone call and made the instant decision to have his private jet fueled up and ready to leave JFK airport by eight that evening. The flight itself was well under an hour, and Lennon really could have simply flown out early the following morning, but he was beyond curious and couldn't wait to meet the gameshow people.

Instead of rising to Jilly's bait and kicking off a poolside argument in front of the kids, Lennon simply replied, "Thanks for understanding, babe."

"That's what *I* do, isn't it?" Although not directly picking a fight, Jilly appeared determined to make her point; passive-aggressive should have been her middle name.

"I've still got all of today with you guys, and I'll be back in a couple days," Lennon reiterated before laying back down on his lounger. His body language for *I'm done*.

Sadly, his wife was not.

Jilly gave him that dismissive smile of hers and said, "Maybe you should go now, babe. You know how you prefer to be early for these things."

The kids had been similarly nonchalant at their father's premature departure. He'd gotten hugs, of course, but couldn't shake the feeling that they were just too used to him letting them down like that and to him being absent from their lives. They'd resumed playing, laughing and splashing around in the pool before Lennon had even gone inside to pack.

So, Lennon had left Bayside Drive early, not wishing to stick around in the awkward atmosphere Jilly had deliberately created, and hung around the airport while they got his plane ready. A few drinks, a fast-food burger, and fries, and he'd been feeling nice and relaxed by the time he'd boarded.

The guilt had niggled at him all the way to JFK and onto the Cessna Citation. There, Lennon stared out through the window as the plane taxied out onto the runway and made ready to take flight. The full, ice-cold champagne flute in front of him served well to assuage his conscience at having left the kids, although they'd seemed blissfully unmoved at him leaving so soon in their vacation time.

Perhaps *that* ought to have worried him more than Jilly's non-argument?

As the Citation taxied along the runway in a quiet corner of the Northeast Philadelphia private airport, all thoughts of Jilly and the kids slipped from Lennon's mind. A few more sips of the sweet, sparkling wine helped, as did the gentle tug of momentum as the Cessna took to the sky. On the horizon, the sun, bloated and a most spectacular peach color, made ready to begin its descent; it would be dark when Chase Lennon got to Philadelphia.

Chapter 4

It was a far cry from the overly loud mix of music, vomit stink, and piss stains of Bourbon Street, but Privateer Place on the shores of Lake Pontchartrain was still very much New Orleans. Built specifically to house the city's university students, Privateer Place more resembled nice, middle-class apartments than the stereotypical frat houses and cold, damp student homes; there was even an on-site laundromat and community pool.

Through the window of the third-floor student accommodation, the cop gazed absently out at the famous causeway that sliced the lake neatly in two and he considered the endless streams of vehicles; people going about their day-to-day business.

Naturally, they were all blissfully oblivious to the brutal tragedy that had brought him to the apartment before the sun had even had the chance to peek over the horizon; it was most likely for the best, the cop thought to himself.

"The CSI team is here," one of the uniforms said to the detective as he stepped gingerly around the threadbare couch that took up the center of the room, his black size-eleven shoes clad in blue paper bootees. "You said to let you know when they turned up…"

Distracted, Detective Broussard offered only a vague nod. His gaze remained fixed upon the rod-straight stretch of roadway across Pontchartrain. It was so much better than dwelling upon what he'd had to face in the apartment at such a ridiculously early hour that morning. "Thank you, Officer…"

"Pascal, sir," the uniform prompted, as if concerned the detective might forget his name and how well he'd done his job.

"Yeah, Pascal. Good work today."

Chest puffed out, beaming at the acknowledgement, Officer Pascal made his way to the apartment door, no doubt pleased to be out of the God-awful meat-stink of the bloody carnage inside.

Alone once more, Broussard—Theo, short for Theophile, although only those closest to the cop knew it—forced himself to turn his attention back to the murder scene he'd been called out to attend in the painfully early hours of that morning. Unmarried, unattached, Broussard had become the precinct's go-to for all the unpleasant jobs and unsociable hours that were called in; kinda went with the territory.

It also helped that he had an incredibly keen mind for joining the dots and sniffing out the bad guys, which is how he'd risen so quickly through the NOPD ranks to achieve the rank of Detective III a year before, a little after his thirty-fifth birthday. The rumor mill had run rife, of course, with jealous gossip spread around that he'd only been fast tracked because of his skin color, family history, and Cajun lineage.

Considering himself above such maliciously unfounded tittle-tattle, Broussard chose to ignore that.

Slim, five-nine in his socks, Theo Broussard was what most would consider 'classically handsome,' which to him meant he had a face only a mother could love. He knew the assessment was unduly harsh on himself because he'd had little problem attracting potential suitors through the years but it had more to do with how he felt on the inside.

He had dealt with the nastiest side of humanity too long to feel any other way. And he'd chosen to remain unattached because he witnessed first-hand the absolute devastation his father's untimely death in the line of duty had on his poor mom – a brutal pain that lasted decades after Detective Broussard Sr. failed to come home from a night patrol in the French Quarter.

There were three bodies in the apartment's living area: two girls, one guy, all young, all piled together onto the blood-drenched couch. All three were entirely naked and, judging by the clothing, bottles, and marijuana paraphernalia scattered about the room, they had been in the middle of one hell of a party when they'd been so rudely interrupted by the perpetrator.

Broussard had attended murder scenes before, more than he cared to recall, but he couldn't remember having seen so much blood in one place. The stuff was sprayed across the walls, spattered upon the white stucco ceiling, soaking into the cheap, garishly patterned carpet, and splashed on every stick of furniture.

Broussard knew the distinctive pattern of arterial spray when he saw it, and it looked like all three victims had been stabbed in either their carotid or femoral arteries; it was impossible to tell for sure given the amount of drying, congealing blood covering the stiffening corpses and the multitude of stab wounds covering them. Broussard huffed; that was one for the medical examiner to figure out.

It was likely the partying trio had been murdered somewhere around one, one-thirty, that morning; Broussard had noted the stiffness of the bodies, the lividity that had set in, and how all but the thickest patches of blood had dried upon exposed skin.

Whoever the killer was, they had launched a frenzied attack on the students with the determination to cause as much damage as possible; it was definitely someone who had enjoyed what they were doing. Chances are, Broussard made a mental note, if they hadn't done this before, they'd most definitely be doing it again… unless he tracked them down first, of course.

Still, given the brutality of the killing, the killer had taken the time afterward to place the bodies upon the couch, piling them neatly on top of one another with the guy sandwiched between the two young ladies. It was like a bloody tableau of a grim three-way laid out for some ghoulish art class.

The killer had also removed an eye from each of the victims: left from the girls, right from the guy. No doubt that carried a deep meaning to someone, the same someone who would enjoy reliving the moment over and over until the thrill wore off and, without a doubt, they'd be out looking for their next fix. Broussard had learned in training that was why killers typically saved some kind of trophy from their victims: a psychopathic *aide memoir*, if you will.

"Sickos," Broussard let the word slip out as he crossed the room. It was all such a terrible waste of young lives, and for what? All that human potential gone in a few manic minutes just to sate somebody's warped bloodlust.

Ducking beneath the yellow police tape, out in the hallway, and mercifully away from the rank, cloying, stench of blood and voided bodily wastes, Broussard took in a couple much-needed deep breaths and gathered his thoughts as he made his way toward the stairwell. A quick glance up and he espied the small, black CCTV security camera clinging resolutely to the ceiling at the far corner of the hallway.

He'd not noticed it before, but then again, it had still been dark when he'd gotten to the crime scene and one of the hallway's fluorescent strip lights had not been working. The camera was the type he'd seen a hundred times before; he knew all too well from bitter experience it was the cheap type which saved footage to an onboard memory card and wrote over the oldest files with the new.

Broussard made another mental note, this one to have a deputy get hold of the previous night's footage from that camera and any covering the external doorway before the cheap thing overwrote it.

Chapter 5

He was there in Philly for the opportunity to become richer than even his wildest dreams, to cement a legacy of being among the world's elite. Sure, he'd never quite be Musk, Bezos, or Gates rich, but having those extra zeros on the end of his net wealth would make a heck of a lot of difference to his self-worth as well as his net worth.

Hell, maybe Jilly would even put out a little more often.

But, more than any of that, for Lennon, it was the thrill of the bet, the gamble, that had got his old juices flowing; feeling the same adrenaline-fueled hunger he'd had back in the day when he lived hand-to-mouth hustling at the bottom of the real estate pile which was better than any of the designer drugs he'd experimented with along the way.

Better, even, than sex.

It was late, Philadelphia was quiet, the darkness kept at bay in its streets by the endless rows of glowing lamps.

The charter company had laid on a Tesla model X to get Lennon downtown and to the Pyramid Club. His audition for the gameshow was scheduled to take place there, apparently. A text had popped into Lennon's inbox while he'd still been 41,000 feet over Pennsylvania with the time and location; he was going to make it with five minutes to spare.

The Tesla made its way silently through downtown Philly, smoothly rounding the corner by the huge Macey's store and onto Market Street. The car's lack of engine noise irked Lennon even more than the huge screen that took up most of the dash; he much preferred his vehicles to have a little grunt, some soul, to them – being in the Model X, for him, was like riding a TV set.

Give him the meaty growl of an Aston Martin DB7 or Dodge Viper any day of the week.

As the tall, imposing building topped with the exclusive club eased into sight, Lennon's driver spoke for the first time.

"Looks like we're here, Mr. Lennon," said the middle-aged man with an expensive, dark blue suit and a two-hundred-dollar haircut. The building loomed ahead, taking up most of the view from the windshield.

"Yup." Lennon was in no mood for small talk. He knew the driver had only broken the silence in the hope of earning himself a fat tip. Lennon knew from experience it was strictly forbidden for agency drivers to solicit gratuities but it didn't stop most of them from at least trying it on, even if it could end with the instant termination of their employment.

Done discretely, typically by means of lighthearted chitchat, it was harmless enough; and so what if a rich client saw fit to share the wealth a little?

"I hope you have a wonderful night, Mr. Lennon, sir," the driver said as he drew the car silently to a halt in front of the Market Street building.

Lennon slipped the guy a surreptitious hundred and muttered an absent thank you; his mind was elsewhere and he was as nervous as a fat kid on prom night!

The Pyramid Club was fifty-two floors up, at the very top of the tower, and enjoyed spectacular, panoramic views across the city. It was easy to see why the place was invitation-only and astronomically expensive to be a member—nice, high prices to keep all the proles out, Lennon reckoned.

All in all, despite his nervous excitement, the dry mouth, heart thumping hard against his ribs, Lennon was delighted to have finally made it into the world-famous Pyramid Club. Philadelphia was one city he'd rarely done business in, and the opportunity had just never arisen.

"One hell of a first time," Lennon mumbled to himself with a wan smile as he made his way to the building's main doors.

"Mr. Lennon?"

At first, Lennon thought the Tesla driver was calling him back; maybe he'd dropped his wallet or phone in the back of the car?

But no.

He spun around just in time to see the black car glide away from the curbside and disappear around the corner.

"Mr. *Chase* Lennon?"

He turned around. "Yes?"

"We have been expecting you."

More than anything, Lennon wanted to add "Mr. Bond" to the line, but there was just something about the tall, dour-looking older guy holding open the door for him that suggested the joke would have fallen on stony ground and gone completely unappreciated.

"I'm not late, am I?" Lennon knew he wasn't, but it seemed like the correct thing to say – it was *something* to say.

"You are on time, Mr. Lennon," the man told him without a hint of emotion. "But you knew that already."

Lennon felt his face color up a little. He felt a touch embarrassed at having been caught out; it was not a feeling he experienced all too often and he wasn't sure he much cared for it.

With nary a smile, the man ushered Lennon into the vestibule. The lights there were overly bright and it took a second or so for Lennon's eyes to adjust from the darkness outside he'd just left behind.

"I've never been to the Pyramid Club before," Lennon ventured as he followed on across the expansive, marble floor of the atrium. Why he felt the need to make small talk, he wasn't sure, so he put it down to nerves. Again, an altogether alien feeling for Chase Lennon.

The man was oddly out of place for such a salubrious location; he wore loose-fitting, khaki pants, pristinely white Air Jordans, and a dark gray button down under a navy-blue sports jacket. Lennon mused to himself that, if he ever dared to dress like that at home, Jilly wouldn't let him open the front door, let alone step outside of it!

One thing that could always be said for Jilly Lennon was her sense of what worked and what didn't, her fashion sense impeccable.

"In that case…" the man said with that impossibly straight face, "you're going to be a little disappointed."

And disappointed, he was.

The two rode the elevator in silence; as the car hummed its way up all fifty-two floors of the building, Lennon couldn't help but wonder what the guy had meant by his comment. How on earth could it be possible to be disappointed by one of America's most desirable private clubs?

The place was empty.

Lennon stepped out of the elevator after his guide and into a deserted, silent dining room. Illuminated by dim lights around its periphery, the dining area was deathly still; each table had its accompanying chairs stacked on its cloth-covered top for the benefit of the cleaning staff. It was only ten, the Pyramid Club should have been heaving.

Could that mean the show people had paid to close the place down early? Lennon figured a company offering over a billion bucks in prize money might have the clout to do just that.

"Where is everybody?" Lennon asked, more to break the silence than anything. There was just something about a place like that entirely devoid of people that he found… *unnatural*.

"Everybody?" The flicker of an upturn at the corner of the man's mouth let Lennon know he was playing with him.

"The other contestants?" Lennon pressed. "I expected there'd be a bunch of us here for the audition."

The man shook his head and scratched absently at his left ear. "No, Mr. Lennon. It's just you this evening."

"Oh." It was all Lennon could think of to say.

"I can only apologize for your disappointment, Mr. Lennon." Another voice wafted out from the gloom and inky shadows at the far end of the deserted dining room. Softer than the Air Jordan guy's, the voice was almost feminine in its timbre.

Lennon strained hard and made out a dark shape as it slipped from the shadows and made its way toward him. In contrast to Lennon's guide, the newcomer was of a stocky build, only five seven, eight at the most, and walked with that arms-slightly-out stance of a seasoned bodybuilder. To

Lennon's mind, the body most definitely didn't fit the voice.

"I was just expecting—"

"More auditionees. I heard."

Lennon shook the offered hand. It was warm, smooth, dry. "Call me Chase," he said. Again, something to say.

"Ben Austin. It's so good to finally meet you, Chase." Austin pumped Lennon's hand hard, maintaining firm eye contact as he did so.

"So… what happens now?" Lennon broke the handshake and got straight down to business; it was an old habit that some people he dealt with found to be uncomfortably blunt. Given that, it was how Chase Lennon got business done.

Austin, however, did not appear fazed one bit. "I appreciate you cutting through the platitudes. This is where things start to get a little more interesting, Mr. Lennon," Austin told him.

Lennon wondered if the man had already forgotten the invitation to use his first name, or if he'd deliberately chosen not to. Perhaps the show people preferred to keep things more formal? "Things were interesting enough," Lennon said. "From the time your ad popped up in my inbox, I'd say it's been interesting." He forced a smile; why *did* he feel so absurdly nervous?

Austin mirrored the smile. "As the old saying goes, you ain't seen nothing, yet, Mr. Lennon. That was from *The Jazz Singer*, you know. The original Al Jolson version from back in the day when blackface was acceptable, of course, not that travesty they threw together with Bradley Cooper and Lady Gaga." He pulled a face, as if something unbearably foul had just wafted its way into his nostrils.

"I hope I qualify." Lennon wasn't really sure what the appropriate reply was to Austin's fun fact; he'd never been much of a film buff.

A light, girlish laugh flitted through Austin's lips; he cast a sly glance across at Air Jordan guy, who was in the process of backing away toward the dining room's door, as if eager for the shadows there to swallow him up. "You already *have* qualified, Mr. Lennon," Austin said. "Otherwise, you wouldn't be here. I thought that much would have been obvious to you by now."

And that was the second time they'd made Lennon feel embarrassed.

"This is not *The Price is Right*, you know." Austin spoke softly, with a twinkle of humor, in an accent Lennon was struggling to place: east coast, New Jersey, perhaps? "Do I look like Bob Barker to you, Mr. Lennon?"

Lennon shook his head no. If anything, Ben Austin looked the *least* like the cheesy old gameshow host than anyone he thought he'd met.

"I'll be taking you to your next location," Austin explained as the older guy in the Jordans made his silent exit. He swept an arm wide with a dramatic flourish. "This was just to make sure you came along, if I'm to be perfectly honest."

"Why on earth wouldn't I?" Lennon couldn't imagine anyone giving up the opportunity to become an instant billionaire.

"You'd be surprised how many people get cold feet before they get this far. Way too many cynical people around these days." It was Austin's turn to look disappointed. "But I'm sure glad you did not get cold feet."

"Where are we going?" Lennon tried not to sound too nervous.

"We have a secret location." Austin pulled out what appeared to be a long strip of black material from his pants pocket, much like a magician producing a surprise string of colored handkerchiefs seemingly from nowhere. "And, as it's a secret, I have to ensure it stays that way. I'm sure you'll understand the necessary formality, Mr. Lennon."

Lennon eyed the blindfold with suspicion. Just what had he let himself in for? What if this really was all some elaborate kidnap plot? Of course, Lennon had considered that distinct possibility when he'd decided to fly out alone to Philadelphia; that was why he'd sent all the details he had regarding his impromptu trip to Leibowitz with strict instructions to contact the cops if there was no communication from him within twenty-four hours. And then there was always the tracking app Lennon had installed on his cell phone; Leibowitz had a copy on his company-issued phone, too, and could see where his boss was at any given time.

Naturally, the show people wouldn't be so naive—or dumb—as to believe their potential contestant wouldn't have made provisions for such a possibility and let people know where he was.

After all, they hadn't even taken his phone off him.

"If you wouldn't mind…" Austin stepped around to Lennon's rear with the blindfold held at head height; he stood a good few inches shorter than Lennon and had to reach up a little to tie the soft cloth in a neat ribbon at the back of his head.

With the blindfold firmly in place, Lennon could see absolutely nothing; zilch. In the movies, there always seemed to be a convenient gap where cloth didn't fit snug to the nose, or the blindfold itself was just flimsy enough to allow the compromised protagonist to at least make out the fuzzy outlines of the bad guys and where they were taking him.

But no.

Lennon stood in pitch black darkness.

Ben Austin had clearly done this before.

As he was led out of the Pyramid Club by the crook of his elbow, Lennon wondered just how many potential contestants for the mysterious millionaire's gameshow had been blindfolded in Philly's most exclusive private members' club. And how many of those had gone on to realize the dream of becoming a fully-fledge *billionaire*?

He also couldn't help but be curious as to the true purpose of the trip all the way up to the club; he'd been there barely ten minutes and the place had obviously been closed for his benefit. It hardly seemed worth all the effort.

Maybe that was the whole point? A first show of power on behalf of the gameshow producers?

Somehow, the trip back down in the elevator seemed much quicker than it had taken to go up the fifty-two floors; most likely something to do with being blindfolded, Lennon reckoned.

Then they were out of the elevator and into what was likely the building's underground parking garage, if the resonant echoes of their footsteps were anything to go by.

"Please, take a seat, Mr. Lennon." Austin's invitation was accompanied by a light-but-firm hand to the top of Lennon's head.

Lennon slipped into the plush rear seat on the limo that awaited him in the parking garage. He didn't have to see the vehicle to know what it was; Lennon had been a passenger in enough stretch limousines in his time to know exactly how they felt, even how they *smelled*.

And, judging by the height of the thing, Lennon surmised they were treating him to a stretch Hummer – most likely gleaming black, given the clandestine nature of the whole thing so far.

He heard the distinctive sounds of Austin climbing into the front passenger seat and, as the limo pulled away and made its way out of the garage, Lennon's mind once again returned to the worrying flight of fancy that he could have just walked willingly into his own kidnap…

Would Jilly be receiving his ear by FedEx the next morning? Would that be followed by God-only knew what body parts until she ponied up the extortionate amount of ransom money Lennon had no doubt the kidnappers would demand?

But *would* she pay up?

"Yeah, she would," Lennon muttered to himself. "Jilly would miss me if I was gone."

"What was that, Mr. Lennon?" Austin's voice sounded tinny over the car's intercom.

"Nothing." Lennon was embarrassed he'd been caught talking to himself. It was a habit he'd never allowed to show itself in public because he'd always been taught that people who talked to themselves were just one short step away from straight jackets and rubber-walled rooms.

"We're almost there."

"Thank you." Lennon wasn't too sure what he was thankful for, other than having the foresight to let his old accountant know where he was going.

Chapter 6

Austin allowed Lennon to remove the blindfold upon exiting the limo. In doing so, Lennon was pleased to find he'd been right about the vehicle: it was, indeed, a stretch Hummer, only in white. Still, he'd been blindfolded, so guessing the color incorrectly really didn't count. The limo drove smoothly away and Lennon noted the absence of license plates.

No surprise there.

"Please, come this way, Mr. Lennon." Austin guided his guest toward the revolving door at the entrance to what appeared to be a generic, unremarkable office building; a bit of a letdown after the opulence of the Pyramid Club.

The office block was the kind of multi-use office building that festooned every large town and city in the country; the kind which were home to a whole host of businesses from family lawyers to tax accountants to recruitment agencies and graphic designers. The place caught Lennon with an unexpectedly warm wave of nostalgia; it was in a building much like this one that Imagine Real Estate had been born.

Following on obediently along the long, ground-floor hallway, Lennon peered through the windows of the darkened offices that lined it. Again, nothing remarkable to see, just cluttered desks, lifeless computers, and water coolers.

He pictured how the place would be during the middle of a business day; filled with voices, the shrill trilling of phones, and the bustle of honest, hardworking folks enjoying the excitement of making a buck or two. Admittedly, there were times Lennon genuinely missed those early, stress-filled days of not fully knowing where the next paycheck was coming from.

"It's just down here." Austin's voice echoed slightly along the deserted hallway. "We're in the office at the very end."

Lennon wasn't entirely sure why the guy felt the need to announce that. It was obvious where the destination was, as there was only the one office with light filtering through its frosted windows.

The door opened.

Harsh, fluorescent light flooded out from the office to illuminate the dimly lit hallway with its stark, white glow. A blonde-haired woman stepped out through the doorway, leaving the door open behind herself. She strode quickly, purposefully toward Lennon and Austin.

The welcoming committee?

Lennon sure hoped so: The woman was attractive enough and he guessed her to be late twenties, early thirties. She strode tall in vertiginous, spiked heels, and had a slim figure which was enhanced to perfection by a tight, scoop-necked white T-shirt and faded skinny jeans with a fashionable rip above the left knee. She embodied sex appeal and Lennon couldn't take his eyes off her.

He couldn't help himself; he'd always had a thing for slim blondes.

Austin gave the woman a respectful nod as she rushed by. Lennon treated himself to a less-than-subtle glance backward to see if the young woman's behind showed as much promise as the front.

He was not disappointed to find it most certainly did.

"Mr. Lennon! *Chase!* How good it is to see you!" Lennon's burgeoning fantasies about the young woman were rudely interrupted by an overly exuberant voice.

Snapping his gaze around to face front, a little sheepish at being caught out openly ogling the blonde, Lennon was greeted warmly by a man standing in the doorway of the lit-up office. He had an arm outstretched, hand all ready to shake, and a broad smile on his smooth-shaven face.

He was probably in his late thirties—maybe early forties if he'd had some work done—and was the most unremarkable looking man Lennon thought he'd ever met: medium height, neatly trimmed black hair, blueish-hazel eyes, and a physique that could only be described as *average*.

Sure, his personality appeared friendly enough, his smile warm, but he had a look as generic as the building in which they stood. He was pretty much just the kind of guy one would walk by in the street a thousand times without noticing. Instantly forgettable, in startling contrast to the sexy young woman.

"I'm Mercer, the producer of *The Contestant.*" He shook Lennon's hand firmly and all but pulled him through the door and into the office. "Welcome!"

"Thank you." Lennon extricated his hand from Mercer's and took a look around. The office was small, no more than thirty-five square feet, a perfect square, and contained a duo of matching office swivel chairs behind a thin, wooden desk, upon which sat a projector and thin Dell laptop.

The projector, hard wired to the laptop's USB port, beamed plain, white light onto a vinyl screen at the other end of the room. There were no windows to the outside of the office building, nothing to let daylight in during working hours. Those at the opposite side to the hallway looked out onto an atrium that housed a chic coffee bar and a row of vending machines. All as dark, lifeless, and silent as the rest of the place, of course.

And that was it.

The show people certainly enjoyed their contrasts, Lennon mused. The office building could not have been more removed from the salubrious Pyramid Club if they'd dropped him off outside a two-man tent in the desert.

"Sit, please." Mercer indicated the swivel chairs with a theatrical sweep of his hand.

"Thank you for accepting my application." Lennon made himself comfortable in one of the office chairs. He glanced over at the office door—still open—and saw Austin standing sentry just outside it. Lennon thought the man looked kind of sinister standing there stock-still with his hands meshed in front of his crotch like some hired goon in a cliched mob movie.

"I'm sure you must be wondering what our show is all about," Mercer began with a warm smile.

"You could say that." Lennon assumed much of the theatrics was for the benefit of the show, and his journey from the airport to the dull little office, via the Pyramid Club, had been filmed for some behind the scenes footage. He reckoned it would be much like those real-life sob stories they put out ahead of a contestant's performance on *America's Got Talent, American Idol*, and the myriad other trash TV shows Jilly and the kids were often glued to in the evenings.

"Well, first things first, I'd like to welcome you to our show, *The Contestant*." Mercer beamed and sat himself down next to Lennon. "I'm the creator and producer, and very proud of my baby."

"*The Contestant*?"

"I get it. You were expecting it to be called something more inventive, more remarkable, given its unusual nature and more-than-generous prize money." Mercer sounded apologetic. "But, when you're dealing with such a unique concept on an unprecedented scale as ours, there really is no need for a fancy or clever name. We let the show's engaging and incredibly exciting content speak for itself."

Lennon wondered just who had force-fed Mercer a thesaurus; it was rare to come across such a vocabulary. "How come I've never heard of your show before? I'm not a big gameshow fan, to be honest, but my wife watches just about all of them. Is it a new one?"

Mercer laughed. "Oh, heavens, no." He rubbed his hands together as he spoke, which looked to Lennon like a nervous habit. "*The Contestant* has been running for quite some years now. Having said that, you won't have happened across it on any of the networks or streaming services because we prefer to keep it exclusive. Our viewers are strictly by invitation only. Much like our contestants."

Lennon's unintentional glance around the sparsely furnished office gave his thoughts away before he had the chance to voice them.

"Oh, this is not our real office," Mercer clearly read his guest's mind. "We borrowed this one especially for tonight; secrecy is a big part of what we do on *The Contestant*, Chase. Once you find out more about what you're signing up for, you'll understand. Actually, our offices are situated in a private studio in Los Angeles; I can actually see the Hollywood sign from my desk!"

"Nice." Lennon had never cared much for LA. It was too much crappy air and equally crappy, superficial people for his tastes. There was good money to be made selling real estate there, of course, and the LA branch of Imagine Real Estate had contributed nicely to his personal wealth in the five years since he launched it. He just made sure to not visit the place any more than was strictly necessary.

"Before I get into the rules and particulars of the game itself, and the necessary signing of your contract and waivers, of course, there's a presentation I like to show all participants – it will give you a feel of what you're playing for."

With that, Mercer tapped his forefinger on the laptop's track pad. In an instant, a dramatic swell of music blared out from the Dell and the projector shot a bright splash of vivid color onto the screen.

Immediately, Lennon's eyes were drawn to the screen and the sweeping, panoramic view of a sun-kissed, beach of golden sand and gently swaying palm trees. The beach itself was deserted, apart from a tall, bronzed, bare-chested man surrounded by a bevy of equally sun-kissed, bikini-clad beauties.

The guy, clad only in miniscule Speedos, was easily in his fifties—his thick, curly chest hair a shocking splash of white against his tanned torso—and looked to be having the time of his life watching a trio of young ladies cavorting together in the crystal blue sea while the other four caressed his exposed body with perfectly manicured fingertips. As the camera panned by the man, he gave a broad, cheesy grin and two thumbs up; life was clearly going very well indeed for him.

The movie then jumped to a snow-covered mountain dotted with tall, frosted pine trees. In the background sat a cluster of huge ski chalets, their inimitable style immediately giving the location away as Switzerland. A couple skied into view, pulling up directly in front of the camera, their skis spraying up arcs of pure, powdery snow. Lifting her ski mask, the woman of the pair winked and grinned at the camera.

"As you can see, *The Contestant* is open to both women *and* men," Mercer spoke over the music that blared from the laptop. Coming from immediately in front of Lennon, the music itself sounded disjointed, not particularly relevant to the opulent scenes being played out on the screen. "In fact, we welcome any sexual orientation – and there are so many of those to choose from these days, don't you think?"

Lennon half-nodded, eyes glued to the screen, ears assaulted by the music, which sounded tinny and cheap, like something purchased for a few bucks from a royalty-free website.

"I hope you're enjoying the music, too, Mr. Lennon." Mercer read his mind yet again. "It was actually composed by John Williams especially for us; he said it was some of his best work since *Jurassic Park* and *ET*. I'm afraid this setting doesn't really do it justice, though. We really ought to invest in better audio-visual equipment for these presentations."

The skiing woman was very quickly replaced by a bulky-looking, older Black guy smoking a fat Cuban cigar in front of a mansion that actually looked more like a small country house hotel. Next came a handsome young man climbing the steps up to what was clearly a private Lear jet. Waiting for him at the door stood two ridiculously stunning, young air hostesses in short, black skirts that put their endless legs on display.

The stewardesses' smiles let the viewers know they'd be taking care of more than the young man's drinks and salted peanuts during the private flight to some no-doubt exotic location.

After that came a plump Hispanic couple driving up a long, gravel driveway in a vintage Rolls Royce Silver Shadow to what appeared to be a large Scottish castle. Lennon figured it was safe to assume, given the context, they owned the place.

Next came an arial view of a yacht that seemed to go on for miles – it reminded Lennon of the boats he'd seen moored in St. Tropez and Monaco on the last vacation he'd taken with Jilly and *sans* kids. That seemed such an awfully long time ago.

As the film zoomed in on a handsome, middle-aged guy relaxing in the yacht's hot tub next to an ice bucket containing an opened bottle of 2013 *Gout de Diamants* champagne—which Lennon knew was $2.07 million per bottle—Mercer spoke again to state the blindingly obvious. "All these men and women are previous winners of *The Contestant*," he informed his audience of one. "And, as you can see, they are all enjoying their winnings to the full."

"Weren't they rich to begin with, though?" Lennon couldn't keep the cynicism from his voice; while he could never stump up over two million for a bottle of bubbly, he made sure he lived a good life. He eyed the hot tub guy, who had bandages around his face and bruising beneath both eyes; obviously he'd had quite a lot of work done, and Lennon couldn't help but wonder what he'd looked like *before* the expensive rejuvenation surgery.

The supposed John Williams music lowered. On the screen, a handsome, elderly lady with silver, shoulder-length hair stood in front of her collection of a dozen or so vintage Ferraris and Aston Martins parked up in an underground garage, each one polished to gleaming and most likely rarely driven.

"As are you, Mr. Lennon." Mercer spun his chair a half-turn to look directly at his guest. "And yet, here you are here."

Touché

"I was curious." Lennon knew how feeble his defense sounded the moment it left his lips.

"Ahh, I like to think it was more than mere curiosity that brought you here this evening," Mercer pressed. "Take a look at the people on the screen, Mr. Lennon – a *proper* look."

Lennon scrutinized the next in the seemingly endless parade of men and women, young and old, who were all more than happy to show off the opulence they'd won, courtesy of *The Contestant*.

"What do you see, Mr. Lennon?"

Mercer's near-constant use of Lennon's name was beginning to wear thin. He guessed it to be, most likely, some psychological game the guy liked to play prior to the show starting up yet he couldn't figure out what. All it served to do was grate on his nerves – almost as much as the tinny music wafting out from the laptop on the desk.

"Looks just like folks showing off their money to me."

"Ostensibly, yes," Mercer conceded. "But, it's all so much *more* than that. As you so astutely pointed out, each and every one of the men and women you are meeting in our presentation was wealthy *before* taking part in *The Contestant*. Every one of them was just like you, Mr. Lennon, a self-made multi-millionaire.

"They didn't *need* the money at all. Heck, they all had more than enough for at least a lifetime or two and to ensure their children and grandchildren would never have to work, should they so choose. There's only so much money one can spend, only so much of the stuff your kids will need to get them through the best colleges and to give them a good start in their young lives.

"Did you know Richard Branson and Bill Gates made the decision to have their children make their own way in life? No inheritance, no handouts. Nothing?"

"I'd heard that." Lennon also thought that particular philosophy went directly against the whole point of the exercise: wasn't the future success of your DNA supposed to be the ultimate end game in life?

"But I digress." Mercer's smile made him look like a genuine gameshow host – one of the sorts who populate the trashy early evening TV schedules. "What motivated those people, and so many more just like them, is not the money, it's the *earning* of the money. Sure thing, the opportunity to become a billionaire is one hell of a carrot to dangle to the rich; it certainly caught *your* attention. But it's the chase, the gamble, the having a lot to lose, the danger of *not* winning... That's what motivates our contestants, Mr. Lennon. Wouldn't you agree?"

It was a loaded, rhetorical question.

"Are you a gambler, Mr. Lennon?"

"I'm here, aren't I?"

"Indeed, you are."

"So, what am I signing up for here?" Lennon turned to face Mercer. The film had switched back to the yacht guy, and the stream of smug, smiling faces and scantily clad women on the screen was wearing thin. Lennon had always preferred to revel in his own success and money rather than that of other people.

"The reason *The Contestant* chooses people like you, Mr. Lennon, is because you don't need the money, per se. Of course, having an extra billion or so in your offshore bank accounts will be nice, but it really wouldn't make much difference to your life, would it now?"

Lennon was about to contradict Mercer: there were myriad things he'd love to do with over a billion dollars!

"Of course, there *are* so many things you could buy with that amount of money. Ridiculously huge yachts, a private tropical island or two, maybe even a trip into space." Was Mercer *actually* reading Lennon's mind? "But that wouldn't change *you*, would it? *The Contestant* is not about changing lives, Mr. Lennon, it's all about changing *people*."

Mercer paused.

The movie came to an end, the shiny screen plain white once more, the room silent.

Had Mercer actually timed his little speech so perfectly as to end in synch with the film of previous show winners?

Not possible, surely.

"You really haven't explained much about any of this, Mr. Mercer." Lennon broke the awkwardness. He was beginning to feel more than a tad antsy. Perhaps the whole show thing was one big con after all; he'd already parted with ten grand, how long before Mercer had his hand out for more? "All you've shown me is some of your supposed past winners and treated me to...*this*." He lifted a hand, to indicate the less than salubrious surroundings.

Now, had Mercer's little presentation been given at the Pyramid Club, Lennon would have been far more impressed.

"Well, we have definitely ascertained that you have the correct level of motivation." Mercer appeared unfazed by Lennon's growing impatience. "The show itself is really quite simple."

Lennon sat up in the office chair. His ass was growing numb.

Here it comes – the part where Mercer would demand money from Lennon for the honor of participating in his gameshow. Had he really been dumb enough, desperate for a little excitement, to fall for what was beginning to look like something akin to a timeshare scam?

"You, the contestant, will play the part of a fugitive. All you have to do is evade capture for seven days, and you win."

"That's it?"

"That's it."

"And this will be in Los Angeles, I assume?"

Mercer shook his head. "That would be a tad too obvious, don't you think, Mr. Lennon? No, we pick a different city for each new contestant to start off in. We find that keeps things fresh and interesting for our viewers."

"Who do I have to avoid?"

"The contestant is chased—hunted, I suppose—by ex-military, law enforcement, that sort of thing," Mercer explained. "People who are very good at what they do."

"So, it's like *The Running Man*?"

Lennon's comparison with the Stephen King book and old Schwarzenegger movie appeared to tickle Mercer's funny bone. "I guess you could say the basic premise is similar, but no, it's most definitely not the *Running Man*, Mr. Lennon. For a start, you don't get shot if you are captured. We like to compare it more with *The Trueman Show* or *The Game*. All far more civilized."

"So, what does happen if I'm caught?"

Another chuckle from Mercer. "Nothing at all. You just get to go home empty handed and with the knowledge you failed at a fairly simple challenge."

Lennon snorted. The more Mercer spoke, the less the whole thing appealed to him. There were no high stakes, other than the supposed prize money, and the 'game' itself was more like a trumped-up version of hide-and-go-seek than *Squid Game*. And Mercer was right, he didn't *need* the money. It was hardly adrenaline-pumping stuff.

"I really don't think—"

"You're wondering what's at stake, Mr. Lennon?" Mercer smiled once again. "Don't worry, you all do. The contestants, that is. And a great many do actually walk out at this stage in our proceedings. So, how about personal pride and that ego of yours for a start?

"How about living the rest of your life with the knowledge that you have not only backed away from the opportunity of a lifetime, but from *yourself* as well? Trust me, Mr. Lennon, walk away now and, no matter how much wealth you accumulate in the future, how many worthy charities you donate your fortune to, and how many expensive trappings you surround yourself with, you will always *feel* like a failure."

"Maybe I can live with that."

"But what if you can't?" Mercer countered. "You will never get this opportunity again, and you will regret having not grasped it. Believe me. Everyone who has turned us down to date lives with their regret. But, if that's your decision..." Mercer stood; his chair rolled back a few inches on its casters.

"I'm not saying I'm turning you down," Lennon backtracked. Faced with being taken out of the running, he found it meant a hell of a lot to him to stay in. All part of Mercer's psychological game-play? "I just need to know more about what I'm letting myself in for here. I'm sure you can understand that."

"Of course." Mercer remained standing. "Your progress will be closely monitored by hidden cameras and incognito cameramen; you'll never know if or when you're being filmed. And we won't make it easy to evade capture; there'll be plenty of twists and turns and red herrings to keep you on your toes and our viewers guessing and, most importantly of all, engaged."

"Might I ask who your viewers are, exactly?" Lennon felt a touch more comfortable getting down to the nitty-gritty.

"Our viewers are an anonymous bunch of individuals who are incredibly secretive. They come from all around the world and share only wealth and invisibility in common. They view on an exclusive, private streaming channel known only to them—and we producers of the show, of course—which is encrypted beyond all military grades and impossible to access for anyone outside of *The Contestant's* elite network. A lot of money is wagered on the outcome of the game—on *you*, Mr. Lennon—which makes the whole thing so incredibly lucrative for us."

"That's where the prize money comes from? Illegal gambling?"

"We do take a cut from all bets placed, but the majority of our income and the $1.2bn prize fund, comes from the prohibitive subscription fees our loyal band of viewers pay to remain in such an exclusive club."

"And how exactly do I know you are good for that amount of money?"

"You don't, Mr. Lennon." Mercer clasped his hands together, as if he was praying. "And isn't that what makes it all so *very* exciting?"

Flashing Mercer a cynical smile, Lennon was forced to admit to himself that yes, that did actually make the whole unlikely scenario just that little bit more exciting. After all, wasn't that what had hooked him in the first place? The thrill of the new, the excitement of the unknown, a gamble like no other? Lennon already felt the adrenaline seeping through his veins, his heart quickening its beat.

No matter what, Chase Lennon knew perfectly well at that point he was all in and fully committed.

"So, where do I sign?" Lennon asked. "You said something about contracts. I'm *assuming* there is a proper contract for all this?"

Mercer shot his guest an acid look; he actually appeared to be offended, as if the very suggestion his precious gameshow could be anything less than above board. "Of course we have a contract for you to sign, along with all the necessary waivers, too. We've found it's always best to be prepared for any and all eventual outcomes."

Lennon opened his mouth to ask what outcomes exactly had Mercer and his crew experienced in the past, but he stopped himself Surely, given the show's format Mercer had briefly described, along with the colorful depiction of its past winners, there wasn't much risk of anyone getting hurt.

Was there?

Despite the slight niggle that settled at the back of his mind, Lennon decided against voicing any concerns and kept his mouth shut.

"Let's get this show on the road, then," Mercer declared with a clap of his hands. Then, reaching into the inside pocket of his exquisitely tailored jacket, he pulled out a sheaf of letter-sized paperwork. A dozen or so sheets in all, held together by a trio of brass brads along the left-hand side. From his other pocket, Mercer produced a dark blue Parker pen.

Gently, he placed both items on the desk in front of Mercer, next to the laptop's dark screen; he acted like he was afraid the contract and pen might break.

"I'd usually have my lawyers look through this." Lennon leafed through the double-sided papers before him. The print was small, tightly packed, and somewhat impenetrable—typical legal stuff. He'd never really had the mental bandwidth or patience to plough through legalese like this, which was precisely why he had expensive lawyers on retainer.

"And what do you think their advice would be, Mr. Lennon?" The tone in Mercer's voice had a mischievous flavor to it. It sounded a lot like a dare to Lennon, like they were a pair of middle school kids egging one another to eat dirt.

Is Mercer taunting me here?

"They'd tell me not to sign anything until they've given it all a thorough run-through and performed due diligence." Lennon knew by rote Mackenzie Crail and Associates' stock answer to everything he stuck under their fifteen-hundred-dollar-an-hour noses.

"Then perhaps we ought to wait…"

Now Mercer was baiting him and not even attempting to try hiding it. Lennon's common sense told him to back the hell off; anyone pushing their wares so hard and expecting him to either read through a dozen pages of legal small print or blindly sign on the dotted line seemed sketchy to say the least.

"Is there anything illegal in here?" Lennon pretended to scrutinize the block of text at the top of the third page; it was all quite incomprehensible to him, but he figured it was worth asking the question.

Mercer shook his head. "Were we to force you, contractually, into any form of illegal activities, that would void the contract, Mr. Lennon."

"That doesn't answer my question." Lennon may not have been a legal-eagle, but he knew how to pick apart a business proposition in his damned sleep.

"I can assure you, Mr. Lennon," Mercer's tone was sharp, "you will not be expected to do anything against the law during the course of your time on *The Contestant*. However, if you'd prefer to have your lawyers—"

Lennon flapped a dismissive hand at Mercer. "That won't be necessary," he said, picking up the pen; he noticed it had the gameshow's name printed along one side in plain, silver lettering. Leafing through the contract, Lennon searched for the places to sign and was pleased to see Mercer had thoughtfully highlighted those parts in neon yellow for the sake of convenience.

Was he actually going to do this?

A brief hesitation, pen poised above the first highlight, Lennon checked himself one last time. He was astutely aware what he was about to do went against every instinct that had brought him so much success in business, and which had made him wealthy enough to be invited to participate in the exclusive game that promised to make him rich beyond his wildest dreams.

But, and this was a big 'but,' everything he'd seen and heard from the moment he'd stepped inside the depressingly generic office building had contradicted Mercer's sales pitch: The cheapness of the venue, the vagueness of Mercer's dismissive description of the show itself, the obvious display of luxury in the presentation—even the pen was little more than some cheap, promotional biro; Lennon would have expected a *Mont Blanc* fountain pen at the very least, given the prize money up for grabs and the vigorish Mercer claimed they were making from *The Contestant*.

It all screamed, *don't do this!*

Maybe, though, it was all part of the audition process? A few things to test his mettle before anything was signed?

This is crazy.

But wasn't that what made it all the more exciting?

"Is everything okay, Mr. Lennon?"

Mercer's prompt jerked Lennon back into the moment, contract, crappy pen, and all.

"I'll be happy to stay here for as long as you need if you'd like to read through the whole contract." He placed emphasis on *whole*. The inference was clear: Mercer would actually be far from happy to wait there until the small hours for Lennon to pour over his comprehensive contract.

Lennon nodded. "Yeah, it's all good." With that, he scribbled his signature on top of the first highlighted line and rifled through the remaining pages, signing on the dotted lines as he went.

The contract, duly signed by first Lennon, then Mercer, was spirited away back inside his jacket pocket, along with the pen.

"An official welcome to *The Contestant*, Mr. Lennon. You have made a wise decision."

"I sure hope so." Lennon made light of what he'd just done with a half-hearted smile, even though his brain admonished him for having been so stupid and giving in to his ego—none of it being about the money.

Mercer patted the slight bulge over his chest where the contract nestled. "I guess we can get started in earnest now," he said with a cheesy smile.

"Now?" Lennon was taken aback.

"Right now."

"As in, the game itself?" Lennon's heart rate spiked; surely there ought to be a cooling off period, or at least time to let people know why he'd be out of pocket for a week.

"What else could I possibly mean?" Mercer fished around in his pants pocket as he spoke.

"I'll need to tell my family and business associates where I am, for a start."

"No need to worry about any of that," Mercer reassured with that cheesy smile again. "We will take care of everything. You can let them know once you arrive at your first destination, of course. How excited are they all going to be?"

It was a question Lennon hadn't even considered until then; Jilly would be furious that he'd taken off in the middle of a family vacation, ostensibly for important business, only to turn up on some dumb gameshow hiding from fake cops and bounty hunters.

Yeah, it really wasn't going to go down well with the wife at all. The kids would love it, though; Dad being on TV – assuming, of course, they'd be allowed to watch it, given the show's apparent secrecy. Nonetheless, Chad and Casey would be suitably delighted at having a famous father; at their age, literally *everyone* on TV was a world-famous celebrity!

As for Jilly…

I'll deal with her when I return home in a week or so a billionaire. Lennon placated himself. *That amount of money will soon make her forget about me disappearing without notice for a while.*

"Are you ready, Mr. Lennon?" Mercer held out his right hand, palm up and open. In its center sat a small, blue capsule similar to the nighttime flu meds he'd taken countless times in his life. It looked harmless enough.

Nonetheless, Lennon raised a quizzical eyebrow.

"I know, it's all a bit *Matrix*, I get it." Mercer laughed a little at Lennon's obvious discomfort. His hand remained outstretched, though.

"What is this?" Once again, Lennon questioned his own hasty decision.

"Nothing to be overly concerned about," Mercer told him with what Lennon guessed was meant to be a reassuring smile. "Given the secretive nature and the surprise element of *The Contestant*, we require you to be asleep for transportation to your location. It's nothing more than a sleeping pill. I'm sure you understand."

Lennon eyed the capsule with growing suspicion. "I'm not sure I do, Mr. Mercer."

"It's all in the contract." Mercer slipped his free hand inside his jacket, as if making ready to pull out the paperwork he'd secreted within. "On page six. You signed your name after the appropriate clause; would you like me to point it out to you?"

For a heartbeat or so, Lennon considered insisting that yes, he really would like the producer to show him precisely where he'd just agreed to be drugged in the interests of the gameshow. But something about the guy's confidence left no doubt in Lennon's mind there was such a clause and he'd find his name scribbled next to it should he choose to take a peek.

So, instead, Lennon plucked the capsule from Mercer's hand and popped it into his mouth.

Oh, what the hell? Lennon inwardly dismissed his own reticence as he swallowed the thing down dry. *Nothing ventured, nothing gained, right?*

With that, Chase Lennon fell into a deep and dreamless sleep.

Chapter 7

The first thing Lennon became aware of as he stirred from the deep, unnatural sleep was the overpowering reek of damp, decay, of rotting wood and mold, and of some cloying, earthy odor his drowsy mind couldn't quite place. Next came the stark, blinding sunlight that assaulted his opening eyes as it stabbed through the uneven gap between the frayed, faded curtains.

Snapping his eyes tightly shut, Lennon groaned loudly and rolled over. He buried his face in the rough pillow that prickled his skin with myriad tiny feather shafts and assaulted his nose with more of that musty damp aroma and something unmistakably *human*.

It was evening; it *felt* like the evening, the low-slung sunlight was bright, dull orange, the day itself *tired*. What particular evening it was, and just how long he'd been asleep after taking Mercer's blue pill, Lennon had no way of knowing. He could have been out for just hours, or *days*, for all he knew, especially given the rumbling growl of his empty stomach.

Just as Mercer had promised, the game had obviously begun.

Forcing his eyes open once again, Lennon sat up in the bed. The mattress was soft, unsupportive, and decidedly saggy in the middle. The age-yellowed sheet covering it was stained with patches of stuff that Lennon didn't care to contemplate.

"Where is this?" Hearing a voice, albeit his own, brought Lennon some comfort as he fought hard against the sense of being totally alone, the isolation of not knowing where he was, or how long he'd been there. It was all terribly disorienting, but he reckoned that was probably the point of the exercise.

Lennon had seen enough reality TV shows to know how effective the psychological games they played were— all in the name of creating dramatic viewing and hiking up those ever-important viewing figures and advertising revenue.

There'd be cameras everywhere, Lennon figured. Hidden, of course, secreted in nooks and cervices in strategic places to capture his every movement, expression, and disorientation for the show's elite viewers. The cameras would be practically impossible to spot, Lennon knew that, as they made them so friggin' small these days.

From what Mercer had told him, Lennon figured it would be safe to assume he'd be on camera pretty much all the time; hopefully not in the restroom, though; they even avoided filming in those on the shamefully intrusive *Big Brother* show. Lennon made a mental note of that. If ever he needed some privacy, the toilet was most likely the place to go.

And that was to be his life for the next week, or at least until Mercer's hired hunters caught up with him. Nope, it was *definitely* for the next week, this being something Lennon was determined to see through to the end.

No matter what it took, or what he was forced to do, he was going back home to Jilly and the kids a billionaire, *period!*

Lennon rubbed his knuckles hard into his eyes and squinted through slitted lids at his surroundings. He was in a grim, down-scale motel or hotel room, that much was for certain. He'd spent more than his fair share of time in such places back in his early days to recognize the look, feel, and smell of them.

He'd discovered during his more hedonistic days they were all pretty much the same wherever he went, be it for business, pleasure, or in the interests of illicit sex with some lady whose circumstances meant she had to be discrete. And, Christ knows, there had been plenty of those during Lennon's married woman phase what seemed like another lifetime ago.

The room itself was quite spacious, which somehow made the few sticks of furniture it contained appear small, even though they were constructed of what looked to be solid dark wood; either the hotel had obviously once been a nice place to stay or the owners had bought up a job-lot of quality furniture on the cheap.

There was the bed, of course, which was a twin-sized affair with a low, solid frame, a pair of nightstands—one on either side of the tall headboard—a large, wafer-thin, flatscreen attached to the wall directly opposite by means of a black, swing bracket, and a long, low cupboard containing a sextet of battered drawers.

Perched on top of the cupboard was a plastic tray containing a small, black kettle that had seen far better days, a pair of light blue tea cups, and a dusty selection of teas, coffees, and tiny plastic pots of creamer.

"What the—?" It was then Lennon espied the odd array of items sitting next to the tray. Climbing from the bed, his head fuzzy and spinning a little from whatever Mercer had given him to sleep through transporting him to the show location, Lennon padded across the tacky carpet to take a closer look.

There was a matt black Smith and Wesson revolver, a coil of rope, complete with a neat hangman's noose tied at one end, and a generic brown plastic pill bottle; lid off, laid on its side. Five small, white tablets had spilled out of the bottle. Perfectly round, each one had that handy, tiny groove along its center to make splitting in two easy for those wishing to take a half dose. They actually appeared enticing, much like Alice's cake in Wonderland.

Eat me.

The collection of pills seemed to Lennon to have been carefully staged for effect, most likely for the benefit of the show's viewers.

"Nice touch." Lennon wrinkled his nose at the grim selection of items. "Just what am I supposed to do with these, guys?" He peered around the room, as if talking to the viewers at home.

So what if he broke the fourth wall?

It was a valid question, though: what *did* they expect him to do with a gun, noose, and a bottle full of pills? It could well be that they wanted him to do nothing, and they'd been put there simply as props. That made the most sense to Lennon—why else would a gameshow put what was essentially a suicide kit in his hotel room?

Assuming, of course, he *was* in a hotel room…

It occurred then to Lennon he could well be in a well-presented studio *made up* just like the grubby hotel rooms of his younger years, the ones Jilly could never know about.

Aware he was clad only in his boxers, Lennon gingerly pulled open one of the floor-length curtains. Some part of him expected to be met by a studio audience, all sitting in neat, tiered rows with vacuous grins on their faces as they all eagerly waited for him to do something for their entertainment.

But no.

The hotel room's window looked out onto a small, unassuming courtyard, in the center of which was an unpleasantly green-looking pool and a haphazard array of empty, white plastic sun loungers. He was three floors up, and the rooms on all three sides of him were red brick, French-colonial style, and sported a small balcony with white-painted, iron railings. There was a familiarity about the place, which Lennon's fuzzy head couldn't grasp.

"I need to pee." Lennon had no idea why he felt the need to narrate his actions. Then again, he'd never been on any kind of reality TV show before. Nonetheless, the sound of his voice remained comforting; he was so used to background noise at home and at work that its absence made him lonely and more than a little lost.

Opening the door and switching on the light to the cramped bathroom, the first thing that hit Lennon was the smell. It was a nauseating mix of stale urine, cheap bleach cleaner, and that same rank odor he'd picked up in the bed.

Stench aside, Lennon really did need to use the toilet.

The cracked tiles in the bathroom were chilly beneath his bare feet, and the humidity in the air made them feel ever so slightly moist, clammy, like dead skin.

Not the nicest of sensations.

Almost to the toilet, peering down at the black, crusted ring circling the bowl's discolored water, something in the sink caught Lennon's eye. Turning his head to see, he caught a glimpse of himself in the mirror above the sink, and then he saw what the sink contained.

"What the –!"

Lennon's bladder let go.

"No!" He was painfully aware of just how shrill his panicked voice sounded within the confines of the small restroom; he sounded eerily like Casey whenever she happened upon a spider in the bathtub.

Taking a step or two back, narrowly avoiding slipping on the newly wet floor, Lennon composed himself just enough to put a stop to the warm flow cascading down the inside of his leg.

No!

He'd just peed himself live on TV!

Lennon took in a long, deep breath and dared himself to take a second look in the sink.

There, a trio of disembodied eyeballs peered back at him from the blood-spattered porcelain. One was brown, one hazel, one blue, and they had been deliberately propped up against an ivory-handled lock knife so they all appeared to be gazing up at Lennon.

"You got me there, guys!" Lennon addressed his imagined audience with a nervous laugh, in the hope of distracting from the fact he'd just wet his pants. "Fake eyeballs… You got me!"

The eyeballs certainly *looked* real enough. Among the bloody shreds of muscle surrounding each one, Lennon easily made out the stringy, white optic nerve snaking out from the back, and they definitely *smelled* real. He was getting the earth, raw-meat stink that had permeated through to the bedroom, only it was far stronger within the confines of the tiny restroom. Lennon wondered just how long the eyes had been sitting there, just waiting for him to stumble upon them.

Naturally, he had no idea know what genuine, real-life, plucked-out human eyeballs should *actually* look like. It was not as if Lennon had seen anything like them outside of Halloween props and the hokey horror movies he loved to watch as a kid, although he vaguely recalled the preserved sheep's eye he'd dissected in tenth-grade biology. These looked nothing like that one; they looked… *fresher*.

Gathering courage, upon closer scrutiny, Lennon saw what he thought was a dried-up contact lens on the blue eye. It resembled an impossibly thin, tiny disc of clear Seran-wrap curling up at one side.

"Nice attention to detail," Lennon praised the show's special effects team. They really had gone the extra mile to scare the crap out of him.

That was it, he decided: the eyeballs were gruesome props, nothing more.

Had to be.

"Jeeez," Lennon sighed to himself. "You *really* did have me going there, guys." A glance down at the hairs plastered to the inside of his leg, glistening wet, reminded Lennon he'd embarrassed himself like a naughty toddler, and hoped against hope there really were no cameras in the bathroom.

As he relieved himself what remained of his pee into the toilet bowl, Lennon became hyper-aware of his heart thumping hard and fast. The burst of adrenaline his body had experienced upon seeing those freakin' eyes had forced him fully awake and had his senses on high alert. As perverse at it seemed, it was the best he'd felt in a long, long time.

Done, Lennon flushed, stepped out of his sodden boxers, set the shower running to warm up the water, and padded naked back into the bedroom to grab the kettle. He figured strong coffee was much needed, even if it was crappy hotel instant; the adrenalin would wear off sooner rather than later and he had no idea what he'd be in store for once the gameshow *really* got underway.

The TV burst to life the moment Lennon picked up the small, travel-sized kettle. It was a deafening cacophony of noise that startled him so much he jumped, his body tensed, and he dropped the kettle.

"*What the –!* It was rapidly becoming his catchphrase; Lennon hoped the folks watching at home approved.

Ignoring the kettle, Lennon scanned the hotel room for the TV remote. The sound blaring from the thing was way too loud and the voices coming from it terribly distorted. So much so, it made Lennon's eardrums ache and he couldn't make out a single word of what was being said.

Mercifully, he located the remote, a slender, black affair with bright colored buttons, on the left-hand nightstand. Wincing against the noise, Lennon darted across the room, grabbed the remote, and hit the volume button.

The color contrast on the screen was way off, the picture contained far too much red for anything to appear natural, but Lennon's eye was immediately drawn to the attractive young anchor in the news studio. The caption beneath her read: Brheanna Boudreaux.

Brheanna's heavily made-up face and bottle-blonde hair were immaculate, marred only by the Monroe-sized mole on her left cheek. Lennon figured she wore that proudly as a kind of trademark. The anchor's expression was somber, as befitting of the headline news she delivered.

"*This is WWL-TV, bringing you all the latest news from New Orleans. Tragedy struck the normally peaceful neighborhood of Privateer Place late last night. Three of its residents, all sophomore University students, were brutally murdered by an unknown assailant.*"

The woman's words meant little to Lennon, other than to let him know he'd woken up in the Big Easy, but the images of the three victims that popped up around her perfectly coiffured, wavy hair caught his attention. Two of the pictures appeared to have been taken at some student party or other, the third came from a drivers' license or passport and showed the kid's dour, unsmiling face in a most unflattering light.

None of the trio were the best of pictures, but certainly enough for Lennon to see that one of the kids had blue eyes, one hazel, and the other, a deep, chestnut brown. The girl with the blue eyes, quite a cute-looking chick with her chic, bob-cut, black hair wore gold, wire-framed glasses.

"Police have issued a statement asking the public to be vigilant and not go out alone, especially younger citizens who are being asked to stay in groups of two or more or to remain home until the killer is found."

"Didn't do those three any good sticking together at home," Lennon heard himself saying as his mind snapped back to the three disembodied eyes sitting in the bathroom sink only a few feet away. Could it be that glasses gal sometimes wore contacts?

The screen switched from the nicely easy-on-the-eye Ms. Boudreaux to an outside shot of a well-maintained building framed by yellow police tape flapping in the stifling evening breeze; Lennon thought it strange how the place actually *looked* hot and humid on camera.

Other than a handful of uniformed cops, only one other person could be seen milling about behind the tape. He wore a well-fitted, light gray suit, appeared to be of average height, and the dark skin on his handsome face was shiny with sweat.

An assorted collection of nosy looky-loos was rubbernecking from the other side of the tape, and Lennon wondered if the killer was among them—like they always seemed to be on the TV shows; something about not being able to resist reliving the thrill of their crime. The caption at the foot of the flat screen told him the TV station was transmitting live from the crime scene.

"Police were called to this normally quiet apartment block in Privateer Place in the early hours of the

morning..." a different voice, this one a man with a rich, baritone timbre, told the viewers at home who were no doubt making ready to head out to work or otherwise start their day; the tiny digital readout in the left-hand corner of the screen gave the time as 7:32 AM.

"*A roommate of the two victims discovered their bodies after his calls went unanswered. Police have yet to release details at this time, but some say the students' bodies were found to be mutilated. Now authorities are asking the public for their help...*"

Lennon fiddled absently with the TV remote as he watched the report. Behind him, the shower was steadfastly filling the bathroom with steam, which puffed out into the bedroom in thin, white clouds, and he had yet to locate his clothes. Surely Mercer the show people didn't expect him to participate in just his boxers – especially wet ones?

"*...New Orleans Police have issued this picture of the alleged attacker, caught on CCTV leaving the premises...*"

Was that him?

"*Oh, hell no...*" Lennon dropped the remote onto the floor.

"*If you see this person, please call 911 or the special incident number on the bottom of the screen. It is strongly advised that no one approach this individual, as he is believed to be armed and extremely dangerous...*"

Lennon stared in horrified disbelief at his own picture up there on the flat screen. Sure, it was a grainy image taken from security camera footage, but it was undeniably Chase Lennon.

Hell, he was even looking directly into the camera like he knew he was being filmed and was determined they capture his best side.

Raw panic gripped Lennon's chest, like an icy claw clutching at his heart. Other than waking up in the grubby hotel room ten, fifteen, minutes ago, he had absolutely no recollection of anything that had happened after taking the pill Mercer had offered him upon signing the contract.

Lennon's mind was a complete and utter blank.

Could it be possible he'd killed three young people in cold blood in the middle of the night and not remember doing so? Without knowing the drug Mercer had administered, it was impossible to tell, although Lennon was certain such drugs did exist in the movies, at the very least.

Could those eyes in his sink really be *real*?

They sure as hell *looked* the part.

What *was* in that innocuous blue pill?

"Is this all part of your sick gameshow?" Lennon asked Mercer as if the guy was standing right there in front of him. "Is this what it's all about?"

Heart racing, mouth dry, Lennon hunted around for his clothes as the TV droned on. They'd now cut from the student deaths to something else; his mind was too preoccupied to register exactly what, but he was grateful not to be confronted with his own face up there. What he did know was he *had* to get out of that hotel room; suddenly it felt unbearably claustrophobic, as if the dingy, stained walls were closing in on him. He also had the overwhelming urge to call Jilly, to hear her familiar, soothing voice telling him everything was going to be alright.

Chase Lennon had never felt so unsure of himself, so friggin' terrified, in his entire life.

The room's landline telephone didn't work. Of course, it didn't – that would have made things far too easy for him. Nevertheless, Lennon jabbed his finger on the cradle buttons until it hurt, but the receiver remained deathly quiet. He double checked the phone was plugged into the socket on the wall behind the nightstand and then gave up. He was not supposed to use that particular phone, then.

Lennon finally tracked down his clothes to the third drawer down of the four in the worn-out cupboard. They were the same jeans, short-sleeved shirt, and Vans sneakers he'd been wearing when he'd set out to meet with the show people at the Pyramid club which now seemed like a lifetime ago.

And the same clothes you're wearing on the CCTV footage, Chase, my friend.

Doing his best to push that thought to the back of his mind, Lennon dressed quickly. With no choice but to go commando, he pulled on his pants and padded the pockets for his wallet and cell phone; his wife was only a phone call away.

Of course, it's not there.

His pockets were empty, save for a plain, dark gray credit card.

Lennon turned the thin plastic card over in his fingers. It was a Mastercard and had his name in raised gold lettering on the front. His signature—a near-perfect likeness of the real thing—was already scribbled on the strip at the back next to four neatly handwritten numbers, which he figured would be the PIN. So, he'd signed the card at some point during his trip from Philadelphia to New Orleans, and they'd taken his cell and wallet; clearly the mysterious gray card was his only means of paying for anything he might need as he evaded the show's hunters.

Running on the heady mix of pure adrenalin and absolute panic, Lennon returned the credit card to his back pocket, picked up the room's keycard from the nightstand, and headed for the door.

Something made him pause by the low cupboard. There, Lennon contemplated the small, snub-nosed gun that sat there. The rope and pills were of no use to him, as far as he could see, but he was all alone in a strange city and had no idea what Mercer had in store for him. Plus, if the gameshow people didn't want him to have a weapon, they'd not have provided one, would they?

It's for just in case.

Lennon grabbed the gun, checked to see that each of the half-dozen chambers were occupied, and tucked it into the waistband at the back of his jeans. He then yanked open the hotel room's door and made ready to leave. Behind him, the shower's steam continued to fill the grim room with billowing, wispy clouds. Any other time, Lennon would have doubled back to switch it off, but he was acting on self-preserving instinct. And besides, the steam hid those awful eyeballs and congealing blood in the sink.

The approaching dusk filled the street outside the hotel with long shadows. The air was hot, humid, and had Lennon's shirt clinging to his back before he'd so much as turned the first corner. Keeping his head down, taking care not to look anyone in the eye, Lennon slipped into the crowded anonymity of the French Quarter.

First priority was to find an ATM and get some cash in his pocket. Lennon figured he'd be able to do that with the card the show had so thoughtfully provided; he'd not get far without money, and where would be the fun in that for the discerning viewers?

Next, he'd find a payphone and call home. He'd been gone from home we'll over twenty-four hours, and Jilly had to be worried sick about him.

Especially if she's seen the news.

Lennon shook that thought from his mind and pressed on.

The first ATM he happened upon was at a quiet little gas station on Decatur Street. Tucked away near the back of the place, next to the make-it-yourself coffee machine, the ATM was nicely hidden from the street. Sure, there'd be a camera next to its screen recording each transaction, but he was certain no one would be watching the camera feed;

they were only viewed if a crime was committed against the ATM.

After feeding the gray card into the slot, Lennon punched in the PIN he'd memorized from its back, and a screen popped up to inform him there'd be a seven-dollar-fifty-cents charge for taking money out, plus whatever deduction the bank deemed reasonable at their end. Then another screen appeared, this one from the show people to let him know he could only take out fifty dollars every twenty-four hours – not including the service charge.

How the hell did they do that?

Conveniently, it didn't give Lennon the opportunity to request any money. Instead, the machine simply returned Lennon's new card and spat out two twenties and a ten.

Making his way toward the Bourbon Street crowds, Lennon knew he'd be able to lose himself among the raucous revelers, find a quiet bar, and call home. He made a mental note to ask Jilly to give him Mackenzie Crail's number – he'd put in a call first thing in the morning.

"Perfect," Lennon told himself as he rounded the corner onto Frenchman Street. There, a little way ahead, was a cozy drinking hole called The Stripey Cat. It was still early for Nola, the bar almost devoid of customers, and the ubiquitous New Orleans' trad jazz band hadn't hit the stage.

"Shiner Bock." Lennon waved his ten-dollar bill at the barman, a tall beanpole of a guy with a mousey-brown, wispy goatee, and horn-rimmed glasses. "You have a payphone?"

"Over by the restrooms." The beanpole up-tipped his fluffy chin in the general direction of the rear end of the bar.

"Thanks." Lennon paid for his beer—apparently expected to swig it straight from the bottle like some common hipster—and made his way over to the phone bolted to the wall over by the gentlemen's restroom door.

Pausing by a small, iron-topped table at the side of the low stage, Lennon gulped down a mouthful of chilled beer and fought hard to compose himself. And then another, which made his empty stomach ache a little. He'd pretty much acted without thinking since seeing himself on the news report as his fight-or-flight survival mechanism had gotten itself firmly stuck in *flight* mode. Now, far enough away from that God-awful hotel, hidden among the drunken tourists, he relaxed just enough to allow himself to process.

Common sense told him there was absolutely no way he'd killed those three kids, no matter what the news report said.

But what about those eyeballs, Chase?

There was no doubt in Lennon's mind it was his face up on the TV screen in the hotel room. Either that or his doppelganger—hadn't he seen that in some made-for-TV Stephen King movie once? Sure, it was possible, a seven-billion-to-one coincidence, but it was more likely it *was* his face.

Which doesn't necessarily mean you were there, buddy.

That was it!

Somebody had put his face onto that of the real perp,' or had added all of him to the CCTV footage outside the murder building.

Like, perhaps, Mercer's gameshow people?

At that thought, Lennon began to feel a tad dumb. The eyes in the sink *were* fake, and the alluring Ms. Boudreaux's report had to be bogus. After all, it was not beyond the bounds of possibility she was in on the gag and most likely had accepted a fat paycheck for pre-recording the fake news because who knew what reach a show offering a $1.2bn prize would have?

As for the crime scene broadcast, just how hard could it be to string up some fake police tape, organize a few extras, and create a realistic on-site report? Thinking about it more, hadn't it been just a little bit *too* convenient the hotel's TV had switched on the second Lennon had been standing next to it in all his naked glory? And that the news report had played from its beginning so he didn't miss any of it?

Especially his own appearance as man of the moment.

"You got me again, guys. You really freakin' did." Suddenly feeling decidedly foolish, Lennon peered around the dingy bar, expecting to spot someone surreptitiously filming him.

"You okay?"

The voice, out of nowhere, startled Lennon.

Turning around, he found himself staring into the gray-green eyes of the young woman standing close behind him, uncomfortably so. His first instinct was to check his back pocket to make sure his cash and credit card were still there.

"Are you high?" she asked.

"Umm, no." Lennon eyed her with suspicion. She had a sweet, round face, which was quite beautifully made up, if a tad plain, and a shock of unnaturally red hair. She wore a skimpy, white tank top and short leather miniskirt, which showed off a neat cleavage and slim, tanned, bare legs respectively. She stood no taller than his shoulder, her diminutive height exaggerated by patent black, four-inch spiked heels.

"Would you like to be?" She gave Lennon a broad smile and knowing wink. "I know a nice place we could go and have a little fun together…"

"Thank you, I'm good." Lennon knew he sounded blunt, rude, and instantly felt bad. After all, she'd been concerned enough to check in on the spaced-out guy, even if she was now openly propositioning him. "I… I have to call my wife," he told the woman.

She nodded gently. "Maybe when you've done that, you can buy a girl a drink?" Reaching out, her hand gently brushed Lennon's arm. Her skin was warm, soft, slightly damp with sweat; he smelled the subtle undertones of her vanilla perfume and enjoyed his bird's eye view of her cleavage more than he felt he should. It felt good to have some human connection, albeit such a random one.

"Maybe." Lennon had no intention of doing any such thing. He knew her sort all too well. She was most likely a hooker, and even if not, he'd definitely end up paying for her company in one way or another.

And what would Jilly say?

"If you'll excuse me…" He popped his beer back down on the table and pointed at the payphone to finish the sentence.

"I'll wait for you at the bar." The woman turned on her vertiginous heels and sashayed away.

Lennon ogled her taut butt as it wiggled beneath the tight, black leather, and realized he already missed the tempting caress of her skin.

He couldn't remember the last time he'd ever used a payphone. In fact, he was surprised to see the things actually still existed; surely the mobile communication revolution ought to have rendered them obsolete by now? At that particular point in time, Lennon was incredibly grateful it had not.

And thanks to his reliance upon his cell phone, the only number he knew by heart, other than his own, was his wife's, because they'd bought their phones through the joint plan together, and Jilly's number was just two digits different from his. Not understanding why he felt nervous about making a phone call—this was all just part of the TV show, right?—Lennon stuck a few quarters from his bar change into the slot, waited for them to rattle down, and punched in the number on the metal keys.

"Hello? Jilly?"

"Chase?" The tone to her voice had Lennon worried. Was she annoyed he'd taken all this time to call her? That was most likely it, although it wouldn't be the first time he'd been gone a couple days on a business trip without calling; she knew all too well how distracted her husband got when he was chasing a deal.

"Hey, I'm so sorry I've not called, babe. You'll never believe—"

"What have you *done*, Chase?" Accusing.

"I signed up for this gameshow…" Should he tell her they'd drugged him and dumped him in New Orleans? Or that they'd concocted some fake murder story to set the scene and get him running? It all sounded far-fetched as he ran it through his mind.

"How could you do such a horrible thing? I thought I knew you, Chase." Jilly hawked back what sounded to be snot and tears. Was she crying?

Lennon was perplexed. Sure, he knew he could be thoughtless at times, especially when it came to keeping Jilly informed as to his whereabouts. But she had to know he'd never be unfaithful to her, even if he wasn't above lying about the reason for his trip to Philly. Those days were well behind him, behind *them*, and Jilly knew that.

Taking in a deep breath to counter the bubbling annoyance at his wife's overreaction, Lennon made ready to smooth things over and explain everything to her. Hell, he'd put in a call to Charlie Stubbs at the dealership first thing and buy Jilly that red Mazda sportster she'd been dropping less-than-subtle hints about for months.

"I'm in New Orleans right now and it's a long story, but—"

"I know where you are, Chase." Jilly sounded angry. "You're all over the news!"

"What?"

"I said, you are all over the news, Chase." She paused ever-so briefly between each word, as if talking to a slow kid.

The show people broadcast Brheanna's fake news report in New York? Why on earth would they do something like that?

Then it dawned on him.

"You're in on it, too?" he said. "Jilly?"

"I'm in on *what*?"

"The show. They're putting you up to this – pretending you believe I did something terrible."

"Those poor kids are *dead*, Chase," Jilly snapped. "I saw your face on the news. Do you think I don't know my own husband when I see him? I won't stay married to a monster, Chase."

"It's all part of the game, babe." Lennon struggled to maintain his composure; she was evidently playing along, and he didn't want to look like a complete gullible idiot to his viewers.

"You killed three college kids! That's not a game!" She was sounding hysterical; had Mercer given his wife acting lessons in addition to coercing her to play along?

Certainly made sense.

"I didn't kill *anyone*. I told you, I signed up for this gameshow, and I have to evade capture for a week. I guess this is all part of it."

"You're scaring me, Chase."

"There's nothing to be scared about, Jilly, I promise you."

"You need to give yourself up, turn yourself in to the police. If you've had some sort of mental breakdown, we can get you the help you need… and a good lawyer. Not Mackenzie Crail—a proper, *criminal* attorney."

"But, I haven't—"

"Come home, Chase," Jilly urged. "Please. Come home before it's too late."

Click.

Lennon stood there awhile with the payphone's dead receiver held to his ear, his mind whirling. His wife had put on one hell of a performance there: so much so, Lennon found himself beginning to wonder if she really had seen the news report and was genuinely thinking he was capable of murdering three people. Was it possible Mercer's people had streamed the fake report directly into the TV back at the beach house? Or had it gone out everywhere?

Now, that *would be crazy.*

Replacing the phone onto its tarnished cradle, Lennon returned to the table to find the last half of his beer had been whisked away by the overzealous bar staff. So, with a soft sigh, he made his way back to the bar and chose a stool respectfully away from the young woman in the tight skirt. She sat quietly on a barstool close to the door nursing a whiskey on the rocks and fiddling around on her cell.

"Same again?" Beanpole appeared as if from nowhere, iPhone pressed tight to his ear.

"Sure." Lennon offered a wan smile, but the young man seemed not to notice.

Lennon had barely had the chance to swallow his first cold mouthful when the young woman slipped off her stool and made her way over.

"Looks like you could use some company." She clambered onto the stool next to Lennon's; her skirt, riding high up her smooth thighs, threatened a glimpse of tomorrow's laundry.

"Not really."

"Call to the missus not go so well?"

Lennon shrugged and sipped at his beer to avoid having to reply.

"From where I was sitting, it looked like it wasn't a very good conversation at all," the woman said with a wry smile. It flashed just the tips of startlingly white teeth between plum-painted lips. "Have you been a naughty boy?"

Lennon shook his head. "I'm sorry, but I really am not in the mood to talk."

"I think you need a friend right now and you're just too much of a macho man to admit it." She fiddled with the neckline of her tank top, exposing just a hint more of that wonderful, tanned cleavage.

"I don't need anybody." Lennon was growing impatient. "I just got some crap going on right now."

"If you don't need to talk, I can think of plenty other ways I can help alleviate all that pent-up stress you've got going on…"

And there it was.

The hustle.

Lennon would have been lying to himself had he'd said it hadn't crossed his mind to take the young woman up on her offer. He really could have done with some distraction, some relief right then and there, but he very much doubted the forty bucks he had in his pocket would buy him much by means of her services. And, if the show people had shown Jilly the news report, there was no guarantee they wouldn't stream him live to the beach house TV picking up a hooker.

"I'm trying to be polite here, lady," Lennon growled, doing his best not to come over as aggressive; last thing he needed was her kicking up a fuss and screaming *assault*. *#metoo* certainly had a hell of a lot to answer to. "I'm *really* not looking for company right now, especially the kind you're offering. So, if you wouldn't mind—"

The woman looked honestly offended. "You think I'm a *hooker*?"

"Well, aren't you?" Lennon took another swig of his beer. He'd always taken pride in himself for his innate ability to accurately read people and stood by the initial impression he'd formed of his unwanted bar companion. Her pretend offence was most likely all part of the ruse: make the john feel guilty for the insult, then hustle him for business, anyway.

"I suppose you're making that sweeping assumption about me based on what I'm choosing to wear?" She fiddled absently with her glass, its contents almost gone. "Do you have any idea just how inappropriate that is in today's world? Also, is your self-esteem so low you automatically jump to the conclusion that any attractive woman trying to make conversation with you is nothing more than sex-for-sale?"

Lennon pegged her for a smart one, that was for sure; she'd read him as accurately as he thought he'd read her. She'd only missed his trust issues; Lennon knew from bitter experience how some people craved his company only because he had money. However, this woman had no idea who he was or that he only had a few dollars to his name right, then.

"I'm sorry if I offended you," Lennon lied and chugged at his Shiner.

"Buy me a Bourbon and I'm sure I'll find it in my heart to forgive you."

"You really don't give up, do you?"

"Nope." The woman shook her head and smiled at him; her eyes twinkled in the dim, crappy light of the bar.

"Another one of whatever the lady's drinking, please." Lennon waved over the beanpole, who was still chatting on his cell. If any of Lennon's employees ever showed such unprofessionalism toward paying customers, he'd have fired their sorry ass on the spot.

"Thank you, kind sir." The woman drained her glass and slid it across the sticky bar for the bartender to refill

Lennon snorted and forced a thin smile by means of reply. He fished out one of the two twenties he'd gotten from the ATM and paid for the woman's drink. The truth was, even though he knew damned well she *was* a prostitute after his money, Lennon was genuinely grateful for the company after the shock he'd had earlier of seeing himself accused of triple murder.

Naturally, he had no intention at all of paying her for sex, or anything else, for that matter, but a young woman in a short leather skirt was a welcome distraction and very easy on the eye.

Is she part of the game, too?

Of course, that was a consideration, and another good reason for not entertaining the woman. Although, it would be interesting to see what her part might be, if she was in the game rather than *on* it. Buying her a couple of drinks would still irk Jilly if she was watching back home, but she'd take him to the cleaners in the divorce courts if he ever took things further.

The bartender topped up the woman's glass and retreated to the far end of the bar. He'd finally finished up his phone conversation and busied himself by tidying the whiskey bottles behind the bar into a neat, straight row.

"Drink up," the woman said. She downed her fresh drink in one and plonked the glass down hard on the counter.

The sudden, loud noise startled Lennon. "I already told you, I'm not—"

"Look outside."

Lennon did as instructed, peering through the bar's dirty window, and saw what appeared to be a pair of cops standing outside the bar looking in; they were most likely part of Mercer's team, Lennon reckoned. One, a stocky Black guy, made the briefest of eye contact; it was enough to alert Lennon to the fact they were searching for him.

The next part of the game is on!

"Are they after you?" The woman's eyes scrutinized Lennon's.

Lennon nodded yes. "It's not what you think, though," he offered. "It's all part of a—"

"Save the BS for later, we can take the back door." The woman slipped from the bar stool, her skirt riding up once more to flash a whole lot more honeyed thigh. She grabbed Lennon's hand, held it tight.

Lennon rested his bottle on the bar and stood. It didn't occur to him to wrest his hand from hers since holding hands in such circumstances seemed the natural thing to do.

The cops made their way into the Stripey Cat the moment Lennon allowed the woman to lead him away from the bar and back toward the restrooms. From the corner of his eye, Lennon saw the beanpole tip a nod to the cops and glance in his direction. Was *that* who he'd been talking to, tipping them off about the fugitive in his bar?

Was there a bounty on his head already?

"Come on!" The woman tugged impatiently at Lennon's hand. Much stronger than she looked, she almost pulled him off balance.

With the restrooms in sight, the two broke into a walk-run, and as they entered the narrow passageway, the back door came into view.

Behind them, the police officers hurried through the bar, catching curious glances from the few patrons scattered between the tables, nursing their drinks. Lennon admired the cops' commitment to the game – they definitely looked and acted like the real deal.

"No!!" The woman yanked hard on the metal bar that ran across the door. The thing was locked, despite the notice screwed to the door making it abundantly clear it was to remain unlocked during business hours.

There was no time for Lennon to question the Stripey Cat's blatant violation of fire safety codes; the cops, fake or otherwise, were almost upon him.

Can't let the game end this quickly!

In his panic, Lennon became acutely aware of the small gun tucked into the back of his pants and covered by his shirt. It had been there since the hotel, of course, but he'd all but forgotten about it.

Only now it provided him with an option.

Or did it?

For all he knew, the revolver was loaded with blanks; he couldn't imagine Mercer letting him run around New Orleans with a loaded gun, especially with the cops on his tail. Having said that, what was to say the two cops wouldn't fall and play dead if he fired in their direction? All part of *The Contestant's* drama.

That would buy him some time to get away, for sure.

Then again, what if some do-gooder decided to get involved and take down the guy shooting at cops in the French Quarter?

Deciding against pulling out the gun—for now—Lennon pulled his companion into the women's restroom just as the Black cop caught hold of his free arm. Instinctively, Lennon yanked his hand from the woman's grasp and took a swing at the cop.

Sharp pain shot through Lennon's knuckles as his fist connected with the cop's cheek. The hard, unyielding bone beneath the pudgy flesh hurt his hand like hell, but the cop let go and staggered back, reeling from the blow.

That gave Lennon just enough time to drag the woman into the restroom and slam the door shut behind them. He twisted the lock and leaned his weight against the flimsy door, fighting to get his bearings. In the movies, there was always a handy restroom window to escape out of, but the one facing him was high up and would definitely present a tight squeeze for him, if not the slim woman by his side.

"Open up! Police!"

Fists pounded heavy and insistent upon the door.

"You have a plan?" The young woman looked around the small restroom. She didn't appear to be panicking quite as much as Lennon; likely didn't have as much to lose as he did—a billion dollars and change was plenty to get panicky about.

Unless she was part of the game, of course.

"I was hoping the window…" Lennon's words were punctuated by the thumps on the door. The cops weren't about to give up easily.

"Looks like we have no choice," the woman said. "You kinda got us cornered in here."

Lennon was embarrassed. What on earth had made him think he could evade capture for a whole week? It had all sounded so easy when Mercer had him signing the contracts, but the minute stuff got real, he was going to end the game in a dive bar toilet.

"I'll never fit."

The young woman looked Lennon up and down and led him by the arm to the window. "Yeah, you will." Lacing her fingers together to form a step, she positioned herself directly beneath the window.

"You're joking, right?"

"Open this door!"

"Got any better ideas?"

Lennon realized he most certainly didn't. All he could do was hope her assessment of his size was correct.

Placing his foot in the human stirrup, Lennon hoisted himself up to the window. First, he pushed it open, then pulled himself up using the peeling wooden frame. It was hard work, much harder than expected, and beads of sweat dripped into his eyes and trickled down his back.

The thumping on the restroom door intensified. The cops' patience was clearly running out. How long before they quit the pretense and just kicked the freakin' door in?

Half in, half out of the window, Lennon sucked in his gut the best he could and rued the day he'd quit going to the gym. It was a tight squeeze, the rough wood of the window frame scraped at the skin on his belly, but it would seem his companion had been right.

There was a dumpster just below the window, much to Lennon's relief. Headfirst, he shimmied out through the window, rested his hands on the top of the dumpster in an awkward handstand, then let his legs drop from the ledge. It was far from elegant or acrobatic, but it got the job done.

"Hey!" the woman hissed. She sounded distressed.

As he righted himself, it crossed Lennon's mind to jump down from the dumpster and just leave his unwanted helper there in the restroom. Even if she wasn't part of Mercer's game, he hoped the cops were, and she'd be just fine.

But what if she's supposed to be part of it?

And what if she isn't and the cops are real? She'd be hung out to dry for aiding a fugitive.

Lennon leaned back in through the window to offer his hands. "Grab hold. I'll pull you up."

The woman didn't need asking twice. The pounding on the door had stopped and the indiscernible sound of angry chatter filtered through to the restroom.

Mindful of scraping her exposed skin on the window frame, Lennon pulled the woman up slowly, carefully. She was heavier than she looked.

She was half in, half out of the window when the restroom door burst open. The Black cop stormed in, his left eye already swollen shut from Lennon's punch. The guy looked truly pissed. *"Stop right there, miss!"*

"Pull!" the woman urged.

Lennon braced himself against the dumpster top and hauled her out through the window with one last hearty tug. She fell into his awaiting arms like some soppy heroine in an old black-and-white romantic movie as the cop yelled frustrated obscenities after her retreating legs.

"Hey!"

Of course, the other cop had gone around to the back of the building. He ran into view along the alleyway, gun drawn and pointed to the ground by his side; they evidently weren't as dumb as they were portrayed on the movies.

Lennon helped the woman down from the dumpster and eyed the opposite end of the alleyway. There was a gap in the buildings halfway along, which led to a narrower, darker alley.

"Hold on," the woman grasped Lennon's arm. Bending slightly at the waist, she lifted a leg behind her, almost touching her ass, and hooked her spiked shoe off with her thumb. The second shoe followed suit, and she was suddenly so much shorter in bare feet. "Now I can run," she explained, as she slipped her hand back inside his.

Lennon set off toward the narrow gap of the alleyway with the cop in hot pursuit. Lennon was banking on it being unlikely the cop would shoot at them, since it was part of Mercer's gameshow, but he couldn't be entirely sure.

Should have read the fine print, Chase.

"Stop right there!"

Lennon and the woman ducked into the inky shadows and continued running. A quick glance behind, let them know the pursuing cop was refusing to give up; there could be no doubting his commitment to the role. Lennon pulled the woman into another alley, and then another after that.

He planned on losing the cop in the confusing maze of French Quarter back streets, even if it meant getting lost himself. Between him and the young woman, Lennon was confident they'd be able to find their way back once they lost the cop.

Back to where, exactly?

No time for that. Lennon still had the cop to shake off, and he was getting the impression his new companion was flagging. He was *pulling* her a little more with each step, and, once again, Lennon thought he may well be better off cutting her loose and taking his chances alone.

"Stop." The young woman echoed the cop's shout. Only hers was more pleading than a frustrated command. She tugged on Lennon's hand and slowed her step as they slipped into another shadow-filled alleyway, this one catty-corner from the last.

"We can't…" Lennon panted, his lungs struggling to take in the hot, humid air. He'd developed one hell of a stitch, too, which had him grateful at the brief pause. "We gotta go…"

The woman remained defiant. She let go of his hand and turned to face the way they'd come. She stood, legs slightly apart, bare feet planted on the cold stone ground, eyes fixed on the narrow entrance to the alleyway.

"What are you doing?" Lennon hissed, trying to keep his voice low. "We can't stay here."

"Shhh!"

The cop's heavy footsteps and rasping, labored breathing grew closer. He'd quit shouting now, no doubt because it was so dang hard to breathe; the alleys and back streets of New Orleans were soaked with stale, wet air that smothered the lungs.

Closer, closer still, the cop's shoes echoed between the dank brick walls. He'd be upon them any second.

Lennon braced himself to run and leave the woman to it.

This was her choice, not his—he had over a billion reasons, after all.

As the cop rounded the corner to their alleyway, the woman sprang into action, aiming a vicious kick directly between his legs. The grunt of exertion that came from her told Lennon she'd put every ounce of her remaining strength behind it.

The top of her bare foot connected squarely with the cop's balls, and he let out a loud, wheezy *ooof!* and crumpled to the ground before he'd even quit running. Eyes bugging out in pain, the cop grasped at his crotch with both hands, and his gun clattered harmlessly away into the shadows. The woman landed another well-aimed kick at the cop's flank, her toes digging deep into the flab there. She then turned her attention to his face.

"That's enough!" Lennon grabbed hold of the woman's arm, yanking her backward. "You'll kill him!"

The woman snapped her head around and, for a fleeting moment, Lennon got the notion that's precisely what she *wanted* to do.

Mercifully, the moment passed, and the woman allowed Lennon to lead her away from the fallen cop. He hoped whatever Mercer was paying him was worth a hard kick in the nuts like that.

They emerged from the rabbit warren of tight alleyways onto Dauphine Street, within sight of the Museum of Death. From there, the woman took the lead, and the pair chanced a walking pace to catch their breath.

"I have a place not too far from here," she informed Lennon. "You'll be safe there."

Lennon shrugged. He was tired, all run out, and figured he may as well play along. Whether she was part of

Mercer's game or not, she'd helped him evade capture, and that was good enough for him.

Her place was less than a block away. It was a small, grubby apartment above an old, closed-down voodoo store. The acrid stink of incense and skunk hung thick in the air.

"Barbara," the woman said once they'd settled down in the cramped living area with a generous tumbler of Bourbon each. They sat side by side on the only seating in the place: an ancient, ratty love seat-style couch covered with once-colorful crocheted throw blankets.

"Chase."

"It's good to meet you, Chase." She made a big show of shaking hands, as if they'd not just run through the French Quarter together, holding hands like star-crossed lovers in some cheesy romance movie.

"You don't know who I am?"

"Should I?" Barbara raised a quizzical eyebrow.

"You said I'd be safe here. I assumed you'd seen the news."

"Never watch it," Barbara smiled. "It's all far too depressing these days. If it's not Trump playing fast and loose with his stupid mouth, Putin bombing the crap out of innocent people, or the Gaza Strip getting bombed into oblivion, it's COVID this, cyber-attack that. That's all crap I can do without. I figured that, since the cops don't just chase random white guys through New Orleans for the fun of it, you were in some kind of trouble. Whatever it is, you're welcome to stay here until you figure stuff out."

Ever the cynic, Lennon still looked around the dingy room for any tell-tale red LEDs of hidden cameras. Nothing caught his eye.

"So, you're definitely not part of this?" He tested the water, looking for any reaction that might give her away.

"Part of what?" If she was bluffing, Barbara could make a good living as a poker player.

"Mercer's game." Lennon studied her eyes for a flicker of recognition at the name. Nothing. "All of this, the cops, the news report, *this…*" He pulled the revolver out from the back of his pants and placed it carefully on the arm of the couch. "It's all part of an odd gameshow I kinda got myself involved in."

Barbara's eyes flicked to the gun, then back at her guest. Was that a glimmer of nervousness he was seeing?

"Got yourself *involved* in?"

"Okay, I signed up for it." Lennon was embarrassed at not taking ownership for his actions; he'd hardly had a gun held to his head when he'd blindly signed that contract. Yes, he'd gone into this thing with Mercer feet-first and eyes wide open. "It's big money, and all I have to do is not get caught for a week."

"Easier said than done, eh?" Barbara chuckled at Lennon's expense and took a sip of her drink.

"It is when they put out fake news reports labeling me as some murderous psychopath. That makes things more than a tad difficult, to be honest."

"How so?"

Taking his cue, Lennon launched into the shortened version of the mysterious email, his meeting with Mercer, Brheanna Boudreaux's report, how they somehow got pictures of him at the supposed crime scene, the severed eyeballs in the sink…

As Lennon talked, Barbara left the couch to retrieve something from the small kitchenette: an old cigar box. When she brought it back and lifted the lid, Lennon was assaulted by the unmistakable aroma of good-quality weed. He'd actually smoked a fair amount in his day, right up to when he'd met Jilly, because it helped him destress. Sadly, she didn't approve of such illicit pleasures, and that had been that.

"Did the report go out on *real* TV?" Barbara rolled a fat doobie with expert, nimble fingers.

Lennon heaved his shoulders. "I honestly couldn't say. I do know Jilly saw it, though—"

"I figured… that certainly explains your phone call at the bar now."

"Exactly. But, if they can stream it directly to our TV at the beach house, they could have done the same to my hotel room. Only show it to people involved in the game which makes more sense."

"You do realize all this *they* talk is making you sound like some crazy conspiracy theorist?" Barbara lit the spliff, drew in a long, slow lungful, and passed it over to Lennon.

"I guess it all does sound crazy, huh?" He hesitated for a beat or two, then took a lengthy, sweet drag for himself.

You've earned this, Chase, old buddy.

"I'd say just a little."

"So, why are you helping me? I'm either crazy or a sociopathic serial killer—take your pick—and you invite me to your home?"

"Or… you could be telling me the truth." As Barbara took the spliff from Lennon, her fingers brushed gently against his. "You don't look much like a killer to me, Chase. Or a crazy person. So, I'm happy to do what I usually do with people, trust my gut, and take you at face value."

"You sure you're okay with me laying low here?" A mellow warmness spread through Lennon's brain; perhaps things were going to work out just fine after all and he'd be making it home to Jilly with one hell of an explanation and an even fatter bank account.

Barbara nodded. "I wouldn't have offered if I wasn't one hundred percent. You can't certainly go back to the hotel *they* arranged for you," she tipped a mischievous wink, "that would make it far too easy for them to find you.

But I only have the one bedroom, one bed, and this couch is way too small for you…"

"Are you propositioning me?" The words slipped out before Lennon could stop them. Mentally, he kicked himself.

Thankfully, his hostess wasn't the easily offended type. Smiling, she retorted, "Will you quit with the hooker talk already? I was going to say, my bed is a king, and there's plenty of room for the two of us. I think I can be trusted to keep my hands off you."

That wink again.

"You can trust me, too." Lennon felt it was something he was expected to say. The truth was, in any other circumstance, in his earlier years, he'd be pulling out all the stops to get the woman into bed.

And yet, here she was, *inviting* him.

Funny how things change when you're on the run.

Barbara smiled at him. "You saw what I did to that cop, right?"

"Yeah. Poor guy." Lennon winced at the memory of the cop's face when he went down; surprise and agony blended into one horrified expression.

The two shared a strained laugh.

Barbara rummaged around in her cigar box amid the weed paraphernalia. Lennon looked over her shoulder and saw tiny baggies of buds, papers, cigarette roller, lighters, a half dozen ready-rolled reefers, a syringe filled with amber cannabis juice… he really had to admire Barbara's dedication to the craft.

"Here you are," she said to the small, clear baggie she'd located beneath the debris. It contained a dozen or so tiny white pills similar to the ones the doc had prescribed Jilly to keep her cholesterol in check.

Barbara fished four out of the bag and placed two in Lennon's hand.

He eyed them with suspicion.

"They really have got you all paranoid and jumping at shadows, haven't they?" The corners of Barbara's eyes crinkled with her smile.

"What is this?"

"Just to help you sleep," she told him. "All that adrenaline in your system, you'll be buzzing for days no matter how tired you feel. Then exhaustion will kick in, and I'm guessing you'll need to keep sharp if you're going to survive a full week out there."

Lennon remained skeptical, and was painfully aware it showed on his face.

"It's to take the edge off, nothing more, I promise. I don't often partake, but, then again, it's not every night I rescue a fugitive and get chased by the cops." Barbara popped two pills onto her tongue, swilled them down with the last of her Bourbon, and opened her mouth wide for her guest's benefit.

All gone.

She then took another deep toke from the joint and held it in her lungs.

"Why are you helping me, Barbara?" Lennon asked again as he gulped his pills down. A momentary taste of bitterness on his tongue, then they were gone. It was true: he *really* could use some relief from his predicament and needed to get a decent night's sleep if he was going to last more than a day on Mercer's show. "Are you *sure* you're not in on this?"

Barbara placed her hand on his. It was warm, soft, comforting. Focusing his fuzzy vision on it, Lennon saw how fuzzy the woman's fingers looked, how the edges of his vision were getting gray and blurred.

"I'm really glad you're not part of this..." Lennon slurred, but he was unconscious before he knew for certain Barbara had lied to him.

Chapter 8

"You got a call about last night's case, Sergeant Miller," the uniformed cop called across the small office.

"Take a message."

"He says it's important. Reckons he's got some information you might be interested in."

"Does he now? Just say I'm busy, for Christ's sakes." Sgt. Trae Miller slumped in his chair and rubbed at his jowls with his hands. His face was rough with bristles because he'd not been home last night and some asshole had taken his razor from the staff bathroom; kinda went with his unruly mustache and dire need of a haircut.

He'd not gotten a wink of sleep either, nor left the precinct after his shift when the call came in; he'd headed straight out to the crime scene and stayed there, sweating his ass off in the dry desert heat 'til the sun came up.

Much of Miller's night had been taken up waiting for the chief medical examiner to show and keeping the KCBD news crew from getting too close and contaminating the crime scene. Just how those vultures caught wind of a ratings-grabbing murder as quickly as they did was beyond him. Miller struggled to imagine why in hell anybody would want a job like that.

Of course, Margaret was pissed when he called her from the car. It was their 25th wedding anniversary, and she'd booked them a table at the Double Nickel Steakhouse for a nice, romantic dinner. Miller's wife wasn't much of a red meat eater, which was seen as peculiar in Lubbock—in all of Texas, for that matter—but the place was his favorite, and she'd wanted to spoil him a little.

Fat chance of that, now. He knew he'd be lucky if she was still talking to him when he finally crawled back home with his hollow apologies and gas station flowers.

"He's *insisting*, Sarg." The cop's face was red, sweaty, like he was on the verge of having a heart attack, despite his youth. He leaned back in his chair to address Miller over his shoulder. "I really don't think he's going to give up until he's spoken with you."

"Oh, for the love of God—" Miller reached for his desk phone.

"Want me to put him through?"

Miller grumbled to himself that, no, he didn't want Garcia to put whoever the hell it was through, that he'd had enough of *everything* for twenty-four hours and just wanted to go home to sleep. "Sure, why the hell not?" he huffed.

The young cop sighed in relief. He patched the call through to Miller and scampered off to the safety of the coffee machine.

"This is Detective Miller."

"Thank you for taking my call, Detective Miller. I'm Detective Theo Broussard, New Orleans Police Department."

"What can I do for you, Detective Broussard?" Miller really was not in much of a mood for idle chitchat. He leaned forward in his chair, elbows on the desk, and cradled the phone's receiver between his shoulder and right ear.

"Call me Theo."

An attempt to be friendly?

Again, Miller was in no mood.

"My officer said you have information about the murder we had last night."

"I caught the report on the early news here," Broussard explained. "It might be nothing more than a hunch, but—"

"You're calling me because you got a hunch?" Miller growled. "This is not some seventies' cop show, Detective Broussard." He all but spat *Detective*.

Broussard clearly decided to ignore the jibe. He went on, "We had a murder case here a coupla days ago; three victims."

"Three in one day?"

"All in the same place, same perp' as far as we know. Did you not see the news report?"

Miller snorted. "I don't have the time to keep up with all the Lubbock news, let alone whatever you got going on over there in Louisiana, Detective Broussard."

"Three young people , all students, were killed in their apartment. We even got a clear CCTV picture of the killer on his way in."

Miller's interest was suddenly piqued at *students*. The victim they'd found last night all sliced up in Prairie Dog Town Park had been a senior at Baylor University, a chemistry major who'd come back to her hometown to visit with family. She'd last been seen alive at the Buddy Holley

Center on Crickets Avenue showing her boyfriend the sights. "So, you know what he looks like?"

"Better than that, Detective Miller." Broussard sounded pleased with himself. "We got his name, too. Chase Lennon. He's some big-shot real estate guy from Upstate New York. Give me your cell and I'll send you what we got."

Miller gave Broussard his number and fished his phone from his inside pocket. He noted with an all-too-familiar sinking feeling in his stomach there'd been no calls or texts from Margaret. Boy, she really was *pissed* this time.

The phone pinged with Broussard's text. Miller opened it and saw Chase Lennon staring back at him. The guy was handsome and looked regular enough, but, then again, most sociopaths did. It's what helped them blend in with the rest of society and get away with their appalling behavior.

Another ping.

This time, it was a crime scene picture: Three blood-soaked bodies in an apartment: two girls, one guy, all naked. Looked to Miller like their killer had put a permanent dampener on what had been planned to be one hell of a fun-packed evening.

Three more snaps came through from Broussard: close ups of each victim, their ruined faces with black, empty eye sockets pooled with dark, congealing blood.

Miller gently placed his phone face down on his desk next to the pile of reports he'd promised to get around to by the end of the week.

He'd seen enough.

"Okay… so what makes you think he's *our* guy?" Miller spoke quietly into the desk phone's receiver. "Lubbock is a helluva long way from New Orleans, Broussard. Shouldn't you be looking for him over there?"

"The report said the killing appeared to be a random stabbing and that Kirsty Boule's body had been mutilated."

Miller shuddered at the still-fresh memory of that poor girl's body. What kind of monster would do something like that to another human being?

"We kept the specifics away from the media," Miller said.

"As did we, Detective." There was Broussard's self-congratulatory tone again. He really was beginning to rub Miller up the wrong way. It was standard practice in cases like the Boule girl to withhold certain details from the public; it helped prevent copycat murders and came in useful in instances where there might be a possible serial killer at large. Pretty much policing 101, *Detective Broussard*.

"Did your killer take the girl's eyes, Detective Miller?"

Miller sat up straight. "And her face," he said quietly; even the uniforms at the precinct didn't even know that much about the case yet. "He also cut off both her breasts."

"He took them?"

"No." Miller felt the coffee he'd just drank to keep him awake gurgling up his gullet at the thought. That poor young girl had barely looked human after what that sicko had done to her. "We found those stuck onto a prickly pear cactus at the periphery of the park."

"I think we may both be looking for the same guy, Detective Miller." The smartass tone was gone from Broussard's voice.

"It's certainly looks to be pointing in that direction," Miller said. "But if he is our man, and he's come all this way from New Orleans to kill some random student here, it's across state lines."

"Which means FBI." Brussard sounded quite disappointed.

"Yup."

"I guess I'll put in a call," Broussard said. "Thank you for sharing your information, Detective Miller—"

"Hold on, Broussard." Miller had a strong feeling he was going to regret the next words out of his mouth; didn't he have enough mess to deal with already? "I have an old friend in the FBI, Ty Eubank, he used to work this precinct 'til they dragged him off to Quantico. He's based out of D.C. now, and I reckon he'll keep you and me in the loop on this one if I tip him off now."

"That'd be great," Broussard said. "I'm invested in this one, and I'd sure love to be there when they catch up with this Lennon guy."

"Yeah, the forensic psychologists are gonna have a field day with this one,provided the Feds don't go in all guns blazing like they do."

Broussard laughed. "Amen to that, Detective Miller."

"I'll be in touch, Broussard."

Miller hung up the phone, retrieved his cell off the desk, and scrolled through his contacts to E, and then to: Eubank, Tyrone.

Chapter 9

Jilly tensed when her phone rang, the breath caught in her throat. She'd been expecting the call since her tense conversation with Chase when he'd called her from New Orleans. That had been a couple days ago now, and she'd grown ever-more anxious with each hour that passed by. Of course, Chase was going to call her again, who the hell else did he have to turn to, given the mess he'd created for himself?

Her husband hadn't even bothered to give Mackenzie Crail a call. Jilly had checked in with them first thing Monday morning to see if anyone at the firm had heard from their biggest client.

They had not.

So, Jilly thought it safe to assume Chase had not contacted any other attorney as she'd suggested. And that planted yet more doubt in her mind: if he was truly innocent of the terrible things the reports had accused him of, why hadn't he lawyered up and come home to fight the accusations?

She picked up the call, thumbing her iPhone screen hard.

"Where are you, Chase?" Jilly didn't give her husband time to draw breath, let alone speak. "It's been two days… *two days!*"

"I… I don't know where I am, babe." Chase sounded bewildered, as if he was badly hungover or under the influence of some powerful narcotic or other. "I just woke up in the middle of nowhere."

Jilly fought hard to conceal the derision in her voice, and Chase was making it difficult. "What happened to you in New Orleans?" she demanded. "Why did you—?"

"I *didn't* do anything!"

"You were all over the news, Chase." Close to tears, Jilly's voice waivered. "I told you to turn yourself in, get a lawyer, do *something…*"

"You asked me to come home."

Jilly's next words, so carefully rehearsed over the last few days, caught in her throat, as if reluctant to be heard. "I think it's too late for that now," she told him. "I have Casey and Chad to think about. You can't bring all… *that* back home with you now."

"But I haven't done anything, Jilly." She heard the awful desperation in her husband's tone. He was a drowning man clutching at the side of the boat with wet, slippery fingers while the sharks circled. "I didn't kill those kids, you gotta believe me, babe. It's all part of this game I'm in. I really don't believe anyone was killed at all – it's all faked for effect."

"So why not go explain all that to the police?"

Silence.

"I could come home…"

"I already told you no, Chase." Jilly stood firm. It hurt her to do so, but she really had no other choice. "I've managed to keep the children away from the news so far—Casey is pissed I took her phone away—and I can't have you bringing all this trouble back here and have them knowing what you've done."

"But—"

"Save it, Chase," Jilly snapped. "I know what I've seen, and you're doing nothing concrete to refute that. An innocent man would have come forward by now."

"Is that really what you want me to do?"

"What other options do you have?" Jilly was quite matter of fact, the time for emotion slipping by. "They're going to catch up with you sooner or later. Hopefully sooner, and before you can hurt more innocent people."

She heard a long, drawn-out sigh.

"I guess there is one other option…" She spoke softly, her voice barely above a whisper.

The unfinished sentence hung in the air between husband and wife like some dark, malevolent cloud.

"It would be better than facing life in prison," Jilly replied. "Or worse."

"Seriously?"

Jilly swallowed hard. "It was your suggestion, Chase. I'm just thinking about—"

"The kids. I know." He made it sound like a bad thing.

"What else am I supposed to do here?"

"Support me."

"When you won't do anything to help yourself and you keep rambling on about some stupid gameshow. Do you have any idea just how crazy and deluded you sound right now?"

"Babe…"

"I thought you were having some kind of breakdown, Chase, and I felt sorry for you. I really did. But now, now I think I don't know who you are and probably never really did, I do believe you killed those poor kids."

There, she'd come right out and said it.

Jilly thought she heard a sniffle at Chase's end. It broke her heart.

"I'll call you later." Her husband's voice was barely audible.

"No, Chase," Jilly replied coldly. "Please don't."

***

Lennon threw the burner phone down hard onto the passenger seat next to him. It bounced off the gray-blue cloth and into the footwell, where it disappeared beneath the seat. He wiped his hands, sticky with old blood, down his red-stained shirt.

"Christ!" Lennon hissed. The word bounced loudly within the confines of the car that was completely alien to him. All he knew was it was a Ford—given away by the blue oval logo in the center of the steering wheel—and whoever had dumped him there in the middle of nowhere had thoughtfully left the engine running and the AC on.

He'd called Jilly almost immediately after waking up in the driver's seat of the car that most definitely wasn't his; a green sticker just below the small LED screen on the center dash told him it was a rental. He figured the show people would have organized the vehicle, stuck him in it, and dropped him there. All he could see out the windows were trees, shrubs, and scruffy undergrowth. He was, evidently, at the edge of a woodland God only knew where.

Lennon wasn't entirely sure what he'd expected from his wife when he called her, but what he'd gotten certainly wasn't it. Even though things had not been peachy between them of late—there had been building friction in the past year or so Lennon had become painfully aware of, despite his usual denial of anything emotional—Lennon had at least thought Jilly knew him better than to think him capable of cold-blooded murder.

She *actually* believed he was capable of murdering a random bunch of college kids! Lennon found *that* impossible to comprehend. He thought he knew Jilly well enough after all their years together, certainly enough to expect she would believe he was telling her the truth.

As it had turned out, Chase Lennon did not.

So, now what?

His brain was foggy, to say the least. Up until the moment Jilly had chastised him for not being in touch, Lennon had no idea how long it had been since New Orleans. *Two days!* He remembered waking up in the grubby Big Easy hotel, seeing his own face blown up on the widescreen TV, running from the cops, making his way into the city, and meeting some random woman as he slurped on a much-needed cold beer. After that, Lennon's recollection was beyond fuzzy, it was nonexistent.

And that left two whole days in which he could remember absolutely zilch.

Before calling Jilly, Lennon had taken a few minutes to check out the car in which he'd awoken. There was nothing on the back seat except a copy of the New Orleans Tribune with his face on the front page, and on the front passenger seat, he'd found the cheap cellphone, credit card, and the few bucks cash he had left over from the bar.

He'd also noticed the bloody fingerprints on the glove compartment door, but he really didn't have the stomach to open it. Memories of disembodied eyeballs in the hotel sink staring up at him accusingly flooded Lennon's mind, which had his chest tightening with the all-too-familiar grip of panic.

Clearly, he was *meant* to open the glove compartment—no doubt, part of Mercer's show—so, with a futile glance around for any hidden cameras that may not have been hidden too well, Lennon pulled the handle and dropped open the small door.

"Oh, Jesus Christ!"

Lennon shot back in his seat in shock and scrabbled for the door handle. The car's door flew open and he tumbled out onto the dry grass outside, cracking his knee hard on the steering column as he fell. Turning his head just in time to avoid hitting his soiled shirt, Lennon heaved up an acrid stream of bile into the dirt.

He waited awhile for the nausea to pass, poised for another wave he was sure would come. Dry heaving a couple times, his stomach already empty, he wiped his mouth on the back of his hand and struggled to his feet. His knee throbbed where he'd hit it and his legs wobbled. The sight of the bloodied plastic baggie in the glove compartment had truly shaken him up. And, there, next to it, neatly arranged, was a silver, snub-nosed revolver, a length of rope, and a plain, brown bottle containing white, round pills.

It was déjà vu, and the recollection of what he'd found in the New Orleans hotel had Lennon's heart pounding and his armpits feeling uncomfortably moist.

Daring himself to peer back inside the car, and into the opened glove compartment, Lennon studied the eyes that peered lifelessly back at him through the blood-smeared clear plastic. The irises were hazel in color, the blank pupils dilated and glassy, the eyeballs themselves surrounded by ragged shreds of muscle.

It looked as if they'd been *ripped*, rather than cut out. By far the worst thing was the eyes were nestled within a clump of skin, sticky with drying, clotted blood; it had lips, eyebrows, and the outline of a collapsed nose.

Oh, sweet Jesus, it was someone's face.

It all looked so brutally real, as if the show had *actually* butchered somebody for effect. Another dry heave wracked the entirety of Lennon's body. He doubled over, clutching at his stomach. It hurt like hell, but he was grateful there was nothing left to come up.

"No, no, no, *no…*" Lennon reached into the car and, for a moment at least, considered yanking the baggie out and tossing it away into the bushes.

"It has my prints all over it," he told himself. Hearing his own voice brought a little comfort, as if he wasn't entirely alone. It also occurred to Lennon he was talking to the unseen cameras he was convinced were watching his every move. "This is all part of Mercer's show," he reminded himself. "Just one big special effect."

So, instead of disposing of the baggie and its gruesomely realistic contents, Lennon slammed the glove compartment door closed with two fingers and slumped himself back into the driver's seat.

A cursory glance at his face plastered across the Tribune – blown up so big it was a tad grainy, but still undeniably his – informed Lennon he'd no doubt be featured in the news wherever he was now. He guessed he was no longer in or near New Orleans as the morning heat outside the car lacked the cloying Louisiana humidity.

It was hot, alright, but this was a dry, breath-sucking heat that reminded Lennon of the time he'd spent backpacking on the periphery of the Gobi Desert in his gap year.

"Well, I can't stay here, that's for sure. There *has* to be a crappy motel around somewhere. It's that kinda place." Lennon realized, once again, he was talking to his imagined audience and, not for the first time, he wondered just who the hell they were.

He'd signed on Mercer's bottom line to take part in what he'd been led to believe was a simple cat-and-mouse style gameshow, only to find himself at the center of what was, ostensibly, a murder investigation.

Unless, of course, that, too, was all part of the show?

Modern technology and AI being what it was, Lennon knew it wouldn't be too difficult to print up a fake newspaper and conjure up a pretend newscast. As for the body parts, for as real as they appeared to be, they could still be just very convincing fakes. He'd seen enough stomach-churning horror movies in his time to understand just how realistic they could make practical gore effects.

Which left the question hanging in Lennon's mind: just what kind of individuals actually got off watching this kind of reality show crap?

Chapter 10

Mercer paced the floor, his pristine, white, Air Jordans squeaking on the polished tiles. Things were going well, he thought, despite the one slip up: Jilly Lennon had pushed the suicide angle far too soon, despite the thorough briefing he and the show's production team had given her.

"Did I do okay?" Jilly was asking him. She looked up at Mercer from the white leather couch with wide eyes, like a puppy dog desperately seeking approval and a pat on the head.

"Yes, ma'am, you did just fine," Mercer lied—something he'd become unnaturally good at. "Maybe next time, don't be too quick to hint at… the *alternative* option."

Jilly shrugged and looked a little downcast. "I'm sorry… I figured it was not such a big deal since you'll pull him out of the game before he actually goes that far. You *will* stop the game before anything happens, right?"

"Of course we will," Mercer reassured her. "And I do see your point."

More lies.

"But… we don't want your husband getting to that juncture too soon; the game has only just gotten started. We have to think about—"

"The viewers and your viewing figures," Jilly regurgitated the line Mercer had trotted out to her when he'd first appeared at the beach house with his two young dogsbodies; the three of them had more resembled a mafia hit squad than TV show people.

"Absolutely, Mrs. Lennon." Mercer's smile was insincere, to say the least, but he figured Jilly hadn't caught the nuance. She simply smiled back at him, showing teeth that were a shade *too* white for his liking. "I would like to call you Jilly, if that's okay with you."

Jilly nodded and flashed that smile again; like a little kid who'd just gotten a smiley face sticker from her favorite teacher. "I'd like that," she replied. "Mrs. Lennon makes me feel like an old woman… which I am most definitely not." Straightening her back, Jilly puffed out her chest, which Mercer considered to be impressively perky for a mother of two kids.

Which reminded him…

"I'm thinking Chad and Casey should be here for the next time Chase calls," Mercer said. "The dog, too – our viewers always love to see *all* a contestant's family. It kinda makes the guy they're rooting for all the more relatable, more… *human*."

Jilly's smile wavered a little. She'd been doing well at keeping up her façade and playing along with his instructions; Mercer had even picked up on what he'd interpreted as a flirtatious vibe or two when they'd discussed her relationship with Chase; he was surprised to learn all was not as rosy in the Lennon marriage as he'd initially been led to believe by the brief he'd been given.

In fact, Mrs. Lennon had seemed eager to not only float the notion of suicide to her husband as a way out of the mess he'd ostensibly gotten himself into, but had also thrown the notion of a divorce around with more enthusiasm than he'd expected – even though that particular threat had been part of the show's ploy to push the contestant ever closer toward the edge of despair.

Either the woman was a dang good actress who'd gotten into the part with gusto, or she actually relished the thought of being free from Lennon. No doubt, there'd be a fat settlement in the cards for her and she'd walk away from the marriage a very wealthy woman indeed.

Not as wealthy, though, as she would be if—*when*—Chase Lennon delivered his own *coup de grace.*

All that considered, Mercer made a mental note to fire the researchers just as soon as Lennon's game was over.

"I already told you I sent them to visit with my parents." Jilly was defensive. "The police suggested I keep them away from the internet and TV news because of what they're all saying about Chase. Mom and Pop have taken them camping up at Pine Lake; it's the Southern Adirondack Pines campground they used to take me and my brother to when we were kids. They have a strict no electronics rule up there; Chad and Casey are used to that and Casey is happy—kinda—to do without her cell phone for a few days."

Mercer offered a sage nod. Naturally, the cops had paid Jilly a visit once the news broke about her husband; it would have appeared odd had they not. But, apart from a preliminary interview to ask the usual questions: had she noticed any recent changes in her husband's behavior that may have led to him committing such heinous crimes, how long had he been gone from home, had he been in touch since the news broke about the killings? Of course, Jilly had answered the questions in all innocence and had omitted to tell the detectives about her husband's claim it was all some ridiculous gameshow. She'd sent them on their way with a sincere promise to call them when or if Chase made contact again.

And that had been that. The police had not been back, nor had they asked for permission to tap Jilly Lennon's phone.

Mercer had seen to that.

The last thing the show needed was the authorities sniffing around and making waves with the contestant's wife. Mercer had to keep Jilly under control and saying all the right things to keep the game flowing smoothly, just as he'd managed to do for so many others throughout *The Contestant's* successful run.

It was his job to ensure nothing got in the way of the viewers' enjoyment and subsequent financial speculation, and if that entailed manipulating, intimidating, or buying off local law enforcement, then so be it. The truth ran far deeper than bribing a few bad cops to look the other way, of course; the show's reach had extended over the years to include the highest-ranking officers of police departments across the country.

It was something of which Mercer could be particularly proud.

"I still think it would be a good idea for you to bring Casey and Chad back from their trip," Mercer insisted. He tried his best not to sound *too* pushy, as he knew from experience the importance of keeping the contestant's spouse on side, but he evidently needed to emphasize the fact he was not making a suggestion here. "It's important for the show, Mrs. – *Jilly*."

"I'm not sure if I can reach them, Mr. Mercer," Jilly shuffled nervously on her obscenely expensive couch. It was clear she was intimidated by her house guest and his accomplices.

Good.

"I'm sure your parents are sensible enough to have a means by which to communicate." Jilly was really trying Mercer's patience now with her dumb excuses. He understood she wanted to protect her children, but that really was not his problem. He had far more important matters to think about.

Like his paying viewership and the fat side bets they were placing on the outcome of the Lennon game. It was more money in his pocket than he'd know what to do with.

"Well, I can *try*." Jilly had a guilty look on her face, like she'd just been caught out in a huge lie. "I think Pop might have his emergency cell with him."

"I can definitely see where you get your smarts from, Jilly." Mercer hoped he hadn't come across as *too* condescending. If he had, Jilly appeared not to have noticed, which he found to be quite ironic.

"I'll call him now." Jilly stood from the couch and made her way across the room, past Mercer's people who'd been observing the exchange with stony faces.

"Get the production room on the phone," Mercer barked at the two. "I think it's time to throw a little excitement into Mr. Lennon's day…"

***

It had been five, maybe six, years since Detective Miller had found the need to visit Lubbock Preston Smith International airport, and the place really wasn't all that different to how he remembered it. Sure, it looked like they'd given it a new lick of paint and swapped out some of the old, worn seating at the gates—no doubt thanks to the $8.7m, highly publicized, government cash injection it received five years before—but it somehow still managed to appear second-rate and tired, despite the too-shiny floors. Still, at least the place was air-conditioned, which made for a welcome respite from the relentlessly baking Texas heat outside.

Miller's last time at the airport had been when he'd surprised Margaret with what was supposed to have been a romantic getaway for some anniversary, or birthday, or some such. He'd booked a couple cheap flights out to Puerto Rico, along with a week's stay in a moderately priced hotel not far from the beach out there – it was as much as his cop's salary would stretch to at the time.

As things worked out, Margaret had been stricken with a severe case of *e-coli* from some poorly prepared lettuce on their first night, and Miller had been called back to his precinct in Lubbock because they'd made a break in some big credit card fraud case he'd spent over nine months investigating.

That had been the last time he'd attempted to surprise his wife. Miller also had the suspicion that disastrous vacation had been the beginning of the rot that had crept into his marriage like some insidious black mold on a tenement apartment ceiling.

"Trae Miller!" The voice from his right startled Miller from his miserable woolgathering. Spinning around, he saw the familiar face of his old friend and colleague.

"Special Agent Ty Eubank, how the hell are you?" Miller gave the guy a warm, genuine smile.

"How long has it been?" Eubank gave Miller a firm handshake and hearty slap on the shoulder, which landed far stronger than his thin, wiry frame appeared capable of delivering.

"Far too long, my friend."

The two then hugged in that awkward man-hug way of grown men the world over, before making their way through the arrivals lobby.

"I have to say, you're looking good, Trea," Eubank said as they walked. He carried a bulging, navy-blue sports bag and nothing else; the FBI agent had always preferred to travel light.

"That's horsecrap and you know it," Miller replied with a self-deprecating laugh. He knew he looked a mess: he still needed a haircut, his graying moustache hairs were creeping into his mouth, and he was suddenly conscious of the extra weight he carried around his gut. Years ago, Miller had played college football as the biggest linebacker on the team. Built like a brick outhouse and almost preternaturally fast, there had been little that could get in the way of Trae 'The Pantry' Miller.

Of course, all that had gone to hell in a handbasket over the subsequent years, and much of the bulk that had once been taut, powerful muscle had turned to wobbling flab. And, as much as Miller tried to drum up the motivation and enthusiasm to get himself back into shape, he always found excuses as to why he couldn't and therefore failed miserably

His former best friend and colleague, Ty Eubank, was about as much a contrast as it was possible to get. A skinny five-seven versus Miller's six-two, Eubank weighed in at what Miller guessed to be no more than a hundred-fifty pounds soaking wet, fully dressed, and with his shoes on. The guy still had the pasty, smooth complexion of his youth, along with a thick thatch of neatly combed black hair, not a single gray strand in sight. His arms still looked to be too long for his body, as did his thin legs: the man reminded Miller of the stretchy guy he'd once seen on the *X-Files*.

The two of them together made for quite the comical duo.

"Nah, you're looking terrific, buddy." Eubank wasn't about to be contradicted. Some things never changed. "Looks like Lubbock PD is suiting you well. Any sign of the chief's position yet? It must be time they gave Lubowski his gold watch and gave you a go in his chair."

Miller shook his head and gave Eubank a wry smile. "Nah, that stubborn old coot is never gonna retire – he's even said it himself that they'll have to carry him out feet first in a black bag before he hangs up his boots."

"Well, if that's what it's gonna take to get you where ya belong, I'm more than happy to make a few calls…"

Just for a heartbeat or two, Miller thought the guy was serious. Eubank always did have the perfect face for poker, along with that acerbic sense of humor of his.

"I'm ok to wait it out, thanks," Miller replied with a hearty laugh. "I'm not quite ready to finish up my days on the force behind the chief's desk just yet, no matter how cute his secretary is."

"Just say the word, bud." Eubank's lips curled upward in the slightest of smiles. Perhaps it was to let Miller know he was joking and he wouldn't really intervene to remove Lubowski, even if it was within his means to do so.

"You got it, my friend." Miller reciprocated the earlier shoulder clap and almost knocked Eubank off his feet. "I'm guessing the FBI life suits you. You're definitely looking well on it, Ty."

Eubank shrugged. "It's okay, I guess. They say ten years is more than enough for a field agent—too much, if I'm really honest—and I'm almost there."

"Has it been that long already?"

"Yup. Come this December tenth, it's gonna be ten years to the day I shipped out to Quantico and started my training. Can you believe that?"

Miller shook his head. Time really had flown by.

"It's not all chasing serial killers and other bad guys, all guns a-blazing, you know." Eubank sighed and his slim shoulders slouched a tad. "You think the paperwork is a pain in the ass back at the precinct, you should see the mountains of it I have to deal with. I'd say the most dangerous threat I face day-to-day is carpel tunnel!"

The two laughed together as they made their way out of the concourse and on toward the oppressive heat awaiting them outside.

Old friends, old times.

"You know there's never a day goes by without me regretting not joining you at the Bureau." Miller pushed open the wide glass door for Eubank, reaching with little effort over the smaller guy's head to do so. The brutal outside heat hit them both hard. "But you know how Margaret is… wild horses couldn't get her to leave Texas, even if Tom Cruise himself was riding 'em."

That brought a broad smile to Eubanks' face. "And how is your lovely wife?"

"How the hell do you *think* she is?" Miller grumped. "This is Lubbock, remember. Nothing ever changes here."

"Last time I saw your wife, she was still quite the catch. As I recall."

The agent's comment elicited a wry smile from Detective Miller. "Well, maybe *some* things do change, then."

Miller had parked up just outside the terminal building—the typically over-vigilant airport wardens fended off by the *police business* card he'd had printed up himself—and he ushered Eubank toward the car.

"Still driving a Camry, I see," Eubank nodded at the maroon sedan sat baking in the midday sun over by the curb.

"Boxy but reliable," Miller said as he pressed the well-worn button on the key fob. The Toyota beeped and flashed its lights as if happy to see him. "These things'll go round the clock three times if you take care of them right."

"I hear that," Eubank agreed. "It's not the black Corvette you always planned to get, though, is it? You really ought to spoil yourself sometime, Trea, before it's too late."

Miller pulled open the passenger door. It squeaked, barely audibly. "I suppose you're driving a 'Vette now?" He caught the tinge of jealousy in his voice and hoped Eubank had not.

"Nah," his friend replied with a grin. "I'm still humping around in the old Camaro. Single man's life and all that. The chicks kinda dig it, though."

Eubank climbed into the old Camry, kicking aside the heap of trash that hid the brown carpet to find a place to put his feet. Diligently securing his seat belt, he cradled his travel bag across his knees like an old dowager would an elderly lap dog.

There had been plenty of times over the bast near-decade Miller had been genuinely envious of his erstwhile colleague. After all, the guy had the dream FBI job, a sexy condo in D.C., as much female company as he could shake a friggin' stick at, and no wife to hold him back and tell him what he could and couldn't do. This was definitely turning into one of those times.

"So, what brought you to Texas?" Miller asked as he settled himself in behind the steering wheel and gunned the engine. "I was surprised to have caught you in Dallas."

"Yeah, talk about luck of the draw, Buddy." Eubank checked the wing mirrors and rear view as if he was the one about to pull away from the curb. "Another couple hours, and I'd have been on a plane. I was actually in an Uber on the way back to Dallas Fort Worth when you called me."

"Official business?"

"You know I can't tell you anything about FBI business," Eubank teased. "Or, if I did tell you, I'd have to kill you afterward."

Miller laughed along with the old joke. It was beginning to feel like they'd not been apart for the better part of ten years; the time really had flown by in a heartbeat.

"So, what have *you* got for *me*?" Eubank deftly switched the subject. Evidently, he was keen to get down to business, now the pleasantries were duly dispensed with.

Earlier, on the phone, Miller had made noises about them both having Chinese food, a few beers, and a proper catch-up later that evening; he'd even warned Margaret he might be home late, but that remained to be seen. Eubank had been cagey at the time about when he'd be needing a ride back to Preston Smith International.

Tipping his head back to indicate the back seat, Miller said, "I started a file after Broussard called me this morning."

"Broussard?" Eubank grabbed the beige card folder from the backseat. It was frayed around the edges, stained with coffee rings, and had its previous title scribbled out with black Sharpie: Lubbock PD was big on recycling.

"*Detective* Broussard," Miller huffed. He hated having to repeat himself. "The guy in New Orleans I told you about on the phone."

"Ah, yes," Eubank replied, distracted, as he leafed through the file's contents. "He's the one who tipped you off about the potential serial killer. *Jesus*!" He came to the crime scene photographs Broussard had emailed and Miller had printed out: the bloodstained walls, the carpets sodden and red, the victims' mutilated bodies. All had been painstakingly photographed by the crime scene crew and laid out in glorious technicolor in the name of evidence. "This is some mess."

"The guy's name is Chase Lennon, and, yes, he loves to cut up his victims." Miller kept his focus on the road ahead. He had little desire to see those bloodied corpses with their hollow eye sockets again.

"You sure it's the same guy you have here?" Eubank flicked back and forth between the photographs as he spoke.

"He was caught on camera outside the student apartment before the killings. He was filmed going inside and then coming back out again twenty-two minutes later with blood on his clothing." Miller snorted as some asshat in a white mom-mobile cut in front of his car without using her blinker; she was too busy with her animated cell phone conversation to bother, by the look of things. "Yeah, I'm pretty sure he's our guy."

"Looks like he enjoys taking his time." Eubank flipped back to one of the more gruesome photographs: this one a full page of a girl's face, mouth slack and gaping, eye sockets filled with congealing blood that looked so much like dark red Jell-O.

"I guess so," Miller replied with a sideways glance. He'd studied the photographs Broussard had sent over earlier until they'd made him sick to his stomach. Compared with those his guys had taken over at Prairie Dog Town Park in the early hours of that morning, there was no doubt in his mind at all they were looking at the same perp'. "The CSI guys reckon the eyes were cut out with some degree of precision – the muscles and optic nerve were all carefully incised, rather than just being hacked out and pulled."

"Your man obviously knew what he was doing, then." Eubank pulled out the sheet of paper that clearly showed Lennon making his way out of the apartment block in the early hours. He was looking directly into the camera with a cheesy, smug grim across his face, blood smeared down his left cheek. At first glance, a layman might surmise he knew the camera was there and recording him and he *wanted* to show his face. "Does he come from a medical background?"

Miller shook his head. "He's a realtor," he told Eubank. "Can you believe that?"

"How'd Broussard find him so quick?" Eubank narrowed his eyes, scrutinizing Lennon's face.

"Guy's all over the internet." Miller pulled off the main road and aimed his Camry toward a neat, leafy suburb. "He's some kind of big shot in the realtor universe – worth an absolute fortune according to what Broussard dug up. Made his money selling stupidly expensive properties the likes of you and I wouldn't even be able to afford to drive by on a cop's salary. Look him up when you get a few; his company is Imagine Real Estate."

"Imagine," Eubank mused. "Lennon – I get it. Clever."

"Not really." Miller huffed. "Ya know something, Ty, even if I did this damn job for another fifty years, I'll never be able to figure out what makes guys like him do things like this. I mean, I get the low-lifes, the junkies and dealers, the looney-tunes, but a self-made millionaire with a successful business, cute wife, and young kids…"

"Yeah, beats me, too," Eubank added. "Maybe the burden of making all that money finally got to him and he just snapped. It does happen, and I reckon I get to see a lot more of that at the bureau than you do out here in Hicksville."

That made Miller chuckle. It was a welcome relief from the gravitas of what he was facing: a disturbed serial killer was on the loose in his hometown, and he had no idea where to even start looking.

"Less of the Hicksville, if you don't mind," Miller replied with a smile. "You seem to forget where you came from, Mr. D.C. And let's not also forget one Charles Hardin Holley hailed from this very corner of Texas!"

Eubank's eyes twinkled, and Miller caught sight of his old friend in there for the first time since the airport. "That's nigh-on impossible," he laughed. "His name's plastered everywhere you care to look. I mean, heck, the guy died decades ago, and Lubbock is still riding his cold, dead coat tails – move on, already!"

It was an old routine between Miller and Eubank, one that dredged up old memories of cold, dark nights in the patrol car, hot, humid days moving panhandlers along from the intersections and writing traffic citations for the seemingly endless stream of incompetent drivers who plagued Lubbock. Those days had been so much simpler, happier, and without the sinister overcast of a brutal killer and young lives cut so mercilessly short.

Miller kinda missed them.

"You reckon the eyes might have some deep meaning for him?" Miller asked.

Eubank shrugged. "Who knows with people like that?"

"You're FBI, I was sort of hoping *you* would."

"I'm not the Behavioral Sciences Unit, Trae," Eubank said. "Those guys don't even talk to guys like me in the lunchroom."

"Lennon takes his time and great care cutting out his victims' eyeballs," Miller stated the obvious. "I saw that myself with the Boule girl."

"Your park student?"

"Yeah." Miller gave a sad nod. "Almost surgical precision. Like he'd had a lot of practice. There's no mention of any medical training whatsoever in his background – he's all over Wikipedia, too – but I got one of my guys checking into him just in case."

"You're thinking New Orleans wasn't his first time?"

"Always a possibility," Miller said. They were five minutes from the precinct, and he was in desperate need of strong, black coffee. "I was hoping you'd pull some strings and expedite a look into anything unsolved involving removal of a victim's eyes, especially in the New York State area."

"I'll put a call in." Eubank peered out through the Camry's dusty windows at the Lubbock streets that had changed so little since he'd left. "Could be that any previous victims haven't been found. Might be buried or burned or something, and they'll never be discovered."

"If Lennon's been a closet murderer for some time, and he's been careful enough to cover his tracks—"

"Then how come he's gotten sloppy now?"

"Yeah," Miller sounded out. "He's made no attempt to hide the bodies at all. In fact, he's pretty much made a display of them;– he sliced off Kristy Boule's face and left her tits skewered on a cactus, for Chrissakes! And I'd swear he *deliberately* looked into the CCTV camera in New Orleans. The sicko wants us to know what he's done and who he is."

"So why the sudden change in MO?" Eubank seemed clueless, too.

"Unless there *are* no previous victims."

"And he just happens to have a natural aptitude for eye surgery?"

"Is that even possible?"

Eubank eased back in the cloth-covered seat and sighed a weary sigh. "My friend," he said, "if there's one thing I've learned working for the FBI, it's that *anything* is possible. The human spirit seems to know no bounds when it comes to being a psychopath. Could be, your rich-boy realtor just so happens to have a knack for cutting out eyeballs – like some people just happen to be good at shooting pool or doing mental math."

"But *why* eyes?" Miller was convinced there had to be some deep, meaningful reasoning behind that. Sure, he knew serial killers took trophies; anyone who'd sat through *Silence of the Lambs* knew that much, but there was usually an inbuilt reason behind *what* they chose to take.

"Windows to the soul? Maybe he wants to take that away from his victims. Either that or he didn't want them to see him." Eubank offered.

Miller winced at the thought. "You think he could have done that to his victims while they were still alive? They *were aware* of what he was doing to them?" Miller immediately felt the all-too-familiar nausea creeping back up his gullet, and he remembered another reason he'd turned down the opportunity to join Eubank at Quantico.

"I doubt it, very much." Eubank's words gave Miller little reassurance. "They'd have to be at the very least unconscious for him to have done such a neat job. Imagine trying to slice out somebody's eyes nice and tidy like this when they're fighting back."

"Good point." The thought sat just a tad easier with Miller. "Still leaves us with the question of *why*, though."

"Maybe you'll never know." Eubank closed the beige file and held it firmly on top of his carry-on. "Unless he decides to talk after he's caught. You'd be surprised how many just love to discuss their crimes once they're hauled in. It's like they're getting to relive every gross detail all over again, and they get a big kick out of it."

"That's sick."

"Never said it was healthy, Trea. That's the last thing psychopaths like your boy Lennon can ever be. Whatever his reasons for killing those kids and taking their eyeballs, the priority right now is making sure he doesn't do it again."

Miller didn't have to be told that. He knew all too well, the minute Chase Lennon had decided to commit his next brutal murder in Buddy Holley's birthplace, the burden of responsibility rested upon his shoulders, and that of the entire Lubbock police department.

And it was pulling him down like a lead weight

"Is there a chance of catching him quickly?" Miller asked. "He doesn't seem too shy about letting us know who he is."

"Difficult to tell," Eubank replied with a frown. "Sometimes you just get lucky, or they make a mistake. Or, more often than you might think, they *want* to be stopped, so they make it easy for you. Or, he may just disappear, or…"

"Stop himself?"

"It's been known," Eubank told him. "Sometimes the burden of living with what they're doing, what they feel *compelled* to do, becomes too much and they do what they feel is the decent thing."

That was a conclusion Miller would be only too happy to see. That they'd find Lennon's body with its wrists slashed or the top of its head blown off out in the desert somewhere was something he'd happily live with, even if it meant he'd never find out *why* he did what he did.

"From your mouth to God's ears," Miller said as the precinct loomed into view.

Miller's phone rang out, startling both him and his passenger. He fished it out of the cupholder in the center console and immediately recognized the precinct's number. He thumbed the green button that flashed on the screen.

"This is Detective Miller."

"It's me, Officer Garcia. At the station."

"Yes, Juan." Miller sighed. For a youngster, Garcia seemed to have little idea of how cell phones and caller ID worked. "What is it?"

"Lennon's rental car just showed up on a traffic camera." Garcia sounded like an over-excited six-year-old. "Out by the Executive Inn on Q."

Miller hit the brakes. The Camry juddered to a halt, much to the annoyance of the truck immediately behind. The driver blared his horn as he swung out and zoomed past.

"I'll be there in five, get backup."

"You got it."

Miller hung up.

"Good news?" Eubank asked.

"I'm hoping so," Miller said. "Traffic cameras just picked up Lennon. Looks like he's going to ground."

With that, Miller swung the car around and set off the way he'd just come, leaving the drab, gray precinct building in his rear view.

Chapter 11

Sticking to the speed limit to avoid attracting unwanted attention, Lennon drove the rental car past the House of Furniture on Avenue Q. The last thing he needed was to be pulled over by some over-enthusiastic traffic cop looking to break up the monotony of the day, especially considering what he had concealed in the glove compartment.

Having said that, Lennon was mentally prepared to at least use the handgun as a threat, should things come to that. Lennon reckoned they'd stop the show before anyone got *really* hurt, but then he'd lose.

And a billion dollars was a billion dollars, after all.

The road itself was quiet, with only a handful of other vehicles to be seen – most of them dusty trucks and well-worn SUVs. As he drove, Lennon's mind churned over the conversation he'd just had with his wife.

There'd been something different about Jilly, something intangibly *off* – even more so than the time before. Naturally, Lennon figured she'd be under a huge amount of stress about the whole situation, and with him being away from home and the kids, but surely Mercer, or at least his show's lackeys, would have explained the whole deal to her by now. They'd have to in order to get her to play along.

Wouldn't they?

She'd hinted at divorcing him, and there had been something in Jilly's voice that told Lennon she'd actually meant what she'd said. It sure as hell didn't sound like she was sticking to some script or pre-agreed brief.

Like she *believed* he'd committed murder.

Surely not.

Then that would mean the news reports had gone out to more than just the TV in the motel room, and *that* meant whatever sick things he'd supposed to have done to result in the nasty mess in the glove compartment baggie had also been plastered all over the national news.

Lennon cracked a wry smile. This was only a dumb gameshow, nothing more, despite its supposed exclusive viewership, and no matter how realistic Mercer and his crew made it seem, that's all it was ever going to be.

Lennon shook his head to clear his mind.

Ahead, a squat, ugly, one-story motel came into view. Constructed of red brick what could easily have been back in the early fifties, the place sported sickly, lime-green painted woodwork, and an old-style hording next to the entrance boasting the Executive Inn had cable, HBO, and a refrigerator in every room. As for the small parking lot, it had only two occupants: an ancient, three-door Jeep with a canvas top, and a newish Chrysler sedan.

The odd pairing put Lennon in mind of as illicit afternoon liaison between some ageing, long-married businessman and his money-grabbing, young mistress.

Reminded him of the good ole days.

Lennon slowed down and swung into the Executive Inn's lot. The place was undistinguished, anonymous even, and, more importantly, looked cheap enough for him to afford with the meager allowance the show allowed him.

It would be perfect for freshening up, regrouping, and making decisions on what his next move ought to be. He was pleased they'd seen fit to provide a change of clothes; he'd discovered the bundle stuffed beneath the rental's driver's seat. It would make for a quick capture if he were forced to walk around in bloodstained clothes.

And where would be the sport in that?

He parked at the far end of the lot, in front of room six and out of sight from the road. Lennon had no doubts at all the local cops would be looking out for him. Whatever crime scene Mercer's team had set up to incriminate him, Lennon had to assume it, too, would be all over the news.

It was a short walk from the car to the cramped, dingy office, but Lennon's fresh shirt was quickly soaked through with sweat by the time he made it inside the chill, air-conditioned foyer. His body just wasn't used to the blistering heat and humidity in the high nineties. Lennon wondered how the Texans managed to put up with it.

The motel's foyer appeared not to have been changed in decades. The floral wallpaper was decidedly sixties, garish, if somewhat faded, the brown carpet worn, its pile trampled flat by countless feet, and the once-white paint yellowed with years of cigarette smoke.

"I'd like a room, please," Lennon told the gray-haired old dear behind the Perspex-fronted counter. He leaned in toward the small, metal grille set in the transparent barrier and spoke clearly into it. Appearing silently beside a clear plastic display case of Lottery scratchcards on the reception counter, the woman looked to be a hundred years old at least, with cotton-candy, white hair tied up in a loose bun, wrinkled, weathered skin that resembled old boot leather, and a tiny, fragile-looking body that couldn't have weighed more than eighty pounds.

Despite that, there was a fearsome fire sparking in the old gal's eyes that told Lennon—and no doubt anyone who dared mess with her—she would be a formidable force to be reckoned should he get on her wrong side.

Not that Chase Lennon had any such intention.

"How many nights?" The old lady's voice was light and rang with the distinctive Texas twang Lennon thought only existed in the movies.

"Just the one." Lennon was in no mood for chitchat with the woman and was relieved to find she was not the chatty type. She was likely more interested in getting back to the daytime soap on the portable TV in the gloomy office behind the counter. Playing loudly, no doubt to accommodate the woman's ancient hearing, it was some over-the-top Mexican melodrama, which Lennon found surprising.

"Forty dollars. No pets." The woman pointed her boney middle finger at the neatly printed yellow sign to her right.

"Does that include taxes?" Lennon rummaged around in his pockets as he spoke, suddenly aware of the fact he might not have enough money to pay for a room even as cheap as hers.

"With cash, yes." A twinkle in the old gal's eye.

Ignoring the credit card the show had provided, Lennon pulled out the wad of cash from his pocket. It was damp with his sweat and felt soft. Suddenly self-conscious, he unfurled each note in turn and laid them out on the countertop. After what seemed an impossible age, Lennon counted out the forty and slid the bills through the small opening in the Perspex.

They were snatched away in the blink of an eye.

Lennon eyed the woman, and half expected her to tuck his crumpled wad of cash into her bra for safe keeping. But, no, she tucked them away into some unseen receptacle secreted beneath the counter.

"Receipt?"

"Thank you, no," Lennon replied.

"I can put you in room 3."

"Could I have 6, please?" Lennon didn't want to be next to the occupied room, especially if there was likely to be sexual athletics going on inside. He needed time to think. Plus, three would put him in full view of avenue Q.

"Six?"

"I parked my car outside 6." It was a weak excuse, and Lennon knew it. More accustomed to overly accommodating five-star hotels, Lennon actually felt as if he was putting the old lady out by requesting a room different than the one she'd offered. "It's kind of a superstition I have," he added, as if that would help.

"Makes no difference to me," the woman said with a derisory snort that certainly indicated otherwise. Turning her back on Lennon, she shuffled back into the office. There, the grainy old TV blared out a dramatic, blazing row between two of the soap's characters on a sweeping staircase. It really couldn't have been more cliché if they'd tried.

"Room 6." The woman returned and slid the key over to her guest. It was attached to a large, wooden fob with the motel's address branded into it. "Checkout's at eleven."

"Thank you." Lennon snatched up the key, pocketed it, and was about to ask if there was a telephone in the room when the old lady turned on her heels and shuffled her way back to the small office.

She closed the battered door firmly behind her; the interaction was evidently over.

"Have a nice day, yourself, ma'am," Lennon called after her as he walked out of the office and back into the heat.

He stopped by his car to retrieve the revolver. As much as he hated carrying the thing, Lennon had a niggling feeling he was *supposed* to. Something had happened before, a memory lurked at the periphery of his mind that made sure he grabbed the gun from the glove compartment. Of course, he took great care to *not* look at its fellow contents; Lennon wanted nothing to do with any of that. He did check the gun's six chambers were full before tucking the cold, heavy metal into the back of his jeans' waistband.

The brass key on the end of the ridiculously sized fob worked hard to unlock the door to room 6. Stiff in Lennon's hand, it felt as if the lock had not been touched in a long, long time, and he feared what he might be faced with once he finally got inside.

As it was, the room was not as the motel's exterior had suggested. Sure, the plain taupe walls and dull green carpet looked tired, the single bed was pushed up against the corner, at its foot sat a silent window-mounted AC unit, and there was a thin film of dust on top of the single nightstand, credenza, and TV, but otherwise the place appeared clean and bug-free.

Plus, he reckoned because he'd not woken up in the place, and he'd chosen both the motel and room 6 randomly, there'd be no hidden cameras capturing his every move; not even Mercer could have second-guessed this move. Although, Lennon figured it a safe bet that the rental car was likely wired and tracked, so they'd know where he was. Even so, he was confident he'd bought himself at least a short period of alone time and anonymity.

Lennon found himself drawn to the TV.

Something stirred within him, like some old, long-forgotten memory struggling to surface, and he found himself surprised to see it was one of the older flat screens. Matt black, a couple inches thick, it sat on the credenza supported by a pair of thin plastic feet.

It wasn't brand new, nor was it mounted on the motel room's wall.

Why would he have expected it to be?

Shaking his head to rid himself of the invasive, unwanted déjà vu, Lennon grabbed the remote and flicked on the TV.

The screen burst into life with the same raucous, overly dramatic music the old lady at the reception desk had been tuned into. The suddenness of the sound disrupting the quiet jarred Lennon's nerves and he thumbed the well-worn button on the remote until he found a local news channel.

"Oh, dear lord…" Lennon groaned as his face appeared on the TV. It was a recent picture, plucked from Imagine's company website. Alongside it was a long shot of sparse vegetation, an expanse of sand, and bright yellow police tape which sat, unmoving, in the glaring sun.

They were looking for him already.

Lennon's mind filled with mental images of waking up in the rental car, the blood, the gun, rope, that sinister small, brown bottle, and the severed eyeballs in the baggie. And, once again, surged that overwhelming sensation of it all feeling so terrifyingly familiar, as if he was living out some grim *Groundhog Day* and was destined to do so in perpetuity.

New Orleans interspersed Lennon's more immediate memories. Another dingy hotel room, pursuing cops, a darkened bar, muted jazz music, and cold drinks with a stranger.

As the thoughts swirled through his mind, a hot wave of nausea swept through Lennon. His stomach flipped in synch with his pounding head and his tongue suddenly felt unnaturally dry and far too big for his mouth.

Switching off the flatscreen, Lennon threw the remote onto the bed and raced into the motel room's cramped bathroom with a hand clamped firmly to his mouth. Even in his panicked state to reach the toilet bowl before the inevitable occurred, Lennon couldn't help but cast a passing glance into the stained sink on his way by, as if he was expecting to find something awful lurking there, waiting to catch him unawares.

Save for a long-dead, desiccated cockroach laying on its back, legs crossed, the beige porcelain was empty.

Lennon flipped the toilet lid up, dropped to his knees, and heaved until his stomach emptied and his abs ached.

Clearly, he'd not eaten much since blacking out in New Orleans. Pretty much all that splashed into the scummy water at the bottom of the toilet bowl was bile and well-digested mush that could have been anything. The whole disgusting mix burned Lennon's throat and filled his mouth with a nasty, acidic taste that stung his nostrils and had his eyes watering.

Pulling the handle, Lennon flushed.

Waited for the cistern to refill, then flushed again.

Satisfied there was nothing left to empty from his stomach, even though the sick feeling persisted and his head pounded, Lennon eased himself upright and chanced a handful of water from the facet above the deceased cockroach. Mouth only slightly refreshed after that, he then wobbled back into the bedroom. There, Lennon flopped down heavily onto the bed, sending up a cloud of gray dust from the dark green bedspread.

"Ow!" A sharp pain in the small of his back had Lennon roll over onto his side. Reaching around, he fished out the revolver from the back of his pants and placed it gingerly onto the nightstand next to the old boxy radio-

alarm clock that rhythmically flashed 12:00 in red, LED numbers.

Rolling onto his back, the pain gone, Lennon stared up at the ceiling and cursed himself for not having switched on the AC unit to combat the dry, stale heat before laying down. He tried his hardest to recall any of the events that had brought him to that grubby little motel in Lubbock, Texas.

But, as much as he tried, and for the sparse smattering of snippets from the Big Easy, all Lennon could remember was his conversation with Mercer, the TV news reports showing him on some grainy CCTV footage, and the fraught telephone calls with Jilly.

Other than that, all Lennon had was a bunch of infuriating black holes in his memory and an overwhelming urge to run and just keep on running.

Wasn't that all part of Mercer's twisted game, after all?

A knock on the door.

"Housekeeping!"

Lennon jolted upright. His eyes flicked to the gun on the nightstand.

"I'm all good. No, thank you," he called out, his voice a touch croaky.

No sooner had the words left Lennon's lips than the room's door handle twisted and the door swung open with a bright, sudden burst of sunlight and heat.

"I said no—"

The maid bustled in wheeling her cart crammed full with cleaning supplies. She was petite, maybe late twenties, with an unremarkable, makeup-free face, mousey-brown, bob-cut hair, and an ill-fitting dark gray uniform that appeared to Lennon to be a size and a half too big. "I'm so sorry," she sputtered, eyes alighting upon the revolver.

"I only just booked in," Lennon instinctively reached for the weapon to hide it, even though the maid had quite obviously seen the thing and was surprised to see her recoil in horror. "Why would I want my room cleaning now?"

"Please…" the maid took a step backward toward the door, which stood ajar.

Lennon was about to reassure the woman he meant her no harm when a movement outside in the motel's courtyard caught his attention.

Freezing, his fingers tightened around the revolver's handle.

Staring over the maid's shoulder, Lennon made out the distinctive shapes of two men talking to the old lady from the Executive Inn's reception. The three stood next to a maroon Camry that clearly had its best days behind it; one of the guys was built like a brick outhouse, if somewhat gone to seed, the other, a wiry weasel of a man with a pinched face and ill-fitting Ray Bans.

The two couldn't have looked more 'cop' if they'd had the word emblazoned across their sweat-soaked shirts in neon lettering.

The only uncertainty in Lennon's mind was, if they were part of the game or just a couple of locals who got lucky?

Panicking, Lennon pointed the revolver at the maid.

"Close the door," he ordered.

Looking close to tears, face drained of color, the maid did as she was told. "Please, don't hurt me." She spoke quietly, her voice barely above a whisper. "I'll do anything you want…" Her eyes left the gun's muzzle only just long enough to look into Lennon's.

The suddenness of the connection startled Lennon. He all at once felt guilty for roping the poor maid into his game, while at the same time experiencing that flash of déjà vu once again.

Did he know the woman?

Had they possibly met back in New Orleans?

Snapping his mind back to focus upon the problem at hand—namely the pair of obvious cops outside who were undoubtedly looking for him—Lennon told himself there'd be time to contemplate his foggy, unreliable memories later on, once he'd evaded the police and kept himself in Mercer's game.

"You have a car?" Lennon asked the maid.

Nodding, her attention remained solely upon the gun in Lennon's hand.

With a sick feeling in the pit of his gut, Lennon wiggled the revolver toward the maid's cart. "Let's go get it, then."

Chapter 12

"You sure he's in 6?" Miller asked the old woman.

"What?" Cupping a hand to her ear, she leaned in toward the detectives.

"Are you positive the man in room 6 is this one?" Eubank thrust his cellphone under the woman's nose so she could better see the smiling picture of Chase Lennon adorning its screen.

Squinting at the image, she replied firmly, "Yeah, he *insisted* on that room, too."

Miller was satisfied: it looked like they had their man. He glanced across the dusty blacktop of the motel's courtyard at room 6. It looked as quiet and unassuming as the rest of the place, save for the rental car parked up outside its closed door and the maid trundling her cleaning cart along the walkway.

"You got a master key we could use?" Miller asked. "Save us busting your lock."

"What's that stupid girl doing now?" the old woman mumbled, handing over a single key on an old, tarnished chain to Miller. "She knows darn well she's to start at room *thirteen* today. If you two gentlemen will please excuse me…" Wrinkled face screwed up with intense displeasure, she set off toward the maid with a briskness that belied her advancing years.

"We should wait for backup" Miller said.

"I think we got this," Eubank told him.

"You've seen what the guy's capable of."

Eubank nodded. "He's a surprise attacker who preys on students. Mostly girls, at that," Eubank replied. "In my experience, perps like him either lie down and present their wrists for cuffing the second they see a cop, or they do the decent thing as soon as the net starts tightening."

"They kill themselves?" Miller was surprised by that information; it wasn't a story that often hit the news.

"Cowards, the lot of them." Eubank wrinkled his skinny nose. "One look at you and our boy'll not be able to get a gun in his mouth quick enough."

"If he's armed, we really ought to wait till the boys get here." Miller was alarmed; Eubank's eloquent turn of phrase conjured disturbing mental images. Plus, the last thing he needed right now was a gun fight at the Executive Inn corral.

"I was speaking metaphorically, Trae." Eubank gave a wry smile that Miller thought quite condescending. It pulled him straight back to their days working together at the Lubbock precinct – friend or not, Eubank could really be a dick when he put his mind to it.

Following Eubank's lead, Miller pulled his gun from the well-worn leather holster under his armpit and approached room 6 with all his senses on high alert.

"Maintenance," Eubank said, rapping his knuckles gently upon the door's faded green paintwork.

The two waited, stock-still, in silence.

Nothing.

"Hello? Sir?" Eubank's raised voice carried across the parking lot and mingled with the old lady's ignored calls to the retreating maid.

Miller pulled the master key from his pocket and dangled it in front of Eubank's face. "Perhaps he's not home. We should check."

He shook his head and readied his Glock with a grin. "It's not often I get the opportunity to do this anymore, Trae," he whispered. "Sure as hell not gonna pass up this one."

With that, Eubank shouldered the motel room door with a grunt. *"Police!"*

Miller bustled into the dim, musty room after Eubank, genuinely surprised the skinny agent had it in him. Perhaps they taught the weedy guys extra-special door-bursting techniques back at the FBI training school?

"Clear." Eubank declared as the two scanned the cramped motel room. It really didn't need to be said, but Miller took that as his cue to check out the bathroom.

That was empty, too. Plus, there were bars on the outside of the window, which meant there was no way Lennon could have escaped that way.

"So where the hell is he?" Eubank huffed. "No way he went out."

Miller shrugged. "Obviously, he did."

"Dammit," Eubank growled and stepped back outside, scrunching his eyes against the sun's glare.

Miller was on his heels. There was no point in hanging around the motel room; he'd checked the tiny closet, and the bed was too low to the floor for Lennon to be hiding beneath it.

The guy was gone. But how, and to where?

"The maid!" Eubank's sudden exclamation startled Miller. "He's got the maid!"

Turning his head to where the special agent pointed, Miller eyed the young housekeeper. Still pushing her overladen cart, she had slowed up next to a white Chrysler sedan at the opposite end of the lot.

And, as the two men looked on, and the motel's ancient owner caught up with the maid, a man stepped out from where he'd been crouching down behind the cleaning cart.

"Lennon." Miller recognized his quarry immediately. The CCTV pictures Broussard had emailed over didn't do him justice. Chase Lennon was one handsome devil.

***

"Get in," Lennon growled at the maid and pulled open the Chrysler's passenger side door. The two guys he'd figured as cops were eyeballing him across the parking lot. They clearly knew exactly who he was. They just *had* to be law enforcement, and they were making no attempts to hide the fact. The only unknown for Lennon was he couldn't be sure if they were part of Mercer's game or real-life police.

Either way, Lennon knew he couldn't afford to be caught.

"Are you sure you don't want me to drive?" The maid did as she was told and clambered into the shotgun seat. "I'm assuming you don't know your way around Lubbock."

"You can navigate." Lennon lifted the front of his shirt to show her where he'd secreted the revolver and climbed in behind the wheel; did she really think he was *that* dumb?

The maid shrugged and strapped herself in. The seat belt sat snug between her breasts, separating them in her loose-fitting uniform.

"You! Miss!" The motel's elderly owner scurried toward the Chrysler waving an arm over her head as Lennon slammed the door shut and gunned the engine. In the rearview, Lennon saw the two guys race across to the Maroon Camry and jump in.

Reversing the Chrysler, Lennon swerved to narrowly avoid colliding with the old woman. She appeared to have no intention of moving out of the way until the vehicle was almost upon her. She was far too focused on Lennon and her maid as they made their getaway.

"Who are you?" the old woman shouted after the Chrysler as it sped from the parking lot. She did stand aside for the Camry, however, and stood, clearly out of breath, watching the two cars speed off with one hand shielding her eyes from the sun, the other on her scrawny old hip.

"Take a right here," the maid said.

"You sure?" Lennon eyed the turn with suspicion. It seemed like a busy street; he'd much rather have taken some quieter backstreets where it would be easier to lose the cops.

"You're the one with the gun," the maid said with a nervous glance toward Lennon's waist. "Do you want to shake those guys or what?"

Grunting, Lennon followed the instruction and took the right. The back wheels spun a little on the dusty road and the rear end of the Chrysler wobbled as the car rounded the corner tightly and sped off down the long, straight street bordered by small stores.

"Left at the lights."

A better choice, in Lennon's opinion. This one was a narrow side street sandwiched between a thrift store and a small, provincial bank. A quick glance in the rearview mirror told him the Camry was still hot on his heels: it came into view around the corner behind him as he slowed up just enough to take the tight turn into the side street without slamming into the thrift store's red brick wall.

"Where are you taking me?" Lennon growled as he hit the gas and sped along the street. It was devoid of traffic; he had it to himself. "If you're thinking about directing me to the nearest police station…"

"Again, you're the guy with the gun, here." The maid stared straight ahead, eyes wide, yet eerily calm. "Straight on at the lights at the end, then take a sharp left."

The Camry behind hit the side street and closed the gap between them. Lennon leaned on the gas pedal as hard as he dared. His tail was close enough behind now to make out the two faces through the windshield. They appeared to be having a heated discussion of sorts, and Lennon hoped they were arguing about the questionable safety behind high-speed car chases through downtown Lubbock for a dumb gameshow.

Then again, Lennon reckoned the whole episode would make for exciting viewing indeed for *The Contestant's* mysterious subscribers.

"Where the hell are you taking me?" Lennon snapped.

"I know a place," she replied quietly. Either the young woman had nerves of steel or simply didn't realize the gravity of the situation he'd put her in; Lennon found it impossible to tell. "Right at the gas station."

Lennon tapped the brakes and swung the car wide around the corner. Had there been anything coming in the opposite direction, they'd have both lost front bumpers. "Give me more notice next time," Lennon growled.

"Why? You want to use your blinker?"

Was that a smile playing on her plump lips?

Lennon hit the gas pedal and the Chrysler jerked forward, speeding along the straight stretch of road. Ahead lay what appeared to be the edge of town: the small stores gave way to ramshackle two-story, white-sided houses, dead gas station, a dive bar, and a handful of abandoned shotgun shacks.

He questioned his reasoning behind entrusting the maid to get him away from the two guys he was increasingly convinced were gameshow cops. What was he thinking when he made her get into the car? Why couldn't he have just left her back in the motel lot and figured out his own way to get out of Lubbock? It would have given him one less thing to worry about.

What was he supposed to do with her once he'd evaded the police?

"There's a train coming," the maid announced flatly and pointed out through her dust-smeared window.

Upon glancing to his right, Lennon espied the hulking shape of a freight train looming a little ways in the distance. The thing was moving fast, much quicker than the lumbering giants he was used to seeing, the ones that crawled along like giant, mechanical snakes and seemingly went on forever.

"Dammit." Lennon's attention turned to where the rail tracks crossed the road ahead at a poorly marked crossing without barriers, and his mind did the quick calculation. There was no way he could see how he could possibly beat the train, and the only intersection was four, maybe five hundred yards beyond the crossing.

And that meant the cops would definitely catch up to him, and it would be, *literally*, game over.

"You can make it." The maid's words of encouragement seemed odd, given the circumstances. Did she *want* him to lose their tail? Was she not concerned that, if Lennon tried to beat the train and didn't quite make it, she'd die alongside the man who'd just kidnapped her at gunpoint?

"No freakin' way," Lennon snapped. "I'm gonna have to stop."

"She's got more in her than you think." The maid patted the car's center console with some affection. "Open her up. Let's see what she's got."

Is she actually enjoying this?

Lennon pressed the pedal to the metal and the speedometer needle crept its way past the one-twenty-five mark as the Chrysler's engine strained to reach its maximum output and the vehicle's chassis shuddered. Lennon had driven a good many performance cars in his past, and he knew the sound of an engine nearing its limits. Having said that, the Chrysler was carrying more power under the hood than he'd given it credit for.

The car lurched forward and on toward the railroad crossing. To its right, the train hurtled onward, oblivious to the impending potential for absolute disaster. To the rear, the Camry fell back just far enough for Lennon to feel like he was actually going to pull this off.

The whole thing felt so strangely surreal, like he was living inside of some big-budget Hollywood action movie. Only, it wasn't Tom Cruise or Jason Statham bravely doing his own death-defying stunts in front of a CGI green screen, it was Chase Lennon, real estate entrepreneur, risking his life by racing against something that could so easily smoosh both him and his reluctant passenger like bugs on a windshield.

In the rearview mirror, the Camry grew larger. Evidently, it, too, had found its second wind, despite being older and worse for wear than the maid's Chrysler. Maybe the cop driving it reckoned he could beat the train, too, and had no intention of allowing his quarry to escape.

Holding his breath, Lennon ground his teeth together and pushed his foot down harder still on the gas pedal, even though it was already mashed into the Chrysler's carpet and had no place else to go. The tires bump-bump-bumped over the iron rails embedded into the road surface, and the train let out a cacophonous, mournful hoot, and its colossal front filled Lennon's side window.

Heart pounding, he braced himself for the inevitable impact.

Then it was over, the rails gone, the train behind him. He'd made it!

Letting out his breath in a long, snorting sigh, Lennon eased off the pedal some and fought to control his nerves.

The train rattled along the track behind him, crossing the spot where he'd been only moments before, its bulk shaking the ground.

And there, outlined against the huge cylinders and rectangular metal haulage containers, was the Camry.

The cops, too, had taken a chance and beaten the train's unstoppable advance.

"Dammit!" Lennon floored the gas once more. The Chrysler's engine complained loudly and the vehicle lurched forward toward the only intersection in the long, straight road ahead.

"Keep straight." The maid read Lennon's mind. He was contemplating taking a last-minute, sharp right at the intersection in the hopes of putting some distance between himself and the rapidly approaching Camry. After that, the best he knew he could hope for was that the cops hadn't called for backup and they'd run out of gas before he did.

Desperation was creeping in. Like some malevolent, black fog smothering the back of his mind, it told him it was all over and why didn't he just stop the car, hand himself over to the cops he hoped were part of *The Contestant*, and go home from Mercer's game an empty-handed loser?

Ahead, the lights at the intersection turned green and a white, double-wheeled RAM truck eased to a stop on the road to the left.

"Thank you, God," Lennon mumbled beneath his breath. Finally, something was going his way.

In a heartbeat or two, Lennon pushed the Chrysler through the intersection at breakneck speed. He kept one eye on the Camry following closely behind, gaining on him once more.

Lennon had barely left the intersection when the Camry raced through the green lights behind him and the white truck lunged forward, despite the red lights that were supposed to be holding it back.

The RAM hit the Camry's rear end with a loud, metallic *clang*, which had it spinning out of control across the road in a thick, red cloud of dry desert dust and a shower of broken glass that glinted like tiny diamonds in the harsh sunlight.

Lennon cringed as he looked back at the carnage behind him. The truck was at a standstill, chrome front bumper mashed in, driver's door wide open. The driver, already out of his vehicle and assessing the damage to his truck, stared over at the Camry, which had come off far worse in the collision.

Its course had been halted by the sturdy metal pole that held the traffic lights over the road. The pole itself leaned at a crazy angle, the lights no longer working. Thick, white steam plumed out from the Camry's crumpled hood, the trunk smashed almost beyond recognition, and its driver's side tires both shredded and pancake flat.

As relieved as Lennon was to finally have the two cops no longer on his tail, he kind of hoped they were ok. Whether they were part of the game or not, Lennon figured nobody deserved to get badly hurt or even die for a gameshow, no matter how high the stakes.

"Follow that track there." The maid pointed to what amounted to little more than a pair of grooves in the dry dirt off to Lennon's left. Either side of the track stood a pair of thick wooden posts—the vestiges of an ancient gate long-since rotted away.

"Are you serious?" Lennon brought the Chrysler to a halt amid a billowing cloud of dust. It crossed his mind the maid might just be leading him into some kind of trap here – or was he just being paranoid?

"Do you want someplace to hide out or not?" The maid nodded down to where Lennon's gun hid beneath his shirt. "What do you think I'm going to do? You're the—"

"The one with the gun. Right." Lennon gave the young woman a half-smile and noticed for the first time she had a strange attractiveness about her, despite having initially appeared somewhat plain.

"Exactly," the maid replied. "And, don't worry, the car'll make it."

With little other choice but to put his trust in his hostage, Lennon yanked the steering wheel hard left and touched the gas pedal. Soon, the Chrysler was bouncing along the rough track like some pioneer's wooden-wheeled wagon.

Beyond Lubbock's outskirts, the terrain had turned hilly. Hunks of barren, dry rock dotted with tenacious shrubs and fat cacti poked up through the dirt and, between the rocky hills, winding tracks led off through narrow valleys and seemingly into nowhere. As far as Lennon could see, there were no dwellings at all, no clumps of trees in which to hide a cabin, no caves.

"Where exactly are you taking me?" he asked.

"Someplace safe," the maid told him. "You're the one on the run from the cops, not me. I'm only doing as I'm told."

"I'm not really on the run…" Lennon stopped himself there. He wasn't entirely sure how much of his story the maid might know; that would depend upon what the TV stations and other media had put out about him on behalf of Mercer and *The Contestant*.

Having kidnapped the poor woman at gunpoint, Lennon figured she'd be the more scared of the two of them, and now was hardly the right time to try explaining he was part of some bizarre gameshow and not *really* a psychopathic killer.

"That's not what it looked like to me." The maid stared out through her window. "You seemed keen enough to me to get away from those two cops."

"I was not even sure they were cops at first."

The maid snorted, her breath adding a little fog to the window. "Oh, come on. They *reeked* of law enforcement. I had them made the second I saw them on the motel's parking lot."

"I'm guessing you've had more experience with law enforcement than me, then."

Nodding, the maid replied, "And you'll have to get wiser if you're going to survive being on the run. Otherwise, your next encounter with the police might well be your last."

Lennon, about to defend himself, realized the young woman was correct. So, he kept his dumb mouth shut.

"There." The maid tapped a neat, plain fingernail on her window to get Lennon's attention.

He looked across and saw, nestled in between two rocky outcrops, a ratty, single-wide trailer. It appeared to have been standing there for a hell of a long time: its sidings were warped and blistered, the screen door swung at an impossible angle off its one remaining, rusted hinge, and the tires were rotted into almost nothing.

"Home, sweet home," Lennon grumbled as he pulled the Chrysler up in front of what may have once been a small front garden decorated by bright, neatly-tended flowers. Now, the desiccated plants were nothing more than a handful of neat rows of dried stalks poking up out from the dust.

"They'd never think of looking here, even if they could find it," the maid announced with confidence. "This place has been used as a hideout for as long as I can remember."

Before Lennon could question her further—he had at least a dozen things running through his mind—the maid had gotten out of the car and was making her way along the short dirt pathway to the trailer.

Is this the trap?

Was it possible she had some dangerously lunatic guy sitting with a loaded shotgun just waiting to offload it into her kidnapper?

Or could this be another part of Mercer's game, and he was well-and-truly caught?

Heart pounding, hands clammy with sweat, Lennon fumbled the revolver out from his waistband and climbed out of the car. Even with everything he'd been through the past couple days, this was the most afraid he'd felt. If whoever might be waiting for him beyond that rickety old trailer door was not part of Mercer's game, Lennon couldn't shake the sinking feeling Jilly and the kids would not be seeing him again.

"Are you coming in, or not?" The maid held the door open for Lennon, one hand on her hip. "If we're lucky, there might be a bottle of cheap bourbon inside."

That was music to Lennon's ears; he sure as hell could use a drink.

Stepping inside the hot gloom of the trailer, Lennon contemplated returning the gun to the back of his pants but decided against it. While the fear of what he might encounter within that single-wide had proved unfounded, he reminded himself the maid was only being accommodating because he had her at gunpoint. For all she knew, he planned to do unspeakable things and leave her corpse to rot in the dust-laden trailer for the ants and other desert critters to pick at.

Her outwardly compliant behavior was little more than a textbook ruse to keep herself alive long enough to seize a chance of escape. Lennon had sat through enough movies and cheesy TV crime shows to recognize that much.

"We might as well make ourselves at home." The maid sat herself on the overstuffed couch dominating the trailer's lounge area; a thick puff of white dust rose up around her. "Have you thought about what you're going to do next? You can't stay here forever, and the cops will have the plate and description of my car."

Lennon sat at the opposite end of the couch. The dust irritated his nose and made the back of his throat tickle. He shrugged. "I just needed to get away and give myself time to think." Sure, had the trailer been anywhere near habitable, he could have simply hidden out there and waited out the required length of time to win Mercer's game. But even a cursory examination of the place told him that was never going to be a possibility.

"You're gonna have to think fast, mister." The maid reached a hand down the side of the couch.

Lennon tensed. His hand gripped the revolver's rubberized handle, his pointer finger instinctively seeking out the trigger.

Seemingly oblivious to Lennon's reaction, the maid lifted a half-full bottle of Jack Daniels and rested it on the arm of the couch. "What say we take the edge off?" She eyed the gun in Lennon's hand and a momentary look of alarm flittered across her face; had she realized just how close she'd come to being shot?

Lennon nodded and mentally forced his finger away from the trigger. He had no real intention of harming the young woman but understood now he'd have no hesitation in doing so should the need arise.

And that thought frightened him more than anything so far: just what kind of sociopathic monster had *The Contestant* turned him into?

"There should be some glasses here somewhere." The maid stood from the couch and walked the half dozen or so steps into the tiny kitchenette. Opening the crumbling cupboard above the small, stainless-steel sink unit, she fished out a pair of grubby mason jars. "I guess these will have to do." Lifting the skirt of her baggy uniform, she wiped each glass in turn with its hem to clear out the dust they'd accumulated after God only knew how long.

At that, Lennon caught sight of the maid's leg, clad in thick, unflatteringly beige hose. The uniform had clearly hidden her slim figure and perfectly defined legs, and he couldn't help but wonder how the rest of her looked under the drab garb.

"Don't know about you," the maid said once she'd finished with the rudimentary cleaning and returned to the couch, "but I really need this." She unscrewed the cap off the bourbon and poured a good couple inches into one of the mason jars.

Lennon nodded; the amber liquid looked incredibly welcoming.

She poured an equal amount into the other jar and handed it over. Taking it from her, Lennon put the glass to his lips.

Pausing, he sniffed at the drink.

Of course, Lennon had no idea what he was smelling for. If the booze was laced with something, how the hell would he even know? He'd read somewhere that a small percentage of the population carry the gene that helps them sniff out cyanide, but he wasn't at all sure exactly *what* cyanide was supposed to smell like.

And what if the bottle was dosed with a poison with no smell or color, or some date-rape drug to render him helpless? For as much as Lennon needed that drink, his survival instinct—*paranoia*—had taken over.

As if sensing her guest's reticence, the maid took a hearty swig of her own bourbon. She gulped it down noisily and finished off with a satisfied, lip-smacking *ahhhh*.

"Good?" Lennon asked.

"Better than," she replied. "Especially after the day I've had. But you know all about that, don't you?" A sardonic smile.

Put at ease, Lennon took a hefty sip of his own Jack. He relished how the amber liquid burned his lips and tongue, and how warm it was as it ran down every inch of his gullet. It brought back memories of happier, more carefree times, of loose women, gambling, running wild with old friends. It had Lennon missing the old times so freakin' much.

Another sip and his portion in the old mason jar was over halfway gone. Lennon hoped there was more booze hidden somewhere in the trailer. Half a bottle of JD hardly seemed adequate to contend with the level of stress he was experiencing.

"I'm really sorry," Lennon broke the silence.

"For what, exactly?" draining her glass, the maid reached for the Jack Daniels bottle.

"All of it, I guess." Lennon felt like a little kid caught shoplifting for the first time. "For making you come with me when I could have just taken your car, for running from the cops… I really don't know what I was thinking." He wiggled the revolver he still had resting in his hand.

"Kidnapping me at gunpoint?" The maid winked as she topped up her glass. She held the bottle out toward Lennon.

Nodding, holding up his almost empty mason jar and glancing down at the revolver, Lennon said, "Yeah, this. I don't think I'd actually use it, if that helps any."

"Not really."

Lennon sipped at his drink and contemplated telling the maid all about *The Contestant* and how it was just a dumb gameshow he hoped to get stinking rich from. Then he realized he was still pointing the revolver at the poor woman and he'd not even bothered to ask what her name was.

Too late now.

"I'm thinking I should rest up here until it gets dark." Lennon noticed how his words came out a touch slurred; the JD was obviously starting to kick in. Hardly a surprise, given he couldn't remember the last time he'd eaten anything. Hard liquor on an empty stomach was never going to be a good combination.

Agreeing, the maid craned her neck to peer through the dirt-encrusted window. From outside came the unmistakable growl of an engine and the crunch of heavy tires on dry dirt and stones.

Lennon tensed, trigger finger once more at the ready.

They had company.

"Put that down, Chase," the maid told him as she put down her drink and stood up from the couch. "You're not going to be shooting anybody."

Lennon complied, even though his every instinct told him otherwise. He placed the gun gently down on the couch cushion and put his bourbon down on the dusty arm. He miscalculated, and the glass, just a touch too close to the edge, teetered before tumbling off onto the filthy carpet. Jack Daniels splashed everywhere and Lennon just stared dumbfounded at the mess, his mind fuzzy, swirling.

The maid was exiting the trailer, out through the shabby door. It closed behind her with a loud rattle and

Lennon was left all alone. Instinct screamed at him to get out, and fast, his mind telling him those two cops had caught up with him somehow, despite their wrecked Camry.

It took Lennon three abortive attempts to get to his feet. But his legs were Jell-o, his mind fading out and worryingly gray around the edges. It didn't take a giant leap to figure out the maid had, indeed, slipped him something in the bourbon – but couldn't quite figure out what, or how.

He'd watched the young woman like a hawk from the moment she'd produced the bottle of Jack from beside the couch to grabbing the mason jars from the cupboard to wiping them both clean on her skirt, and then to pouring out two generous helpings of the amber liquid for the two of them.

Hell, he'd even made sure she drank the booze first, just to be extra-sure.

Finally up onto his unsteady feet, Lennon wobbled his way to the window. He was forced to use the trailer's thin, grubby walls for support as his legs threatened to betray him. There, he heard voices drifting over from outside; one, he recognized as the maid's, the other gruff and decidedly masculine.

"What the—?" Lennon slurred to himself as he peered out through the window, convinced his drugged mind was playing tricks on him.

Where he'd fully expected to see the two cops and their beat-up maroon sedan, there stood a large, white truck, one of those the Texans loved, with the double wheels at the back. The vehicle's front chrome bumper was badly damaged, seemingly clinging on by only the brackets at one side.

Striding away from the truck, and toward the maid and her Chrysler, Lennon's fogged brain vaguely recognized the driver as the guy he'd seen at the intersection following the collision with the cops. The man sported a full, bushy red beard, wore faded jeans, dusty, well-worn cowboy boots, white T, and a sleeveless denim jacket. He smiled at the maid like they were old friends.

Behind the truck's driver, a pair of stocky, younger men appeared as if from nowhere. They wore pale blue T-shirts, jeans that looked brand-new, black training shoes, and a brown Stetson; looked like they were trying way too hard to fit in with Texas. The pair followed the driver over to the maid's Chrysler and stood on either side of its rear end as she pointed the key fob at the vehicle to pop the trunk.

"No..." Lennon could barely utter the faint whisper. As he did so, he was aware of warm drool dribbling down his chin; his mouth was uncomfortably numb and out of control.

As the maid and her bearded friend looked on, the two younger men reached into the Chrysler's trunk and pulled out a body.

Retching, Lennon doubled over and heaved up the sour, reeking contents of his stomach. The purge came as a relief; perhaps he'd ridded his system of enough of whatever the maid had slipped into his drink to allow him to escape?

The body was that of a plump Hispanic-looking lady. Middle-aged, slack-faced, her eyes glassy and half open, she was clad only in white, utilitarian underwear, and a small hat askew and tangled in her long, tousled, raven hair.

Just the sort of uniform hat hotel maids wore.

"Oh, sh—" Lennon retched again and nothing came up except for the acid sting of bile that scorched the back of his throat.

How dumb had he been? He should have seen the big, red flag right there in front of him – no maid at some two-bit fleabag motel could possibly ever have afforded a Chrysler like that. Nope, the woman he'd taken hostage had evidently murdered the real maid, stolen her clothes, and assumed her identity. Most likely, Lennon's diminishing mind suggested, the poor woman had traveled to her death on the bus.

Which could only mean the maid he'd kidnapped was part of Mercer's game, along with the truck driver who'd just so happened to miraculously appear at the perfect time to throw the cops off Lennon's trail.

Which also meant the driver's two accomplices who were busy bundling the deceased maid into the back of the RAM were also part of it. Was it too much for Lennon to hope the maid was not *actually* dead? That they'd drugged her as they'd drugged him? Or perhaps she was merely acting for her part of the show?

As much as he wanted to believe that, Lennon doubted it. That still-eyed, blank stare in the poor woman's eyes, the way her arms flopped and body sagged as the two men carried her to the white truck sure made her look very dead to Lennon.

It meant Mercer wasn't above killing innocent people for the benefit of *The Contestant*.

The gray fuzz around the periphery of Lennon's brain closed in and quickly turned black as he watched the men heave the corpse into the back seat of the white truck. He was unconscious before his body hit the floor.

Chapter 13

"You need more coffee?" Eubank asked Miller. The two were back in Miller's office at the precinct, nursing the minor bumps and bruises they'd sustained in the collision with the truck.

Shaking his head, Miller replied, "What I need is a coupla beers and that idiot's plate." His hands were still shaking, and he was incredibly pissed about having his beloved Camry written off by some randomer in a truck. Especially when it meant losing Chase Lennon in the process. Also, his wife was never going to let him hear the end of trashing yet another personal car for his job.

"Isn't there a camera at the intersection?" Eubank said.

"This is Lubbock, Tyrone." Miller shot his old colleague a world-weary smile. "Not DC – there's no need for CCTV every six yards. You sure you didn't even catch a partial?"

Eubank shook his head. "You saw how quick it all happened. Guy just came outta nowhere and hit you."

"No, he didn't." Miller furrowed his brow and gave the special agent his best Clint Eastwood, narrow-eyed stare. "He was waiting at the lights then jumped the red. It was like he was just waiting there making ready to hit me."

"Lights must have changed," Eubank sat himself down next to Miller.

"You think I wouldn't have noticed that?" Miller was getting angry now: weren't FBI special agents supposed to be highly trained in observation and memory techniques? Eubank had been sitting beside him for the entire duration of the Lennon pursuit – he'd seen everything just as well as he had.

They'd both watched the truck's driver walk across the intersection toward the Camry – just close enough to see the two cops sitting behind deflated airbags. He'd stopped halfway across the road, stroked his beard as if deep in thought, then turned on his stacked heels, climbed back into his truck, and left the scene.

"Like I said, Trae, it all happened so fast… You were focused on Lennon as much as I was. Too bad he got away."

"I got a bunch of uniforms scouring the area," Miller told him. "He can't have gotten too far. Even if he's gone to ground somewhere, he'll turn up sooner or later."

"Listen, Trae," Eubank leaned in, voice low. "One old friend to another, are you a hundred percent *sure* it was actually Chase Lennon you were after?"

Miller could hardly believe his ears. Had Eubank gotten himself a concussion in the accident? "You saw his face on the traffic cam photograph I showed you before we left here." He grabbed the file from his desk, opened it, and leafed through it to retrieve the photograph to emphasize his point. "You can't tell me that's not the same guy we saw at the Executive, Ty."

Eubank scrutinized the blown-up, black-and-white image in Miller's hand. "It kinda looks like Lennon, but these things are never as clear as we want them to be. Besides which, we only had eyes on him for a second or two before he ran."

"It's *definitely* him." Miller closed the file. His patience with Eubank was quickly running thin; he was beginning to recall what a pedantic asshole the guy was back in the day – that was probably what had made him the perfect shoe-in for the Bureau. "I'd stake my reputation on it."

"I'd hate for you to do that, Trea." Eubank eased forward in his chair with a wince. He rubbed at the small of his back as if it were bothering him. "If it *was* Lennon, how the hell did he get all the way from New Orleans in time to murder and dismember your young woman last night? It's one heck of a drive, Trea, and not one camera picked him up. I mean, he must have stopped for gas at some point, right?"

"Well, that's something I'll make a note to ask Lennon when my boys catch up with him." Miller threw the beige file back onto his desk; it made a satisfying *slap*.

"I guess I don't have to remind you that if that *is* Chase Lennon, and he's responsible for New Orleans and your murder," the special agent said as he stood from his chair with a barely audible grunt, "that makes it cross-state, which means the case will fall into FBI jurisdiction."

"Yeah, I get that." Miller felt the hard knot of disappointment in the pit of his stomach. The first taste of a big case he'd had in as long as he could remember, and Tyrone Eubank and his Bureau cohorts were going to get their jumped-up, sticky little hands all over it. Miller, along with the rest of the Lubbock police department, would be relegated to little more than lackeys at the whim of the FBI.

And that stuck like a fish bone in the detective's throat.

"Well, I guess I should be going." Eubank made for the door. He was carrying the hint of a limp in his right leg, and Miller surprised himself by just how much satisfaction that brought him. "I think I'll pay the chief a visit and say hello – maybe see if he wants to have a beer or two at Millie's Place. If it's still there, of course."

Miller snorted. "It's still there," he said, "and yeah, why don't you do that."

"Lemme know if—*when*—you catch up with your fugitive, Trae." Eubank paused, hand on Miller's doorknob. "And if it's Lennon, I'll make sure you get some credit for bringing it to our attention."

As Eubank left, Miller was relieved to have his office back to himself. He needed time to think, to second-guess where Lennon could have possibly gone to ground. There were only so many places to hide around Lubbock, but there were a whole bunch of locations so remote out there in the wilds, only the foolhardy had set foot in them in decades.

His neck twinged a reminder he'd just been T-boned and really ought to get Dr. DeSanto, the precinct's physician, to check it out. Miller hoped it wasn't whiplash, because he didn't relish the idea of having to wear one of those dumb collars like some freshly castrated dog for four to six weeks; he had enough crap to put up with as it was, and Chase Lennon to find.

Closing his office door, Detective Miller reopened the beige file and pulled out the crime scene photographs to study Chase Lennon's nauseating handiwork.

Chapter 14

"Try to get all the sand off your feet, first!" Chris Mitchell barked at the kids as he tried to remove the dried salt scum off his glasses with a damp handkerchief. He'd spent a ridiculous amount of money getting the Tesla cleaned out after the family's last trip to the beach and wasn't in the mood to spend more.

If Emma hadn't decided to suddenly go to the mall with her girlfriends in the Toyota SUV, which he'd specifically bought as the family vehicle, he wouldn't be getting all stressed out over his precious Model S right now.

"It won't come off," Phillip whined as he brushed frantically at his sandy soles with one hand while supporting himself against a fence post with the other. Behind him, the sea lapped lazily at the shore and sand pipers darted and bobbed in the froth. Even though he was about to turn thirteen, two years his brother's senior, Phillip was by far the more immature of the two.

"I'm all done," Sam piped up. He lifted each foot in turn to prove his point and clambered into the car.

Mitchell let out a loud sigh at the sight of the hiney of his younger son's swim trunks: damp from the sea, generously coated with a thick layer of Gulf Shores' finest golden sand. Weary from his day at the beach with the boys, skin clammy with sea air and sunscreen, Mitchell just wanted to drive the ten minutes up the 59, grab a hot shower, and retreat to his den to catch up on the news.

"Just get in the car, Phil," he said, resigned to having to call the mobile car detailer out once again. At least the guy did a good job, and the Tesla didn't even have to leave the driveway. Mitchell kinda liked that.

Emma's blue RAV4 was parked up in front of the house when Mitchell and his kids got there. It was a touch after six and the sun was slumping its way down toward the horizon, which likely meant Emma had been home for some time. Mitchell hoped she'd prepared something for dinner, even if it was only PB and J sandwiches; he was pooped and in no state to rummage around in the kitchen to feed the boys.

"Hey, honey, we're home!" Mitchell announced his arrival as he stepped through the front door and tossed his keys onto the faux-antique mahogany table by the bottom of the stairs. It was something he and Emma said every time one of them came home, just like on the old sitcoms. It had been their thing since before they were married, and somehow never failed to raise a smile. The boys trotted into the house behind him, trailing fine sand in their wake upon the immaculately polished, dark wood hallway floor.

"Where's Mom?" Phillip asked, slipping off his Crocs to place neatly on the shoe rack in the understairs cupboard. "I'm hungry."

"Me too," Sam echoed. Barefoot since leaving the beach, he simply tossed his white Crocs into the cupboard, narrowly missing his brother's head.

"Probably shopped herself into a coma." Mitchell's comment was meant to be funny, but there was too much truth to it for that. Emma's spending had been getting out of hand lately, and Mitchell knew he was long overdue speaking with her to rein it in before she shopped them all out on the streets. "You guys go grab that leftover pizza from last night, and I'll go wake Mom up."

Phillip and Sam grumped a little and headed into the kitchen. Mitchell reckoned they were hungry enough to eat day-old pizza cold, and that was just fine with him.

The landing at the top of the stairs was gloomy, with just a thin sliver of light glowing out from beneath the bathroom door. "Honey?" Mitchell called out; wasn't this the part in the movies where the unwitting husband caught the unfaithful wife *in flagrante*? Usually with some slick, tanned, billionaire lover or the hunky pool boy.

Mitchell allowed himself a wry smile at that thought. To begin with, living so close to the beach, the Mitchells had no need for a pool, plus there was a definite lack of billionaires in Gulf Shores, Alabama. There was also the fact he trusted his wife of fifteen years implicitly; he gave her no reason to stray and knew Emma was more than happy with their cozy family life together and albeit vanilla sex life.

His only slight worry was she might have hit the Pinot Noir early and fallen asleep in the tub again. On the other hand, there was always the chance Emma was playing her game and waiting for him to find her nude, soaking in the tub, and reading one of her favorite erotic romance novels. A sure-fire signal that Mrs. Mitchell was, as she liked to put it, *in the mood.*

That thought quickened Mitchell's step, and he thanked God for the cold Little Ceasar's Supreme in the refrigerator. Between that and cable TV, the boys would be occupied for more than enough time for him to have some spontaneous tub fun with his sexy little wife.

"I hope you're still awake in there…" Easing open the bathroom door, Mitchell was hit with a cloud of steam, which fogged up his spectacles in an instant. He picked up the sound of the shower running and felt a twinge of disappointment: he much preferred sex in the tub because thrusting away, standing up, at Emma in the cramped shower stall was always guaranteed to aggravate his old lacrosse knee injury.

Still, Mitchell was never one to complain when Emma initiated intimacy, even if it was only to soften him up for the no-doubt substantial dent she'd put in the credit card.

"You need anything soaping up in there, my love?" Mitchell closed the bathroom door behind himself and removed his steamed-up glasses.

And the sight that met Chris Mitchell had his legs buckling beneath him. *"Oh, dear god, no…"*

Head spinning, Mitchell grabbed the side of the bathtub to prevent himself collapsing onto the warm, damp tiles of his bathroom floor. "Emma?" He prayed for his wife to reply, to turn her head toward him, fix his eyes with hers, and give him that salacious, inviting smile that let him know she wanted him to climb into the tub with her.

But Emma was dead.

And those beautiful eyes were no longer there.

The tub's water, filled almost to overflowing, was stained red with a whole lot of Emma's blood. Her head lolled back, bobbing gently, showing the broad, ragged tear across her throat, which ran ear to ear. Mitchell saw his wife had been sliced open from between her breasts all the way down to her navel, and her water-filled body cavity was efficiently emptied of its organs.

As Mitchell threw up next to the bathtub, his mind swirled with the old black and white photographs of Jack the Ripper's victims he'd seen in books as a kid.

They were images that had never left him, stark pictures of brutality that had triggered his lifelong horror of death. The ever-elusive serial murderer of Victoria London was renowned for disemboweling his prostitute victims and artfully arranging their entrails about the room in which they'd perished at his brutal hands.

Whoever had killed Emma had done the same, as if they'd somehow been able to tap into Mitchell's inner fears and brought them to full, gruesome, bloodied life. His wife's intestines—large and small—were draped around the expansive bathroom mirror like bizarre, fleshy garlands, her liver and kidneys occupied the faux-marble sink, stomach and lungs were placed neatly atop the vanity unit, and her heart perched upon the toilet seat in a thickening puddle of its own blood.

And there, balanced side by side on top of the toilet cistern, as if overlooking the whole gruesomely staged scene with twisted approval, were Emma's beautiful gray-green eyes.

A loud crashing noise, followed by the sound of something heavy scraping across a wooden floor, below him brought Mitchell to his senses, triggering his paternal protectiveness.

The boys.

There'd be time to mourn Emma once the remainder of his family was safe; whoever had done this to his wife could still be in the house and planning a repeat performance with his children.

Making every effort to avert his eyes from the horror in the bathroom, Mitchell made his way out through the steam and into the hallway. Closing the bathroom door with his butt, Mitchell wiped his glasses dry on his shirt and headed down the stairs. He took them two at a time despite his trembling legs.

"Come in, Mr. Mitchell." The voice welcoming him into his own dining room was cold, detached, had a definite southern twang to it; Mitchell half-expected the guy to end the sentence with *y'all*.

"Dad?" Phillip said as Mitchell walked in.

"Is that you?" Sam joined in. His voice was quiet, shaky; he'd been crying.

"It's me, guys," Mitchell reassured as best he could. Then, "What have you done to them?" he asked the intruder as he took in the sight of his sons, who were duct taped to a dining chair each with a black hood covering their heads.

"Don't worry, Mr. Mitchell, they haven't seen anything that will put them in danger." The guy pointed a silver six-shooter revolver directly at Mitchell's chest with one hand, stroked at his full ginger beard with the other. He looked like he was contemplating something really deep and philosophical. Behind the boys, silent, black ski masks hiding their faces, stood a pair of shorter men clad all in black. "You, on the other hand…"

"Please, no," Mitchell stammered, thoughts of what they'd done to his poor Emma playing fresh in his mind. He couldn't even bring himself to imagine what such sick people might have in mind for him and his children. "You don't have to do this."

"Ah, but I do." The bearded guy raised the gun so Mitchell could see directly into the dark eye of its barrel. "It's all part of the game, I'm afraid to say. And you have been selected."

"*Game*? What game?"

"I really do wish there was time to explain, Mr. Mitchell."

Mitchell followed the guy's sideways glance to the recumbent figure beneath the polished pinewood dining table. At first, he thought the man was dead, but the faint rise and fall of his chest showed him to be only unconscious, though deeply so.

His clothes were stained with blood and looked like he'd lived in them for days. Even with his eyes closed, mouth dropped wide open, face slack in sleep, Mitchell was sure he recognized the man from somewhere. It was then he noticed the coiled rope and plain, brown plastic pill bottle on the table, next to the display of white silk geraniums Emma had insisted on buying so many years ago.

The bearded man cocked the revolver's trigger. It made a metallic, ominous *click*.

"No!" Instinctively, Mitchell raised his hands in front of his face, as if flesh and bone really could prevent the inevitable.

"Dad!" the boys cried out in unison.

Then, without further ado, the guy with the red beard squeezed the trigger.

Chapter 15

Lennon's head hurt like all hell, but not quite so bad as the previous times he'd woken up in a strange place, and for that he was grateful. His back ached, too, the hard floor upon which he lay flat out was cold and unforgiving; it felt as if each single ridge of his vertebrae was bruised and chilled by the smooth tiles.

As he eased his eyes open against the dull throbbing that pounded away in his temples, Lennon was greeted by a lifeless strip light on the ceiling above him and, to his right, a double-door stainless steel refrigerator and row of pale green, antique-style cupboard doors with dulled, brass handles designed to resemble knives, forks, and spoons.

A random thought struck Lennon from out of the blue: *He remembered the previous times.*

Rolling onto his side with a loud groan, Lennon struggled himself upright with nebulous images of a dingy motel room and an unfamiliar car swirling around in his foggy brain. The thoughts were definitely connected somehow, yet Lennon couldn't quite grasp how – perhaps all would become clear once his head sharpened a little more?

Sitting upright on the kitchen floor, Lennon glanced down at the gaily patterned tiles drawing his body heat away; they were brightly painted with an array of Mexican motifs, which put him in mind of a *Día de los Muertos* celebration in Chiapa de Corzo he'd enjoyed with Jilly long before they'd even considered having kids. His heart ached for such simpler times, and Lennon had a sick, sinking feeling things would never be the same again, even when the game was finished.

Again, the fog clouding his mind made the details haunting him elusive, even though there was something *there* this time. He remembered, of course, Mercer and his Faustian contract, along with fragments of strange places and a dingy hotel room.

It'll all come back once my head clears.

Grunting, Lennon forced himself to his feet. He had to get moving, do *something*. The more he attempted to mentally track the memories, the farther they slipped into the recesses of his brain, and the more likely they would be to drive him crazy.

The all-too familiar butchers-shop stink of freshly spilled blood threatened to put Lennon right back on the kitchen tiles. Gagging against the cloying reek that conjured snippets of bloodied corpses, blood-splattered walls, and dead, staring eyes, Lennon caught hold of the marble kitchen countertop to steady himself.

"Please, God, no," Lennon whispered beneath his breath as he fought back the waves of nausea that swept through him. Had his stomach not been so obviously and completely empty, he'd have thrown up.

A quick check of himself showed Lennon he had no blood on his hands or clothing – neither his own nor someone else's, which meant the sickening, coppery smell was coming from elsewhere within the stranger's house.

Working purely by instinct, his logical brain frozen, unable to form a single coherent thought, Lennon made his way toward the glass-paned door at the far end of the kitchen. He walked slowly, eyes fixed upon the splash of verdant green that lay beyond the door. Once he got outside, Lennon promised himself he'd take as much time as he needed to clear his head and formulate a plan for what he should do next.

For now, though, his main priority was to get the hell out of the house and away from the sour stink of death that clung to him like some nefarious veil.

He'd do whatever he had to do once he could think straight.

A noise.

It came from somewhere behind.

Quiet, muffled, *nearly* a voice.

Spinning around too quickly to home in on and identify the sound had Lennon almost landing his ass back on the floor. He muttered a quiet prayer of thanks for the cool, stone countertop that prevented his fall.

That noise again, from a room beyond the bare brick archway at the opposite end of the kitchen to where the sanctuary of outdoors lay. It sounded to Lennon like stifled sobbing, wet sniffles. It sounded like…

Children.

"God, no," Lennon groaned out loud. For as much as he wanted—*needed*—to flee what his sense of smell told him was nothing he wanted to confront, some innate instinct urged him to turn on his heels and make his way toward that heartbreaking sound. And yet, even as he walked toward the dense, cloying stink, Lennon's mind

screamed at him to get the hell out because something even worse awaited him, because of the game he was playing.

There was a corpse in the dining room, of course, laying supine with its legs beneath the grand dining table, which had been fashioned out of a huge slab of tree, complete with rough bark, and polished to within an inch of its life. The dead body, a man in his early thirties, Lennon guessed, was sprawled out where he'd fallen. He had a wide, ragged hole between raw, empty eye sockets and a drying pool of blood around the back of his head that resembled a ghoulish, dark crimson halo.

Lennon caught sight of the pink-gray globs of brain matter and glinting shards of skull spattered across the floor and all over the chintzy floral curtains at the same time he espied the large blood stain on the ceiling above him.

Wide, misshapen, it had evidently soaked through from the floor above: Fat stalactites of blood congealed on the white stucco, all ready to drip down as a dire portent to what horrors may lay in wait up there.

It was then Lennon noticed the two pairs of eyeballs— one pair green, the other brown—nestled between the silver revolver, coiled rope, and plain, brown bottle of pills on the table top.

As the flood of churning, sickening images returned, Lennon became aware he was not alone in the dining room. There, in the corner opposite the dead man sat two small figures bolt upright on the high-backed chairs that corresponded with the gaps in the seating around the long table.

Kids.

Lennon's gut lurched once more and a sharp pain stabbed at the inside of his chest. He could only hope the latter was acid reflux and not something altogether unhealthier, given the immeasurable stress he was under.

A pair of young boys stared at Lennon across the shining expanse of the table with wide, terrified eyes. Their mouths were sealed shut with silver duct tape, which had also been used to bind them to their respective chairs; much of their small, thin chests were covered by the stuff. The tape covering both boys' mouths glistened wet with tears and snot.

To complete the sickening tableau, the boys' wrists and ankles were taped to the arms and legs of the dark wooden chairs, thus rendering them entirely immobile.

"Hey…" Lennon lifted his arms to show empty hands and stepped gingerly over the congealing pool of blood. "It's gonna be okay."

Hollow words.

Nothing about what was happening was ever going to be okay. It seemed safe to assume the corpse half under the table with the back of its head shot out was the boys' father, and Lennon reckoned it highly likely the two kids had witnessed his brutal slaying. The absolute horror etched on what little of their young faces were not covered by silver tape painted a heartbreaking picture indeed.

A sudden flashback to a large, out-of-place flatscreen and news report showing his face jolted Lennon out of his compassion. The kids had gotten a good look at him standing over their dead parent's body, and who knew what manipulation Mercer's cohorts could have put into place to have them identify him as the killer?

If they were capable of an outright deep fake fabrication of a CCTV recording in order to put him in the frame to add excitement to the gameshow, then Lennon could only guess at what else they'd be capable of.

Was it possible the kids didn't actually belong to the dead guy? Could they have been brought in as stage dressing to add to the drama and heap more pressure on the contestant to have him panic and make a dumb mistake that would lead to his capture and lose him the game?

It also occurred to Lennon, as he approached the whimpering boys, it was also entirely possible he *had* pulled the trigger and murdered their father in cold blood. After all, the gun was right there on the table, and common sense dictated it was the murder weapon.

He'd clearly been drugged, which was the only way Lennon could explain the fogged recollections and infuriating black gaps in his memory, so he could very easily have killed the man and not remember.

If the two kids had actually *seen* Chase Lennon blowing their father away, there would be no more relying on cooked-up camera footage because there would be actual witnesses to point the accusing finger at.

Lennon stopped dead in his tracks at that thought.

There were likely to be Mercer's cameras dotted around the house, invasive electronic eyes capturing his every move.

Suddenly, Lennon felt like a rat caught in a trap.

His gaze flicked once more to the gun that sat silver, glinting, on the blood-spattered table top. Beside it, the plastic pill bottle and rough-hewn rope appeared almost innocuous by comparison. The dark, perfectly round muzzle stared blankly at Lennon, much like the hollowed eye sockets of the man he may well have murdered. The weapon seemed so very inviting, a simple way out of the impossible predicament the game had placed him in. Just slip that shiny steel muzzle in his mouth and pull the trigger…

So much quicker, albeit not cleaner, than the pills or the rope. Lennon didn't much relish the thought of slowly strangling himself to death or drifting off into some drug-induced sleep from which he had the chance of waking up and having to face the horror in that house all over again.

It had come to this already?

Lennon's fantasies of winning Mercer's game and the ridiculously fat prize were crowded out by the fragmented memories and the overwhelming feeling of being trapped with no place to go, no one to turn to. Even Jilly had turned her back on him and not-so-subtly hinted that he take this way out.

With an apologetic look at the kids immobilized in the dining chairs, Lennon reached for the revolver. Naturally, he wouldn't do the deed in front of them, he figured they'd be traumatized enough as it was.

As Lennon's fingers brushed against the gun's ridged handle, a movement in his peripheral vision made him freeze.

There was somebody else in the house.

Instinctively, Lennon snatched the revolver up off the table and did a half-turn toward the narrow, arched doorway leading from the dining room to the hallway beyond. And there, framed by the red brick, stood a cop with her service pistol aimed squarely at Lennon's chest.

Chapter 16

So, the game was up?

Caught unawares, Lennon thought it highly unfair he'd hardly been given the opportunity to make good his escape from the house of horrors Mercer had him awaken in. Whatever it was they'd drugged him with had barely had time to wear off.

And now the cops had caught up with him—endgame indeed.

Staring at the cop across the blood-spattered dining room, startled by just how young she looked, how perfectly proportioned in her dark blue uniform with shiny brunette hair tied into a heat ponytail that disappeared behind her back, another thought crept into Lennon's mind:

What if this wasn't *the end of the game?*

The silver revolver suddenly felt unnaturally heavy in Lennon's hands, heavy and *purposeful*. Sure, the cop had her black Glock trained on him, but if he could distract her just long enough for him to fire off a shot or two, he might just be able to get himself out of the situation.

A fraction of a second was all he'd need to turn this whole situation around. She was, after all, alone. And, even if she had a colleague waiting in a car outside the house, Lennon reckoned he could get himself out through the kitchen door as he'd originally planned before Cop Number Two got into the house, guns blazing.

"Don't." The cop's voice was barely a whisper, but her intention was as clear as her finger on the Glock's trigger: she wouldn't hesitate to defend herself, should Lennon try anything stupid.

Shaking his head, Lennon kept hold of the revolver. His mind was doing its best to convince him he had a chance, even though the steely look in the cop's dark brown eyes told him otherwise.

"Put the gun down, Mr. Lennon, and come with me."

The cop's voice was soothing, calm, quiet, and she made no attempt to step into the dining room to close the gap between them. It was as if she preferred the relative sanctuary of the hallway and her weapon.

Lennon turned his attention from the cop's face to her gun, his mind still weighing up the feasibility of using his own and getting the hell out of there. What troubled him was he felt entirely capable of pulling the trigger, gunning down a cop in cold blood, all in the name of Mercer's sick game.

Did winning money, no matter how big the pot, really mean *that* much to Chase Lennon?

"Give it up, Mr. Lennon." The cop was most insistent, that infernal Glock unwavering in her rock-steady hands.

One of the kids let out a whimper, his voice muffled by silver tape.

An involuntary reaction, Lennon's eyes switched to the two small boys, to the absolute terror in their young eyes. He couldn't begin to imagine what the trauma of all this was doing to their impressionable minds.

"They'll be okay," the cop reassured. "They will be taken care of. You just need to put the gun down and come with me. Please, Mr. Lennon…"

Finally, Lennon decided to do as he was told.

Even in his heightened state of adrenaline and determination not to lose Mercer's game, his common sense won out—there really was no conceivable way he'd be able to shoot his way out of the house; in his gut, he knew the cop would put three slugs in his chest before he'd even had time to point his revolver in her direction.

Slowly, not daring to take his eyes off the cop, Lennon put the gun back down next to the rope and tablets.

Lowering her weapon, the cop twitched her head to beckon Lennon over. She remained rooted to her spot in the hallway, sensible, flat shoes not moving an inch.

Despondent at having lost the game, Lennon stepped gingerly over the corpse and around the dining table to make his way to the archway where the cop waited for him. Glock still in hand, her finger lay stiff and straight along its body and no longer on the trigger.

"This way," the cop urged once Lennon was out of the dining room and through the red brick arch. He'd turned in the direction of the house's front door, but it appeared the officer had other ideas. She pointed her gun toward a white-painted door at the opposite end of the hallway to the front door, and then at Lennon, her intention crystal clear.

Compliant, defeated, Lennon made his way to the door and, upon opening it, discovered it led into a spacious double garage. Feeling the hard nose of the cop's gun prod gently into his ribs, Lennon stepped into the empty garage, followed closely by the cop. She pulled the door closed behind them and flicked on the strip light.

It buzzed and flickered into life.

"What's going on here?" Lennon eyed the cop nervously. She'd not holstered the Glock, nor had she cuffed him or recited his Miranda rights. That, coupled with the fact she was so obviously working alone, brought Lennon to one inescapable conclusion.

"Are you… is *this* part of the game?" he asked.

The cop said nothing. Instead, she crossed the garage and pushed at its side door that opened out into a narrow passageway between the house and a seven-foot wooden fence, which in turn conveniently concealed them from the overlooking neighbor's two story. Then she ushered Lennon through the iron gate at the end of the fence and out into the street to the left of the house.

"If you're expecting me to go anywhere with you," Lennon took his chance, stopping as he spoke, "you're gonna have to tell me if you're part of Mercer's game or not. And if you are, does this mean I just lost?"

"We really don't have the time for this, Mr. Lennon." The cop was visibly exasperated with him. She fidgeted with the gun in her hand, which Lennon was beginning to think might just be a fake. Or, if it wasn't, that she had no real intention of using it on him. "The cameras will be back online any minute now, and we need to be gone by then."

So, she *was* part of the game! But she was still a cop, which, according to the rules Mercer had explained what seemed like a thousand years ago, meant he'd been caught fair and square.

It was game over, whichever way he looked at it.

Except it somehow didn't feel like the game was over. Lennon was forming the impression there was more to come, and he was still very much in the running. Perhaps this was some 'unexpected' twist thrown in purely for entertainment value?

Let the viewers at home think he'd been caught, only to return in some contrived way to keep them watching and paying those all-important monthly subscription fees. Either way, second chance or otherwise, Lennon knew he had no other choice than to play along with the cop and continue to wonder if she was the genuine article in on the ruse or some actor paid to play the part.

"I'll explain everything to you when we get to someplace safe." The cop nodded toward the black-and-white that sat empty by the curbside. "If you'd like to get in the back, please, Mr. Lennon, that would be very much appreciated."

Chapter 17

"Are you sure you're sure about this, Broussard?" Trae Miller let out a long, weary sigh and eased his bulk back in his chair; it creaked its protest loudly. Waving a hand at a young, uniformed officer making her way toward the precinct's utilitarian kitchen, the detective mimed to her his urgent need for a strong, black coffee. Already it was turning into one hell of a day.

The uniform, a homely-looking gal with a mousey-brown bob cut and thick-rimmed glasses, nodded her acknowledgement as she disappeared into the kitchen. Everybody at the Lubbock police precinct knew exactly how Detective Miller liked his coffee; pretty much the opposite to how he liked his women.

"As sure as I can be without seeing the crime scene first-hand," Broussard was saying. "I got some photographs that are pretty damn convincing."

"Send 'em over. I'll take a look." Miller had little desire to take a look at whatever the New Orleans detective had gotten his hands on this time, but felt obliged to lie, given that Broussard had gone to the trouble of calling him. "How the hell did you hear about this in New Orleans, anyway?" Miller asked, breathing heavily into his cellphone. "We've not heard as much as a whisper over here."

"I keep my ear to the ground, Detective Miller." There was the slightest hint of playfulness to Broussard's tone. "Especially with a case like this; it's not every day I get to investigate a suspected serial killer. I'm sure it's the same for you guys over there, too."

Broussard was right, naturally. The murder the week before, allegedly by Chase Lennon, was the first time Miller had come across anything even remotely akin to a serial killer's work –if that's what it was, of course. Lennon had dropped off the radar as soon as he'd given Miller and Eubank the slip at the railroad crossing. The detective had no idea anyone could disappear so effectively, not in this day and age of almost omnipotent surveillance and CCTVs absolutely everywhere.

"I know a few people in other states," Broussard continued. "I have a coupla good friends over in Tennessee who caught wind of what went down in Gulf Shores this morning. I'd put the word out after Lennon did his thing here and down your way. I had a hunch he'd strike again."

"*If* it's him." Miller never liked to play Devil's advocate but, then again, he'd never had a potential serial killer to deal with before.

"It's him." Broussard seemed annoyingly sure of himself.

"Similar MO?"

"Yeah, he even took the eyes out. Left 'em on the dining room table, right in front of the kids, too. And what that monster did to the wife…"

"Who the hell does that?" Just the thought of having to view the crime scene images Broussard had promised to text over had Miller feeling sick to his stomach. He'd seen enough brutal carnage between what Broussard had sent over from the Nola crime scene and the God-awful mess that had been made of poor Kirsty Boule to last him a lifetime.

"There are some sick, sick people out there, Detective Millier." Broussard sounded older, the wiser of the two. "Chase Lennon being one of them. The guy's on an inter-state killing spree getting a kick out of murdering innocent people and tearing up their corpses. We may very well have another Israel Keyes on our hands here. I wouldn't be surprised if it was some weird sex thing; seems these things usually are."

Miller had read somewhere that, at any given time, there are around twenty or so active serial killers in the United States alone, and that just about everyone has come into contact with one at some point in their lives, albeit unknowingly.

The very notion terrified him.

"I saw the guy close up, remember?" Miller said. "He looks a hundred percent normal to me, Broussard."

"You know how it goes, Detective Miller," Broussard replied. "When a killer like this is caught, everybody and their dog who ever knew him comes out of the woodwork to say what a swell guy he was, a veritable pillar of the community, someone who wouldn't even hurt a fly. It's all: 'he was a marvel on that suicide hotline,' and 'he was a wonderful clown at my kid's birthday party,' and 'he was just the guy next door.' Except for Dahmer, of course.

Everybody who knew that guy said what an oddball freak he was."

"I'm just saying maybe Lennon's not your man."

"Then why did he run?"

"No idea – maybe he's caught up in some tax avoidance scam or some such; could explain why he's popping up in different states. You know how those rich guys are."

"No, I do not." Again, that tinge of mischievousness. "But what I *do* know is he's killed in at least three states now, and he's escalating. His face is all over the CCTV footage, Miller, you can't refute evidence like that."

Miller thought back to the Chase Lennon he'd seen in the motel parking lot what seemed like only yesterday. Sure, the guy had appeared to be spooked, but who wouldn't be when confronted by a pair of cops? Maybe the guy had been visiting an out of state mistress… Jetsetters like Lennon were bound to have a woman in every port, so to speak, but, unless it was some bizarre fetish Miller had not been made aware of, why would someone with Chase Lennon's money be holing up in some fleapit Lubbock motel?

Plus, there was the missing maid to consider. Miller and his old FBI friend had been the last people to set eyes on the woman as she'd climbed into what had turned out to be a stolen Chrysler sedan. He'd put out an APB on the young woman, using black and white, grainy footage from the Executive Inn's solitary security camera.

As he'd perused the fuzzy video for a suitable still, the motel's ancient owner had glibly announced that the woman leaving with the suspected serial killer was not actually one of her maids, and where the hell was Juanita?

So, *two* missing women, then.

Miller, listening politely as Broussard continued to join the dots for him, wished for the conversation to be over.

The more he thought about the mess of unanswered questions Lennon had left behind him in Lubbock, the more frustrated he became. He'd have loved nothing more than to have earned his Chief of Police stripes hunting down a brutal murderer, but Lennon had taken that away from him the moment he disappeared without a trace only to reappear in Alabama, of all places.

"Dick," Miller mumbled beneath his breath.

"What was that?" Broussard stopped mid-sentence.

"Not you, Detective," Miller felt his face flush. "I was just thinking about the FBI getting all the glory for our… *your* hard work.

"Copy that. But as long as the guy is caught and the killing stops, right?"

"Right." Miller could practically taste the resentment in his mouth. "Let's not forget what's important here, Detective Broussard."

Broussard laughed, a breathy chuckle sounding more like a static hiss coming through Miller's phone than anything akin to true humor.

"I guess I'm obliged to call Eubank now," Miller grumped. "In case his department at the Bureau haven't caught wind of Gulf Shores yet. You know how slow those guys can be at putting the pieces together."

"Amen to that."

"Send over the crime scene pictures now, and I'll hit Eubank up."

"Will do, Detective."

Broussard hung up the call without a goodbye; it would appear that was his thing. Maybe they did things differently over in the Big Easy. Even so, Miller got the impression Detective Thepohile—*call me Theo*—Broussard was just the kind of guy he'd like to have a coupla beers and chew the fat with one evening.

As he searched for Eubank's number in his call log, Miller's text notifications began to ping, letting him know Broussard was making good on his promise to send over the Alabama pictures he, in turn, had been sent from Gulf Shores PD. Miller had no real burning desire to actually view them, but there was no escaping the inevitable.

"Trae! Great to hear from you again so soon! How're you doing, my friend?" Special Agent Eubank sounded far too jovial for Miller's liking. The tone grated terribly against the mood that had settled over Miller during the conversation he'd just endured with Broussard.

"I just got a call from my contact in Louisiana," Miller began. "Figured I'd give you the heads-up so you can earn yourself a couple gold stars or whatever it is they give you Feds these days."

"I'm listening."

"Looks like our old friend, Chase Lennon, has been up to his tricks in Gulf Shores, Alabama," Miller went on. "Husband and wife this time, kids left unharmed but traumatized beyond belief. It's a similar MO with indications of escalation. My contact is sending over crime scene photos right now. I'll text them over to you as soon as I have them all."

"Thanks, Trae, but there's no need for that." Eubank sounded as cheery as ever. "I'm already at the scene—it's one helluva mess over here, I can tell ya!"

Miller hung up.

FBI, getting all the glory.

Chapter 18

The cop took Lennon a ways out of Gulf Shores, to a place due west signposted as Orange Beach. Quiet, picturesque. The town overlooked Wolf Bay, and felt conveniently far away enough from the carnage Lennon had woken up to earlier that morning.

Neither Lennon nor the cop spoke a word during the drive. Lennon was too deeply wrapped up in his own thoughts, disturbed by what he'd been witness to in the house they'd just left, and still trying to figure out if this was all part of *The Contestant* or a for-real arrest. Whichever it was, he remained un-cuffed and the cop definitely wasn't transporting him to the nearest police station for questioning.

As for the cop, Lennon just figured she had nothing much to say to him, and he was in no mood to attempt any form of conversation.

Eventually, they arrived at a modestly sized, single-story house at the very end of Bay Circle, which appeared to be a small, exclusive bunch of homes well away from the beaten track. Each one was nicely private and far enough from its immediate neighbors to avoid nosey stares and awkward questions.

Had she pre-planned this?

The cop pulled her car onto the driveway of the house, which served to hide it from view, and killed the engine.

"We're here." She pushed open the door and got out. "After you, Mr. Lennon." The cop opened the rear door and gestured for her passenger to join her.

There was a *For Sale* sign in the front yard, complete with a picture of the broadly smiling realtor, one Ms. Suzie McIntyre, and a key box attached to the front door handle. The cop punched in the six-digit code into the keypad, retrieved the key secured within, and ushered Lennon inside with a quick glance down the eerily silent street.

Inside, Lennon's professional eye noted, the house was of the modern, open-plan design with plenty of natural light and a stunning view over the bay. Had Imagine Realty been tasked with selling the property, they'd have definitely got top dollar for sure.

"I could use a drink," Lennon said, as much to break the loaded silence between him and the cop as to slake his nagging thirst.

The cop shook her head. "That wouldn't be wise, Mr. Lennon," she replied, her face stern, "you need to keep your wits about you, right now."

"I meant water. I could use a drink of *water*," he offered a half-smile. "Although a single-malt scotch-rocks would go down really well about now."

"Sit down, Mr. Lennon." The cop pointed to the cloth, floral couch dominating the living room.

Lennon did as instructed—she was the one carrying the gun, after all. The cop walked over to the refrigerator to retrieve a couple bottles of water. Other than a half dozen or so bottles of spring water, as far as Lennon could see, the fridge was empty.

"I'm sure you have a lot of questions, Mr. Lennon." The cop sat on the opposite end of the couch and passed over one of the bottles.

Lennon nodded at her understatement; he hardly knew where to start.

"Does this mean I've lost? The game, I mean." Predictably, Lennon's first thought went to the money.

"Not necessarily." The cop cracked her water bottle's cap and downed half of its contents in one chug. "It all depends."

"Depends on what?" Lennon followed suit with his water. Perfectly chilled, it was like cool nectar to his sandpaper throat.

"On you."

Was she being deliberately curt or simply trying her best to infuriate him? Either way, Lennon really wasn't in the right frame of mind to play games.

"Mercer's rule is that once I'm caught by the cops, or anyone in on the game, I guess, I'm out. End of." Lennon decided to let the cop's obtuseness slide, for now, at least. "I'm assuming you're not a real cop, so where does that leave me?"

"You have been caught, Mr. Lennon. The cop smiled at him. "But not in the way you might think. Although, if you'd procrastinated any more back at the Mitchell's house, you'd have been in police custody by now."

Putting a name to the dead guy and his wife and those poor kids made the whole situation a thousand times worse for Lennon. He still couldn't truly comprehend how *The*

Contestant would actually murder real people for the sake of the game. It was beyond sick.

Yet, here he was, desperate to stay in it.

"So, this *is* part of the game," Lennon said. "Rescued by a fake cop – seems all a bit contrived to me."

"Well, it is and it isn't." The cop smiled uneasily and sat forward on the couch.

"Are you going to give me any straight answers, or not?" Lennon snapped, his patience dangerously thin.

"I'm sorry. I've never done this before in all my time working on *The Contestant.*"

"You work for Mercer?"

"Not directly, but yes, I'm part of the ground crew."

"Meaning?"

"Meaning I stay close to the contestants and make sure certain things happen, or *don't* happen."

"So, *who* the hell are you?"

It was the cop's turn to show impatience. "I'm just a small cog in a very big machine, Mr. Lennon." She spoke quietly, softly. "I have to be very careful, right now. This is unchartered territory for me, as I explained—"

"Can you at least give me a name?"

The briefest of hesitation, then, "It changes every time we meet, Mr. Lennon, even though you're unlikely to ever remember it even if I told you. But, in the interests of building trust here, you can call me Lol. It's short for Lolita."

"Lolita?" Lennon couldn't help but smirk.

Lol nodded with an air of resignation. "My parents were big fans of Nabokov's book, and, yes, I've heard all the jokes."

"You said *every time we meet*?" Lennon leaned forward in his seat and scrutinized the young woman's face. That unsettling sensation of déjà vu swept through him, although it remained infuriatingly vague. "I *knew* I'd seen you before," he growled. "Good to know I'm not going crazy here."

"No, you're not going crazy."

"How come I don't recognize you, then, if we've met before? I have a photographic memory when it comes to people; it's kind of essential in my line of work."

"The drug the show administers wipes very specific parts of your short-term memory, including recalling faces and particular details. It's a proprietary thing Mercer's pharmacists perfected years ago, especially for *The Contestant*. I made sure you got a lower dose the last time you took it by adding ipecac to the whiskey you drank back in the trailer. It's a fast-acting emetic."

"I know what ipecac is, thank you." Lennon had figured they'd been drugging him; it was the only way he could see how they got him to wake up near or *in* the horrendous crime scenes they set up. That train of thought triggered a whole bunch of different questions, which Lennon chose to ignore.

For the time being, at least.

"How come the viewers at home don't recognize you every time you pop up on their screens?" Lennon wanted to know. "Surely you can't just change costumes and fool 'em all." He eyed Lol's police officer uniform which, he had to admit, did appear pretty damn convincing.

"Oh, that's the easy part," Lol replied with an awkward, lopsided smile. "They deep fake all the ground crew associates so no one catches on. Mercer and his company have driven a large part of AI deep fake technology over the years. From behind the scenes, of course."

Of course!

"That's how they got me on the CCTV videos?" Lennon felt some relief at the revelation. It meant he hadn't been directly responsible for killing any innocent people. "I saw it on the news; I figured it was just for my benefit at first."

Lol drained her water bottle and scrunched up the flimsy plastic bottle with one hand. She screwed the cap back on so the bottle remained balled up and rested it gently on the couch's arm.

"It's for *everyone's* benefit." Lol looked down at her feet, at the sensible flats beat cops all across the country wore. "The news reports are for real."

"So, the whole country thinks I'm a psycho killer?" Lennon struggled with the concept. Up until now, he'd assumed he was existing in an isolated bubble created by the gameshow and he was being pursued by actors – *ground crew*, as Lol called them. To discover that was not the case terrified Lennon.

"That's the game." Lol's voice was flat and completely without irony. "You really should have read the fine print, Mr. Lennon."

"The game is to set me up as a psycho murderer and have law enforcement hunt me down for real? Mercer sold all this to me as some campy version of *Running Man*." Lennon's voice trembled as the realization that Jilly, too, really did think him capable of such heinous crimes. After all, video evidence didn't lie, did it?

And that went some way toward explaining the last conversation he'd had with his wife.

"No, the Stephen King movie is just that, pure science fiction fantasy. This is the real world, not Hollywood. The objective of *The Contestant* is to put you under such pressure, back you into such a deep hole of despair, that you end the game yourself and not simply get caught by actors pretending to chase you or real cops." A self-conscious glance down at her uniform.

"Suicide?" Lennon replayed the last phone call with Jilly through his mind. He'd convinced himself at the time he'd imagined her alluding to suicide, but now he doubted that. Had his wife *really* suggested he kill himself to spare the family?

"Of course, why else would we leave a choice of means?" Lol sounded so matter-of-fact it came across as trite. "Huge wagers are placed upon which point of the game a contestant finally gives in and puts a permanent stop to their torment.

Interestingly, the men mostly opt for the gun, while women prefer the gentler out the pills offer. Not many have chosen the rope over the years, I guess it's just too gruesome to contemplate. Imagine strangling yourself to death?" She pulled a face. "Jeffrey Epstein was one notable exception, of course."

"Seriously?"

Lol gave a sage nod. "Jeff was a renowned, respected financier and friend to the rich and powerful until he joined *The Contestant*. The lure of so much money was more than he could resist, even with his wealth, much like yourself."

"But I'm not a kiddie fiddler," Lennon protested.

"That's the point," Lol replied. "Neither was he until we began fabricating the false narrative around him. The clientele were all disappointed he gave in quite so easily. We are having fun with the royal prince though – Jeff let his involvement slip in his early days on the game, and Andy so desperately wanted in. Mercer just couldn't turn a golden opportunity like that down. I'm assuming you know how that one is going?"

Lol's impish smile flipped Lennon's stomach over.

"I was told the contestants only had to evade capture for a week to win. The Prince Andrew thing has been going on for years now. And as for Epstein and Maxwell…"

"You were told that *you* had to see out a week," Lol corrected Lennon like a stern schoolmarm. "Contract lengths vary contestant to contestant. It all very much depends upon who they are and how long Mercer feels they will continue to be entertaining to his clientele.

"Public figures such as Epstein, Madoff, Cosby, Clinton, and the British comedian tend to have higher staying power and generate a great deal more income for the company. Epstein bowed out well before Mercer thought he would; cost him a hell of a lot of revenue, that one."

Listening to the woman in the fake cop uniform reel off the list of famous, discredited, names had Lennon's head spinning. Just who the hell else had been involved in *The Contestant*?

"So, they're trashing my name and reputation to drive me to kill myself?" Lennon knew he was stating the obvious, but the idea still sounded unbelievable when spoken out loud. "Even Jilly thinks I'm a deranged serial killer?"

Lol fixed Lennon with a thin-lipped smile, her eyes glistening. "Mercer will have gotten to your wife very early on in the game, Mr. Lennon," she told him. "He will have identified her as a key player from the outset."

"So, she knows this is all just faked?"

"She knows people are dying." Lol looked away, and Lennon imagined he caught a hint of guilt in the young woman's face. "And it's quite likely Mercer told her you are responsible for the killings because you've gone too far in the game you're caught up in. It's a tack he's used before with contestants' families and it works well."

"Do you know what he's told my wife?"

Lol shook her head no. "I'm not party to everything that goes on at the higher levels," she explained. "I'm barely ever a producer on the show."

"Which means what?" Used to knowing every nuance of any given situation in which he found himself, Lennon didn't much care for the fact he was so obviously immersed in a world completely alien to him.

"A producer *produces*." Lol said that as if it clarified everything to Lennon. To the contrary, it was just another riddle to him. Evidently picking up on her audience of one's blank expression, Lol went on, "And that means we make things happen."

"How so?"

"We scout out the best locations to stage scenes, help set up cameras, microphones, and such. We also find places like this," she spread her arms to emphasize their tasteful surroundings, "which are well away from the show's prying eyes. We manipulate the contestants into performing how we want them to perform by popping up here and there to help move things along a little where, and when, necessary."

Perform.

Lennon thought it was an interesting choice of words, and for the first time since learning the true nature of the sinister gameshow he'd so blindly signed up for, he felt like a seal in an aquarium performing demeaning tricks for a handful of rotting fish.

"*We*?" Lennon's brain shot off at a tangent.

"Pardon me?" Lol look puzzled.

"You said *we* when you talked about the show's producers."

Another nod and Lol's gaze returned to Lennon. "Yours is not the only game being played out, Mr. Lennon. Mercer likes to give his clientele an entertaining selection of different games around the world to choose from – both long and short-contract. Hell, I'm not even the only producer on *your* game."

"I've met others?" Lennon searched his memory for other instances, and was surprised to find a few of the gaps were beginning to fill in.

"Not that you'd recognize or remember," Lol said. "Our primary objective, to paraphrase *Star Trek*, is to observe and interact in such a way that we are not obvious and don't interfere with the natural order of things."

"So, why are we *here*?" The more the woman spoke, the more confused Lennon became. Was she deliberately talking in riddles to achieve just that? For all he knew, this whole soul-searching, eager to come clean schtick was all part of the act.

After all, hadn't she just told him her job was to manipulate the game-players? For all Lennon knew, the supposed safe house she'd brought him to under the auspices of rescuing him from inevitable capture was yet another part of the ruse.

And yet, there was just something about the young woman in the police uniform that had Lennon *believing* her, and not simply because he so desperately needed someone he could trust.

"I am the only one you can trust right now, Mr. Lennon." Lol read his mind. "And I do appreciate just how difficult it is for you right now. Mercer's games tend to have that effect on those who play them."

"Only, this is not really a game, is it?" Lennon finished up his water, which had grown tepid in his hand. "People are actually getting killed. Unless that's all as fake as the cops and… well, *you*."

"There's nothing fake about what happens to those people. I can assure you of that. Otherwise, we would have to stage them and involve every level of law enforcement and the media to make it *seem* like there are nasty sociopaths running amok state-to-state." She snorted, as if the very notion was derisible. "And can you even begin to image the costs and effort involved in generating such a widespread deception? Not to mention the public outcry when the Prestige was finally revealed?"

"*The Prestige?*" Lennon vaguely recalled having snoozed through the movie with Jilly one cold Saturday evening date night. He had never understood its title.

"The *reveal*, Mr. Lennon." There was the merest hint of condescension to Lol's tone. "In magic, it's when the magician reveals the true nature of his illusion. In *The Contestant's* case, it would be when the fact it was all staged and the general public had been terrified and rendered paranoid for no other reason than entertainment value.

Not to mention it could only ever be done one time. Once the game was up, so to speak, and everyone knew what was going on, there'd be no point in even trying to run it again. Imagine *The Bachelor* where the first girl the guy met was *always* the one he ended up with."

Lennon shrugged. He'd never been much of a fan of the reality shows Jilly loved to waste her time glued to. And, yes, he did get the irony of that.

"Exactly." Lol seemed to be on a roll, as if spilling the beans on *The Contestant* was somehow cathartic for her. "Mercer's clientele would never subscribe to another game once the jig was up, and they'd definitely not bother making their substantial wagers."

"And that's where Mercer makes his money?" The revelation surprised him.

"Like you wouldn't believe, Mr. Lennon." Lol said. "Mercer handles most of the book, and takes a handsome vigorish for the privilege, too. Although, there are plenty of side bets between the more competitive clients, no matter how much Mercer tries to put a stop to it: Who's going to shoot a cop, how long before a contestant sleeps with someone, when someone will try hiding from the game… even dumb stuff like what their first or last meal is going to be. Despite all his money and power, Mercer's dealing with people far wealthier and infinitely more powerful than he is. Even he knows how to choose his battles and cut his losses. Besides, Mercer and his company make more than enough from the likes of you."

Are you judging *me, young lady?*

"The likes of me?" Lennon couldn't help but take the bait.

"Rich, greedy people." Lol kinda looked down her nose at him, which Lennon didn't much care for.

"I don't think that's a fair assessment…" Lennon knew, of course, the woman was right.

"You have more money than anyone could possibly ever spend in a lifetime if not more, and yet you willingly signed on the dotted line for the chance to win an even more obscene amount. So much so, you went against everything you know about business, all your instincts, and never even bothered to read the fine print."

Lennon couldn't argue with that.

"It's about more than the money," he protested. "It was the chance to do something—"

"Exciting?"

"Yeah, I guess so."

"And how is that working out for you, right now?"

Was that a smirk?

"How do you think?" Lennon caught the tremor in his own voice. "I'm being hunted as a serial killer and my wife wants me to kill myself. I'd say it's not going well at all, wouldn't you?"

"I love the understatement." Lol shifted in her seat. "The way it's going, this really isn't going to end well for you, Mr. Lennon."

"You're writing me off already?" Lennon was offended by Lol's inference. It had been a long, long time since anyone had even dared suggest he might fail at something. "I've managed to not get caught so far."

"Only because *I* didn't want your game to end too quickly." Lol played with her fingers as she spoke, intertwining them in a way Lennon thought ought to be sensual, but seemed to be more…

Nervous?

"You're saying you've *helped* me escape?"

"If I hadn't pulled you out of the house back there, you'd be in the back of a police car by now— game over. And if I hadn't played the helpless maid at the motel when I did… same result, I'm afraid." Lol told him, matter of fact.

"And then what?" Lennon asked. "Mercer pays off the authorities and I walk?"

"Not quite."

"So, I don't walk?"

"Have you not stopped to think why each stage of your game is held in a state that still actively carries out the death penalty?"

Lennon took in a deep breath. He'd been so immersed in what was going on with the game, the sickening deaths, Jilly, he'd not stopped to consider that. "I'm guessing that's deliberate?"

A nod.

"You get convicted of what they think you've done, and you'll be fast-tracked for lethal injection before you know what's happening. Although, I hear state execution by firing squad is gaining in popularity at the moment." Lol seemed uneasy at the notion. "Especially with Mercer's involvement. It's a neat way of getting rid of the losers who don't have the balls to do it themselves and keeping them quiet, of course."

"He can do that?"

Lol nodded. "You'd be surprised just how far the show's influence goes. There are people involved in *The Contestant* that would shock you. It's developed into so much more than a crazy, high-stakes gameshow."

"And what happens if I win?" Lennon had to ask. He still felt he had a chance of waking off into the sunset with the fat check. "Do the winners all end up being kept quiet?"

"If he's nothing else, Mercer is a man of honor, one who *always* keeps his word." Lol appeared offended on her boss's behalf, which made Lennon wary of her. Mercer was clearly a monster who thought nothing of slaughtering innocent people and destroying lives in the interests of ratings, subscriptions, and his own bank balance, and yet she'd just described him as a *man of honor*. Perhaps Lol couldn't be trusted, after all?

"So, what does happen to the winners, then? How come nobody ever hears from them? Dirt has a tendency to stick, especially if you're labelled a psychotic murderer by every media outlet and social media platform."

"*The Contestant* winners are incredibly few and far between, as you can imagine. But, for the handful who do manage to evade capture and not kill themselves, the prize money is real enough. There's a hell of a lot you can do with over a billion dollars. Plus, there's a watertight NDA in that fine print you didn't read: you breathe one word about *The Contestant* or Mercer to anyone and your status as winner is immediately terminated."

"He takes the prize money back?"

"You've seen what Mercer is capable of. He can do more than just rescind your winnings."

Lennon decided upon not pressing for details; he had a damn good idea what Lol was alluding to and didn't have the stomach to hear the words out loud.

"But…" Lol continued, "It's so very easy to disappear, create a new identity; Mercer will introduce you to the right people for that and even a touch of plastic surgery to really seal the deal. Our winners can so very easily become entirely new people."

"That's encouraging."

"I really don't think you have much of a chance, though." Lol spoke softly. "I've worked the show more years than I care to recall now, and I know a winner when I meet one. You just don't have what it takes to see this through – one way or another. No offense, Mr. Lennon."

"None taken," Lennon lied. How dare some woman gussied up in a fake cop uniform like some cheap strip club dancer tell him he didn't have what it takes to see things through to the end? He had a mind to tell her to get lost and quit helping him, and they'd see just how far he'd get without her help.

Although, deep down, Lennon's common sense was telling him Lol was right. He'd already considered, albeit fleetingly, turning that ubiquitous silver revolver on himself.

That he recalled the revolver being present in the other locations came as a revelation to Lennon. Little by little, fragments of memories of previous scenes Mercer had dumped him into were creeping back, although not all of them welcome.

"So why *are* you helping me?" Lennon asked. "If I'm such a dead cert' to get caught or end it all myself, why go to all this trouble?"

"I'm not helping you."

"That's not how this looks from where I'm sitting." As Lennon scrutinized the young woman, his eyes flicked down to the neatly bridged fingers resting in her lap. They appeared a tad less in focus than they had just a few minutes before. "You just told me if you hadn't pulled me out of the house back there, I'd have been caught."

"What I'm doing is for *my* benefit, not yours." Lol smoothed out an imaginary crease on the thigh of her utilitarian cop pants. "I have my reasons for making sure you stay in the game… for now, at least."

"Reasons?" Lennon felt uneasy. Lol clearly had a motive for being so infuriatingly evasive with him. "What reasons, and how do I know this is not just part of the show to keep me going out there for Mercer's benefit?"

A flicker of a smile, a look of determination. "All I can do is reassure you that this is definitely *not* any part of how *The Contestant* is meant to play out," Lol said. "My brief—all producers' brief—is to keep a distance and help things along as and when necessary. And that doesn't include bailing out a hopeless contestant."

Lennon opened his mouth to defend himself, only to close it again as words failed him.

Hopeless?

"Don't take it personally, Mr. Lennon." Lol offered a smile, which Lennon thought was intended to be placating. "I appreciate a man like you is used to winning, coming out on top every time which made you rich, after all. But *The Contestant* is something entirely different."

"I'd say that's a bit of an understatement." Lennon attempted a smile back, but his face felt slack, unresponsive.

As Lol fiddled with her belt, Lennon idly wondered if the gun it held was for real, or just some dumb TV prop. "As for my reasons, I'm afraid we don't have the time to go into that right now. All I will say, though, is I think Mercer has gone too far and has to be stopped. For now, though, I have to get you to your next location. We can discuss everything in detail the next time we meet."

"Time to go?" Lennon made as if to stand from the couch, only to slump back down into the soft embrace of its plump cushions.

Lol stole a quick glance at her wristwatch and nodded. "I need to get you into the car while you can still walk," she told him.

"You *drugged* me? Again?" Lennon slurred the obvious. "How did you manage…?"

Lol eyed Lennon's empty water bottle. "It's nothing to worry about, I've kept the dose very low this time."

"You don't trust me?" Lennon slurred.

"It's not a matter of trust, Mr. Lennon." Lol stood. She seemed so incredibly tall, preternaturally so. "It's all about keeping up appearances. If I fail to do what's expected and Mercer's people catch on—which they will, I can assure you—everything I've been working toward with you falls apart in a heartbeat."

"So, you drugged me?" It was a struggle to get the words out, and Lennon knew they were barely understandable.

"No other choice, I'm afraid," Lol made her way over to where Lennon was slumped upon the couch. "If we're going to make this work, it's all got to look authentic."

"So, you *don't* trust me?" Lennon repeated. He was beginning to see a gaping hole in the woman's story about helping him. Was he about to wake up in the middle of yet another murder scene? Or was she simply setting him up to be caught by the real cops and carted off to death row somewhere?

"I'll trust you as much as I need to, Mr. Lennon," Lol said, again with the mysterious act. To Lennon, her words had an unpleasant echo to them and seemed to be coming from someplace far away from her mouth as if she was *thinking* them and he was reading her thoughts. "I've adjusted the dose this time around, so you'll be aware of what's going on around you and *to* you."

"What did you give me?"

"It's sort of my own concoction." Lol appeared pleased with herself, smug even, although her face and its expressions were growing increasingly nebulous for Lennon. "My own very special blend of a muscle relaxant based on *botulinum* and Gamma Hydroxybutyrate – GBH to the uninitiated."

Once again, Lennon attempted to speak as Lol spoke to him like a sommelier explaining the intricacies of a fine wine blend.

Not a sound. Lennon's lips were unpleasantly numb, his tongue frozen to the roof of his mouth.

"The relaxant will give you the appearance of unconsciousness; you'll have control over your eyes and eyelids, though, so use that carefully and don't get caught peeking. The GBH will help you to stay relaxed and might affect your short-term memory. Although, at this dose, it really shouldn't."

Lennon had read about GBH—what father with a young daughter hadn't?—and understood it explained how come he'd had no recollection of getting to any of the crimes Mercer's people had framed him with. It also explained the fragmented flashes of recollection triggered by Lol's intervention: sometimes, with the right stimulus, memories wiped by GBH came back.

"Okay, let's do this." Leaning over, Lol grabbed Lennon's forearms and heaved him upright. Remarkably, he found he could stand on his own two feet, albeit incredibly wobbly. It was as if his legs were made entirely of rubber, held together and moved only by a scant network of tendons.

Lol draped Lennon's left arm around her slender shoulders and maneuvered him toward the door. The young woman was surprisingly strong, Lennon thought. He guessed he outweighed her by a good fifty, sixty pounds, but still she managed to get him outside and into the black-and-white with what seemed to be very little effort. Maybe she'd grown accustomed to manhandling all the contestants she'd drugged over her years on Mercer's gameshow?

With Lennon safely ensconced in the back of the police car, Lol eased herself into the driver's seat and gunned the engine. As the vehicle juddered to life, she twisted around to face her passenger.

"You'll sleep for a while." Her voice echoed around Lennon's skull. "Just long enough to get you where we need to be. You'll remember me at your next location, of course, unlike the previous times. Maybe then, you'll believe what I'm doing here is not part of Mercer's plan."

The woman's lips moved, her words registering moments later in a weird, echoing time-lag. Mustering up what control he could over his failing body, Lennon forced himself to form a few words.

"Please, call me Chase."

Then everything faded out.

Chapter 19

"Who the hell does something like this?" The crime scene investigator fought the urge to throw up his morning coffee into the blood-stained toilet to his left. But that would mean lifting its lid, which would also mean removing what appeared to be the dead woman's uterus and fallopian tubes from it first. Naturally, that was a no-no because, while his team had photographed the entire bathroom, all the body parts had to be bagged and tagged before anything could be moved.

It was sure as all hell gonna be a long day.

"You'd be surprised what an honest-to-God psychopath can do for kicks," the skinny FBI agent told him as they scanned the room in unison. "I have actually seen worse, believe it or not, Mr....?"

"Davison." He'd *definitely* told the special agent his name when they'd met downstairs; it irked the CSI the guy hadn't been bothered to remember it. After all, he'd remembered the FBI guy's name, even though Special Agent Eubank hadn't struck him as being all that memorable.

"CSI Davison," Eubank repeated to himself, a tried-and-trusted memory technique. "Have you unearthed anything that might help us here?"

Davison shook his head. Surely someone from the Bureau would know it was far too early in the investigation to separate what was meaningful from what was not. The only thing for certain was someone with considerable strength and unnatural bloodlust had dismembered poor Mrs. Mitchell and decorated her fancy marble bathroom with her innards. They'd then laid in wait for her husband and young sons to come home before making the kids orphans.

"I understand one of the neighbors saw a cop car leaving the premises not long before the bodies were discovered," Eubank pressed.

"You'll have to speak with Detective Perez about that." Davison had little desire to step on the lead cop's toes and didn't relish getting involved with the FBI. He just wanted to bag and tag and get himself back to the comfort of the laboratory. Sure, he'd be taking the scattered parts of Mrs. Mitchell back with him, but out of the context of her bathroom, and neatly sealed in clear plastic baggies, Davison would be able to disassociate himself from the brutality inflicted upon her.

"Was it a cop who called it in?" Eubank ignored Davison's direction.

"Friends of the kids, as far as I know. Called round to play and found the two boys tied up and the father shot dead." Davison gave Eubank what he'd gleaned from the uniformed cops downstairs in the hopes of the agent leaving him alone.

"They came up here?" Eubank turned slowly around to study how Emma Mitchell's lower intestine was woven between the row of bare lightbulbs surrounding the large mirror over the quaint his-n-hers sinks.

"Thankfully, no. They called 911 as soon as they freed the kids. They're still traumatized at having seen the father, of course. Lucky for them he was only shot in the head and left face down, I suppose."

Eubank gave a barely imperceptible nod. "Silver linings, I guess," he said quietly. "Lord only knows what effect all *this* is going to have on a coupla kids. Can't begin to imagine the years of therapy, can you?"

Davison nodded his agreement, even though it seemed a peculiar segue to make. Still, in his experience, FBI special agents were usually an odd bunch to begin with.

"And where would I find Detective Perez?" Eubank asked.

"He's around somewhere," Davison told him. "He was taking a look around outside when you came in."

"Maybe I'll go look for him, then."

Davison felt a ripple of relief at that. There was just something about Eubank which set his nerves on edge the moment they'd first met downstairs. The guy had just wandered in, flashed his badge at the uniforms on the door, and started asking his questions.

Why he'd homed in on the CSI team was a mystery to Davison – it was as if the man didn't want to speak to the detective leading the investigation. And that was the correct protocol in these circumstances. What also troubled Davison was how the FBI had shown up to the crime scene so quickly.

"I just happened to be in Pensacola International when I got the call," Eubank had told Davison, even before the CSI had asked.

"I'm sure you'll find him. He can't have gone too far," Davison urged, keen to have the pallid-faced man and his expensive suit out of his space. He just wanted to do his job and get the hell out of the literal bloodbath.

As Eubank nodded a cursory goodbye to Davison, his cell rang.

"Gotta get this." Pulling the phone out of an inside pocket, he thumbed the screen to answer and held it to his ear. "Trae, I was just thinking about you."

Having no interest in the agent's call, Davison returned his attention to the job at hand. He'd have to wait for the ME to turn up to take what remained of Mrs. Miller's hollowed-out body out of the bathtub and away, of course. The fact she looked so much like a meticulously dressed stag carcass, all emptied out and drained of blood, didn't help Davison's queasy stomach any.

Then, it would be a matter of picking up the pieces, so to speak, and remembering the woman's eyes were still on the dining table downstairs. The memory of those disembodied eyeballs next to her husband's would stay with Davison for a hell of a long time, that much he knew for certain. And yet, in a tragic kind of way, there was something about it that was almost romantic.

"Yeah, I just got here," Davison heard Eubank lie. "I can let you know more when I do. No, no, there's nothing to suggest it's Chase Lennon again, although they've not looked at the security footage yet."

Eubank flapped Davison a half wave and stepped out of the bathroom, conversation in full flow. "Yes, I understand Detective Broussard *believes* it's your man, but there's nothing to say—" The FBI man sounded more than a tad irritated. "Okay, okay, I'll definitely keep you in the loop, Trae, and you be sure to keep me up to date with any developments on your end. I'm looking for the lead detective here, and as soon as I find him, I should know more. Okay? Gotta go."

CSI Davison listened to the special agent's footsteps retreating down the polished wooden stairs behind him, and breathed a long, loud sigh of relief that he was gone.

Chapter 20

Lennon floated back into consciousness after what seemed an eternity. The concoction of drugs the young woman had slipped into his water had filled his sleeping mind with a whole host of vivid dreams filled with death, blood, and the claustrophobic, panicked sensation of having his every move watched and scrutinized, of being... *hunted*.

The woman's name swam lazily into Lennon's memory: Lol. *Lolita*, like the book and the Jeremy Irons movie Jilly had found so distasteful. So much so, she'd made Lennon switch it off halfway through and insisted they watched *America's Got Talent* instead, as a palate cleanser.

Only, Lol—*his* Lol—was nothing like the pre-teen Dolores Haze. No, she was a full-grown woman who'd apparently been popping up during his time on *The*

Contestant to ensure his continued success at evading capture, only to drug him when it came time to move on.

Lennon recalled with ease her slender frame and soft voice, but her face remained out of focus in his mind, infuriatingly out of reach.

Opening his eyes to dispel the cloying darkness and shake out the splintered fragments of those terrible dreams, Lennon winced at the brightness of the daylight that assaulted them.

Imagined he winced: Lennon's face, along with the entirety of his body, remained paralyzed, wholly unmovable.

It was a strange sensation, that of being aware of his body but unable to move any part of it, except for his eyelids and eyes. When Lol had told him about the muscle relaxant, just as it was kicking in, he'd imagined it would be like a dentist numbing the mouth prior to a root canal, only on a whole-body scale, that he'd be unable to *feel* anything, along with losing power over every muscle.

Instead, Lennon was aware of everything, from the crick in his neck from laying across the gray cloth back seat of the small car with his head pressed tight against the door, to the dull ache in his back and throbbing pain in his folded-up calf muscles that threatened the agony of cramp. In all, Lennon's body felt just the same as it always had, only he couldn't move it. So, if a cramp did take root in any of his muscles, there would be nothing he could do about it except suffer through the agony.

He'd not even be able to scream.

A fresh wave of panic gripped Lennon's gut. He'd read stories before about people who'd woken up during surgery to find themselves unable to let the doctors know they were awake. Eyes taped closed, all muscles taken out of their control, there was literally nothing they could do to communicate with the people slicing them open. With morbid fascination, Lennon had learned how such unfortunate people were aware of every cut of the scalpel, every clamped artery, every sawed bone; he could only begin to imagine the sheer terror they must have experienced throughout hour upon hour of such excruciating pain.

Until now, of course.

Voices.

Muted, they came from outside the car, which was surprisingly cool even though the engine was switched off. He'd not been in there long at all.

"That's the best you could do?" A man's voice with the slightest hint of a southern state's twang.

"Short notice. You know how it is. I had to ditch the black-and-white – far too conspicuous." The woman's voice, Lennon recognized immediately: Lol. Relieved her drug cocktail had not wiped his memory of their meeting in the for sale house, Lennon wondered if she was still wearing the cop uniform.

A flash of returning memory: Lol in an ill-fitting maid's outfit.

"Poor guy's been squashed up in this thing for over an hour," the male voice was closer now. "Mercer's not gonna be pleased with that."

"It's hardly my fault you took your own sweet time getting here for pick up. I can't imagine Mercer being delighted about *that* fact, either." Lol sounded defensive and more than a touch exasperated.

"Okay, okay, don't get your panties in a bunch, missus," the man countered as he pulled open the rear passenger door of Lennon's prison.

Lennon closed his eyes as light and warm day air filled the confines of the vehicle and his head lolled out against the door frame. A sharp pain radiated out from his temple as skull connected with metal, twinkles of light danced in the darkness behind his eyelids.

"See what you did?" The man admonished Lol. "Coulda cracked his damned head open."

"He's perfectly fine," Lol defended with a grunt. "Just get him out and into your SUV before anyone comes by."

"Nobody's coming by here," the man argued as he lifted Lennon's head from the door frame, cradling his limp neck in what felt to be an enormous hand. "You picked a good spot here – middle of friggin' nowhere. No wonder I had trouble finding the place."

"You never heard of GPS? So much easier than maps and guesswork." Lol was closer now. Lennon caught the sweet, vanilla scent of her perfume.

"Mercer doesn't like us to use GPS, you know that. Too easy to track." The man had his hands under Lennon's armpits now and was heaving him from the car.

As his body unfolded and Lennon embraced the sweet relief in his legs, he heard footsteps.

"You two. Come give me a hand over here," the man called out with a grunt of exertion. "This one's heavier than he looks."

Lennon noted how both the man and Lol were careful to not use names at all. Were they wary of such detail sinking into his subconscious as he slept?

Then, more hands were on Lennon's body, manhandling him up from the cloth seat, supporting his weight as he was carried away from the car in the sunlight. As the warm breeze caressed Lennon's clammy cheeks and forehead, he became aware of his body being damp with sweat. He figured it was most likely a side-effect of Lol's drugs combined with being stuck in the compact car for an hour or so.

"One, two… *three*." The man let out a loud groan and Lennon was deposited onto a cool leather car seat, this one considerably roomier. Lennon's legs were stretched out to be comfortable, and a soft cushion was placed under his head. There was a distinctive *new car* smell to the vehicle, which always triggered the word *success* in Chase Lennon's mind.

"Sleeping like a baby," a new voice, deep, resonant, declared with satisfaction. "How long's it going to last this time?"

"Long enough to get him to the airport," Lol replied, climbing into the SUV's shotgun seat. "Providing you don't get us lost again."

The man harumphed and mumbled something beneath his breath that sounded to Lennon a lot like *uptight bitch.*

If Lol heard him, she chose to let it slide. "We'll meet you two at Mobile Regional. Should take us around an hour, depending on traffic." She addressed the others in her party like she was running the show; was it possible her role was far more than that of a background player who made things happen? Lennon heard nothing by means of complaint from them - just footsteps and a car's doors opening.

Once the SUV was on its way, Lennon chanced a peek around, cracking his eyes open a smidgeon at a time, one after the other.

With his head being behind the driver's seat, Lennon was confident the driver wouldn't be able to see his eyes open. If he strained them to the left, Lennon was able to just about make out the side of the man's head and thought he recognized the full ginger beard and white T-shirt.

A nebulous recollection of the bearded man outside a trailer, a woman's corpse being pulled from the trunk of a sedan.

Lol sat silently beside her driver, focusing on the road ahead as if making a determined effort not to look behind at their passenger. Lennon figured she'd know he was taking a look around and had no desire to draw attention.

He saw she'd changed out of her police officer uniform into faded blue jeans and a pale pink tank top with spaghetti straps that showed off slim, tan shoulders and toned upper arms.

Without the ability to move his head or neck, Lennon soon grew tired of peering around the SUV. From what he could tell, it was a white Toyota, it had beige leather seats and probably looked just like all the millions of other nondescript Japanese SUVs out on America's roads. Perfect for blending in.

Closing his eyes again, Lennon focused on the bizarre sensation of being aware of every bump in the road, the gentle rocking motion of the vehicle, the coolness of the seat, all without being able to move. Concentrating his mind inward just as his sensei had taught him so many years before, Lennon battled against the rising panic threatening to overwhelm him.

The absolute loss of control was far more disturbing than Lennon had imagined, and he wished Lol had deprived him of consciousness as she had the other times she'd drugged him even if it meant waking up in another bloody murder scene and not knowing how the hell he got there.

Lennon must have dozed off, because the next thing he was aware of was the SUV gliding to a gentle stop and the sound of aircraft roaring overhead.

"You're gonna have to help me get him out," the bearded man was saying. "God only knows where those two have gotten to."

"They had the cop's car to dispose of," Lol snapped back. "Cut them some slack, will you?"

"How long does it take to lose a piece of crap like that? You ask me, they're just taking advantage."

"It takes as long as it takes. Can we just concentrate on getting the contestant on the plane?" Lol opened her door and climbed out of the vehicle. The conversation was clearly over, as far as she was concerned.

Lol and her associate skillfully maneuvered Lennon from the back seat and carried him the short way to the awaiting jet. Of course, Mercer used a private jet, it really was the only way to move contestants quickly around the country, and undetected. Lennon was surprised he'd not worked that out much sooner.

A keen small jet enthusiast, Lennon risked a clandestine glimpse of the plane and saw it was a Cessna Citation, most likely the XLS model, in pristine white. The Citation was one of the more popular models among private jet owners—another smart ploy by Mercer's people to not stand out in the private airfield. Personally, Lennon had always dreamed of owning the Dassault Falcon 8X, but with a cool $50m price tag, so it still remained uncomfortably out of his reach.

Maybe he'd spoil himself with one when he won *The Contestant*, along with the yacht he'd always promised himself he'd buy and name *Lady Jilly*?

Both big ticket luxuries together would barely even put a dent in a billion dollars plus

It was disappointing that he wasn't able to enjoy the luxurious comfort of the small jet. Both Lol and her bearded cohort had seated themselves close by and he couldn't risk opening his eyes and giving himself away.

He'd always loved flying private and at that moment would have loved nothing more than to sip on chilled, ridiculously expensive champagne, nibble on delightful canapes, and take in the sumptuous surroundings as the plane soared high into the clouds. After all, owning his jet was one of the perks of being rich.

Instead, though, Lennon pulled his thoughts inward once more, and somehow managed to fall asleep.

Chapter 21

The jarring bump and squeal of tires on tarmac woke Lennon from his deep and mercifully dreamless sleep. Momentarily forgetting himself in his waking fog, he allowed his eyes to open.

Thankfully, Lol and the bearded man were otherwise occupied; both stared out of their respective windows as the ground rushed up to meet the small jet. Their two suited associates had evidently made it to the jet in time for takeoff – they both dozed, open-mouthed and gently snoring, in their seats at the rear of the plane.

"Showtime," the bearded man said with a thin smile.

"I guess it is." Lol yawned, her voice weary.

"We've landed at Henderson Executive airport," the pilot's voice over the intercom startled Lennon. He snapped his eyes shut, then opened them just a crack. "Local time is 3 PM."

So, they'd transported him all the way to Las Vegas for the next segment of *The Contestant*. They'd flown him into the smaller airport, of course, no doubt having paid off the officials there to keep schtum, which made much more sense than using Harry Reid International. Even with Mercer's seemingly endless pots of money to grease the wheels, Lennon knew it would be the Devil's own job to fly under the radar at such a major airport. Literally.

Vegas had to be one of Lennon's most favorite places in the world. He'd partied there a great many times over the years, both before his success with Imagine Reality and after. More often than not, he'd visit the party city *sans* Jilly, preferring to enjoy himself than have the old ball-and-chain holding him back.

There were far too many hedonistic delights to be savored in Las Vegas to be hobbled by the wife, and, thankfully, Jilly was smart enough to know better than to ask her husband what he got up to on his trips there.

What happens in Vegas, stays in Vegas, right?

Only, this time it was going to be vastly different and far from pleasurable. Knowing what lay in store for him had Lennon questioning Lol's decision to not render him totally unconscious for this particular round of the game.

A big part of him would have chosen to be oblivious to what was going on and have simply woken up in whatever scenario Mercer's minions had prepared to further sully his name and have him running like a terrified animal. Still, he reckoned the young woman had her reasons, and he hoped she'd stick to her word to explain them the next time they got together.

Unless, of course, her ruse was just that: another convoluted part of *The Contestant*?

Despite Lol's ostensibly sincere motives, that grain of doubt still festered at the back of Lennon's mind. However, he had other choice than to go along with her plan;

whichever way the game was playing out, he was nothing more than a pawn at this point.

All he *could* do was follow the young producer's lead and hope everything somehow worked out in his favor.

"I'll leave you to it," Lol said to her bearded cohort with a cursory nod toward Lennon's ostensibly sleeping body. "I have things to prepare." Unbuckling her seat belt, she stood and stretched her arms above her head to reveal an unflattering couple day's armpit stubble.

"You always do," there was a touch of humor in the man's voice. "Typical woman, leave all the heavy work to the menfolk."

The two shared what Lennon thought was a strained, awkward laugh as Lol stepped away from her seat and made her way to the door in synch with the pilot opening it. Hot, dry desert heat filled the cabin as she stepped out into the sunlight.

"Come on, you two," the bearded guy roused the two suited men. Again, no names. "We gotta get our lucky contestant to his next magical destination."

"They'd better have a car ready for us this time," one of the guys moaned.

"And not some piece of crap electric thing, neither," his compadre added. "Took us an hour to charge that last one up."

Peering out through one of the Cessna's small windows, the bearded man put their minds at rest. "Mercer's organized us a Hummer," he said with a satisfied smirk. "Most likely LPG, but at least ya don't have to plug the mother in like a kiddie's toy to make it go."

That appeared to placate the two younger men. They then turned their attention to Lennon, who squeezed his eyes tight and continued to play possum.

"We'll grab him, you go get the Hummer fired up." Lennon heard one of them say.

"I wasn't gonna carry the big lug, anyway," the bearded guy snapped. Any trace of humor he'd had for Lol was well and truly absent with the suited pair. "You two just do your job and quit telling me what to do."

With that, the bearded guy's footsteps retreated from the cabin and on down the steps to the tarmac. Then, as the two suited men lifted his flaccid, supposedly unconscious body between them, the awaiting Hummer sprang to life outside.

"Any idea where we're taking him?"

"No, sir. I guess we'll find out when we get there."

"Nothing ever changes, certainly not in the whole seven years I've been working on this dumb show."

"Might be different once we're producers. They *always* know what's going on."

"You've seen the stuff the producers make us do for the show." There was lethargy to the man's tone, along with a slight breathlessness through the exertion of carrying the dead weight of Lennon's limp body. "You wouldn't want that job in a million years."

"Must be good money, though. I reckon that takes the sting out of most of it."

A long, world-weary sigh. "I wouldn't bank on it, buddy. They couldn't pay me enough to have all that psycho stuff on my conscience."

Sunlight warmed Lennon's face as he was carried down the jet's steps and bundled into the Hummer. The Nevada air was unbearably hot in his lungs after the cool comfort of the Cessna's air conditioning; it was as if Las Vegas was offering up its own personal welcome.

Chapter 22

"So, I caught my best friend in bed with the wife," Dickie Kaye—plain old Matthew Smith offstage—related the joke's setup to the sparse audience of no more than a couple dozen. Ticket sales had been on a downward slump the past six months or so, and Circus Circus management were starting to get antsy.

"So, I said, 'what are you doing, humping my wife, you dumbass? I *have* to!'"

Pause for the ripple of light laughter. Most of the audience were well on their way to being nicely drunk on the casino's cheap cocktails and free beer, even though this was only the early evening performance.

"…'and will you please stop while I'm talking to you!'"

A marginally bigger laugh that time; the hilarious mental imagery that went along with that line was one of Dickie's favorites. It tickled him every time he wheeled out the well-worn gag, which had been twice a day and three times on Saturdays for the past three years.

"So, I dragged his naked ass out of my marital bed and down into my tool shed in the backyard." Three years dredging up all the old material was a hefty comedown for *the* Dickie Kaye, who'd appeared on SNL more than a dozen times back in the 80s *and* had his own show on ABC – the unimaginatively titled *Dickie Kaye Show*.

He'd been a big name back then, when all the new big names were only just getting started in the biz. Those same names who overtook him and went onto fame and unimaginable fortune while he dallied with women, booze, and the white showbiz powder.

"I stuck his dick into my vice, tightened it up, and snapped off the handle…"

Titters of anticipation spread through the audience. They knew full-well what was coming, yet the expectation still excited them. To Dickie Kaye's mind, it was akin to seeing the Stones live in concert and praying they'd play *Satisfaction*, even though you'd heard it a million times before.

"Then I pulled out a box cutter…"

More titters.

"You're not gonna cut my dick off, are you, Dickie?"

Make with another comedic pause. The anticipation in the room was palpable.

"I told him, no, you are… I'm setting fire to the shed."

And step back to revel in the laughter and adulation.

As drunk as they were, Dickie's audience absolutely *loved* the gag and adored him. Some got to their feet, applauding wildly, whistling raucously, and others followed suit. Soon, everyone joined in the standing ovation for the one and only Dickie Kaye, comedic star of yesteryear.

"Thank you, and goodnight!" Dickie popped the mic back on its stand and repositioned it center stage for the next act, a Canadian feminist comic who Dickie didn't find the least bit amusing, what with her period jokes and all.

Now, *that* was why ticket sales were down the freakin' toilet. It was the likes of Jenny Roslin with her unshaven pits and potty mouth that were putting the paying public off the comedy shows. And to think Circus Circus was supposed to be a family hotel!

Dickie made his way off the stage as the applause died down. The shed gag had been his second encore and he'd had enough. Leave 'em wanting more, and all that. He was done, for now at least – his next forty-five minutes was at eleven.

Plenty time to enjoy a few complementary drinks, a cheap steak dinner, and the couple hookers he'd had one of the hotel's concierges arrange. He'd slipped the guy an extra fifty to make sure the young ladies—one Black, one Chinese—would be waiting for him in his suite for a little fun time straight after the show.

Just what Dickie needed.

"Thanks, Sasha." Dickie smiled at the stagehand who looked far too young for the job, for *any* job, come to think of it. Still, she was exceptionally good at making sure everything ran smoothly behind the scenes *and* she was easy on the eye. A tad *too* youthful for Dickie's discerning tastes, but give the gal a year or two…

"See ya tonight, Mr. Kaye," Sasha trilled after him. "You did good out there."

Dickie flapped a hand at her by means of goodbye and strode toward the fire door. He *refused* to use the same exit as the audience, they'd only want to stop him for autographs and tell him how much they loved the *Dickie Kaye Show* back in the day.

And he didn't need that, not when there were two hot, more-than-willing babes waiting for him.

Dickie's suite was on the 30th floor of the West Tower, which made for quite the walk when he was tired and his arthritic knee was playing up. It was one of the older rooms, which needed refurbishing and still smelled of stale cigarettes even though they'd banned smoking years ago. Dickie made a mental note, as he did every night, to ask Management if they could move him to a room that didn't stink and was closer to the gigs.

Finally at his room, 3032, Dickie slid his keycard in the slot and, taking his cue from the tiny green light, pushed open the door.

"What the—?"

"Come in, Mr. Kaye, close the door."

The comedian's first reaction was that he'd stumbled into a carefully staged, albeit elaborate, prank the likes of which they used to do on *Candid Camera* a long, long time ago. If it wasn't for the redneck guy with the long, ginger beard, wearing nothing but tighty-whities and pointing what appeared to be a black Smith and Wesson handgun at his face, of course.

Dickie Kaye did as he was told, shocked into complying by the sight of the two naked young ladies hanging together by their ankles from the chandelier in the center of his room. They slowly rotated like some ghoulish art centerpiece. Both were dead, quite obviously so, their bodies slit throat to pudendum, innards heaped and entwined on the blood-soaked carpet beneath them.

As Dickie stumbled toward one of the suite's couches—he *had* to sit before he fell over, even though it meant dumping himself down on the expansive blood stain that soaked into the cushions—the girls rotated to face him. To his dismay, Dickie saw they had no eyes: dark, hollowed-out sockets stared across the room at him.

He also noted at the back of his mind that, while one of the girls was deliciously dark-skinned, the other was definitely Korean. That pissed him off, he'd specifically requested a *Chinese* girl!

Odd what goes through the mind when faced with gruesome absurdity and a gun in the face.

"What is… *this*?" It was all Dickie could think of to say as he flopped down onto the couch, trying to take in the surreal horror in the suite he'd called home for the past three years. A large part of his racing mind still attempted to convince him it was all just some kind of sick, elaborate hoax, even though common sense told him otherwise. The blood, the gore, the stink of spilled blood and the contents of ripped bowels assaulting his senses were all too horrifically *real*.

"It's all part of the game, Mr. Kaye." The bearded man was remarkably soft spoken. "You're about to become very famous indeed."

Dickie opened his mouth to tell the intruder he was already famous enough, thank you, but thought better of it. He figured sarcasm wasn't the best ploy in any attempt to talk his way out of whatever it was that was going on.

The guy with the ginger beard was not alone. There were two younger guys in dark suits standing statue-still in the background, over by the floor-length curtains covering the windows looking out onto the back of the hotel— management were far too tight-fisted to give Dickie Kaye a room with a view.

They held their hands folded in front of them, as if protecting their respective crotches from some expected menace. There was also a young-ish woman hovering in the doorway to the ensuite bathroom. Sweetly attractive under thickly applied makeup and fake lashes, she was dressed only in black panties and a bra so skimpy almost all of her breasts were on show.

She reminded Dickie of so many of Vegas's aging hookers he'd become acquainted with over the years. Only, she lacked the ubiquitous deadness in her eyes and track marks up the insides of her arms, which had Dickie wondering just what the hell she was doing in his room.

And then there was the other guy, the one sleeping on the couch opposite. Half sitting, half slumped, eyes tight shut, mouth sagging open, a barely perceptible snore rattled in his throat.

He looked kind of familiar. Dickie had the feeling he'd seen him on the TV recently but couldn't quite place the show.

The guy with the beard walked across to stand over Dickie, the gun aimed directly at him.

"Welcome to *The Contestant*, Mr. Kaye," he said. "I'm sure you'll appreciate the audience you're getting tonight. They are an exclusive bunch, but very attentive." He glanced around the room. It was a gesture Dickie got the understanding he was supposed to follow.

Tiny red dots of light peppered the hotel suite, each one giving away the location of what Dickie knew were miniature spy cameras. He'd secreted enough about his room, especially in the bathroom, over the years to know a spy camera LED when he saw one. Just who the hell was filming this hellish scene, and, perhaps more importantly, *why*?

"Who are you people?" Dickie finally managed to form the words. "What do you want with me? I don't have money, but I can get my hands on some…"

Dickie Kay's name still carried enough weight in town to allow him to get his hands on hard cash if he ever needed it. Sure, the interest rates were criminally high, but that was par for the course when none of the banks in Vegas would touch him with a ten-foot pole.

A gentle laugh, muffled through the bushy beard. "We're not here for your money, Mr. Kaye," he said. "But thank you very much for your kind offer, all the same."

"Then what—?" Dickie's heart pounded, his mouth was desert-dry, he couldn't stop his hands from trembling. He knew he was in deep trouble, the kind of trouble that would probably end up with him dead or spending the rest of his life in jail, or maybe even worse. How could he even begin to explain two dead, eviscerated hookers in his room? Would anyone ever believe he'd just walked in to find them disemboweled and hanging like that?

It seemed highly unlikely.

"I just need for you to stay calm, Mr. Kaye," the guy said. "All this will be over soon enough." He shot a fleeting glance across the room at the fake hooker in the black bra and panties.

Dickie saw his chance, most likely the only one he'd get, and moved far quicker than he ever thought his sixty-nine-year-old body was capable of.

Jumping to his feet, Dickie made a grab for the gun. His hands clasped the bearded guy's and he pushed the gun to the side, toward the new flat screen TV, which had somehow replaced the old tube TV that had been there when he'd stepped out to do his show.

The gun felt cold, hard, and heavy, the man's hands warm and soft. Dickie focused on keeping the weapon pointing away from himself as he used his body weight to force the gunman backward in the hopes of making him lose his balance and hit the carpet. If he could, Dickie figured he might just have a chance of getting out of the room.

The bearded man was much stronger than his wiry frame intimated. Grunting loudly, he fought against Dickie's grip to maneuver the gun back between them, this time pointing at the comedian's rounded beer gut.

"Enough!"

The new voice came from one of the suited men by the window. His attention distracted, Dickie looked over and saw they had both reached inside their respective jacket pockets and pulled out a gun each—both identical to the one their bearded colleague had prodding into his stomach—which were pointed directly at him.

The woman had ducked back into the bathroom, no doubt to avoid becoming collateral damage should fingers become too trigger-happy. It was like a scene from the hackneyed Scorsese movies he loved to watch on the hotel's pay-per-view when he wasn't entertaining hookers.

"Sit down, Mr. Kaye." The guy jabbed his gun's muzzle into Dickie's belly.

Hard.

Defeated, Dickie did as he was told. As he sank back down onto the couch, he eyed the gun pointing once more into his face and figured he'd blown his one and only opportunity to get himself out of whatever he'd gotten himself into this time.

Now what?

"We really need to get going with this," the bearded guy said. Dickie couldn't be sure if he was addressing him or the guys in suits.

Most likely the latter, Dickie thought, as the two made their way across from the window, guns still trained on him.

A flash of movement, of bare skin and black lace, and the woman reappeared by the bathroom door. Deliciously barefoot, she padded across the room to where the sleeping guy lay, her trim body a wonderful distraction. In any other circumstance, Dickie would have been turning on the old charm and flashing what cash he could muster in an attempt to get her out of those tight panties.

There came a sudden, loud *click* as she opened the black-handled switchblade she'd been hiding in her hand.

Its keen, silver blade glinted wickedly at Dickie, so full of malicious promise.

Starting at the harsh, metallic sound, in his moment of panic, Dickie realized where he recognized Sleeping Guy from. He was Chase Lennon, the dangerous fugitive law enforcement across at least three states were looking for, the rich realtor turned brutal serial killer who left nothing but a trail of corpses behind him.

And, as the sleeping murderer began to stir, as the woman in the black underwear approached with the knife, Dickie Kaye understood fully there was no way he was leaving his cheap-ass suite at Circus Circus alive.

Chapter 23

L ennon shifted his right leg ever so slightly, surprised to discover the leaden limb actually moved under his command. Trying his arms, he was pleased to discover mobility was returning to those, too.

Of course, he had to maintain the illusion of unconsciousness in order to not give the game away to Lol's accomplices, even though he had been fully awake and aware of everything going on around him since coming to on the jet and being transported to Circus Circus.

Which meant, unfortunately, he'd been witness to everything the man with the ginger beard, Lol, and their goons in overly expensive suits had done in that hotel suite.

Sneaking furtive peeks to avoid detection from where they'd deposited him on the suite's couch, Lennon had looked on as Lol helped her team set up the miniature cameras around the room before retiring to the bathroom. Lennon had been surprised at how the four had worked in a well-coordinated silence, as if they'd gone through this routine a thousand times before. Barely a word had passed between them, and when they did speak, as always, names were never used.

Then, once the suited pair had hidden in the bedroom, the two real hookers had arrived. They'd appeared quite unfazed to be greeted by Lol clad only in her underwear, along with an equally disrobed bearded guy wearing only white boxers, and not the famous Dickie Kaye – seemed to Lennon like the comedian was one of their regular clients.

"Tonight's a very special night for Mr. Kaye," Lol had reassured the girls as Lennon admired her trim, toned body through slitted eyelids. "He said we're to make ourselves comfortable and wait for him to come join us."

"This is gonna ya cost extra." The Chinese hooker spoke around the wad of gum she'd been chewing, her accent distinctly east-coast.

"A *lot* extra," her Black friend chipped in. "I don't usually do orgies, or girl-on-girl, for that matter." Lennon watched her reach out to stroke Lol's bare arm. "But I guess I could make an exception for you, sugar."

"Another two grand." The Chinese girl had insisted as Lol smiled suggestively at her companion. "*Each*."

"That won't be a problem, ladies," the bearded guy told them as he brought a pair of full Champagne flutes across from the drinks trolley over by the kitchenette. "Whatever it takes to make you both happy."

Lol had drugged the booze, of course, and before either of the hookers could even suspect what was happening, they were both flopped down and completely immobile on the couch opposite Lennon. They were then neatly positioned by Lol and the bearded guy to look as if they'd simply had too much to drink.

Then Lol had slit the Chinese girl's throat with that onyx-handled switchblade of hers. As cool and calm as you like, she'd jabbed the sharp point deep into the side of the girl's neck and sliced it forward.

There'd been a sharp gasp of air from the girl's severed windpipe and a thick gush of blood stained the hooker's skimpy shirt and bare legs scarlet. It splashed onto Lol's smooth, white skin – clearly her state of undress had been forward planning in the interests of cleaning off inevitable blood splatter. And, for a split second, the hooker's eyes had looked wild, panicked, terrified, before death came for her.

The Black hooker had glanced across at Lennon—the only movement available to her, thanks to Lol's heinous expertise with pharmaceuticals—and their eyes had met, albeit briefly. Lennon caught desperate pleading there, along with a sad resignation that she would share the same fate as her companion.

It was a fleeting moment that would haunt Chase Lennon for the rest of his days.

Then, she, too, was dispatched by Lol and that razor-sharp blade with such uncaring ease. Lennon couldn't help but wonder just how many times she'd performed the same task for Mercer's sick gameshow.

Lennon had closed his eyes after that. More to block out what Lol and her team were doing to the hookers' corpses than to avoid giving himself away. He could *hear* everything, though, and that was more than enough.

As the Black hooker lay dying, gurgling loudly, coughing up dark red foam, as she drowned in her own blood, the other two members of Lol's team emerged from the bedroom to pitch in with the bearded guy hoisting the bodies up from the chandelier while Lol stood back and watched. Lennon didn't peek to see if they, too, were all-but naked. He had little desire to find that particular detail out.

Still mostly immobile and not daring to move what little of himself he could, Lennon had no option but to listen to the wet sounds of rending flesh and guts slopping out onto the floor with a sodden *slap-slap-slap* that conjured a whole manner of grotesque mental images in his sickened imagination. As the stink of spilled blood and ruptured innards assaulted his nostrils, he was actually pleased to find Lol's concoction of drugs had rendered him incapable of throwing up.

"Please, no—"

The ageing comic's desperate plea broke Lennon from his grim reverie. Back in the moment, Lennon couldn't help but look on with morbid fascination as Lol handed the switchblade to her bearded associate. She offered a weak, forced smile that looked to Lennon to be apologetic, sheepish even. Perhaps there was a grain of humanity in the young woman after all?

Lennon certainly hoped so, because his life was literally in her hands right now. Not that he had much choice in the matter, of course, but seeing Lol's hesitation in dispatching the once-renowned Dickie Kaye brought Lennon a little cold comfort.

There was no such hesitation from the bearded guy. Without further ado, and ignoring Dickie's feeble protests, he batted away the comedian's hands with ease and stuck the knife into his exposed throat.

No blood spilled out of the wound until the bearded guy slid the blade back out, at which an arc of bright scarlet shot out to catch him squarely in the chest and paint his wiry body from neck to knees.

Lennon closed his eyes. He'd seen enough death in that hotel room to last him a lifetime and had no desire to watch the old man take his last gurgling breaths as he collapsed sideways on the couch.

"I'll leave you to stage all this." Lennon heard the bearded man say, even as Dickie Kaye still struggled in vain with both hands to stem the pulsing flow of blood jetting from his neck. "We need to get to the next location."

"You know I got it," Lol replied with confidence. "You guys take the cameras."

Lennon chanced a peek, opening his eyes just a crack. A semi-naked Lol, the bearded guy glistening wet and red, and the pair of suits made their way around the hotel room to where the tiny red lights sat unblinking and taking in everything going on, collecting them up as they went.

The bearded guy stripped off his underpants as he strode bare-assed naked and with definite purpose into the bathroom. On his way, he placed Lol's switchblade onto the credenza next to the flatscreen, alongside the two pairs of eyeballs that stared, unseeing, at the carnage he'd helped create.

As the unmistakable sound of the shower wafted over to Lennon and steam puffed out through the bathroom door, Lol made her way into the bedroom. Despite himself, despite everything happening around him, Lennon couldn't help but admire just how good the gal's ass looked, barely contained within those tight, black panties.

"Ya think he's dead now?" one of the suits asked the other as he skirted around the hookers suspended like dressed deer in the center of the room. He eyed the comedian on the blood-drenched couch.

"Looks like he is to me," his companion replied with a flat, disinterested tone. "He's quit moving. That's something, I guess."

"She'll make sure he's gone before she leaves." A nod in the general direction of the bedroom. "Always does."

"Nice gig if you can get it. Producing, I mean."

The suits nodded in unison.

"How long do ya think before we get a chance at that gig?" one asked.

His opposite shrugged. "I've been doing this job four years now, going on five. And not as much as a sniff at a promotion in all that time."

"That sucks, man." The guy plucked one of the diminutive cameras from where it was stuck to the side of a huge, framed print of Siegfried and Roy and one of their white tigers.

"Wonder if this was *the* big cat," one of the suits scrutinized the picture.

"The one that nearly killed him?"

"Serves them right, if ya ask me. Animals like that aren't meant to be performing in a circus or whatever. They ought to be out and running free."

"Like in a zoo?"

"Like in the jungles, idiot."

The two laughed.

"My daddy always used to say: You play with tigers, you get what you get."

"Speaking of which... *she's* looking *hot* today, parading around in her drawers like that. Ought to be a law against it." Another nod toward the suite's bedroom.

"Makes for good TV, I guess," the other suit said. "Easier for her to get cleaned up, too, although it'd be even better if she got *all* naked."

"Hell yeah. Now that's something I'd give a month's wages to see – maybe even two."

At that, Lol reappeared from the bedroom in a flash of gold. She'd evidently ditched the black underwear in favor of a barely-there, gold lame dress that clung to her every curve, rode up almost all the way to the curve of her ass cheeks, and was scooped so low at the front there seemed to be hardly much point to her wearing the thing at all.

She remained barefoot. "You got something you'd like to say to me?" She skewered the suit over by the picture with a withering stare

"N-no, ma'am," he stammered and went about collecting the last of the cameras.

"Let's keep it that way, shall we?" Lol made her way over to where Lennon pretended to be unconscious, strength creeping back into his body with each passing minute. Fishing behind the couch, she retrieved a small, dark blue carry-on case.

"Everything alright in here?" The bearded guy emerged from the bathroom dressed in jeans, white wifebeater T, and dark brown cowboy boots. His hair and beard were wet and plastered down from the shower, which didn't seem to bother him too much. "We gotta get going," he growled at the suits. "You both done here?"

The two told him yes in unison.

"Good." He turned to Lol. "We'll meet you at the next location, then."

Nodding, Lol rummaged through the carry-on and pulled out a small, silver revolver.

Then the bearded guy and his pair of suited lackeys were gone. They closed the suite's door quietly behind them and set off along the hallway. Lennon counted their footsteps until they faded away into the distance.

"You can quit play-acting now," Lol told him as she placed the gun just so next to the TV. "It's just the two of us now."

Lennon let out a loud groan and slowly shifted his arms and legs. They were still somewhat leaden, as if he'd just awoken from a long, deep sleep.

He took in a sweeping look around the room, finally able to take in the full scope of the horror around him.

"So, now you know." Lol produced a length of rope from the bag and coiled it neatly next to the gun. Then she added the ubiquitous brown bottles of nondescript tablets to the grim collage.

"Yeah, now I know." Fighting the rising wave of nausea threatening to swamp him, Lennon truly wished he *didn't* know. "Why keep me awake, though?" he asked. "Through all of… *this*." The vague sweep of a hand in the direction of the two eviscerated hookers and the bled-out comedian hardly seemed enough to emphasize the mess Lol and her associates had left in their wake.

"There'll be plenty of time for me to explain everything later. For now, we have to get you out of here." A tinge of panic edged Lol's voice; she appeared edgier than Lennon could recall seeing her so far. "Can you walk?"

Lennon struggled his ass off the couch and, although his legs felt a tad rubbery, he managed to stand on his own two feet. The act of standing up served to dissipate the remnants of the drug's influence upon Lennon's body, and he was pretty much good to go.

"Good," Lol smiled nervously. "I have a car waiting for us in the lot behind the hotel – I had a contact of mine I can trust park it up a couple days ago. We'll take the stairs – no cameras back there."

"And in here?" Lennon looked around with suspicion, even though he'd observed Lol's goons sweeping the place clean.

Lol shook her head. "I'm supposed to film you waking up." Getting to her feet, she produced a small camera from the bag. "The footage they shot earlier will be edited and AI-ed to make it look like you were the one doing all the killing. It's pretty damn clever what they can do with computer stuff these days."

"And what role are you playing this time?" Lennon eyed the young woman up and down, taking in the clinging gold dress and more than ample amount of cleavage on display. "You're not gonna be all that believable as the maid this time."

Lol nodded toward the deceased hookers hanging from the cheesy light fitting. "I was supposed to tell you I was one of them," she said. "Booked by the late, great Dickie Kaye for an evening of debauched group sex, which was ruined by you forcing your way in here and wreaking havoc."

"Why did I not kill you, then?" It was a plot hole so obvious Lennon couldn't fail to spot it.

"I was in the bathroom when you came in and you never bothered to look in there." Lol gave him a cynical smile.

"Keeping it simple, eh?" It was one of Lennon's favorite business mantras: why over-complicate things when you had no reason have to?

"Exactly." Lol padded softly across to the flatscreen, taking care to step over Kaye's feet and around the congealing bloodstain beneath the suspended corpses. There, she picked up the switchblade the bearded guy had left for her, wrinkled her nose at the drying blood on its keen edge. A push of the silver button and the blade retracted. Without a hint of embarrassment, she reached up the back hem of the dress and secreted the knife in the waistband of her matching gold thong panties.

Ever the gentleman, Lennon averted his eyes.

"Crap!"

Lennon spun around quickly at Lol's exclamation, almost losing his balance. He saw Lol frozen still, staring wide-eyed, mouth agape, at the dark space beneath the TV.

There, Lennon espied what had caught the young woman's attention: a tiny red light glowed out at them both, a glowing, accusing eye. One of her suited colleagues had evidently neglected to remove one of the spy cameras from Dickie Kaye's suite.

"Does this mean they're still watching us?" Lennon already knew the answer to the question but couldn't help but voice it.

Lol nodded and cautiously picked up the tiny camera. It was no bigger than a Bic lighter, but she handled it as if the thing was about to sprout tiny, sharp teeth and sink them into her fingers. She pressed the button at its back firmly, and the little red light died.

She then looked across at Lennon, her face a mask of concern.

Suddenly, the suite's door flew open, startling them both, and in strode one of the suited men. He had a cell phone clutched in one hand, a small, slate-gray Glock in the other, and a sickly, knowing grin plastered across his bestubbled face.

"Gotchya!" He pushed the suite's door shut with a swift backward kick. It closed behind him with a resounding *slam*.

"I *knew* you were up to something." He spoke directly at Lol, his eyes not leaving hers as the two stared hard, menacing, at one another. "The others have suspected things have been off with you since the last show you produced on, but I *knew*. You've been going off script and not dosing him properly."

"I guess that makes you the smart one," Lol said with a cutely disarming smile. As she took a step toward the guy, his knuckles whitened as he gripped the Glock's handle tighter still. "I'll bet the others are really impressed with all your smart insights about me."

"The others don't know."

Lennon scrutinized the suit's face and saw no outward sign of the guy lying. Whether it was a good thing or not remained to be seen. He did note, however, Lol appeared a touch more confident upon hearing the information. She took another couple small steps forward.

"Keeping it to yourself," Lol mused. "Another smart move. And here I am assuming the feed from the camera you accidentally on purpose forgot to pick up was going out live."

"Do you think I'm *that* stupid?" The guy raised his cell phone as if to show Lol something important. All Lennon saw on its screen was what appeared to be a still of the hotel suite, complete with dangling corpses and a dead comedian. "I streamed the feed to here, so I could keep an eye on what you were up to and catch you in the act. It's all recorded, of course."

"Of course." Lol absently fiddled with the low neckline of her dress, which exposed just a touch more of her breasts.

"This is my promotion right here." Again, the guy in the suit raised his phone in Lol's direction for emphasis. "Once this gets back to Mercer, I'll be first in line for your job."

"You're making a big assumption there." Lol inched forward. The guy either didn't notice or didn't care, seeming a little entranced by Lol in her barely-there dress, plus he was the one holding the firearm.

Why should he be concerned?

"Which is?"

"That I'll step down." Lol cast a quick glance in Lennon's direction. He wasn't sure what the hell he was supposed to be doing. All his attention was on that Glock.

"You won't have to." A distinct air of menace to his tone.

"So, that's why you came back?" Pausing, Lol exhaled loudly.

The suit nodded. "To finish you off… him, too." He wiggled the gun in Lennon's general direction. "Then stage the scene like he killed you after finding you in the bedroom and then went ahead and did the decent thing by ending the game."

"You've obviously thought everything through." Lol sounded impressed.

"It's what I do best. I've been staging scenes for a hell of a long time, you know that, planning out all the fine details. I knew it would all come in useful one day."

Lol nodded.

And took a step closer.

Lennon looked on with morbid fascination. The guy in the suit had just announced he fully intended to put a bullet through his brain and make it look like suicide, and yet he found himself more invested in seeing how the dance developing between the suit and Lol was going to play out. Clearly, the guy had more about him than being just a hired goon, but there was just something about Lol's demeanor in the face of adversity that oozed malevolent confidence.

"We should talk about this," Lol was saying. "A man like you could be useful to me; I'm sure there's a deal to be struck somewhere."

In the time to took the guy in the suit to raise a quizzical eyebrow and shake his head, Lol had retrieved the switchblade from the waistband of her gold panties, flicked it open, and launched toward him.

Lennon winced as the knife's blade slid deep into the suit an inch or so below his rib cage on the right-hand side. The guy let out a half grunt, half squeal of pain and surprise as he instinctively clutched at the weapon's black handle.

In the split second he did so, the Glock and cell phone tumbled from his hands and Lol jumped him, using her momentum and body weight to wrestle him to the floor. Lennon guessed the guy had an easy fifty, sixty pounds on the young woman; she'd used the element of surprise to full advantage.

"You wretch!" the suit yowled in agony as Lol pinned him down. Her body had pushed the switchblade deeper into his gut as she squirmed on top of him and clawed at his face with sharp fingernails. Blood bubbled out to stain his white shirt, and the unmistakable stink of excrement wafted across the suite to Lennon. Either Lol's victim had soiled his pants or her knife had punctured his intestines.

For his part, Lennon had no idea what he was supposed to do. Should he wade into the fight and help Lol, who appeared to have the upper hand anyway, or stay well back and avoid getting hurt? Or could he just run and leave all the mayhem behind him?

Somehow, the suit managed to land a hard punch to the side of Lol's head; it connected with a solid *thunk*. She let out a pained grunt and loosened her grip just enough for him to roll her away and wriggle free. In an instant, he was up on his feet, the knife sticking out of his belly like some bizarre, bloody appendage, and kicking at her gold-clad body.

Lol collected herself enough to grab the guy's foot as he swung in for another well-aimed kick at her flank. With both hands, she gave it a vicious counterclockwise twist and pushed it away.

There was an audible *pop* as the guy's knee gave out; it came with another shrill yowl of pain as the suit staggered backward, arms windmilling, fighting desperately to stay upright.

Lol was up on her feet and back on the attack even as her opponent managed to catch hold of the edge of the couch to steady himself. He was ready for her, though, with fists raised before she got to him. He threw a vicious haymaker directly dead center of the woman's face.

Lol turned her head in time to deflect the guy's fist from where it would have surely crushed her nose to the hard bone of her cheek. The punch connected hard, Lennon practically feeling it himself, and snapped Lol's head sharply backward.

She dropped to her knees, eyes rolling.

Seizing the advantage, the suit hobbled toward Lol, his right foot dragging at a disturbingly unnatural angle. He pulled at the black handle protruding from his body, visibly stifling the cry that came with it. Then, knife in hand, its blade dripping with blood and excrement, the suit sprang at Lol.

Anticipating the attack, Lol threw herself into a backward roll like a seasoned gymnast. The downward arc of the knife grazed against her bare foot as she went, drawing a thin line of blood across her toes and knocking it from her assailant's grasp.

Undeterred, the guy rounded on Lol once more with bare fists raised and poised to do serious damage.

Taking no time to gather herself, Lol rolled to the left and sprang to her feet. As she did so, she plucked the Glock from the carpet and swung it around to greet the oncoming attack.

The guy sidestepped with an agility that defied his damaged leg, dodging his own Glock, which was aimed at his chest. In one smooth, swift movement, he caught hold of Lol's wrist, twisted the gun's muzzle away from himself, and slammed the young woman into the wall next to the tacky Siegfried and Roy print.

Drawing Lol's arm back, he then slammed it hard into the wall once, twice, and on the third, the gun fell from her hand. Spurred on by his victory, the guy delivered a vicious downward headbutt to Lol's temple. It connected with a dull, sickening *thwock* that had Lol yelping like a kicked dog. The suit followed on with a flurry of left-handed sucker punches to Lol's torso as he kept her arm pinned hard to the wall.

A surge of adrenaline stirred Lennon into action. Lol no longer had the upper hand in the fight. She was dazed by the headbutt, and the guy was hitting her freakin' hard. Lennon knew he had to intervene, if only for his own self-preservation: if the suit overpowered Lol, he'd kill her and then Chase Lennon would be next on the hit list.

Should have run when you had the chance, Chase, old buddy.

Lennon darted across the room, skillfully circumventing the hanging corpses, and grabbed at the suit's shoulders.

Taken by surprise, triggered by reflex, the guy jabbed his arm backward. The bony elbow caught Lennon square on the chin, which sent a jarring bolt of pain up into his skull and rattled his teeth together. Lennon staggered backward, already out of the fight.

Unfortunately for the suit, that involuntary action meant he let go of Lol's arm and quit pounding at the soft side of her body. With both arms free, Lol slashed at his face with her fingernails, digging them into his cheeks, as she brought a knee up hard into his balls.

The suited guy let out a loud, rasping grunt and collapsed, fighting for breath, at Lol's feet.

Siezing her chance, Lol scooped up the Glock, aimed it at the guy's face.

"Don't!" Lennon heard himself cry out.

Lol ignored him.

The slug hit the guy in the suit a hair's breadth beneath the nose and sprayed the contents of his skull out across the floor behind him. His body went limp in an instant, bladder and bowels letting go with gruesome synchrony.

".38 hollow points," Lol said quietly. "He really did mean business." She turned to Lennon. "You okay?"

"You shouldn't have…" Lennon stared down at the body between them.

"He planned to do the same to us."

"I know," Lennon replied. "But people are going to report the sound of a gunshot in a hotel room, don't you think?"

Lol managed a lopsided grin, which let Lennon know that, yes, she had actually thought of that. "Then maybe we should get going?"

Lennon didn't need asking twice.

Ignoring the dull thumping inside his head from the blow he'd received running to Lol's aid—and not so much as a thank-you—Lennon followed Lol over to the suite's door. "You don't want to get your shoes?" He glanced down at her feet, smeared with fresh blood from the thin cut across her toes.

"Not the ones that go with this get-up." Lol looked down at her dress, which was in disarray, torn in a few places, and splashed with blood. "You try running in five-inch heels." With that, she pulled open the door, took a quick look left and right along the hallway outside, and left.

Lennon followed Lol down the hallway toward the illuminated exit sign. Their footsteps were muted by the short-pile carpet with a psychedelic pattern that looked like it belonged back in the seventies. Doing his best to stay aware of everything around him, keeping a close eye on Lol's shapely behind a couple strides ahead, Lennon noted she still carried the gun she'd used to kill the suit. Was she expecting more trouble?

Lennon certainly hoped not.

As they neared the exit door, the elevator adjacent to it pinged and the doors began to swoosh open.

"Quick!" Lol hissed, grabbing Lennon's hand. "We're taking the stairs."

As the elevator discharged a handful of hotel security guards, Lol pulled Lennon through the fire exit door and into the coolness of the concrete stairwell. Lennon watched through the closing door as the guards dashed toward the suite, drawing their side arms as they did so.

"The cops won't be far behind. We gotta go," Lol urged and began her way down the seemingly endless flight of stairs.

Once they reached the ground floor, Lennon allowed Lol to guide him outside into the spacious, thankfully devoid of people, parking lot behind Circus Circus. The night air out there was warm, dry, and carried with it the unmistakable wailing of police sirens.

"There." Lol pointed at a brown and beige campervan reverse-parked in the middle of the sea of other vehicles, a large number of which were also campers. Nicely anonymous.

"You said you had a *car* waiting." Lennon panted as he jogged to catch up with Lol, who was fishing beneath the van's rear wheel arch. The gal was surprisingly fleet-footed without shoes.

"You want to be pedantic with me now?" Lol replied. "This is better. Gives us somewhere to lie low without using motels."

It certainly made sense to Lennon, who wondered just how long she had been planning to spring him from *The Contestant* for whatever scheme she had in mind. Or even if he was the first contestant she'd tried it with.

That thought made Lennon's blood run cold.

"Get in." Lol retrieved a small metal box from beneath the camper van, fished out the keys concealed within, and hit the button on the fob.

The van's lights flashed twice and Lennon heard the doors unlock. "After you," he said with a chivalrous sweep of an arm.

Lol clambered into the driver's seat, secreted the Glock in the glove compartment alongside an awaiting cellphone and first aid kit, and retrieved a pair of well-worn sneakers from the footwell. Footwear on, she gunned the engine as Lennon took shotgun, pulled the shift into D, and maneuvered the vehicle out of its spot and toward the lot's exit.

****

The man with the ginger beard thumbed at his cell phone as he watched the camper van leave from the shadows at the end of the parking lot. He'd packed his suited associate off to go find out what was keeping his colleague, but he already had a good idea. Hopefully, the surviving suit would have enough sense to make himself scarce before cops swarmed all over the hotel.

Although the set-up with the comedian hadn't gone strictly according to plan, it hadn't been a total bust in the end. They had some good footage to manipulate and implicate the contestant, and more than enough corpses to satisfy the clientele's bloodlust. He'd rather not have lost a good man in the process, but, hey, business was business.

Lifting the phone to his ear, he spoke quietly.

"Looks like they're heading your way," he said, "just so ya know."

Then he hung up.

Chapter 24

"Stay where I can see you both," Jilly called over to Casey and Chad. "Did you remember to pack everything?"

"Yes, Mom," Casey huffed and made with the exasperated eye roll thing she'd perfected since she started hanging out with a couple older 8th grade girls.

Jilly chose to let the attitude slide – just this once. She had plenty on her plate to be dealing with as it was. She looked on in silence as Casey padded back to her room, no doubt to finish up packing her suitcase.

"Are you sure all this is necessary, Agent?" she asked the FBI agent who'd so abruptly woken her up less than two hours earlier and flashed his badge at her through the peephole in the front door. Now, the two of them stood by Jilly's bed as she shoved essentials into her own suitcase.

"I'm afraid so, Mrs. Lennon," Special Agent Eubank assured. "And, please, call me Ty."

Jilly balked at that. The man was a law enforcement official, and she'd been raised to show respect to folks in such positions. She much preferred to call him *Agent* and set a good example for her kids.

"Chase wouldn't hurt me, and definitely not the kids," Jilly said, struggling to comprehend the fact she was actually having to say those words out loud. "I mean, whatever he's done, or *supposed* to have done, doesn't mean he's a danger to any of us."

"I'd really like to think that, ma'am." Eubank's kind eyes fixed Jilly's with a solemn gaze. "But, as far as your husband knows, you've turned your back on him. He's not thinking like a rational person right now; I'd even go as far as to say he's not the Chase you used to know anymore. You've seen the reports, Mrs. Lennon. You've seen what Chase is capable of."

"I really can't believe that," Jilly said. "Whatever he's mixed up in, I'm sure all he wants is to come home."

"You pushed your husband away, Mrs. Lennon. In his eyes, you have betrayed him by telling him to give himself up or…" Eubank left the inference unsaid. "We really don't know how he will have taken that. All we do know is that he's escalating at an alarming rate and not thinking like a rational person. Something made him snap, and he's not the husband you think you know. Up to that point, Mrs. Lennon, Chase was merely playing the game. Now, it's become all-too real."

"I only said what Mr. Mercer told me to say. He told me it was all part of the stupid game Chase got himself involved in." Jilly's temper was rising along with her heart rate and, no doubt blood pressure for good measure. Ever since Mercer's visit and *that* phone call with Chase, things had gotten increasingly out of hand. One thing, though, Mercer had promised her the media would be kept away from her doorstep, and he'd been true to his word with that one, at least.

"I'm sorry it's working out this way." Eubank seemed quite genuine, concerned. "But we really can't afford to take any risks to you and your children. We received intel' your husband may well be heading back this way—"

"Yeah, you said." Jilly snorted. "I thought Mercer was watching every move Chase was making. Isn't that the whole point of the game?"

Eubank now appeared flustered. "From what I understand, Chase went off script a little. He managed to evade the cameras and everyone who was supposed to be following him, and Mercer lost track of him."

"And just how the hell was that allowed to happen?" Jilly spat. She'd had her fill of the ridiculous game Chase had signed himself up for, along with the damage it had done to his reputation and the family name.

A big part of her still refused to believe Chase was capable of any of the terrible things the news was saying about him, and that it was all part of Mercer's sick playtime. She wanted nothing more than to have him back home and for them to get on with their lives. It wasn't even like they needed the prize money; hadn't her husband already made enough of that to last them several lifetimes?

"Honestly, I don't know," Eubank told her. "That's a question for Mercer and his people. Perhaps you could raise it the next time you get to see him? What I do know is your husband might pose a clear and present danger to you and your children, and it's my job to get you into protective custody until matters can be resolved."

A rhythmic knock on the front door jangled Jilly's already-fried nerves. She tensed, her teeth clenched.

"Don't worry, I have police officers stationed outside the front door," Eubank said. "Nobody's getting in here without permission." Turning, he left the bedroom, headed for the stairs.

Jilly followed on, making sure she kept a safe distance behind the special agent. Despite everything, she allowed herself to feel safe in his presence.

Eubank opened Jilly's front door to an elderly man in a bathrobe and fluffy, leopard-print slippers.

"Hello, Mr. Hadid," Jilly greeted him from behind Eubank.

"Is this the gentleman who you told me about?" The FBI man eyed Jilly's elderly neighbor with suspicion.

"I've come for Bingo," the old man offered quietly, clearly intimidated by Jilly's houseguest.

"Come in, please." Jilly pushed past Eubank to usher her neighbor inside. "He's upstairs with Chad. I'll give him a call."

"Not the best guard dog in the world, eh?" Mr. Hadid chuckled nervously as he sidestepped Eubank to make himself at home in the Lennons' vestibule.

"I'm so sorry to have called you so late, Mr. Hadid." Jilly pulled out her cell from the back pocket of her jeans and texted Casey to get Chad to bring Bingo downstairs. Texting the kids in the house was a lazy habit, she knew, but it had become the most efficient way of communicating with her daughter since Chase insisted on buying her the phone.

"Anytime. You know that." Hadid's warm smile reminded Jilly of how she was convinced the dear old man had a crush on her, like he was some over-hormonal teenager and not a septuagenarian. While she found it a tad creepy, Chase had always thought it cute his wife had attracted the attention of the neighbor plenty old enough to be her grandfather.

Either way, whatever the old boy's motivation, it came in useful whenever they needed the dog taking care of or the houseplants watering when the Lennons were out of town.

"You know, I've never believed all the bad things they're saying about Mr. Lennon," Hadid offered. "Your husband has always been a kind and decent man, Mrs. Lennon. If you need a shoulder to cry on, or just somebody to talk to…"

"Thank you." Jilly wasn't sure what she was supposed to say to that. And where was Chad with the friggin' dog?

"It *has* to be a case of mistaken identity." The old man evidently wasn't about to let it go until he'd voiced his opinion. "Somebody who *looks* like Mr. Lennon is doing all those awful things – it *has* to be that."

While Jilly struggled to think of an appropriate reply, Bingo came bounding down the stairs, tail wagging fit to burst, tongue lolling like some crazy person's. The dog was a huge fan of Mr. Hadid because the widowed old man provided undivided attention and spoiled him with treats. Jilly sometimes thought the mutt would be much happier living across the street.

With Bingo safely on his away with her neighbor, Jilly returned to the bedroom to finish up packing. Eubank had told her she would only need to take what would fit in her suitcase, as he hoped they wouldn't have to be away from home for too long. Whether that meant things would blow over and the game at an end or Chase would be caught by the police to face the music, she really didn't want to ask.

The FBI agent poked his head through the doorway, checking his wristwatch with an exaggerated lack of subtlety. "We *really* must be going now, Mrs. Lennon," he told her.

Jilly forced her suitcase shut and ran the zipper along its sides; as always on family trips, she'd packed *way* too much. "I'm sorry." She plucked her phone from her pillow, where she'd tossed it to change her jeans—the black ones far more comfortable for traveling in. Quickly, she tapped out a hurry-up message to Casey and made to slip the cell into her back pocket.

"I think it would be best if you left it here, Mrs. Lennon." Eubank pointed at the phone.

"My husband doesn't track me, Special Agent Eubank, if that's what you're thinking." Jilly was offended at the suggestion: just who the hell did the scrawny little man think he was talking to?

"It's just in case." If Eubank sensed Jilly's irritation, he chose to ignore it. "We can't afford to be careless in situations like this. Make sure your daughter leaves hers behind, too."

Jilly nodded.

"Okay, so let's go," Eubank said with finality.

Chapter 25

Lol pulled up into a rest stop not too far outside Apple Valley on Interstate 15, a stone's throw from Victorville. She'd driven the camper van for a little over four hours from Vegas, determined to get to LA before dawn. It was still the early hours, and the rest stop was nicely deserted, save for a solitary eighteen-wheeler with mauve curtains pulled across its windshield.

"I need a break." Lol rubbed hard at her face, smearing eyeliner down her cheeks. Sitting back in the driving seat, she winced, and Lennon saw she was in some discomfort following the fight she'd put up back in the hotel. Her arms were bruised, along with her right cheek, and there was also a nasty-looking purple patch forming on her left thigh. "I could also do with changing into something more comfortable than this."

Lennon's eyes followed Lol's down to the gold dress, which had seen better days and was struggling to contain her. "I can take over driving," he said. "If you'll tell me where we're headed."

Lol unbuckled her seat belt. It retracted into the door frame with a swift *clack*. "Thanks for the offer, but I got this. Looks like you could use some sleep, too. We got a big day ahead of us." She clambered over her seat and into the back of the camper van. "I have some water and snacks back here, if you're interested. Maybe even a couple beers in the mini fridge, too."

Never one to need to be offered a beer twice, Lennon joined Lol on the narrow bench seat by the tiny silver sink and diminutive refrigerator. It felt good to be still for a while, and somewhere he could feel relatively safe – as far as Lennon knew, no one knew where he was.

Unless the camper was festooned with those tiny cameras, that was.

Lennon studied Lol as she plucked a pair of brown bottles from the fridge and popped the caps with a couple deft twists. It was Mondello Negro, one of his favorites.

"You're wondering if you can trust me?" Lol sat herself back down with a weary thump and grimace. "Can't say as I blame you." She took a hearty swig of her beer, downing half the bottle in one go."

Lennon eyed the bottle she'd given him with suspicion.

"Seriously? You just saw me open it." Lol laughed. "After all we've been through together, you think I'm gonna drug you again without telling you?

Lennon allowed silence to speak for him.

"Okay, I guess I wouldn't trust me, either. It's not like I've not done it before, is it now?" Lol snatched the cold bottle from his hand and put it to her lips.

Lennon scrutinized Lol as she drank some of his beer, still unsure as to whether he should trust her or not. It was always possible she had taken some kind of pre-antidote, or was just some dumb trope they used in the movies? Then again, what other choice did he have? The woman clearly had an agenda, of which he'd inadvertently become a key part, and he was completely in her hands if he was to avoid being captured by law enforcement or Mercer's crew.

Although Lol's reassurances they were on the same side seemed convincing, he'd now witnessed first-hand just what the woman was capable of, and that terrified him. Having said all that, there was no option for him right now than to take the young woman on face value; Lennon knew he wouldn't last a day on his own, especially if Mercer intended to avoid paying out the prize money.

Talk about a rock and a hard place.

As Lennon retrieved his Mondello, his fingers brushed Lol's, and just for a moment, he imagined a spark between them. Of course, it could merely have been the aftermath of the adrenaline overload or the close desperation of his situation, but Lennon was convinced he'd felt *something.*

How about Stockholm Syndrome, buddy?

"You said you'd explain why you didn't put me completely out this time." It was the first thing that jumped into Lennon's mind to say. "Earlier, back in the hotel."

Nodding, Lol took a swig of her beer and replied, "I figured it was important you see for yourself exactly what Mercer is capable of orchestrating in the name of *The Contestant.*" Nursing her beer bottle, sitting so close, her knee rested gently upon his, Lennon, despite himself, couldn't help but take in just how good the young woman looked in that short, golden dress, as disheveled and bloodied as it was.

"I've *already* seen that for myself, remember?" Lennon couldn't help the sarcasm in his tone. "I've woken up surrounded by enough carnage to know exactly what you and your people are capable of. You *actually* killed those girls back there in Vegas and stood by while your colleague cut that old guy's throat. How many more innocent people have you murdered, Lol?"

"They're collateral damage, which is an unfortunate part of my job, I'm afraid. Sacrifices for the greater good, if you will," Lol explained as if she was nothing more than a traffic cop dishing out speeding citations. "If I didn't to do as instructed, I'd be failing to do the job Mercer pays me so well to do."

"And you'd be fired? Just how well do you get paid?"

Shaking her head, Lol placed a hand gently upon Lennon's thigh. It felt warm, quite pleasantly so. "Mercer doesn't fire people." She spoke quietly, deliberately. "You've seen how *The Contestant* plays out. There's always the need for new, fresh victims."

"You mean…?" The stark glimpse of fear in Lol's eyes answered Lennon's question more than words ever could.

"It's why Mercer has to be stopped." Lol fiddled with the hem of her dress, which had ridden up so high Lennon caught a glimpse of the matching gold panties. "He's gone way too far with his sick game this time."

"And you're the one to stop him?"

Another nod.

"Why you?" Lennon eased himself upright on the couch, still not a hundred percent confident with his control over his own limbs. "I get you can't just walk away, but plotting against Mercer? If he's as dangerous as you're telling me he is, then aren't you taking one hell of a risk?"

Lol quit fiddling with her hem. "It's a risk I take every day," she told him. "Ever since I made waves and let it be known I wanted out."

"And you're still around."

"It's been almost two years now." Lol's voice lowered. Her eyes darted about the cramped camper van, as if expecting someone to appear, camera in hand, to catch her out. "I'd gotten to the point where I'd had enough of staging the games for Mercer, and a belly full of the monsters who pull his strings. Every time, it had to be more extreme to keep the viewers hooked and innocent people were dying in the name of entertainment. That's not to mention the absolute destruction of people's lives."

"You actually *told* Mercer you wanted out?" Lennon studied Lol for tells as she spoke. He took pride in his innate ability to know bull crap when he heard it, and as far as he could make out, Lol was not attempting to feed him any.

"He told me I had to at least finish up my contract, which meant two more games, after which I'd be free to leave. Of course, the contracts are water-tight and carry the threat of ridiculously high penalties for breaching the aggressive non-disclosure clauses. It's not that I could go to anyone with my story anyway, I'm just as complicit in all the fabrication and murder as Mercer. If not more so, because he never gets his hands dirty at ground level. Much prefers to leave it all up to his minions.

"So, I did as I was told and played nice, every day half-expecting something unpleasant was going to happen to me. It was obvious Mercer wasn't about to offer me more money to stay on board—that's just not his style—so I kinda thought he'd make sure I was caught and arrested staging a scene, maybe even shot attempting to evade arrest. Mercer and his people have enough law enforcement at every damn level in their pockets to make that sort of thing happen without breaking a sweat."

"I can't see why you don't just walk." Lennon was trying his best to read between Lol's lines but couldn't see past what seemed to him to be the simplest solution to her dilemma. "Surely someone with your resources and… *skills* should be able to disappear. Even with Mercer's reach, there'll be places you can go where his people will never find you. I don't believe the guy is that omnipotent."

Lol's chest rose and fell as she took in a long, deep breath and sighed it back out.

"You're right." Her voice was barely a whisper. "This is about more than me wanting out of this crummy job."

As excruciating as it was, Lennon restrained himself from filling the loaded silence that settled between them. A lifetime in sales had taught him that he who speaks first loses the upper hand.

"After I told Mercer I wanted to quit," Lol picked up again. As she spoke, she clutched her beer bottle so tight her knuckles bulged. "I was assigned a job that kicked off in California – Silicon Valley. The contestant was a stupidly successful tech mogul who'd made her money designing AI algorithms. It was all a bit of a cliché, if you ask me."

Lennon recalled his initial surprise at seeing the footage Mercer had shown him of previous game winners, at least a third of whom had been female. Somehow, he'd never thought women were as greedy or dumb as men when it came to money.

"Mercer said nothing to me directly, but I was pulled off the second scene we had to stage for the woman. We'd started off with fake accusations, along with some very convincing proof Mercer had fabricated, of embezzlement, stock shorting, and outright theft of hundreds of millions of dollars. Her company's share price tanked, and everyone was out baying for Shannon Westerhaus's blood."

"I remember that." Lennon clearly recalled the furor there'd been at the time, a year, maybe a touch longer, ago, along with how excited he'd been when the Sunnyvale branch of Imagine Realty had landed the listing of Westerhaus' $52m house shortly after she turned up dead in a ravine in the Lexington Hills. He also recalled what happened after she went in to hiding following her outing by an anonymous whistleblower in her company.

"Mercer gave the job to Beard to head up," Lol continued.

"Wait…" Lennon interrupted. "The guy's name is actually *Beard*?"

Lol chanced a laugh at Lennon's expense. "We're contractually forbidden to use names, so we kinda make them up as we go along."

"And how do they address you?"

"Woman, Boss, sometimes Wretch," Lol said with no hint of humor. "Depends on who's doing the referring and what the circumstance is."

"I'll stick with Lol, then." Lennon was about to add, *if that's your real name*, but thought better of it in the interests of building some semblance of trust.

"Beard set up the scene at the home of Westerhaus' CFO, the guy she suspected of turning over the company accounts to the SEC. It was all made-up by Mercer's financial people, of course, but it all looked very real to the outside world. And it made for a perfect motive for murder, so when the CFO's entire family were butchered, there was really only the one suspect."

"I remember even the kids were killed." Lennon's thoughts snapped to Casey and Chad.

"The little girl was only two years old." Lol suppressed a sniffle; tears glistened in her eyes.

"Yeah."

"Turns out the guy's wife just so happened to be a good friend of mine. We grew up in the same neighborhood. We were inseparable all the way through school, right up until college. We stayed in touch over the years, I even went to her wedding."

"You think Mercer knew that?"

Lol polished off the remainder of her beer like she really needed it. "I *know* he knew that," she growled. "Mercer orchestrated the whole thing from the beginning. He deliberately targeted Westerhaus to apply to *The Contestant*, much like he targeted you. It's the way Mercer works: it's never the direct approach. He could have had me or any of my family killed, but instead he chose to send me a message instead."

"Would it not have been easier to get you out of the way if he wanted you silenced?"

"*Much* easier." Reaching back into the mini fridge, Lol retrieved her second beer. "But Mercer loves his sick little mind games. And I'm more valuable to him alive and on his payroll. I'm one of the ones who really knows how to make things happen."

"I've seen that." Determined to keep a clear head, Lennon eschewed draining his own beer. "So, why do you need me? You can obviously do everything that's necessary. Why can't you just go stop Mercer yourself?" It was an obvious question: Chase Lennon was a realtor, not a killer or some sinister underworld *fixer*.

"Maybe I don't need you." Lol popped her beer cap. "Perhaps I just wanted you along for the ride, somebody to keep me company?"

"Or to provide a distraction?"

"Got it in one, Mr. Lennon." Lol actually tipped him a wink. "I have more chance of getting close to Mercer with you around. Even if you just keep his security busy enough to not notice me."

Lennon really wasn't surprised by the revelation. It was obvious Lol was more than capable and didn't need a man to get what she wanted. He really could have been any one of the contestants, but he just happened to be in the right place at the wrong time.

"What if I don't want to be any part of your plan?"

Lol smiled a knowing smile. "Then I cut you loose now and leave you to your own devises. Unfortunately, though, you became part of my plan the moment you left the motel back in Lubbock with me. You're complicit now, whether you like it or not."

Lennon shrugged and sipped at his beer. Lol was right, of course, and Mercer's game had taken a definitely unexpected turn.

When Lol leaned in to kiss Lennon, he recoiled. As hot as her trim body was in that tiny gold dress, Lennon had kept his lascivious thoughts to himself by countering them with the all-too-fresh mental images of what she'd done back at Circus Circus.

"That was… unexpected," Lennon said.

"Are you sure about that?" Lol appeared surprised at the rejection. "I thought you've been wanting that since the hotel."

"I'd be lying if I said it hadn't crossed my mind," Lennon confessed.

"It's the hooker persona," Lol replied. "It works every time."

"So, this is not the first time you've tried to seduce a contestant?"

"I don't make a habit of this, if that's what you mean. Mercer would go crazy if he ever caught me having relations with any of the contestants; it's not in *my* contract. Not that it's never crossed my mind once or twice, of course."

"Of course."

"So, what do you say?" Lol stroked along the inside of Lennon's thigh.

"I'm sorry, but I'm beyond tired, mentally exhausted. All I want to do is sleep." He hoped she was buying it. "And there's Jilly…"

Lol moved her hand away and shuffled a few inches away from him. "It's okay. I get it." As far as Lennon could tell, he'd not offended the woman, for which he was grateful. She was a killer, after all.

As bone-weary as he was, sleep evaded Lennon. Instead, his mind tormented him with fleeting images of bloody, desecrated corpses, disembodied eyeballs, and innocent people gasping their last, rattling, breaths right under his nose. While it had been horrific enough waking up in the gruesome scenes staged by Lol and the rest of Mercer's hired thugs, it had nowhere near prepared him to bear first-hand witness to his supposed victims' actual demise.

Jilly and the kids entered Lenon's thoughts, too. He'd vowed to himself a long time ago that he'd never betray Jilly, not again. He'd had his extramarital fun back in the day, when Imagine Realty was just beginning to grow and he spent more time out of the marital bed than in it, and had been proud to have put all that behind him.

He was happy he'd resisted Lol's advances and remained faithful, despite the way Jilly had turned on him. No matter how things turned out, at least he wouldn't have that on his conscience.

Remembering the cellphone in the camper's glovebox, Lennon stepped over the soundly sleeping Lol on the bench seat and made his way to the front of the van with as much stealth as he could muster. The rest area lot remained eerily dark and deserted; it seemed the entire world was asleep.

Lennon fished the cell from the glovebox. It was an older model iPhone that looked well-used. Of course, the thing would have the face recognition security feature to unlock it, and it didn't take too much guesswork to figure out who's face it would be programmed with.

As he thumbed the phone to life, Lennon shot Lol a quick look. She remained oblivious to his absence beside her. Lennon's second piece of good luck was he was one of the few people he knew who still memorized phone numbers. It was an old habit from his childhood when there was no other choice but to carry around a phone book, one he'd never gotten out of.

Cell phone in hand, Lennon clambered back into the rear of the camper van and approached Lol with all the stealth of a seasoned cat burglar. Slowly, ever-so-gently, breath held, he eased Lol onto her back. While she let out a quiet grunting snore and a moan, her eyes remained firmly closed. Lennon noted how her eyes moved around behind their lids, darting frantically to and fro: the woman was evidently having one hell of a dream.

Lennon continued holding his breath as he positioned the cell over Lol's face, fearful the screen's bright glow might awaken her. The phone unlocked in an instant, and Lennon dared to empty his lungs with a soft, silent sigh. He sat himself down on the edge of the bed opposite.

Then, with a furtive look across at Lol, Lennon dialed his wife's number.

The call went straight through to Jilly's voicemail. That surprised Lennon, because Jilly always slept with her cell switched on and by the bed every night in case of emergencies. Her folks were getting on in years, and she bore the constant worry of one of them taking the inevitable fall, which would mean that dreaded one-way trip to the hospital.

Next, Lennon tried Casey's phone. The girl kept odd hours, and even if she was asleep, she'd inherited her mother's habit of keeping her cell close by on her nightstand.

"Hello?"

Hearing Casey's voice snatched the words from Lennon's throat.

"Hello?" She was annoyed now, her tone groggy with sleep.

"Casey?" Lennon finally managed to speak. "How are you doing, baby girl?"

"Daddy?"

"Yeah. It's me. I miss you."

"Miss you, too, Daddy."

"Is your mom there?"

"She's sleeping. So is Chad, and he *never* sleeps on the plane."

Lennon's heart skipped. "You're on an airplane?"

"Yeah. Just a little one, though. It's a bit like yours, but without all the chocolate and chips." Casey sounded like she was talking in her sleep to some imaginary friend. Lennon doubted she'd remember their conversation come the morning, and that made him sad. "Mr. Eubank said he had to take us someplace safe."

"Safe from what?"

"Dunno."

"Mr. Eubank, Casey? Who are you with right now?"

"He's some kind of policeman. FBI I think he said. He told Mom we had to leave home until everything blew over."

Lennon hoped to dear God his kids had not been watching the TV reports about his alleged murder spree. As their father, there'd really be no coming back from that.

"Where is he taking you?"

"Dunno." A voice appeared in the background. A man's.

Casey's phone went dead.

"You're not supposed to use that." Lol's voice startled Lennon. She was supposed to be fast asleep and dreaming.

"They're on a small airplane with somebody from the FBI." Lennon stared at the burner phone in his hand as if expecting his daughter was going to call back any minute. "Since when did the FBI fly around in private jets?"

Lol made her way to the front of the camper van. "*Who's* on a private jet?"

"Jilly and the kids."

"Special Agent Eubank?"

As Lennon nodded, his eyes met Lol's and he caught the distress in there.

"Crap." Lol sat herself in the front passenger seat.

"You know him?"

"He's been in Mercer's pocket for longer than I have," Lol told him. "This is not good news."

"Where's he taking my family, Lol?" Lennon heard the tremble of fear in his own voice.

"He's bringing them to LA, Mr. Lennon." Lol lowered her eyes, like she couldn't bear even to look at the man she'd just been intimate with. "He'll be planning to make them your next victims."

Chapter 26

The guy they all referred to as Beard listened intently to Mercer, phone pressed tight to his ear. Behind him, on the Mach-E's back seat, the muscle in the suit snored quietly, his jacket and pants considerably more rumpled than when they'd high-tailed it out of the Circus Circus parking lot over four hours before.

Somebody in the location department had thought it a good idea to organize the electric Mustang for Beard, and he hated the thing. It felt soulless, like some glorified kiddie's toy, and was like driving a damn TV set with a Mustang badge. It was an absolute travesty to do such a thing to an iconic car, in his opinion. Still, even Beard could see the logic behind the decision: LA was full of the things.

"Yeah, I got eyes on them," Beard told Mercer. "They've not left my sight since Vegas."

"That was a mess somebody's going to have to take responsibility for," Mercer chastised him through the phone's tiny speaker. "How the hell did Lennon get away from there like that?"

"The woman was helping him, by the look of it. One of them killed my assistant, and I reckon it was her. I don't think Lennon has it in him."

"Never underestimate what a cornered animal can be capable of," Mercer told him. "You ought to know that well enough by now."

Beard nodded to himself but chose to say nothing.

"Do you know where they're headed next?"

"I'm guessing in your general direction," Beard offered.

"We don't pay you to guess." Mercer snapped. "Did you put a tracker on the vehicle?"

"Of course." Keeping his reply curt, Beard scratched at his beard, which felt scruffy and unkempt. He was badly in need of a shower and didn't care for the grubby feeling it left him with. Also, it wasn't like Mercer to micromanage like this. The guy was usually more than happy to observe the game's proceedings from his ivory tower and only chip in when he felt it absolutely necessary to move things along or keep the viewers happy.

Which meant Mercer was worrying about how things were going. What with the woman going off script and the loss of the assistant in the hotel, Beard was all too aware things were going slightly awry.

Still, it was nothing he couldn't handle. After all, he'd kept track of Lennon and the woman all the way to LA's outskirts without them realizing it and had even taken a peek inside the camper van when the two were sleeping. He'd had to approach the camper to attach the clandestine tracking device so as not to lose Lennon and the woman in the labyrinth of LA roads and back streets once they left the rest stop.

There was just something about seeing the woman who'd been his superior and called all the shots for the past four years and change in asleep and vulnerable like that. Had Mercer ordered her elimination from Lennon's game, it would have made for the perfect opportunity for Beard to have done so.

But much to his surprise, Mercer had not.

Likely, he was thinking whatever this new direction things were taking would make for compulsive viewing, no matter how unpredictable the woman had become. That she and Lennon were so obviously on their way to the studio and Mercer—and Beard could hazard an easy guess as to their motive—didn't seem to bother the boss one iota. Perhaps because he held the ultimate ace up his sleeve.

"The family will be landing shortly," Mercer continued. "They'll be transported directly to the safe house. I have good people dealing with it all. The best."

"That's great to hear," Beard couldn't quite keep *all* the sarcasm from his tone. He knew damn well Mercer was referring to the overinflated FBI idiot he kept on the payroll. Beard had crossed paths with the guy on more than one game in the past, and it had brought him great satisfaction to have T-boned the Lubbock cop's car with him in it.

"Keep close eyes on her, it's time to turn up the heat. I'm relying on you to ensure everything runs smoothly, of course." Mercer was sounding tired of the conversation now. The guy had a notoriously low attention span.

"Of course."

"I'll send you out another assistant."

"No need," Beard told him. "I got this."

"It wasn't a question." Mercer hung up.

Beard tossed his cell down onto the passenger seat and cussed at Mercer under his breath. Maybe the woman had the right idea in going rogue; it was one sure-fire way of getting out from under Mercer's malignant clutches. Could be she'd manage to make the complete break and get to go live her life someplace where she didn't have to ruin lives and murder innocent people to earn her money.

Despite himself, looking over at the camper van across the rest stop, Beard found himself kind of envying her.

Chapter 27

"Where are we going, Mr. Eubank?"

If the kid asked him that one more time, Special Agent Eubank swore he'd go postal. He'd asked the same damn question at least a dozen times since the jet landed at Van Nuys airport and they'd all got into the awaiting white Chevy Suburban. "You'll find out when we get there," he replied once again through gritted teeth. He hoped and prayed he wasn't going to hear the question again on the ride to Santa Monica.

"Are we going to see Dad?" The young girl looked at him over the back of her seat with a look of hope on her pretty face.

Eubank shook his head. "You'll see your father when everything is sorted out and we know you'll be safe."

"Safe from what?"

The boy *really* was getting on the FBI man's nerves.

"Leave the nice man alone, Chad." Jilly Lennon came to the rescue. "Everything is going to be okay, and we'll be seeing Dad very soon." Her smile at Eubank was as fake as it was possible to get, although the kids seemed to be placated by it. And if that meant no more asinine questions, that suited Special Agent Eubank just fine.

When Eubank's cell phone rang and he saw it was Trae Miller again, he decided to take the call. For as much as he didn't relish sitting in the loaded silence, or, even worse, listening to Lennon's kids whining, he really didn't feel much in the mood to entertain the Lubbock detective. But he figured even that would come as a welcome reprieve, so Eubank picked up the call.

"That you, Ty?" Miller sounded uncharacteristically miserable, even for such an early hour of the morning: it was 4 AM in LA, two hours ahead in Texas. The guy was likely still mourning the destruction of his crappy, old Camry, Eubank mused.

"Yeah," Eubank kept his voice low. Not that he'd ever give anything away, he was too well trained for that, but whatever he had to say to Miller was just none of anybody else's business.

"I heard about the killings in Vegas," Miller told him. "Sounds a lot like our elusive old friend."

Eubank didn't much care for the phrase *old friend* because it made Chase Lennon sound all too familiar, and nor did he like the cop's inference behind *our*, either. It had been a long time since he and Miller had worked together, and Eubank had little desire to relive those god-awful days all over again.

"It's too early to tell for certain," Eubank eyed his fellow passengers in the Suburban. They seemed content enough staring out the windows into California's darkness. "The ME is still working on it."

"Were the victims' eyes removed?" Miller asked. "The reports I've seen don't mention anything about the eyes."

"I really can't answer that, Detective Miller," Eubank replied coldly. "You know better than to ask."

That seemed to flummox Miller. "Of course, but I thought—"

"I really can't divulge any information about the case right now." Eubank fidgeted uneasily in his seat. The safety belt suddenly felt a tad too tight and uncomfortable across his chest.

"Of course, of course." Miller still sounded offended. "You have people with you. I get it. When will you get to the scene? I assume you're going?"

"I'm already there, Trea. I was in the vicinity," Eubank lied. He wondered just how long it would be before his old Lubbock colleague would connect the dots and ask how come the FBI agent always just happened to be in town when Lennon did his thing.

"Give me a call later, then." Clearly, dots had not been connected just yet. "When you can talk."

"Sure thing. Will do," Special Agent Eubank lied again and ended the call.

"Is everything okay, Mr. Eubank?" Jilly asked him. There was sad concern in her eyes.

"Yes, ma'am," the agent reassured her. "We'll be at the safe house shortly. I'll get you and the kids all settled in. It's close to the beach, so I reckon they'll be happy enough."

Even as he spoke to Jilly, Eubank couldn't help but feel a sick twinge of regret at the thought of the unavoidable fate awaiting her and her children once they reached the coast. She had no idea, naturally, she was as much a part of Mercer's game as her husband was, and plans would already be afoot to draw the Lennons' participation in *The Contestant* to a particularly unpleasant finale.

"Thank you, Mr. Eubank," Jilly said quietly and returned her attention to the darkness outside.

Chapter 28

Lol had secreted a change of clothing in the camper van and managed to dress herself in the cramped conditions into faded Wranglers, sleeveless black T-shirt, and a pair of white Nike Air Max; she'd obviously done this all before. She'd topped off the ensemble with a dark gray Vans hoodie, which made for a disappointingly stark contrast from the little gold dress.

Lennon wished Lol had the foresight to have tucked away a few clothes for him, but she'd evidently not even considered he might need some. Then again, considering the situation Mercer had put Jilly and the kids in, fresh clothes were the very least of Chase Lennon's worries.

"Where are we going? Do you know where he's taking them?" Lennon asked as Lol settled herself into the drivers' seat. It was still dark outside, although hints of dawn were beginning to show – the star-speckled sky was taking on the faintly orange glow of what promised to be another baking hot West Coast day.

"Could be anywhere," Lol told him with a loud huff. "Mercer has access to properties all over Los Angeles."

"Then how does he suppose I'm going to get to where he wants me for his people to set me up?" Lennon shuddered at the thoughts those words conjured up: that it was planned for him to wake up alongside the mutilated corpses of his own family, their eyes removed and strategically placed where they could stare at him, made him feel sick to his stomach.

"This…" Lol circled her hand in front of Lennon's face, "was never meant to happen. You were supposed to wake up in the hotel room with the dead hookers and the sad old comic, discover the third hooker—me—still alive in the bedroom and witness to everything, and either end the game yourself or go on the run to avoid arrest.

"Pretty much the same as the other times, but with the net closing in even tighter; that's why Mercer went with a higher profile victim this time – people still remember Dickie Kaye."

"Surely a guy like Mercer would have a backup plan."

"Of course." Lol's eyes rolled upward, as if she was searching behind them for just the right answer. In his professional life, Lennon had always taken that as a sure-fire sign of someone lying, although it didn't quite fit in this instance. "Does your daughter have a phone?" Lol asked.

"Yeah, it was her I called last night." Nodding, Lennon recalled the ruction between him and Jilly at his presenting Casey with a brand-new cell for her twelfth birthday. Jilly had maintained, and still did, albeit with an air of resignation, that a pre-teen was far too young to be exposed to all the evils a smart phone was capable of delivering to her innocent, young eyes.

Lennon countered with the unavoidable fact that *all* of Casey's peers already had a phone and, besides, it would give them, as parents, an early opportunity to warn their daughter of all the inherent dangers that went along with the things.

Jilly had made him promise to install every available parental control app possible *and* ban all social media. He'd obediently done so in the knowledge that every twelve-year-old was more than capable of circumnavigating any and all attempts at censorship.

"iPhone, I presume?"

"Yeah," Lennon replied. "I have a family plan."

"Then we can track her using *Find My Phone*."

"Assuming she still has it with her, that is." Lennon countered; there was always the chance the FBI man Casey had mentioned, real or otherwise, would confiscate the iPhone if he discovered she still had it.

"What teenage girl parts with her cell phone?" Lol said. "She'll still have it with her."

Lennon decided against correcting Lol: it really didn't matter that Casey was still four months away from teenagedom.

Retrieving her phone from the camper's glove compartment, where she'd returned it after taking it from Lennon, Lol fired up the *Find My Phone* function. She tapped in Casey's number from the call log and asked, "What's the passcode?"

"Seventeen-Seventy-Six." Lennon said with a shrug. "Figured I'd use a date both of us could remember."

Unsmiling, Lol punched in the number and stared intently at the screen, her face illuminated in its eerie white glow.

"Got it," she said, after a too-long pause.

"Where are they going?" Lennon craned his neck to get a look-see over Lol's shoulder.

"They're already here, in LA." Lol turned the cell for Lennon to see the small map, complete with a tiny picture of Casey's smiling face. "They're heading toward Santa Monica. It looks like Mercer is planning the finale at the main studio."

"His studio is in Santa Monica?" Given their proximity to Hollywood, Lennon was surprised to hear that.

"It's really a big production suite set up in a stupidly big house Mercer bought years ago," Lol explained. "There's even a couple mockup sets he had installed. It helps with maintaining anonymity. With an underground show like *The Contestant*, it's not really practical to have a studio on Santa Monica Boulevard or on the Paramount lot."

"So, Santa Monica itself, then?"

"Big properties, everyone keeps to themselves, perfect for private security firms." Lol appeared thoughtful, as if the latter troubled her. "I'm gonna have to rethink a little here; it's not going to be as easy to intervene at the studio as it would be at some random house or motel."

"We still *can*, though?"

Lol's nod was not as reassuring for Lennon as she may have meant it to be.

Seeing for himself that Casey and, by default, Chad and Jilly, were on the move had brought a little comfort to Lennon. But at least it meant his family were all still alive, and there was time to put a stop to whatever ghoulish plans Mercer and his sick cohorts had planned for them.

Not much time, but *some*.

And that was all he had to cling to.

Lol gunned the camper van to life, eased it out of the rest stop lot, and back onto the freeway.

Behind them, moving silently, the dark blue faux-Mustang followed suit.

Chapter 29

Mercer half-watched the feed from Beard's vehicle. The guy was keeping a safe distance from the camper van, which maintained a steady sixty-five. It was precisely the speed limit on that part of the freeway; the woman clearly didn't want to draw any unwanted attention from law enforcement.

"Too bad, Lolita," Mercer said to the monitor, which was one of a bank of over a dozen that filled an entire wall of the production suite. "You're going to get some attention, like it or not."

"Go time?" Ben Austin's voice startled Mercer a little. He'd actually forgotten his assistant was still in the room. The guy had an uncanny knack of slipping in and out of places without detection, despite his bulky frame.

Mercer nodded and replied, "Time to give the viewers what they pay a lot of money for." His eyes flicked toward an open laptop sitting on the desk beneath the monitors.

There, on a server, the ultra-secure forum populated exclusively by the anonymous clientele scrolled steadily up as more comments were added.

They had all been enjoying the Chase Lennon season of *The Contestant* – right up until he went AWOL from Circus Circus before security or the police arrived. There had been some dissent, but all were placated now Beard had his live stream on the camper van. "Please make sure they get here in one peace, though." It was almost an afterthought.

"I'll give the green light now, sir." Austin stepped out of the room, already thumbing through his cell phone.

***

Lol cursed to herself. They were headed toward Interstate 10 on the 110, which she had explained to Lennon would circumvent central LA, even if it meant driving by the questionable areas of South Central LA.

"What's going on?" Lennon was suddenly alert, more so than he had been since they'd left the rest stop. Knowing Jilly and the kids were caught up in Mercer's web made him understandably anxious; he'd never once stopped to consider they'd become part of *The Contestant*. Why would he? Because of that, he'd put them all in danger the second he'd signed on the dotted line back in Philadelphia. Now, all he could hope was Lol had a good enough plan to get his family the hell out of Mercer's studio-house before it was too late.

Although, there was one alternative Lennon could think of to prevent his wife and children ending up like the string of random strangers he was supposed to have butchered: if he was to end the game himself and deliver to Mercer's too-rich clients what they'd been gambling on throughout his entire ordeal.

Lennon suppressed an inward shudder at the thought. He wasn't quite ready to make the choice between the revolver, rope, and bottle of pills just yet.

"Cops." Lol cast a nervous glance in the camper's wing mirror and eased off the gas a touch.

Lennon peered out at the mirror on his side to see a black-and-white trailing several vehicles behind, with only a convertible BMW and blue SUV Mustang between them. "We're close to downtown," Lennon said. "There's going to be cops. Maybe you're being a little *too* paranoid?"

As if on cue, the cop car's lights flashed into action, reflecting red and blue in the camper van's mirrors. The light show was followed by the jarring, insistent *yelp-yelp* of the cop car's siren. It pulled out from behind the BMW and SUV and headed their way.

"Too paranoid?" Lol cracked a wry smile, despite her obvious concern. "I keep forgetting this is your first rodeo, Mr. Lennon."

With that, Lol hit the gas pedal and swerved quickly into the left lane, which, according to the signs she flew past, were only for overtaking vehicles. In the camper's wake, an old white Buick that had seen much better days honked and flashed its main beams to register its driver's annoyance at Lol's sudden maneuver.

Lennon was genuinely surprised at just how fast the old camper could go. Up until that point, Lol had kept her speed down, but now the thing was touching ninety. It was almost as if she'd done this on more than one occasion.

"You'd better hold on," Lol warned. Then, before Lennon had the chance to brace himself, she pulled the camper hard to the right and veered it all the way across the three lanes. More honking and flashing lights accompanied the camper as Lol drove it fast over the white crosshatches, narrowly avoiding the crash barrels, and into the sprawling, spaghetti loops of the intersection with Interstate 10.

A glance behind told Lennon she'd still not managed to shake off the cop. His cruiser was clearly more maneuverable than the camper and had the added benefit of the siren and flashing lights to get other road users out of its way. Lennon looked on, heart sinking, as the cop swung onto the frontage road directly behind them, followed them off West 18th Street, and down South Grande Ave.

"Where the hell are you going?" Lennon voiced his concern. He knew from experience South Central LA was notorious for gangs and outbursts of violence that went along with them – he'd once ventured that way by mistake back in his early days in the real estate business and been lucky to live to regret it.

Lennon noticed how the cop on their tail had switched off his siren in the interests of not attracting unwanted attention. They were already getting dangerously close to places which were virtually no-go zones for law enforcement, areas where the last thing a cop needed to be doing was broadcasting his presence.

Perhaps Lol knew what she was doing, after all?

"Best place to lose our tail." Lol kept her eyes on the road ahead as she purposefully ignored the speed limit signs, some of which had what appeared to be bullet holes peppering them. "And I don't want a cop knowing where we're going."

"Is he one of Mercer's people, or a real cop?" Lennon gripped his seat belt tight as Lol swung a hard left and the camper bounced over a myriad potholes.

"Not mutually exclusive," Lol told him. "We have a lot of police forces on the payroll."

It was the first time Lol had referred to anything to do with *The* Contestant as *we*, and Lennon thought that really ought to concern him a little.

"Either way, we can't let him stop us." Lol took a right onto a tight backroad littered with trashed cars, some of them burned into hollowed-out, blackened shells. "Not if we're gonna get to your family…"

She didn't have to say *in time* for Lennon's stomach to lurch. He fought back the intrusive, awful, thoughts of Jilly, Chad, and Casey sprawled out in a blood-soaked mess with their disembodied eyes peering down from a countertop.

Lol took another right and, ahead, an old Cadillac sat diagonally across the narrow street. Raised up on stacked bricks, its wheels were gone, all four doors missing. Next to the car, by the curb, sat a souped-up silver Civic with blacked-out windows, a ridiculously oversized spoiler, gold rims, and wafer-thin tires.

Lennon heard Lol cuss beneath her breath, a hissing snarl too low for him to make out precisely what, but the inference was written all over her face. Digging his feet hard into the footwell carpet, he braced himself for impact.

Hitting the brakes hard, Lol steered the camper sharply to the left, aiming for the Caddy's rear quarter; far better than hitting the engine block, if, indeed, it was still under the hood. Lennon couldn't help but clamp his eyes tight shut, an involuntary reaction, and grit his teeth as the camper van shuddered and trembled in complaint all around him.

They hit the Cadillac with a glancing blow that crumpled the rear quarter, detached the chrome bumper, and knocked the thing off its bricks. Juddering to a brake-grinding halt, Lol's camper shunted the other vehicle twenty yards or so along the litter-strewn street until both came to a stop. A swirling column of white steam hissed angrily from beneath the camper's crumpled hood.

Opening his eyes, grateful to still be in one piece, Lennon looked in the wing mirror and saw the cop, tall, thin, Hispanic, climbing out of his car behind them. Gun drawn and pointed directly toward the camper, he yelled at them to get out of the vehicle.

"What the hell do we do now?" Lennon asked Lol, who appeared remarkably unshaken by the collision.

"We sit tight," she replied with an edgy glimpse in the direction of the garish Honda on Lennon's side of the camper and then at the cop who approached cautiously, weapon at the ready. Lol had obviously chosen to ignore his directions to get the hell out of the vehicle with their hands where he could see 'em.

Suddenly, the cop stopped dead in his tracks and hushed his mouth.

Lennon caught the officer's hesitation in the mirror and saw him take a step backward as the Civic's front doors opened. A couple of swarthy gangbangers stepped out amid a cloud of thick, gray smoke. They, too, carried guns, which seemed far too big for them.

"Surenos," Lol said. "The biggest Mexican gang around here. They're not going to take too kindly to having cops on their turf."

"You planned this?"

"How else was I supposed to outrun the police in this pile of old crap?" Lol patted the faux-leather covered steering wheel. It was an absurdly fond gesture. Then, she leaned across Lennon to reach into the glove compartment and take out the gun secreted there. "When I tell you to get down, you get down and put your hands over your ears."

The gangbangers peered into the camper as they swaggered by to confront the cop. Lennon made every effort to not meet their gaze, figuring it was the best course of action to not antagonize them, although he had a gut feeling they weren't finished with him and Lol quite yet.

"Shouldn't we get out of here?" he asked her.

"And go where?" Lol took an exaggerated look around. "We're boxed in here, and we wouldn't last two minutes on foot. We are hardly gonna blend in in this neighborhood."

"So, you're just going to shoot your way out?" Lennon had mental images of Butch and Sundance's final swansong; was this how *The Contestant* was going to end for him? Mowed down in a hail of drug gang bullets?

Lol's determined expression spoke volumes. Pulling her pistol's slide back to chamber a round, she replied, "If that's what I have to do to get us out of this, then, yes, I'm gonna shoot my way out."

The cop, now shielded behind his car's open door, was saying something to the gangsters, who were already past the rear of the camper. The cop was too far away and quiet for Lennon to make out what. His gun was aimed at the two Mexicans, his face etched with absolute terror.

In return, one of the gangbangers spoke, his voice too muffled for Lennon; he could only see the backs of the two, but their posture oozed menace, especially with those oversized cannons held by their respective thighs.

As the cop began his reply, the gangbanger raised his gun and, without hesitation, shot him in the face.

The gun's report, echoing loudly around the dilapidated buildings, made Lennon jump in his seat. In the mirror, he saw the cop disappear down behind the car door, which had offered him no protection at all; the top of the black-and-white was splattered with blood and pink-gray clumps of brain.

Seemingly unmoved by such a cold-blooded killing, the gangbangers turned on their heels and made their way toward Lennon's side of the camper, guns still in hand.

"Remember what I said." Lol lowered her gun, hiding it from sight behind Lennon, who smiled weakly as the two Surenos came to a stop by his window. The shorter one of the two, a swarthy young man with a wiry beard and round, brown eyes, twirled a pointer finger midair to indicate for Lennon to lower his window.

All Lennon could do was sit there, paralyzed with fear, and smile weakly.

"Get down!" Lol's voice startled him into action.

Even with hands clamped tight over his ears, the resounding cacophony of Lol's twin pistol shots in the camper van's confined space was unbearable and kicked off a loud ringing noise inside his head. Glass fragments from his window pitter-pattered down onto his back like heavy water droplets as the acrid stink of gunpowder groped inside his nostrils.

"You can get up now." Lol's voice was dulled by the high-pitched whistle in his ears. "We *really* need to get out of here."

Sitting back upright, Lennon peered down through the shattered window; fragments of glass clung to the frame in a glittering border that glinted like diamonds in the sunlight. The pair of gangbangers lay in a crumpled heap against his door, one on top of the other. Each had a neat, red hole above their left eye. Lol was obviously one hell of a markswoman.

"You'll need to climb over to this side." Lol stated the obvious as she pulled at the handle on her side and opened the door. There would be no opening the passenger door with a pair of corpses laid against it.

The Civic reeked of acrid weed smoke but was otherwise clean inside. The gangbangers had left the keys in the ignition, obviously having not anticipated being outgunned by a young woman and her middle-aged companion. They'd also left a couple snub-nosed revolvers on the passenger seat; Lennon recognized the brown-handled guns as .38 Saturday Night Specials – he'd done his best to talk Jilly into letting him buy her one, but she'd steadfastly refused.

Taking her place behind the wheel, Lol grabbed a weapon for herself and thrust the other into Lennon's hands. She then stuck the car into drive, maneuvered around the crippled camper van and makeshift roadblock, and headed back toward I10 and Santa Monica with the electric Mustang not far behind.

Chapter 30

"Where are we going, Mom?" Chad clung to Jilly's side like he used to as a toddler. Casey hung back behind her brother with worry on her face.

"Someplace safe," Jilly replied, running a hand through his hair, a gesture her son always found comforting. She felt him relax… just a little.

"Your mom's right, champ," Eubank chipped in. Jilly figured *Champ* was meant to sound friendly, put Chad at ease, but, somehow, it just sounded plain *wrong* coming from the FBI agent's mouth.

"Everything's going to be okay, baby." Jilly tried her best to sound reassuring, but she was barely convincing herself. Eubank had trekked her and the kids to the other side of the country, to a huge, remote house on the Palisades Beach Road, to hide from her husband. It was all hardly conducive to any form of peace of mind.

They were greeted at the huge double front doors by a muscular, middle-aged man who'd introduced himself as Ben Austin. "You guys can call me Ben," he told Chad and Casey, who just stared at him like he was some crazy person. He didn't seem to notice.

Jilly peered around the expansive house as they followed Austin inside, with Eubank bringing up the rear. A touch of paranoia coursed through Jilly, pinging her protective Mom senses, as she felt like they were being *herded* like a small but compliant flock of sheep.

Consciously putting a stop to the thought, Jilly repeated to herself that Special Agent Eubank, and now this gym-honed short guy, were there to keep her and the kids safe and sound. She knew she had to trust they knew what they were doing, even though the surreptitious presence of black suited, surly-looking men and women throughout the expansive house had her nerves more than a touch on edge.

The house, for as big as it was, seemed sparsely furnished and barely decorated, beyond the ubiquitous beige paint everyone put on the walls of their home before trying to sell it. She wouldn't exactly call it Spartan, but it was pretty damn close, especially for a property in such a salubrious area of California. Chase had sold a couple houses in the vicinity back in his early realtor days, and Jilly reckoned the place was an easy twelve, thirteen million.

"Here we are," Austin announced as they neared the end of a narrow hallway that seemed to go on forever. It had no windows, no doors save the one right at its very end and felt like it ran the entire length of the property. Jilly found it most disorienting.

Austin pulled open the door at the hallway's end and stood to one side to allow Eubank to usher Jilly and her children inside the room that lay beyond.

"What is this?" Jilly asked, stepping through the doorway into what appeared to be a hotel room, a second-rate one, at that, complete with dark brown, short-pile carpets and closed, chintzy curtains. Stopping dead a stride or two inside the room, Jilly caught hold of the kids' hands to prevent them going any further.

Austin gave them all a warm smile, mostly directed at Chad and Casey. "The previous owners were a little… *eccentric*," he explained, glancing around the room as if seeing it for the very first time. "They had these rooms built as an exact replica of the hotel in Vermont they stayed in for their honeymoon, apparently."

"Some honeymoon," Jilly heard herself say. She and Chase had spent theirs in a five-star, beach front Hilton in the British Virgin Islands.

Ignoring the slight, Austin went on, "There's everything you're going to need right here: cable TV with *all* the channels, well-stocked fridge and mini bar… not in the kids' room, though."

"Kids' room?" Jilly's eyes fixed on the door in the center of the opposite wall.

Austin nodded. "That's the connecting door. I thought you'd appreciate some privacy, Mrs. Lennon. Assuming Chad and Casey are okay sharing a room, that is. There are only the two, you see, so they can't have one each, I'm afraid." Making his way across the faux-hotel room, Austin clicked the lock and opened the door, which led into a near-identical space. "There's two twin beds on this side," he addressed Chad and Casey. "Just perfect for you guys. If you need anything at all, just ask."

"Is there a PlayStation?" Chad peered past Austin at the huge, flat-screened TV perched on the credenza.

"No, sir," Austin replied with a winning smile, "but that's easily remedied. I'll have one sent over just as soon as I leave you guys to make yourselves comfortable.

Jilly watched Chad visibly relax at news of the game console. The kid was fairly easy to please. What Casey was going to do without her beloved cell phone, though, Jilly had no idea. Eubank had taken it from her before they got into the big house; he'd seemed quite annoyed she'd not left it at home as instructed. But, for now at least, Casey was okay about the whole thing.

"There are cameras dotted about both rooms. Not in the en-suites, of course." Austin pointed up at the corner of what was meant to be Jilly's room. There, above the flat screen TV, a compact, square camera peered down into the room with its tiny red light glowing. "Only for your safety, nothing sinister, I can assure you."

"What are you expecting is going to happen to us, Mr. Austin?" Jilly instantly regretted voicing her concern in front of her children. Both Chad and Casey visibly stiffened.

"Absolutely nothing, Mrs. Lennon," Austin appeared put out by Jilly's formal address after he'd specifically *insisted* they all call him Ben. "But it pays to be extra safe in circumstances such as this."

"Ben's right, Mrs. Lennon," Eubank threw in. "We don't know exactly what we're dealing with here, so it's best we exercise every possible caution."

Even though the agent's words were meant as reassurance, they chilled Jilly to her core. That she and the kids were essentially on the run from her husband's supposed crazed murder spree was far too much to comprehend. It did surprise her, though, that she found the presence of the CCTV cameras quite comforting, even though the whole place had to be the oddest safe house ever.

"There are no windows to be concerned about." Austin pulled aside one of the flowery curtains. Behind it, a bare brick wall. "And that means extra safety. For just in case, that is."

"Just in case of *what*, exactly?" Jilly grew more anxious; just what kind of people rebuilt a sub-par hotel room onto their house and didn't put windows in? "Isn't the whole point of bringing us here that Chase won't know where to find us?"

"That was the plan, Mr. Lennon," Agent Eubank answered for Austin. "But, since someone didn't do as asked and smuggled her cell phone out of your house, it is quite possible your whereabouts has been compromised."

All eyes turned on Casey.

Her cheeks flushed crimson.

"You're saying my husband might have tracked Casey's phone here? Shouldn't you move us someplace else, if that's the case?" Jilly fought hard to keep the accusatory tone from her voice. Casey was only just holding herself together as it was.

"*Anything* is possible, Mrs. Lennon." As Austin spoke, Jilly realized, while he'd introduced who he was, he'd not actually said *what* his role was at the big house. She'd naturally assumed he was FBI like Eubank but now was beginning to wonder. She made a mental note to be sure to ask. "And, no, there's no need to move you. You're all perfectly safe here."

"Okay," Eubank butted in with firm finality to his tone. He took a couple steps toward the door, his intention clear. "We're going to leave you guys to get settled in now."

"Good thinking." Austin joined the FBI agent. He rested a hand on the doorknob. "Be sure to call if you need anything… anything at all." He nodded to the old-style push-button phone on Jilly's nightstand. "There's no outside line, so just dial nine and someone will deal with you."

Jilly opened her mouth to speak. She wanted to ask *why* Ben Austin was so sure they'd be safe there, why there were no windows or outside phone connection, and just who the hell was he supposed to be anyways, but he was already through the door and on his way back down the hallway with Special Agent Eubank hot on his heels.

***

Mercer was busy studying his bank of monitors when Austin and the FBI agent walked briskly into the production suite. He'd been watching Lennon's family make themselves at home as best they could in the mocked-up hotel rooms he'd had built a couple years ago. Mercer had learned from experience over the years it was far better to hold *The Contestant* finale in a controlled, closed-set environment than on location. Far too many variables, far too much to go wrong out in the big, bad world.

He turned around to nod a silent greeting to the two men.

"We're all set," Austin told him.

"So I see." Mercer returned his attention to the monitors. Jilly Lennon lay on her bed with an arm draped dramatically across her eyes as if she was attempting to block out the stark reality of her situation; she put Mercer in mind of the overwhelmed screen sirens of the golden age of cinema. Jilly had happened across the revolver, rope, and pills while snooping around the nightstand drawers and had shown no outward emotion.

She'd simply closed the drawer and lay down on the bed. Mercer wondered what her take on the sinister items would be, if she knew their true purpose. Meanwhile, the kids amused themselves by flicking through the hundreds of TV channels, having had a lively discussion as to who was going to get which one of the twin beds in their room. He'd ordered one of the suits to deliver the boy's PlayStation to the suite within the hour; might as well keep the kid happy.

"What happens now?" Eubank wanted to know. He positioned himself close by Mercer's shoulder, in order to take in the screens, which Mercer found to be disrespectfully inside his personal space. He actually felt the agent's warm, sour breath on his cheek.

As Mercer sidestepped away from Eubank, his eyes flicked to the monitor at the top left of the array. "Looks like they're right on time." He watched as the silver Honda made its way along the narrow road that led up to the house, its progress tracked by the multitude of hidden cameras lurking there, its passengers hidden by ridiculously blacked out windows.

"Yeah, the girl's phone was easy enough for them to track." Eubank cracked a self-congratulatory smile. "She thought I had no idea she'd brought it along, even when she was speaking to her old man on the plane, bless her heart."

"Good of you not to put your safety and wellbeing in jeopardy by trying to take a teenage girl's phone off her, Agent Eubank," Austin laughed from over by the door. Mercer knew his number two had little interest in the monitors. He much preferred real life.

"She's *twelve*." Eubank seemed offended. "And it's *Special* Agent."

Mercer fought back a chuckle. In all his years of show running *The Contestant*, there was nothing that delighted him more than conflict, no matter how small.

"Ahh, there you are," Mercer said quietly as the dark blue Mustang Mach-E drove into sight on the monitor adjacent to where the Civic neared the house. It brought him comfort to see Beard was right on time. The man was a good, reliable team player to have around for the conclusion to a season. Mercer reckoned he'd be good to deal with the woman, too, when the time came.

Lolita had become increasingly troublesome during the past couple seasons, and her going off script during this one had been the straw that broke the camel's back, as far as he was concerned. While she was undeniably one heck of a talented producer, Lolita's unreliability had finally outweighed her usefulness, and the time had come to eliminate her.

It was something Mercer was more than confident he could facilitate during the show's final scenes, while at the same time giving his clientele something that would stick in their minds for years to come. After all, he was the smart one on *The Contestant*, by far the smartest of them all.

"They're here?" Austin asked.

Nodding, Mercer spun around. "Right where we want them," he said. "It's gonna be one hell of a finale, gentlemen."

"Everything's in place." Austin fixed his eyes upon Eubank. "Not sure where you want to be," he said. "Might be best if you stay in here when things start to get interesting."

Eubank shook his head. "And miss out on all the fun? Not after all the work I put in to make this all happen after your guys screwed up like that in Vegas."

"Now is not the time for a peeing contest, not when we're so close to our conclusion." Mercer interrupted the two before the petty squabble could escalate. He had no time for such distractions right now.

"Yessir," Austin replied while Eubank simply pretended to be engrossed in the screens.

"Okay, then," Mercer said. "I guess it's showtime."

Chapter 31

Lennon followed Lol up to the house. She'd parked the Honda up a little ways down the driveway, telling him something about not wanting to get them blocked in should things go south.

"What about this?" Lennon pointed at the .38 he'd tucked into the waistband of his jeans at the front.

"Hide it at the back," Lol told him. She lifted her shirt to show him where her gun was secreted, and Lennon was positive she rolled her eyes at him. He took umbrage at that. It wasn't as if he was accustomed to carrying a weapon, he'd never felt the need to before. The gun felt cold, heavy, and unwelcome next to his skin. Nonetheless, he moved it to the rear of his pants and pulled his shirt down over it.

The door opened just as Lol got to it.

They were expected.

"You know the drill." The solitary security guard's greeting was flat and intimidating. Tall, broad-shouldered, clad in the same style suit as the two heavies back in Vegas, he carried a compact machine gun, which hung over his shoulder by a thin, black strap. Lennon had only seen the like in movies before, and had no idea what type was, other than it wasn't an AK-47. That was the only one he was familiar with – again, from the movies.

Lol nodded and stepped into the spacious vestibule with her arms spread out to her sides. Lennon followed her in and copied her stance as the door automatically eased shut behind them. It closed and locked with a loud *click*, and Lennon suddenly felt the icy rush of claustrophobia.

They were trapped.

"You packing?" The guard stepped up close to Lol, eyeing her companion as he did so. As far as Lennon could tell, the guy didn't view him as a threat. He obviously knew Lol, and was wary of her: while he outwardly appeared nonchalant, his on-edge body language gave him away.

"Just this," Lol replied, the flatness in her tone matching the guard's. Lennon looked on as, slowly, carefully, she reached one arm around to the back of her jeans to retrieve the gangbanger's Saturday Night Special she'd hidden there.

"Slowly." The guard cradled his machine gun, finger menacingly close to the trigger.

"If I went any slower, I'd stop." Lol's sarcasm failed to raise even a flicker of a reaction from the guard. His expression remained fixed, alert, as he watched her produce the revolver from behind her back, gripped gingerly by the handle between thumb and forefinger.

"What about you?" The guard turned some of his attention to Lennon, who looked to Lol for what the hell he was supposed to do next. Was he meant to hand over the gun she'd only just given him, or deny to the guard that he was armed?

In that split second, Lol had her own .38 gripped firmly in her fist and swung it around to smash hard into the guard's face. It connected with a dull, wet *crunch*.

Grunting, the guard stepped backward, blood streaming from his now-crooked nose and onto his expensive suit. His hand, which had slipped from his own weapon, sought the machine gun's trigger.

Startled by the sudden burst of violence and the presence of firearms, Lennon stepped backward until his back was pressed against the door. He'd never felt so much like a coward in his life, and only the thought of his family being somewhere in the huge house kept him from yanking open that door and running until his legs gave out.

Before the guard could swing his gun around to deter further assault, Lol had hold of his lapel and pushed him against the wall. She landed blow upon blow directly into his bloodied face with such rapidity the guy had no chance of even defending himself, let alone retaliating.

Each of Lol's blows elicited a low, pained cry as the bones in the guard's face snapped and crunched and his jaw flapped at a loose, crazy angle, obviously shattered. The final blow was a solid one with the .38's silver butt to the guard's temple, a sickeningly hollow *thunk*. The man's eyes rolled upward and his body went limp. Lol let go of his jacket and stepped back to watch him slide down the wall and slump sideways, lifeless, on the marble floor.

Lennon wondered why Lol had not simply delivered that debilitating temple strike straight away, instead of making such a hellish mess of the guard's face.

An old score to settle, perhaps?

"Let's go." Lol tucked the gore-spattered gun back into her jeans, grabbed the guard's machine gun from around his neck, and set off across the entryway with aggressive purpose in her stride.

Stepping over the guard's splayed legs, Lennon got the distinct impression Lol didn't really care much if he followed her or not, nor if he was reunited with his wife and kids. Obviously, the young woman her own agenda of putting a stop to Mercer's sick games, and she was frighteningly single-minded in its execution.

Lennon had to jog to catch up with Lol, who was already heading toward the sweeping staircase at the far end. She skirted around the walls, on constant alert, the guard's gun poised and ready to fire.

"Where are Jilly and the kids?" Lennon whispered as they stood, shoulder to shoulder, at the foot of the stairs. Instinctively, he plucked the .38 from the back of his jeans. Above them, another suited guard patrolled the balcony, partially hidden by the balustrade.

"Mercer will have them in the studio," Lol whispered back.

"That's up there?" Perplexed at the notion of an actual studio in the mansion, he nodded up the stairs.

"It's on the way." Lol scrutinized the guard above until he moved out of the line of sight, and then, a few seconds later, back into view. "First, we go see Mercer."

"We can't just leave them." Lennon grew concerned it was exactly what Lol intended to do. After all, his wife and kids really weren't any of her concern.

"We won't," Lol hissed. "You know how to use that thing?" She glanced down at the gun clenched tight in Lennon's hand.

"I took lessons," he told her, recalling the six-week gun handling course he'd signed up for what seemed a million years ago. He'd only attended three of those weeks but still reckoned he could point a small revolver at a bad guy and pull the trigger if necessary.

Especially when it came to his family.

The guard upstairs dipped out of sight once more.

"Let's do this." Lol set off up the stairs, taking them two, three at a time, her weapon at the ready.

A deep, terrified breath, and Lennon was hot on her heels and wishing he'd had more time to spend in the home gym he'd spent a small fortune on; halfway up, his breathing was already labored and fat droplets of sweat dripped down his back.

Lennon reached the top of the stairs a second or so after Lol, just in time to see the guard there swing around on his circuit to see them both standing there.

Lennon froze.

The .38 felt unnaturally heavy in his hand, as if all the strength in the world wouldn't be able to lift it.

All he could do was watch as, in his adrenaline-stunted slow motion, the guard reacted to the intruders by lifting his machine gun and opening his mouth to shout out.

A loud, jarring staccato of shots rang out from Lol's gun as it bucked and jerked in her hands. The guard staggered backward with each bullet's punch and the pale blue shirt beneath his dark suit bloomed with circles of red.

The guard had not even hit the floor before Lennon found himself following Lol at a full-on run along one of the two hallways leading from the top of the staircase. It was the one with noticeably fewer doors dotted along its blandly decorated walls. Behind them, Lennon heard shouts, voices both alarmed and angry, and it was safe to assume Lol taking out the guard had alerted every armed suit in the building. There really was no turning back now. As he ran, Lennon chanced a quick look back and saw a handful of suited guards racing across the vestibule below and toward the staircase.

And, in his peripheral vision, the front door opened.

More gunfire from Lol, now several yards away, and Lennon watched another suit hit the floor. A spray of fine, red mist lingered in the air above his crumpled body.

Lennon increased his step to catch up, terrified of being left alone in what promised to be an extremely one-sided gun fight. Ahead, one of the white-painted doors along the hallway swung open and a guard stepped out, gun trained on Lol's back.

Without pausing even to consider the options, Lennon's took aim at the guard and let off a trio of shots before the guard could take Lol down. The .38 had one hell of a kick for a small gun and jumped wildly in Lennon's hand. The first slug caught the guard in the left shoulder, the second and third flew wide and dug into the drywall over the guy's head. Plumes of beige powder puffed out into the big house's cooled air.

With an angry yowl, the guard spun around to face his assailant, gun in hand.

More shots rang out, this time from Lol as she finished the job Lennon had started. She stared with dissatisfaction down the hallway at him as the guard between them collapsed back into the open doorway with his neck a gaping, bloody mess.

Heart thumping, adrenaline surging, Lennon raced to join Lol, determined to not leave her side until the ordeal was over.

The hallway curved sharply to the right at its end, another, shorter, corridor lay beyond that. Even in his panic, Lennon couldn't help but notice the lack of cameras along the hallway; maybe they had an element of surprise after all.

There, Lol stopped. She grasped Lennon's arm to bring him to an abrupt halt, too, and pulled him in close behind her.

They waited.

Sounds of footsteps, the voices again, coming from the hallway. Lennon could barely make the voices out above the sound of his own heartbeat. Hands shaking, he gripped his revolver as a child would a security blanket and reminded himself he only had three bullets left.

Just as the running footsteps seemed to be on top of them, Lol stepped out from around the corner and let loose with four, five, short bursts from the machine gun. Startled screams of pain and dull thumps of bodies on the marble floor were followed by silence as Lol put an end to the pursuit. The harsh resonance of gunshots, along with the sickening reek of gunpowder and blood, hung ominously in the air.

Lol remained still, silent for a moment. Her head tilted ever so slightly as she listened out for more guards on the staircase. Lennon ventured out from around the corner, his stomach turning over at the sight of the half-dozen, dark-suited, corpses strewn along the hallway, and watched as Lol, clearly satisfied there were no more guards coming from that way at least, walked over to the closest body to retrieve its stumpy machine gun.

Bringing it back over, she pressed the weapon into Lennon's hands. He could do no more than stare at the thing as if it was something altogether alien.

"Go!" Lol's growling command jolted Lennon back into action. Struggling to take in the very *realness* of the death around him, he blindly followed Lol as she sped off along the shorter hallway toward a pair of narrow metal doors.

Chapter 32

"What the—?" Mercer turned around from the bank of monitors as the production room door burst open with such ferocity it slammed hard into the wall and dug a handle-shaped divot there. Beside him, Eubank and Austin were similarly startled; they spun to face the disruption and immediately held their hands up, shoulder height.

"It's over, Mercer." Lol looked him straight in the eye, a trait of hers he'd always found uncomfortable. That she also pointed a machine gun directly at his heart did nothing to help with the discomfort.

"I really don't think so." Mercer eyed Chase Lennon, who looked alarmingly haggard. It was a remarkable contrast to how he'd been the first time they'd met, back in Philly. At that time, the guy had struck Mercer as remarkably handsome and oozing with confidence as he literally signed his life away at the bottom of the weighty *The Contestant* contract without bothering to read it.

Had he not watched Lennon following Lolita into the house, Mercer would have been quite surprised to see him still alive and breathing, let alone brandishing an automatic weapon in the production suite like some dime-store Bruce Willis.

"*He* wasn't supposed to get in here." Mercer turned his ire to Ben Austin. Mercer had expected Lol to lead Lennon to the studio to rescue his wife and kids, not the production suite. There'd been no sign of Lennon or his traitorous companion on any of the screens, as there were no cameras along the hallway leading to the room – why would there be?

"I know," Austin replied with a distinct tremor to his voice and a nervous, sideways look at the FBI agent, "but it'll make great TV."

Mercer followed his assistant's gaze up to the small camera up in the corner of the room. He'd not noticed it there before and couldn't recall instructing Austin to install it. He made a mental note to discuss the matter with Austin once things were back on track; he didn't much care for being on candid camera for the clientele; it wasn't his role in this part of the show at all. He'd have his time during the final scenes, and that was more than enough for him.

"You need to let them go." Lol wiggled her gun at the monitors, to where Lennon's wife and kids were going about their business, oblivious to the true nature of their incarceration.

The woman was really starting to annoy Mercer now. He'd been disgruntled enough with her going so wildly off script with Lennon to begin with, although he'd managed to bring that back around and work it to the show's advantage, but now she had the audacity to storm into his production suite waving guns about – it truly was the last damn straw.

"You know that's not going to happen." Mercer's tone was rigid, uncompromising. "He has to finish the game first." His icy look toward Lennon elicited a visible wince from the realtor.

"The game's over, Mercer," Lol was telling him, like she was in some position to be calling the shots simply because she had the gun.

Defiant, Mercer maintained eye contact and made a careful move toward the desk, as if he had a weapon secreted there. Under any other circumstances, such a move in front of a pair of fugitives wielding guns would have been foolish, suicidal, even, but…

Beard had appeared silently in the doorway behind Lol and Lennon, his faithful, suited companion by his side. In the heartbeat it took for Mercer to create the momentary distraction, Beard had rushed into the production suite and cracked the woman's head with the butt of his pistol, and the suit pressed his gun against the back of Lennon's head.

"Drop the weapon." The suit's snarled command left Lennon in no doubt as to what would happen next, should he refuse.

Game over.

Chase Lennon's stolen machine gun clattered to the floor.

Lolita crumpled to the ground like she'd had her legs kicked from under her, much to Mercer's satisfaction.. Her face, pretty in its own way, he'd always thought, smacked down hard with the unmistakable sound of cracking teeth. A thin trickle of blood oozed from the corner of her mouth.

"You took your time," Mercer addressed Beard, who stepped over Lolita's unconscious body and kicked Lennon's gun across the room.

"You know how it is," Beard said, unsmiling. "Gotta build up the tension for the viewers. What do you want me to do with him?" He pointed at Lennon, who stood stock-still and too terrified to move with the suit's gun jammed hard against the back of his head.

"We take Mr. Lennon to be reunited with his wife and children, of course." Mercer was relieved to have things back under his control. For as exciting as the clientele found the impromptu, off-script moments, he was always happier to know exactly what was coming next. "He has an important decision to make."

***

While it was weirdly comforting for Lennon to see Jilly and the kids on the monitors and hear Mercer saying he was finally going to get to see them, there was something to the man's tone that scared him. Call him paranoid, or maybe it was because there was a gun muzzle digging into his scalp, but Lennon was sure he detected more than a soupcon of malice to Mercer's words.

All he could do was hope he was wrong.

"Where's my family, Mercer?" Lennon found his voice as the redneck guy Lol had christened Beard walked by him. "What decision?" Lennon glanced nervously across at Ben Austin, whom he recalled from the very first day he'd signed up for *The Contestant*. He also recognized the runty-looking guy he'd assumed to be law enforcement when he'd fled the motel parking lot back in Texas. Close up, the guy most definitely oozed *cop*.

"All in good time, Chase." Mercer stepped away from the desk, which housed some of the monitors. Lennon figured the man felt safe now Lol was incapacitated and he was held at gunpoint by the silent bodyguard in the company-standard dark suit and pale blue shirt.

Caught in the reflection of the largest screen, now behind Mercer, which showed Jilly laying down on what appeared, worryingly, to be a cheap motel's twin bed, Lol jumped to her feet. She moved with such rapidity, such measured agility, Lennon knew in an instant the bearded guy hadn't knocked her out at all.

Mercer and his two cohorts reacted too late to warn Beard and the suit and, before anyone could utter a word, Lol jerked the suit's arm upward and snapped his wrist with one fluid motion. The gun holding Lennon in place skidded across the floor, harmless and way out of reach.

Lennon spun around to hear the suited guy let out a sharp squeal of pain. He turned on his assailant with his remaining good fist, punching wildly out while the broken one flapped impotently by his side.

Lol dodged the flailing fist with ease and aimed a brutally fast kick at the guy's crotch. Her foot missed his balls by a fraction of an inch and thudded hard into the meat of his thigh. With a winded, guttural grunt, he dropped down to one knee as his leg gave way under him. Absurdly, it looked like he was about to produce a diamond ring and propose.

Turning on his heals, Beard marched back toward Lol, pistol raised. Lennon noticed the redneck was trying to aim past him, and guessed if he'd not been in the way, Lol would have hit the floor for sure that time. Acting against every self-preservation instinct screaming at him to *run*, Lennon grabbed at Beard's gun arm to direct it away from Lol; the suit she'd downed was back on his feet and retaliating with a flurry of left-handed punches.

Beard's gun went off, its report thunderous within the room. The bullet wildly missed its intended mark, instead shattering one of the smaller screens close by Mercer's head.

Beard grunted something obscene in his ringing ear as Lennon grappled with him, using his weight and inch or two height advantage to drag the redneck to the floor. The two crashed down, hands punching and grabbing for one another's necks, bodies writhing, pushing, to gain an advantage.

Lennon barely registered the bearded guy's fists as pain as they pummeled at his face; each one jarred his head, sent stars sparking behind his eyes, and the nauseating taste of blood filled his mouth.

Mercifully, the adrenaline inundating his system held the pain at bay, which allowed him to focus on fighting back. As they grappled, Beard's hand clawed fiercely at Lennon's throat, threatening to choke the life from him, so Lennon did likewise, all the while slamming his fist into the guy's nose and teeth until his knuckles bled.

A short distance across the room, Lol valiantly battled with the suit. His jacket had been pulled off, his shirt torn and bloody, his face a broken mess. Yet still he fought on, determined to take his opponent down, no matter how scrappy their altercation had become. Fists and feet flew, hair was yanked out by its roots, teeth sank into exposed flesh.

Somehow, Lennon managed to roll himself on top of Beard. He pinned the man down to the hardwood floor and sat astride him with Beard's right hand trapped beneath his knee; Lennon felt the small bones of Beard's fingers snap as he bore down with the hard bone of his kneecap.

As Beard yelped, his fingers loosened around Lennon's throat. Siezing the opportunity, Lennon pulled back his fist and aimed it directly at his opponent's Adam's apple, a moving target bobbing with each one of Beard's agonized grunts. It was a move Lennon had picked up from some old Denzel Washington movie years ago.

There came a muffled *snap* as Lennon's fist found its mark, shattering the hyoid bone, and Beard's throat collapsed. Immediately, Beard's attention redirected from Lennon's throat to his own; he clawed frantically at the soft skin there as he fought to breathe, his mouth gaping wide as it failed to draw in air.

Satisfied the bearded man was no longer a threat, Lennon stood and stared down at the harm he'd done. He felt a jolt of self-satisfaction: it was the first time he'd felt anything close to being in control during Mercer's game since waking up in that first grubby motel room.

Lol was still in trouble, though. Despite her fierceness and undoubted fighting skills, the suit was beating her, despite the broken wrist. He had the young woman trapped in a corner and was pummeling the living tar out of her. The best Lol could do was attempt to defend her face and head from the relentless bout of damaging blows.

Even though his own vision remained blurred from the beating he'd just taken, Lennon stepped over Beard, now eerily still and no longer scratching at his own crushed windpipe and retrieved the machine gun Lol had dropped when the suit jumped her. He'd never handled one before, but it was the closest weapon to hand.

"That's enough!" Lennon pointed the gun at the suit.

The guy gave Lennon a contemptuous backward glance and continued his brutal attack on Lol.

It gave Lennon no pleasure to pull the trigger, but Lol was the only one who could get him to Jilly and the kids.

There really was no other option.

The gun kicked in Lennon's hands, jumping to the right as he fought to control the harsh recoil. Lol wrapped her arms over her head and curled herself tightly into a ball on the floor in the corner as the weapon's rapid fire all but hacked the suit in half, hip to shoulder. Mouth agape in shock, driven backward by bullets thump-thumping through his body, the suit collapsed.

"Jesus Christ, Chase!" Lol screamed at Lennon over the cacophony of gunfire as powdered plaster from the ruined walls rained down around her. *"Put the gun down!"*

Broken from the moment, Lennon's finger left the trigger and he dropped the gun, its muzzle smoking, and stared at Lol's angry face. The realization that his thoughtless choice of weapon could very easily have killed her shook Lennon to his core and then came the absurd thought it was the first time the young woman had called him by his first name.

Lol struggled to her feet, wincing from the vicious beating she'd just taken. Looking at Lennon, she managed to say, "Thank you." She spoke softly, her voice strained.

"Can you take me to my family now?" Lennon asked her. "Please?"

Nodding, Lol replied as she peered over his shoulder. "It's not over yet, Mr. Lennon."

Turning around, Lennon saw for himself that Mercer, Austin, and the cop were no longer in the production room.

Chapter 33

Lol was doing her best to walk without limping, but the pain written across her bloodied, bruised face gave her away. She attempted what Lennon interpreted to be a reassuring smile, which showed chipped front teeth. He could only hope she'd not been too badly hurt by the suit – the thug had clearly been well-trained in the art of dishing out effective beatings – and not only because she knew her way around the huge house.

"It's through here." Lol paused by the metal door adjacent and identical to the one leading to the room with all the screens. Lennon was happy to leave the two corpses he was responsible for behind him; it wasn't a good feeling at all to have taken human lives, no matter what the circumstances.

"You sure?" It was a stupid question that slipped out without him thinking. Lennon was lucky Lol didn't take offence.

"Mercer calls it The Studio. It's a staged version of a motel, right down to the smallest detail." As she spoke, Lol double-checked the pistol she'd liberated from the suit. Quite absently, she slid out the clip and eyeballed the bullets nestling there, snapped it back in place, then pulled back the slide to put one in the chamber.

Lennon did likewise with Beard's identical weapon she'd insisted he pick up. There was no way on God's green earth she was going to let him loose with a machine gun again.

"Will they be expecting us?" Lennon was terrified. After everything Mercer had put him through in the name of *The Contestant*, the thought of being reunited with his family was the hardest one to bear. After all, he had no real idea of what Jilly believed he'd done. All she had to go on was the news reports and whatever lies Mercer and his team had fed her. Judging by the last conversation he'd had with his wife, Lennon prepared himself for the worse.

"Of course," Lol replied. "There are cameras everywhere in there. It's very likely Mercer and the others went this way, too, so be prepared to use that." A glance gown at the gun feeling so cold and cumbersome in Lennon's hand.

Lol turned the silver, steel handle and pushed at the door.

It was, of course, locked.

"They're not making this easy," Lol sighed.

"Can't we just shoot the lock out?"

"This is not a dumb TV show, Mr. Lennon," Lol replied without even a hint of irony. "Locks don't work like that. You're gonna have to kick it in."

"Me?" Lennon's day was becoming one of many firsts.

"Look at me."

Lennon followed Lol's eyes downward and took in her slim frame and bloodied, bruised arms. The poor woman really was in no fit state to kick anything in, let alone a steel door.

Taking a step back, bracing himself, Lennon aimed a full force kick an inch or two from the handle. The door rattled in its frame some, and a sharp, jarring pain stabbed at Lennon's knee. Undeterred, he kicked again, and then a third time, until, on the fourth attempt, the metal door crashed open to hang at a crazy angle on warped hinges.

Gritting his teeth against his complaining knee, Lennon followed Lol through the door and down along the dimly lit, windowless hallway he could only assume led to his family. The light was too low to see all the way to the end, although he did spot several cameras dotted along its length, each one given away by a tiny red glow.

They were expecting him, alright.

There was a door at the end of the long corridor. Above it, an illuminated red sign that read, *Silence!*

Without breaking her hobbling stride, Lol burst through the door, which was mercifully unlocked. Lennon's knee really couldn't take any more punishment.

"Chase!" Jilly's strained voice was the first Lennon heard when he ran into the brightness of the faux-motel room. In the handful of seconds it took for his eyes to adjust to the stark studio lighting, Lennon only made out the vague shapes of the room's occupants.

There were three standing, one seated.

"Lose the guns or Mrs. Lennon dies." Mercer stood behind Jilly, who was seated on a well-worn wooden chair, with a gun in his hand. By Jilly's side stood Ben Austin with a revolver held to her head. Its dark gray muzzle nestled in the hair behind Jilly's ear, its end hidden. "Could you take their weapons, please, Special Agent Eubank?" He half-turned his head to address the cop, who stood close behind.

Lennon followed Lol's lead in lowering his gun, and at once felt vulnerable and helpless. The cop—Eubank—strode over to collect the pistols, then returned to his place behind Mercer and Austin like some comically miscast bodyguard.

"Where are my children, Mercer?" Lennon demanded. "If you've done anything—"

"Relax," Mercer said with a hand wave at the room's connecting door. "Chad and Casey are in their own room, all safe and sound."

Muted sounds of what Lennon recognized as his kid's voices crept through to the room. Seeing the motel room set-up in person, instead of up on the monitors, Lennon was taken aback as to just how much it reminded him of the crappy place he'd woken up in back in New Orleans. They'd obviously gone to a lot of trouble to perfectly recreate a grimy one-star motel. Hell, it even *smelled* like one.

"Help me, Chase." Jilly sniffled. Terrified, her eyes were wide and moist with tears, her face puffy from crying. Lennon wanted nothing more than to cross the room, take her in his arms, and assure her he'd not done all the terrible things Mercer's people had set in place. It was important if she was ever to look at him with trust in her eyes again.

But first…

"Let her go, Mercer," Lennon dared a step forward. "I'm not playing your game anymore." He was all too aware of the small cameras scrutinizing his every move and wondered just how much of this set up was for the benefit of Mercer's anonymous clientele.

Mercer shook his head. "Yes, you are," he said. "*The Contestant* isn't over until you achieve your time limit without capture, or…"

"You had no right to get my wife and kids involved." Lennon struggled to hold his contempt for the man at bay.

He'd quite happily rip Mercer's smug face off and make him eat it, given the chance.

If there wasn't a gun at his wife's head, of course.

"We have *every* right, Mr. Lennon." Austin chipped in. "You didn't read the contract, did you?"

Shaking his head, Mercer replied for Lennon. "None of our contestants ever do. All they see is the prize money and all those zeros. That's what pure, unadulterated greed does for you, I suppose."

"You have to stop this, Mercer." Lennon looked on as Lol limped toward her boss with determination written all over her face. "You're going too far, and you know it."

Behind Mercer, Eubank suddenly sprang into action. In the blink of an eye, he had the pistol he'd taken from Lol pointing directly at her chest. His stance, both hands cradling the weapon, let the room know he meant business.

Lol stopped right where she was, her determination deflated.

"How far do you really think is *too far*?" Mercer looked Lennon squarely in the eye. "We have to give our paying viewers what they want, *and* up the game to hold their interest and keep them paying."

"Just let my family go, Mercer," Lennon growled. "I don't care what you do to me."

"That's very noble of you, Chase." Mercer smiled. "But *The Contestant* has to play out to one of its final conclusions to satisfy the wagers. If you want to play the big hero role and save Jilly and your son and daughter, there's only really the one conclusion that will do."

A cold, heart-stopping chill gripped Lennon. Mercer advising him to commit suicide to save his family!

"There has to be another way…"

"There's a hell of a lot of money riding on you taking the decent way out of this, Mr. Lennon. Which is why I've gone to all the trouble of inviting Jilly along."

"Ouch!" Jilly yelped as Austin prodded the gun into her head, as if to underline Mercer's point.

Lennon's mind raced with a myriad of possibilities, all of which brought him right back to Mercer's conclusion. An unarmed Lol was no help, as they were outgunned, and Austin was beginning to look increasingly trigger-happy.

"There are all the familiar implements in the top drawer." Mercer wiggled his gun in the direction of the nightstand by the bed. "May I suggest the revolver? I'm sure your beautiful wife wouldn't want to watch you hang or slowly fade away with pills."

"Go get it." Austin ordered with a snarl. He was a far cry from the affable guy Lennon had first met in Philadelphia.

"Chase, no," Jilly sobbed as Lennon turned tail to collect the silver gun from the nightstand drawer, where it lay next to a well-thumbed Gideon Bible. Mercer's set dressers really had thought of every detail.

"There's just the one bullet in there," Mercer told him. "Just in case you're planning any heroics. You can't kill us all with one bullet." He looked around at Austin and Eubank; the latter's gun was still trained on Lol.

The revolver evoked so many memories in Lennon. Since Lol had held back on the drugs she'd been feeding him throughout his time on *The Contestant*, many of the memories had filtered back into his brain. And the gun he now held in his hand featured prominently as a constant in each one.

Lennon's hand trembled as he slipped the gun into his mouth and aimed it upward. He'd read somewhere once that was the most effective way to get the job done. There was practically no chance of him ending up still alive and a vegetable. His eyes sought out Jilly's, but she had her chin lowered to her chest and was sobbing softly. It broke Lennon's heart knowing he'd put his family through such a horrendous ordeal because of his own dumb greed. Mercer had definitely hit a home run with that particular comment.

"Chase, no," Lol hissed. "You don't have to do this."

"But he *does* have to do this," Mercer chastised. "It's the only fair way to conclude the game. You know that, Lolita."

Lennon gagged on the pungent, metallic taste of the revolver's barrel. He pressed his tongue down to the floor of his mouth, positioned his finger on the trigger, and told himself it was all for the best.

"I can't…" Lennon lowered the gun.

Mercer let out a weary groan and addressed Austin and Eubank. "Kill them both," he said, "we'll have to AI his suicide in post-production."

"No!" Lol's cry was drowned by the sudden *crack-crack* report of twin gunshots.

Jilly's head snapped violently to the side and blood flew from her mouth and nose.

Lol hit the floor.

In shock, Lennon didn't immediately register Ben Austin had fallen forward and away from Jilly's chair, pushed by the force of Eubank's point-blank shot to the back of his neck. Instead, he raised the revolver, its end still glistening wet with his own saliva, and rounded it on Mercer.

"Stop!" Lol clambered back to her feet with a pained grunt; still bloodied and bruised from her earlier altercations, she appeared otherwise unharmed. Lunging at Lennon, she deflected the revolver as he squeezed the trigger, determined to put an end to Mercer's games once and for all. The slug few wide, shattering the flat screen on its way to embed itself in the wall behind.

Confused, Lennon pushed Lol aside and watched helplessly as Mercer raised his own pistol in his direction.

"Put the gun down, Mercer." It only took Eubank one step forward to put his gun to Mercer's head.

Mercer did as he was told, his face suddenly ashen.

Lennon darted across the make-believe motel room, dropped to his knees, and cradled Jilly's lifeless body in his arms. Her blood, warm, sticky, soaked through his shirt to his skin.

"I'm so sorry, Lol," the cop spoke across Lennon. "I really didn't expect him to do that." He nodded down at Austin's body, face down on the ruined carpet, neat red hole at the base of his skull.

"What the hell is going on here?" Mercer snapped. "This isn't part of the show."

Lol made her way over to him. "It wasn't part of *your* show, Mercer." She stood mere inches away, her nose close to his. "We decided to go totally off script and make a few changes. *Permanent* ones."

"We?"

Looking up from his dead wife to Mercer, Lennon saw the abject terror in the man's eyes. Now he was finding out first-hand how horrifying it was to have a gun to his head and his entire world falling apart.

"The two of us," Jilly pointed at the FBI agent, "and the executive producers, of course."

"No… that can't be," Mercer stammered. "They *wouldn't.*"

"But they did, Mercer," Eubank added. "This is where *The Contestant* ends for you. You can't complain too much, you've had a good run."

"Go get your children, Chase. We'll finish up here." Lol helped Lennon to his feet; there'd be plenty time for mourning later. He didn't want to leave Jilly, not like this, but Lol gently maneuvered him toward the connecting door.

"We'll make sure you get your prize money, Mr. Lennon," Eubank called after him. "You've more than earned it."

"It'll be your final job as producer," Lol informed Mercer, who looked in no state to argue. Lennon hoped the man's death would be an unpleasant one.

Lol closed the connecting door behind Lennon, which left him with the aching feeling of having abandoned Jilly. The kids were sat on one of the twin beds, headphones clamped to their ears, playing a PlayStation shoot-em-up game on the big TV. They were blissfully oblivious to what had gone on the other side of the thin wall, and to the fact they no longer had a mom.

Chad and Casey's children's faces lit up when they realized their father was in the room. Dropping the game controllers, yanking off the headphones, they raced over to greet him.

From the room beyond the door, there came the sound of a single, muted gunshot.

The kids didn't even notice.

Epilogue

He'd moored the yacht, a nicely modest 75ft Sunseeker, off the Belize coastline. Lennon had purchased a beachside property there. Also, Mackenzie Crail had arranged a slew of offshore bank accounts and accompanying shell companies to squirrel away his prize money from *The Contestant*, so it made sense to hang around a little while. It was amazing just how much peace of mind $1.2bn could buy, and that *little while* had very quickly turned into six months.

On days like this, with cloudless blue skies and the kids fishing off the side of the boat in clear, azure water, Lennon doubted he'd ever return to the States, let alone New York State.

He had little reason to, now Chase Lennon was officially dead and Imagine Realty was owned by one of the shell companies and thriving under new management.

Special Agent Eubank had taken pretty much all the credit for putting a stop to the Chase Lennon killing spree. The official story was the FBI man had cornered him in some grubby LA motel and shot him dead. He'd magnanimously given a crumb or two of the credit to a couple detectives, one in Lubbock, the other in New Orleans, which Lennon thought was mighty big of him.

Leaning forward in his deck chair to squint against the glare on his wafer-thin MacBook Air, Lennon rubbed at the itch along his jawline. The bandages had been off almost two weeks now, and the skin there still felt tight. The cosmetic surgeon had advised him it might take another couple months or so until the new face felt *right* again, so Lennon had no cause to worry. And besides, they'd done such a tremendous job of giving him a brand-new, younger appearance, even Lennon had trouble believing it was himself staring back from the mirror.

Lennon tapped on the laptop's touchpad to bring up the screen he'd hidden when the kids had been circling round for more popsicles; he'd become a soft touch, unable to say no to either of them because he was the reason they'd lost their mother. There, on the laptop's screen, stood a disheveled, middle-aged man wearing a gray hoodie and dirty, blood-smeared jeans.

The setting, a seedy old motel on the outskirts of Atlanta, was unnervingly triggering to Lennon. As the guy contemplated the rope and shiny, silver six-shooter in his hands, a movement from below decks caught Lennon's attention.

"*Another* mimosa?" Lol made her way carefully up the steps from belowdecks, a too-full crystal-cut glass flute in each hand. "And it's not even ten yet. You should be ashamed of yourself, Mr. Lennon."

"It's orange juice." Lennon smiled. The gal sure looked good in her miniscule, black string bikini, and the orthodontist had fixed her broken front teeth perfectly. Not that he'd made any moves in that direction – it was far too soon after Jilly for him to even think about it, but she made for decent, distracting company and the liked her. Whether or not he'd ever be able to trust an ex-producer of *The Contestant* remained to be seen. "And that's practically breakfast," he said.

Lol returned the flawless smile, delivered the drink, and positioned herself behind Lennon's deckchair with a hand rested gently upon his bare shoulder. She leaned over him to squint at the Mac's screen, and Lennon breathed in the heady scent of vanilla and aloe.

"Only betting ten mill'?" Her breath, warm against his neck, had Lennon stirring uncomfortably in his swim shorts.

"Yep." Lennon was still cautious with spending money, even with a king's ransom of it sitting, tax-free and gathering interest, in the bank.

Lol studied the screen a while longer, taking in the sad-looking face now filling it. "Look, I know Mercer, and he's not gonna last more than another twenty-four hours. Let's make this interesting."

Lennon tapped the touchpad one more time. "Okay, twenty million it is then."

END

About the Author

Blake Rudman enjoyed a former, successful career in executive management, building his own companies from the ground up.

Success or not, Blake's heart has always been in the written word, and the myriad ideas he spent much of his spare time jotting down in notebooks, Post-Its, and scraps of paper whenever the inspiration hit him.

A breakout author of bestselling noir thriller novels, Blake's destiny of becoming a writer of some renown is well under way.

When he's not working diligently on his next novel, Blake spends quality time with his family and reading.

Follow Blake at: blakerudman.com
Facebook: @BRudmanThriller
Instagram: @BRudmanThriller
Twitter: @BRudmanThriller

For all Blake's books, visit him at:
www.hellboundbookspublishing.com/authorpage_rudman.html

Blake Rudman Novels from HellBound Books:

Available in Kindle, paperback, hardcover, and audiobook.

The Gentleman's Choice

"Caught in a whirlwind of adverse publicity following a viewer's death, the streaming show, The Gentleman's Choice becomes the target for a sadistic killer – and it's up to PI Vanessa Young to put a stop to it before more young women are murdered."

A sleazy internet dating show blamed for a viewer's death, a host with a dark, secret past, and a killer with a sadistic grudge…

Someone is kidnapping and murdering previous contestants from the popular streaming show *The Gentleman's Choice* – a strictly-for-adults hybrid of *The Bachelor* and *Love Island.* Private Investigator, Vanessa Young, is hired by a victim's family to infiltrate the show as a contestant to expose and capture the killer.

Vanessa and the show's charismatic star, Cole Gianni, begin to fall romantically for each other, until Vanessa's plan goes terribly awry when they're drugged and taken to a remote location to take part in their captor's own brutal, ultimately fatal, version of *The Gentleman's Choice.*

With the clock ticking toward their fateful final night, Vanessa and Cole are forced into a battle of wills to survive their tormentor and escape with their lives before

NeverEnd

Inexplicably, huge locust swarms of Biblical proportions plague Austin, Texas: a sinister portent of terrifying things to come?

Dr. Jon Edom, hero surgeon, loving father, finds himself unwittingly drawn into the dark conspiracies surrounding the sinister Church of the Resurrected, which has uncomfortably close family ties to his wife, Rochelle.

Rochelle Edom, daughter of the Church's founder, genius creator of the worldwide hit video game, NeverEnd, has left her coding days behind to focus on family life. She laments that the repetitive, highly-addictive game she designed shows an alarming increase in ill effects among its players: they emulate the characters' violent actions with increasingly brutal consequences – which her husband witnesses first hand.

When Rochelle unexpectedly goes missing, along with her and Jon's two young children, Jon all too quickly becomes a suspect once old infidelities are exposed.

As Jon fights to clear his name under seemingly impossible, tragic circumstances, aided by his close friend, Rabbi Max, he becomes inexorably embroiled in the evil undercurrent of the Church of the Resurrected's association with the enigmatic Coppersmith, who has a nefarious agenda all of his own…

Dark Beauty

Tessa and Kristin Morgan are identical twins, exquisitely beautiful, and have the world at their perfectly pedicured feet; they are also profoundly different beneath their stunning facades.

Tessa is the laser-focused academic with her eyes firmly fixed upon a career in neurology, while Kristin exploits her striking looks and undeniable power over men to carve out a single-minded path to fame and fortune as a model and actress; an ambition she also holds for her sister.

But, on the night of the pair's debut as top-tier models, and with a high-profile movie role in the bag, tragedy strikes the twins in the form of a cruel acid attack by an unknown assailant. Thus, a gruesome chain of events begins - one that leaves a trail of blood, death, and devastation behind both Tessa and Kristin.

As Tessa fights to rebuild her life and uncover the truth behind the attack, she finds herself getting closer and closer to an uncomfortable truth about her sister and her search for the truth turns into a nightmare struggle to stay alive.

Goodbye Stranger

"As with *American Psycho*, Blake Rudman's *Goodbye Stranger* has a wealthy, successful man whose wonderful family life masks a much darker side. Throw in a once-trusting, increasingly suspicious wife, and the stage is set for twists and turns you'll never see coming!"

Danielle Harrington has the life many women envy: She's beautiful, rich, has two wonderful children, and is married to *the* Preston Harrington - the handsome, charismatic, retired quarterback who won two Super Bowls.

Unfortunately, something is very wrong with Preston. Having suffered more than his fair share of injuries and concussions, he becomes quiet, withdrawn, and distant. As Preston spends more time away from his family, Danielle begins suspect an affair without realizing her husband is involved in something much, much worse...

Following a series of tragic incidents and the return of an old nemesis from the past, things begin to spiral out of control for Danielle as Preston's dark side puts her and their children in terrible danger.

Redline

"If Lee Childs' Jack Reacher or Clive Cussler's Dirk Pitt tackled a terrorist scheme that utilized subliminal messaging to sow social and economic chaos on a global scale, it would look a lot like *Red Line*." Baltimore Police Detective Mitch Wilson wants a nice day out with his wife and son. Instead, they are all caught up in a catastrophic terrorist attack that has repercussions across the USA and triggers events that could alter the course of civilization.

Having lost everything, Mitch sets out to seek justice – and revenge and stumbles upon a global conspiracy.

On the other side of the world, renowned linguistic professor, Yasaman Karami, flees her native Iran for the freedom of the west; she holds one of the keys to defeating the terrorist organization.

Yasaman and Mitch's worlds collide as, alongside federal agents and allies, they race against the clock to hunt down the terrorist masterminds and prevent worldwide catastrophe.

Kutri

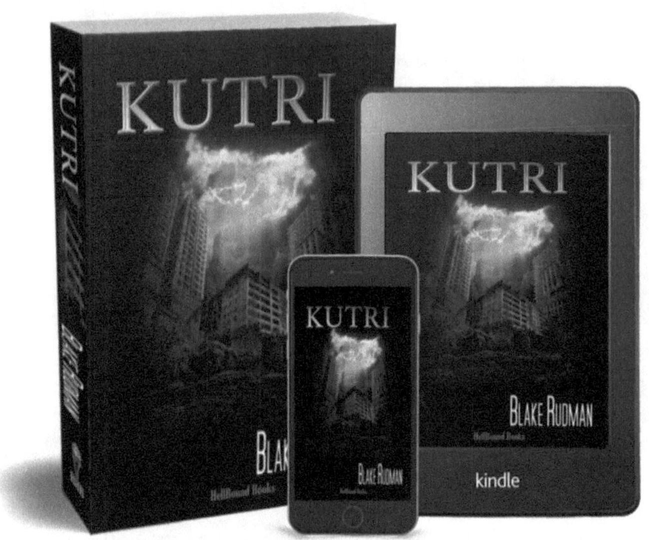

The Slow Plague, a gender-targeting infection with no cure, killed billions of women and girls worldwide and created a dystopian society in which the survivors are treated as highly valuable commodities. Although their market value is high, women's rights decline as they become objects of avarice, awe, and worship – possessions to be owned or won in high-stakes games.

Kutri Chandigarh, a rare beauty, is shipped from her native India to Los Angeles, a shattered metropolis barricaded behind a radiation-proof wall. Within the city stronghold, a bleak, broken, male-led society is mesmerized by stupefying programs pumped out by Little Angel Studios: an endless parade of reality TV shows.

The studio's #1 hit is Good Breeding: a bevy of ethnically "pure" young women compete to marry a chosen suitor and produce a "perfect" family under the scrutiny of the public eye.

Kutri has dreamed of wining the competition since early childhood. But, when she arrives in LA and meets Jakob Freeman, her assigned matchmaker, the fantasy quickly turns sour and twists into a horrific nightmare extending far beyond Kutri and the man she chooses for herself.

As Kutri tries to escape the fate she once coveted, Jakob is swept up in events that threaten him body and soul and spark memories of a past he has so desperately tried to forget.

Follow Blake at: blakerudman.com
Facebook: @BRudmanThriller
Instagram: @BRudmanThriller
Twitter: @BRudmanThriller

For all Blake's books, visit him at:
www.hellboundbookspublishing.com/authorpage_rudman.html
www.hellboundbooks.com

www.ingramcontent.com/pod-product-compliance
Lightning Source LLC
Chambersburg PA
CBHW031154010826
48971CB00012B/290